THE MURDERER YOU KNOW

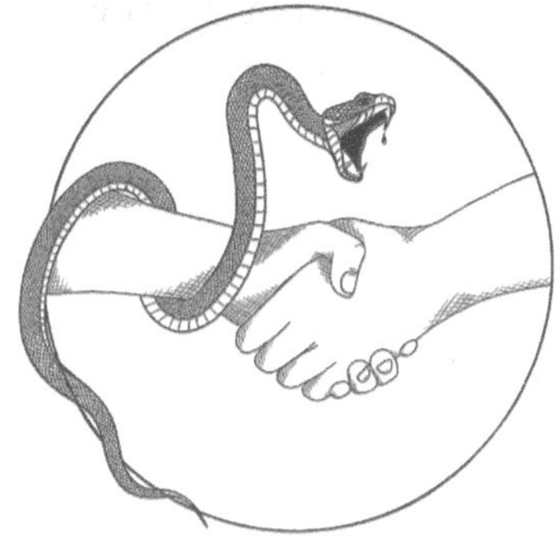

Patti Gaustad Procopi

BLUE FORTUNE ENTERPRISES LLC

Cactus Mystery Press, an imprint of Blue Fortune Enterprises LLC

THE MURDERER YOU KNOW

For information contact:
Blue Fortune Enterprises, LLC
Cactus Press
P.O. Box 554
Yorktown, VA 23690
http://blue-fortune.com

Cover design by The Murderer You Know Podcast/BFE LLC

ISBN: 978-1-961548-27-5

First Edition: May 2025

Fiction by Patti Gaustad Procopi:

Please... Tell Me More
Stop Talking
I'll Get By

Reader reviews:

Please... Tell Me More:
...I can honestly say, after finishing this book, I can sum it up with one word. That word would be amazing. I truly loved reading this book...
Sylvia Jacobs, Goodreads review

Beautifully written story about family ties, tragedy, guilt, relationships and how one gets through all the highs and lows.
Phyllis Bernstein, Goodreads review

Stop Talking
Every time I thought I knew what was about to happen in this ultimately, heartwarming story, Procopi threw me a curve, keeping me turning pages late into the night.
Linda Rosen, author of *The Emerald Necklace*

A compelling and satisfying family drama...
Grace Sammon, author of *The Eves* and host of *The Storytellers*

I'll Get By
A heartwarming story about generational dysfunction and the will to break out of family patterns. Loved the grandmother/granddaughter aspect of the story especially because it reminded me of my own relationship with my grandmother.
Donna Norman-Carbone, author of *All That Is Sacred* and *Of Lies and Honey*

I'll Get By takes you on a generational journey of the ups and downs of relationships in one family and how they deal with their situations. It is a beautifully written story in which the characters are relatable and full of personality...
Kathy Kusinich, author of *Always Remembering*

Dedication

I dedicate this book to the cast of *The Murderer You Know* Podcast:

The Host
The Lawyer
The Mom
and
All the Special Guests

INTRODUCTION

I think most of us are tantalized by mystery and crime, though the closer it is to us the more frightening it can be. In the late 1980s, a series of crimes took place where I live along a road I commuted to work on. While only one murder took place on that road, the four crimes were lumped together under the name of the Colonial Parkway Murders. Everyone who lives in this area, even those born after these crimes took place, knows about the Colonial Parkway Murders.

The first incident happened in 1986, when two women were found dead in a burned out car on the Colonial Parkway. Further investigation determined the women had been murdered.

A year later, a young couple was found shot on a nature preserve. Even though this was miles from the Colonial Parkway, investigators thought the crimes might be linked.

The next year, 1988, an abandoned car was found on the parkway. The car belonged to a college student. He and his date left a party one evening and were never seen again. To this day, their bodies have not been found.

The last incident took place in 1989, when a girl and her boyfriend's brother disappeared. His car was found at a rest stop on the interstate. Their bodies were found buried along a trail in the woods a month later.

Even though there was little tying these crimes together, other than in each case two people were murdered and their abandoned vehicles found, many people believed they were connected.

Rumor and speculation ran wild. People debated if there was one murderer or two working together. Was this the work of a serial killer? Many believed the murderer was either a police officer or park ranger or was disguised as one in order to get people to pull over.

The last murder took place in 1989, and no similar murders happened after that date. Did the murderer move? Die? Reform? No one knew.

The FBI investigated the crimes off and on over the years but until 2024, there wasn't a break in the case. Finally, DNA from a deceased man was linked to the murder of the young man and girl on the wildlife refuge. The FBI later concluded that this same man was probably responsible for the disappearance of the college students as well. He had been a person of interest in that case but had been let go.

The first murder of the two women and the couple that disappeared from the rest stop are still unsolved.

Many books, true-crime television shows, and podcasts have covered these cases in great detail over the years. I was reintroduced to the story when I was listening to my favorite true-crime podcast—The Murderer You Know. In episodes 27 and 28, titled *The Crime that Made Us Obsessed with True Crime*, the host discussed the crimes in great detail. I was surprised by how much I had forgotten over the intervening years.

That podcast (episodes 27 and 28 if you'd like to listen, along with episode 77 which includes the update on the crimes) gave me the idea for writing this book. I had always wanted to write a mystery. I love them and many others do as well.

I hope you enjoy my reimagining of this famous crime.

PROLOGUE

I stood watching the car go up in flames. I was sick to my stomach—but not entirely. What on earth had I done? A thrill of excitement shot through my core.

It wasn't supposed to happen like this. I had no intention of hurting anyone, let alone killing them. But she wouldn't listen to reason. I tried to say I just wanted to talk but they screamed at me, and I lost my temper and suddenly Becky was lying in the grass next to the car, moaning. Then Annie attacked me, so I hit her. With a hammer that was only meant to intimidate them. Show them how serious I was.

After that I really didn't have a choice. I wasn't going to prison for assault and battery. I laughed bitterly. Now I might be going to jail for murder. Annie moaned and tried to get up. Kneeling on her back, I pulled her scarf tightly around her neck. She struggled feebly and then stopped moving. I bent down by Becky. "Get up, we have to go," I said.

She opened her eyes and saw Annie. Crawling over to her, Becky cradled Annie's head in her lap, yelling, "What have you done? You killed her! Are you crazy?"

"I'm trying to save you," I screamed back. I couldn't get her to shut up. A moment later, she was quiet. My brain went into over-drive. I needed a plan. Picking up Becky, I shoved her in the back seat of the car. Then I grabbed Annie and got her in the front passenger seat. I heard a car coming down the road and I ducked down. It drove past. I needed to move fast. The rangers often patrolled River Road after dark, trying to catch kids having sex or smoking pot. If they saw a car in the overlook, they'd stop.

Putting the car in neutral, I thought of pushing it into the river. If it went over the embankment, it might not be found for several days. Suddenly, it occurred to me my DNA was all over the place. I quickly checked around the outside of the car, looking for anything I might have touched. I threw a shoe, a purse and other random bits inside the window. I almost threw the hammer but thought it might be traceable, so I kept it. I began gathering sticks and branches, shoving them inside. I tried not to think about what I'd done. When I felt I had enough flammable material in the car, I pulled out my lighter. I didn't smoke, but my father always said to carry a lighter for an emergency. Well, this certainly qualified.

Lighting a dried leaf-covered branch, I paused until it burst into flames before shoving it into the gas tank. I backed up and waited until the car was fully engulfed. Satisfied, I turned and began walking. I stayed in the shadows. I watched. No one stopped. No one asked me what I was doing there.

No one would ever suspect me. Just one of those random acts of violence.

CHAPTER ONE

"*Rise and shine… greet the* new day."

Amber winced as the bright sunlight pierced her eyes. She yanked the covers over her head and rolled over, trying to blot out the intrusion.

"Time to get up, sleepy head," Aunt Ida's voice continued.

"OMG, you sound like Fluffy. She said those same words to us every morning of our lives. It was annoying then and even more annoying now that I'm an adult and perfectly capable of deciding when to get up."

"Fluffy?" Ida laughed. "You still call your mother Fluffy?"

Knowing she was fighting a losing battle, Amber forced herself to sit up. "Why not? It suits her." Many years ago, when she and her sister Scarlet were in high school, one of their friends nicknamed their mother "Fluffy."

"She's so sweet," the friend cooed. "Warm and cozy. Like a fluffy blanket you could wrap yourself up in." Whenever any one of their friends suffered any kind of emotional crisis, they'd end up at Amber's kitchen table talking to Fluffy, who was always there with advice, kindness, and fresh baked chocolate chip cookies.

From then on, her mother was known as Fluffy to all their friends. Even

Amber and Scarlet started calling her that. Their mother didn't appear to mind.

Another friend, a boy, not to be outdone, decided their father also needed a nickname, and he called Mr. Steen, the "Great Silence." Like Fluffy, this described Amber's father to a T. Mr. Steen hardly spoke. Not to his family, to his friends, to his work colleagues, and least of all to Amber and Scarlet's friends.

He managed to get through life with a series of eye and hand movements and the occasional grunt. He wasn't unfriendly or mean, he just apparently never developed any verbal skills. When Amber and her sister were younger, they often wondered how their father managed to propose to their mother. They decided that after an evening out, he drove her home and shoved a ring box in her hand, pointing at her and then at himself, making sounds that conveyed deep love and devotion. It obviously worked.

Aunt Ida's voice brought Amber back to the present. "You've been wallowing long enough. You need to start getting up at a decent time each day and move on with your life."

"Wallowing?" How on earth could Ida think she was wallowing? She was devastated and rightfully so.

"You're not the only person who's ever had her heart broken," Ida said. "Are you going to spend your life like some Victorian lady collapsed on the couch with your smelling salts clutched in your hand?" Ida's voice trailed away as she headed downstairs.

Amber threw the covers off and marched to the top of the steps. "Is that how you see me? As some melodramatic fainting virgin?"

Ida's voice floated up the stairs. "We certainly know the virgin part doesn't fit, but yes, you are being melodramatic. I know it hurts. I know you were betrayed. But consider the old saying, 'it's better to have loved and lost than spent a lifetime with that psycho.'"

Turning around, Amber went to the bathroom. She brushed her teeth vigorously and stared at her face in the mirror. "Ick." No doubt about it, she looked awful. Pale, with dark circles around her eyes. Twisting this way and that to get a better look, she was baffled. *How did I get dark circles under my eyes when all I do is sleep?*

Amber reluctantly dragged herself downstairs and slumped at the kitchen table. Ida filled two cups of coffee and slid one in front of Amber. "The cream and sugar are on the table."

Sitting across from Amber, Ida spooned a single teaspoon of sugar into her cup. Amber poured a heavy dose of cream and several teaspoons of sugar into her coffee.

"And speaking of Fluffy and the Great Silence, have you told them you're home? Technically not back home, since you're currently at my house, but do they have any idea for the last week you've been less than ten miles from them? Or do they think you're still living the life of a supposed modern-day hippie on a farm in the valley?"

"No, I haven't told them Bruce and I broke up." Broke up? Did that really describe what happened? More like he stole all her money, claiming they were buying the farm together while he was spending it all over town shacking up with various women. She'd had no idea they didn't own the farm until some official-looking guys in suits showed up and told her she needed to leave before they had her arrested for trespassing.

"Trespassing?" she squeaked in outrage. "I...we...own this farm." The bank people rolled their eyes and gave her an hour to clean out her possessions. Then they put a very substantial lock on the door. She sat on the front porch steps with her suitcase and several boxes full of a pitiful collection of personal items and waited for Bruce.

In the hours she'd sat there, she couldn't come up with a coherent plan for the immediate future. Bruce had their only vehicle. He'd convinced her to sell her car. "Babe, we don't need two vehicles. We go everywhere together. More money to put down on the farm." Except they didn't go out together. He went out, leaving her alone at the farm since she had no wheels.

She'd been desperately calling Bruce and leaving messages on his phone, which he ignored. "No service, Babe," she could hear him say. That was always his excuse.

Seeing a cloud of dust coming down the road, she hoped it was him. It was. He pulled up, climbed out of the car, and smiled, the smile that always melted her heart and other parts of her anatomy, "Babe, what's up? Why the long face?"

Amber told him about the bank people. "They said we'd never paid for the farm. Just a bit of earnest money or something. So, after six months, they decided to evict us. Where's my money, Bruce? Where's the money you were going to combine with yours to put a down payment on the farm? That was my inheritance. Left to me by my grandmother. Everything I had in the world."

Bruce's smile slipped for a moment before he managed to resurrect it. "It's a simple misunderstanding, Babe. I'll fix it."

Numbly, Amber stared at Bruce. "What are we going to do? They've locked the doors."

Bruce laughed. "Locks were made to be broken." He started walking up to the porch.

"Absolutely not!" Amber stood up. "I'm not adding breaking and entering to a charge of trespassing. We'll have to find a place to stay tonight and go to the bank in the morning and straighten this all out."

"Okay, Babe." Bruce looked furtive.

Amber climbed in the car and Bruce drove into town.

"Where are we going to stay?" Amber asked. She didn't know if Bruce had money for a hotel. She certainly didn't.

"I have a friend who'll put us up. Don't worry, Babe."

If he says 'babe' one more time, I'm going to scream, Amber thought, clenching her teeth.

Stopping in front of a ratty collection of row houses, Bruce got out and motioned for Amber to follow him. He knocked on the door of one of the units and a young woman with long, stringy hair, wearing a soiled t-shirt and torn jeans, answered. Her wan face lit up when she saw Bruce and quickly turned into a frown when she noticed Amber. "Who's this?" she asked. Amber wondered the same thing.

"A friend. We need a place to crash for the night," Bruce replied.

A friend? Bruce stood aside and held out his hand to welcome Amber into the dingy interior. When the girl turned sideways, Amber noticed she was pregnant. *This is getting worse and worse.*

Amber stood outside the entrance. "Bruce, why don't you introduce me to your friend?" Amber said, staring at the girl's protruding stomach.

"Friend? I ain't his friend. I'm his fiancée. Which still don't explain who the hell you are."

Amber turned, got her suitcase out of the car, and started walking to the bus depot. She called Aunt Ida, who purchased her a ticket home. And she'd been hiding out ever since. Not surprisingly, Bruce hadn't tried to get in touch.

Amber sighed and looked at Ida. "Can't I stay here forever? It's not like Mom and Dad are ever going to visit me in the valley. They never go anywhere. I'll call them once a week and say everything's great."

Ida shook her head and rolled her eyes. "I think you're forgetting your sister, Scarlet. She might visit. Might want a break from law school stress and head up to the Blue Ridge to spend a weekend with her sister, hiking and breathing clean country air."

Amber laid her head on the table. Ida was right. She could possibly pull the wool over her parent's eyes but not Scarlet. And Scarlet wouldn't go along with lying to her parents. Scarlet would probably want to drive up to the valley and beat the shit out of Bruce and threaten him with a lawsuit to get her money back.

Scarlet was a force of nature. The hero child. The straight-A student. The athlete. The soon to be kick-ass lawyer. Amber had trailed in her sister's wake her entire life. Despite being three years behind her sister in school, she had to endure all the teachers' disappointments she wasn't another Scarlet. She was the C student. Average. To her parent's credit, they never compared their daughters and celebrated each one's achievements. And Amber did have some, though not as many as Scarlet. Amber was a gifted dancer, singer, and actress. She always landed the leading role in the school plays and musicals. Sadly, it wasn't going to lead to a career. She had a better chance of being struck by lightning than achieving fame and fortune.

While attending college up in the mountains, randomly studying, with no real idea of what she planned to do with her life, she met Bruce. Sexy, wonderful, charming Bruce, who had this harebrained scheme to live off the land. He bounced between growing organic crops, marijuana, or raising cage-free chickens. Not that he ever actually started any of those things. It was probably not a coincidence he came up with this idea after he found out Amber had a small inheritance.

Her parents were not pleased when Amber announced she planned on quitting college. They consoled themselves with the thought that if she was in love and settled down, grandchildren might come next. That was almost as good as a career, in their opinion. Fluffy couldn't wait to become a grandmother and snuggle little babies and bake more cookies.

Scarlet thought Bruce was a shyster. *Right again Scarlet.* Amber angrily stuffed thoughts of Bruce in the far reaches of her brain. She wished the mind was like a computer and you could simply push a button and delete files forever.

"Amber…?" Ida's voice floated to her as if from a great distance. "What are you planning to do?"

Lifting her head off the table, Amber looked at her aunt. "You're right. I have to tell Mom and Dad I'm home. That Bruce and I broke up." Amber's voice cracked. "I'll call later. I'm not going to tell them I've been home a week hiding out with you. I'll say I got in on the bus last night. Okay? Can you back me up on that?"

"Of course."

CHAPTER TWO

Amber knew her mother would be sweet and kind and concerned. She'd be 'fluffy'. She'd have to gauge her dad's reaction when she got home since he didn't speak on the phone.

Ida got on the phone after Amber told her parents the news and told her sister that she'd bring her youngest over later. Amber went upstairs to take a shower and get dressed. While packing up her clothes, she decided once again her entire life had been ruined by her name. Amber.

Ida laughed at that notion. "Your life was ruined by being named Amber?"

"Yes! It's such a trashy name. My mom named me after her favorite book, Forever Amber, which is some historic drama about a pregnant teenager in London who survives by whoring around."

"I don't think you've ever actually read the book. The 'Amber' in the book survives by her wits to rise above her background and achieve great success. So what if the success is as the mistress of the King? It's not like women had many options back in the day. She wasn't going to become a CEO or start her own business."

Amber snorted.

"Well, your mother also named your sister Scarlet after that most famous of fictional heroines." Ida stared off into space, scratching her chin. "I've never heard Scarlet complain about it. Or moaning about what a manipulative, self-centered bitch Scarlet O'Hara was. The name Scarlet hasn't held your sister back."

Amber hated it when Ida was logical. "Whatever. I still don't like my name. If I'd been named Victoria or Elizabeth, I'd have been a completely different person."

Ida rolled her eyes.

The reunion with her parents went well. Her mom cried when Amber told them Bruce had not been the man of her dreams. That he had impregnated someone else while claiming to love her. Fluffy wrapped her in warm hugs and handed her a glass of milk and a plate of freshly baked chocolate cookies. How was it possible there were always fresh-baked cookies in the house, Amber wondered, biting into the rich, warm cookie. Her father, living up to his nickname, stood silently by, looking angry but supportive of his daughter who'd been wronged.

Ida hugged Amber goodbye, whispering in her ear, "This past week will forever be our little secret." She kissed Amber on the cheek and left. Amber felt incredibly lucky to have her Aunt Ida in her life.

Later, Amber called Scarlet to tell her Bruce was history.

"I am actually happy to hear that. What a sleaze. I couldn't believe you were attracted to him and taken in by his bullshit."

"Let's forget about Bruce or why I was so stupid. I'm embarrassed and humiliated enough."

"Oh Amber. I'm sorry. You deserve someone better than Bruce. You always sell yourself short. Tell you what, I'm going to come home this weekend, and we can hang out; watch old Disney movies, eat popcorn or Fluffy's cookies or both, and give each other manicures."

"Sounds great. Thanks Scarlet."

Amber carried her suitcase upstairs to her childhood bedroom still filled with her stuffed animals, favorite books, art, and posters of her teenage obsessions on the walls. After putting her few things away, she flopped down on her bed. It felt good to be home. Smiling, she realized how lucky she was. She had a wonderful, loving family. A great mother and father who were always there for her. A fabulous sister who loved and cared for her. And when all those people weren't enough, she had her Aunt Ida to turn to. However, there was still the issue of the future. Maybe she could be the old maid sister/daughter/niece living forever in the turret of the castle.

CHAPTER THREE

As promised, Scarlet arrived early Friday afternoon after her last class of the day. Sitting at the kitchen table, she caught everyone up on her studies. She still wasn't sure what kind of law she wanted to practice. "I know I want to do criminal law. Corporate or tax is where the money is, but I have no passion or interest in it. I'm still figuring out if I want to work on the defense side or the prosecution. I'm applying for an internship with the Commonwealth Attorney's office and I'll see how I feel about prosecuting afterwards. Right now, I'm leaning toward defense."

Their father huffed and emitted some kind of sounds that Amber interpreted as a dismissal of Scarlet's desire to defend criminals. He was a law-and-order type guy and probably thought most people apprehended by the police were guilty or the police wouldn't have arrested them. Innocent until proven guilty was merely a momentary speed bump on the way to a life sentence.

Fluffy took advantage of her daughters' visits and cooked a five-course dinner that would have felled an elephant. Afterwards, Amber and Scarlet waddled upstairs to catch up on their own.

Taking out all the manicure supplies, the girls started working on each other's nails.

"So, tell me about your love life?" Amber asked Scarlet. "You can't possibly spend all your time in class."

"Yes, I can and yes, I do. There is no time for love and hardly time for friendship besides the occasional lunch where we bitch about our professors and what hard-ass demanding pains they are. I haven't even noticed if there are any good-looking guys in my classes since my nose is usually jammed in my books."

"Doesn't sound like much fun," Amber said.

"It's all good. When I'm a rich, successful lawyer, I'll have my pick of the crop." Scarlet laughed before turning serious. "Have you thought about what you want to do?"

Amber let out a bitter laugh. "Remember that song when we were younger, and kids would put an 'L' shape on their foreheads to tease other kids? Calling them losers?" She held up her fingers and made an L with her thumb and pointer finger and placed it on her forehead. "That's me. A loser with a capital L."

"Stop. You're smart. You're hard working. You have a million positives. You need to find something you're passionate about. Like me. I've always wanted to be a lawyer. What have you always wanted to be?"

"I wanted to be a singer-dancer on Broadway." Amber's mouth twisted bitterly. "I'm not tall enough to be a dancer, and my voice, while good enough for the lead in a high school musical, is not good enough to beat out a thousand others auditioning on Broadway. Plus, I don't have the patience or stamina to live the life of a starving artist." Amber laughed. "I'd rather live at home and eat mom's chocolate chip cookies."

"I know what you mean. These are some good cookies." Scarlet groaned as she bit into another one. "But think about it. What else are you passionate about?"

Amber was quiet for a long time. "I'm almost embarrassed to admit it, but I am totally obsessed with true crime. I love watching it on TV and listening to true crime podcasts." Amber winced when she looked at her sister.

"Really?" Scarlet looked stunned. "You're the biggest scaredy-cat ever! You were always terrified of staying alone. If you got home, and Mom and Dad didn't immediately yell out a hello, you were convinced there was a murderer in the house and everyone was dead and dismembered."

Laughing, Amber agreed. "I'm still that way. I hated it when we lived out on the farm in the middle of effing nowhere and Bruce would take off, claiming he 'had to' go into town at night. Every noise, every bump scared me to death. At one point I wanted to get a dog, but if the dog started barking and growling, I'd probably pee myself before dropping dead from fear.

"And when I'm driving down the road and I see a large trash bag dumped in the ditch, I'm convinced it's full of body parts. I see murder and mayhem everywhere. I can hardly walk past a dumpster without thinking there's a body in there.

"Despite all that, I am totally obsessed and fascinated by true crime. It's the murderer you know that is the scary part. People are worried about getting killed by a complete stranger when, in fact, most people are killed by someone they love—their spouse, their kids, their friends, or co-workers."

Scarlet nodded. "True. We hear those stats all the time at law school. It's why the police always check out the husband first." Scarlet bit into another cookie. "I guess I should say spouse. It's not always the husband anymore."

"Yeah. Those stories of women being murdered by their husband on their honeymoon are heartbreaking. You wonder when he came up with the idea of doing her in? The minute they met? Or did he get in financial trouble and decide a huge insurance policy on his bride was the solution? And it's always something lame… we were hiking along this cliff, and she suddenly fell over the edge. Really?"

Scarlet agreed. "I know. Buddy, you're going to get caught."

Amber nodded vigorously. "Yeah. So many murderers appear to be really bad at planning a successful murder. They leave evidence. They change their story. They think they're smarter than the police, or teenagers who seem to believe they'll kill their parents and marry their boyfriend, and everything will turn out great. Happily ever after, like a warped fairy tale. No bitch! You're going to jail for the rest of your life!"

"With all the true crime and cop shows on TV, people might get some clues on what not to do," Scarlet said. "I guess it's what keeps lawyers busy. People get caught and go to court."

"I also read some statistic that the average person walks by thirty-something murderers in their lifetime. Hell, some of them are probably living with a murderer and don't know it."

"Like those serial killers? I can't even imagine finding out your significant other is the Blue Mountain Slasher or something." Scarlet shuddered.

The sisters quietly worked on their nails, each lost in their own thoughts. Scarlet finally looked up at her sister and held out her hand, showing off her new nail polish. "We are going to figure out how to turn this obsession slash passion of yours into a paying gig."

CHAPTER FOUR

he next morning, Amber felt a new sense of purpose. Scarlet would figure it out. Scarlet always figured things out for her. She glanced over at the twin bed across from her. Empty. She wondered what time it was and where Scarlet was. Her phone showed it was a little before nine, which in her mind was good. Better than noon, she laughed, though she knew her father wouldn't be impressed. He deemed rising late as sloth and indolence.

Voices floated up the stairs. Everyone was probably downstairs preparing breakfast. Amber hopped up, grabbed her robe, and ran down the steps. She hoped they were still fixing breakfast and not already eating it. Her father stuck to his early morning schedule even on weekends, which meant her mother did too.

Pancakes were being flipped and stacked on a plate. Amber was relieved. She hadn't missed breakfast, her favorite meal, especially if someone else was cooking. And even better if that someone was her mother, who was the best cook ever. Bruce only had coffee for breakfast and made disparaging remarks about people who actually ate food. There were so many clues he was the worst person ever and she'd ignored them all.

"Hi, honey," Fluffy said when she spotted Amber in the doorway. "We have pancakes. I know they're your favorite." Her mother put three large golden cakes on a plate for her. "Syrup and butter are on the table. Coffee's ready and there's orange juice, too."

Amber smiled, taking the plate from her mother. Why had she ever left home? It was wonderful. Sitting next to her father, Amber said, "Good morning," before pouring a generous amount of syrup on her pancakes. Her father's face was buried in the paper, and he merely smiled before looking back down.

Scarlet plopped in the seat next to Amber. Her plate was also filled with a stack of pancakes. "Hey, where's the bacon?" Amber cried.

"Right here," her mother said, placing a platter of crisp bacon on the table. "It just got finished. I know you like it well done and crunchy."

"After breakfast, we're having a family conference." Scarlet announced through a mouthful of pancakes. "It's called, Finding Amber's Passion."

Amber groaned. "No. Please…"

"No really," Scarlet said. "You'll enjoy this. Ida's coming over and we're all putting our heads together to figure out how you can turn your true crime obsession into a paying gig. People do, you know."

Their father snapped his newspaper and refolded it. Amber could tell from the look on his face, he probably thought there was nothing worth discussing. Some deviant commits a crime, is caught, and is hopefully punished accordingly. The death penalty was appropriate for most criminals, according to Dad. He took it personally when the State legislature talked about abolishing the death penalty. Amber once heard him mutter, "death is too good for some people," or maybe she imagined it.

"Speaking of crime," Fluffy chimed in, "they found the bodies of those poor kids who disappeared on River Road four months ago."

This was the second disappearance/murder on that scenic road. The first involved two young women who were found strangled and bludgeoned to death inside their burnt-out car. That was a year ago. Six months later, two college students disappeared. The police found their car parked on one of the park's scenic overlooks, but they were nowhere to be found.

Of course, at the time the police simply assumed the pair had wandered down to the river and drowned. The tide had swept their bodies far out to sea, and they'd never been located.

After the disappearance, she and Scarlet were forbidden to drive on River Road after dark. Up until the first bodies had been found, the most dangerous thing that had happened on that road had been accidents with deer. Amber had always loved taking the wooded, scenic drive that connected their little town of Easton to Westburg, the town on the other end of the road. It wasn't as quick as driving on the state roads, but it was always peaceful and calming. Now her parents acted like The Son of Sam and the Manson Family were hiding along the tree-lined banks of the river.

Swallowing a large mouthful of pancakes, she asked, "Where did they find them? Did their bodies wash up on shore? Were they discovered near their car?"

"No. That's the strange part. They weren't found in the river—they were found miles away. In another county. Some hunters stumbled over their remains in the woods. It appeared they had been dumped along some old logging trail." Fluffy put more pancakes on everyone's plates.

"So, it wasn't an accident," Amber mused.

"No. I always suspected it was murder. Just like the first one." Her mom leaned forward and said in a conspiratorial whisper, "They're talking serial killer."

Dad loudly folded his paper again, and Amber knew he didn't think speaking of serial killers was proper breakfast conversation.

The rest of the meal focused on pancakes and bacon, and Amber ate like she hadn't seen food in months. She loved her Aunt Ida, however, Ida was a takeout, DoorDash, pizza delivery kind of cook.

Scarlet picked up all the dishes and carried them to the sink. "Ida will be over about eleven. Get a shower or do whatever you need to do." Amber headed up the stairs.

Amber was happy to discover her closet and drawers still contained her old clothes. She hadn't salvaged much from the farm when she left. The clothes she'd crammed into her suitcase were worn out, and despite being washed at Ida's, belonged in the Goodwill donation box. She'd left all her other possessions in boxes in Bruce's car. It seemed unlikely that she would ever recover those items, since she never wanted to talk to Bruce again.

After a long hot shower, she picked out jeans and a shirt she remembered from high school. She was pleased they still fit. Riffling through the rest of the clothes, she decided she'd get them organized to see what she needed. Definitely new underwear, she laughed. Fluffy would love to take her shopping. Maybe they could all go to the mall instead of having this dumb, *what to do about Amber* conference. Amber looked in the mirror to see if she was presentable. Fluffy liked her girls to be neat and tidy. She dreaded this. They were going to make her feel like a complete loser, even though it wasn't their intention.

Hearing a knock, followed by Ida's loud hello, Amber quickly ran a brush through her hair and headed downstairs. She was the last to walk into the family room. Ida, Scarlet, and her mom were sitting around smiling. Her father was not in the room. "Where's Dad?" Amber asked, flopping down in the recliner.

"Well, you know your father. He probably wouldn't have much to add," Fluffy said, pulling at the hem of her skirt. Amber's mom was the only person she knew who still wore nothing but dresses or skirts and blouses. She cooked, cleaned, and even gardened in a dress. She wore aprons, too.

"This is the twenty-first century," Amber once said to her mom. "Have you heard of jeans? Shorts? Comfortable casual clothes?"

"I find dresses comfortable. Much less restrictive than pants."

Glancing over at Ida, she was struck again at how dissimilar her aunt and mother were. Fluffy was tiny with small bones. Almost bird-like. She had her light brown hair with gray streaks coiffed once a week at the local beauty shop where they still used rollers, apparently the last salon in the area that did. Fluffy had dozens of almost identical dresses in her closets in various muted colors and patterns. Amber could not remember her mother ever wearing anything with bright, vibrant colors.

Ida was tall, with arms and shoulders more suited to a rugby player. She kept her lavender-tinted hair wacked off in a short, cropped style. She wore what looked like men's jeans, a flannel shirt, and heavy work boots.

Amber wondered why she hadn't noticed the stark differences previously. She knew they were opposite in just about every way, but sitting here it struck her forcefully.

They sat quietly, as if waiting for someone else to come in to start the meeting. Amber's fairy godmother, perhaps? Clearing her throat, Scarlet said, "I'm calling the meeting to order," and laughed before continuing. "Amber and I were talking last night and what we need to do is find something Amber is passionate about that will engage her. I have law. Mom, you have Dad and the house. Ida, you have your garden and your repair shop. Amber has nothing."

"I respectively reject the term *nothing*. I have things," Amber sniffed.

Scarlet raised one eyebrow. "Such as...?"

"Things." Amber shifted uncomfortably as everyone stared at her.

Scarlet continued, as if Amber hadn't interrupted. "Turns out Amber is a huge fan of true crime and, as it turns out, true crime is hot right now. Books, TV, radio shows, and podcasts."

"Oh, you mean she could be one of those influisers?" Fluffy grinned broadly. "I've heard they make tons of money. They have all these followers and—" Scarlet held her hand up.

"Influencers, Mom. Influencers. And no, Amber can't be one of those because she isn't famous and doesn't have a vast following. But anyone can be a podcaster. All you need is a computer, headphones, and a microphone."

Ida and Fluffy stared at Scarlet. "How is that a job? How does one get paid?" Ida said after a long pause.

"Usually, you don't until you go viral. Meaning, once your podcast catches on and you get sponsors and such. Amber will probably have to get a day job, but this will give her something to focus on, and who knows where it might lead."

Amber liked the part about the podcast. That sounded exciting. She didn't like the part about having to get a job. What kind of job? She wasn't qualified for much of anything. Cleaning motel rooms? Lunch lady at the middle school? She gagged.

Scarlet was on a roll, and she steamed ahead. "First things first. We need to come up with a clever name and a unique theme for our episodes. There are a ton of true crime podcasts out there already. What will make ours different?" Scarlet mused.

An hour later, the floor was covered with crumpled sheets of paper filled with rejected ideas. Scarlet finished scribbling on her pad. "Eureka! We've got it!"

Everyone watched her, waiting to hear the pronouncement.

"The name of the podcast will be *The Murderer You Know*, and we'll focus on murderers who were known to their victims."

"Oh, I like it," Fluffy said. Fluffy talking about murder was an alien concept. "I've actually known some murderers."

"What?" both girls shrieked. "You have?"

"Of course. If you live long enough, someone you know will be killed, and you're right, it's usually by a spouse, their kids, or parents."

The girls continued to stare. What creature had taken over and now inhabited their mother's body? This was not Fluffy-type talk.

Ida spoke up. "I've known a few murderers and murder victims myself."

Scarlet looked at Amber. "This will make our podcast stand out. We'll focus on people we know who have been murdered or have murdered."

Our stuck out to Amber. "Our podcast? Are we all in? You guys are going to help?"

"Of course we will. You'll be the host, and I can provide legal opinions. I'm not a lawyer yet, but the audience doesn't need to know that. We won't use our real names. Make it even more mysterious. Mom and Ida can also guest on the program when we talk about the murders they know about."

Their father stuck his head in the doorway and looked around. He was probably not used to his wife ignoring him all day, and it was alarmingly close to lunchtime.

Fluffy looked up, smiling brightly. "Bob. We're planning Amber's career."

Confusion shadowed his face as he stared at the pile of crumpled paper.

"Amber's going to start a podcast about murder, specifically murders done by people we know."

Now their father looked completely baffled. The look on his face said, "That's a money-making career?"

"You actually had a friend, a co-worker, murdered by her son. That poor woman. Allison? You can be a guest on the show and talk about her," Fluffy said eagerly. Amber, Scarlet, and Ida stifled their laughter, imagining the Great Silence snorting, harrumphing, and mumbling through a podcast.

"You can tell us the details and we can do the show, Dad. We wouldn't want to put you on the spot," Amber said.

Their father made his escape.

Having come up with a name and a format, the four put their heads together and started making a list of crimes.

CHAPTER SIX

While they named murderers and victims they had known, Scarlet scribbled them down. Finally, she held up the list. Between them, they had come up with twelve murders in which they either knew the victim or the perpetrator or both. "If each crime takes two episodes, that gives us a good start. And we'll probably remember others while we're recording."

She put the list down. "As decided, we'll start with crimes committed by friends of ours, or friends of ours who were victims of crimes. Then we can go back to older crimes." She smiled. "The first episode is easy. We introduce ourselves—the host and the lawyer. Then Amber talks about her true crime obsession and fears, and then we bring up what kinds of crimes we'll cover."

"What's first?" Amber asked eagerly, ready to put her headphones on and plug in her microphone.

"Hold your horses." Scarlet held up her hand. "What's first is research. You can't go off half-cocked. You need to find out as much about the crimes as possible. Get newspaper articles and police reports and court transcripts about the crimes. Then you have to write the episode. Next, you have to send the trial stuff to me so I can interject intelligent comments on the law and what-not."

"I could talk about crime and the law too," their mother said brightly.

Amber and Scarlet stared at Fluffy. What on earth did she know about crime and the law? Scarlet tilted her head and raised an eyebrow. "Really? What is your expertise in that area, Mom?"

"I have seen every single episode of *Law & Order* at least three times. I learned all those legal terms."

Amber and Scarlet continued to stare at their mother. Was she serious?

Finally, Scarlet said, "I'm sure that will be very helpful. We'll keep that in mind."

Fluffy sat back in her chair with a satisfied smile on her face.

Ida rolled her eyes. "Not sure what my role will be since I haven't watched every episode of *Law & Order*, but tell me what you need, and I'll be there. I do think you should include the impact the victim's death had on their family. And the community at large. The ramifications. Ripple effect. So many lives destroyed. Even the perpetrator's family is destroyed."

Amber nodded. "True. Since some of these crimes involve people we know, we have seen that firsthand. We can talk about it personally."

Scarlet looked at her notepad. "Amber, the first episode is about your childhood best friend, Heather. I think that will be a good title because it makes it sound personal. You knew this person, and the listener will not know at first if she was the victim or the perpetrator. You need some mystery in your mystery."

Amber grimaced. What happened to her friend, Heather, had shocked their little town. At the time of the crime, she and Heather were no longer best friends. They'd met at preschool and had taken dance and gymnastics lessons together for the next seven years. They were BFFs until middle school.

At that point, Heather got in with a bad crowd. Not exactly bad—it was a small-town middle school, after all. They couldn't drive but they were into shoplifting and wearing way too much make-up. Amber remembered

Fluffy being shocked at the change in Heather.

Heather's mother, who had been a friend of Fluffy's, seemed baffled by her daughter's behavior. Heather dropped out of dance and all her other activities and spent her time at her friends' houses. It only got worse in high school, where she got in with the worst crowd. Then it was drugs and drinking and sex.

Sadly, so many kids in their small town went off the rails in high school. Instead of reveling in the dozens of available activities and opportunities, they spent their time getting wasted on the weekend. Or getting wasted every day. Even Scarlet, who hung out with a more sophisticated, motivated peer group, lost friends to drugs.

Scarlet was still talking. "We have twelve crimes, which should take us through a half a year since each murder will be covered in two episodes. In the first we discuss the crime and how the perpetrators were caught. The second episode will cover the trial and the sentence the person received.

"We'll have to keep looking for crimes. Put your thinking caps on. That applies to Mom and Ida as well. If the average person walks past thirty murderers in a lifetime, you must know more."

"What about the serial killer on River Road?" Fluffy said.

"Mom, it might be a serial killer or just a strange coincidence. Plus, we don't know the victims or the murderer. Yet. Let's focus on the people we know." Scarlet sounded a bit exasperated with her mother.

Amber took the list and silently read the names.

CHAPTER SEVEN

$\mathcal{S}$*carlet left late that afternoon* after a sumptuous lunch. "I could stay here forever," she groaned with satisfaction, "but no rest for the weary. I'll order all the hardware this week—headphones and microphones. Amber, start your research and tell me when you have episode one written. Send it to me, and I can start thinking about the legal side and the trial. You should get several written before we start recording. We probably need to record about six episodes to give ourselves a cushion. We need to pick a day to 'drop' them."

Amber hugged Scarlet goodbye. "Thanks for believing in me."

"I've always believed in you."

Amber woke the next morning happy and smiling, which was a massive improvement. She felt energized. Excited. Ready to go out and conquer the world. She was finally involved in something she cared about.

She bounced out of bed and headed downstairs.

"Good morning, honey. There's cereal for breakfast. And coffee, of course." Fluffy said, stirring a pan on the stove.

"What are you mixing if there's nothing special for breakfast?" Amber was a little miffed. She could eat cold cereal anywhere.

Her mother turned around and smiled. "Something special for later today. You'll see."

Amber opened the cabinet door and perused the cereal choices. Of course, they were much better than what she had been able to afford. She settled on some all-natural home-made granola. Grabbing the milk out of the refrigerator, she poured until the cereal reached the edge of the bowl. Then she carefully took her bowl to the table and set it down. Her mother put a cup of coffee in front of her. "Sugar and cream on the table."

They continued their respective tasks in companionable silence until Amber had emptied both her bowl and her cup. "I guess it's time to head out and start researching murder." She emphasized the word *murder* with a deep, scary voice.

Fluffy looked up from her mixing bowl. "Where are you going? Can't you do all that here on your laptop?"

Amber grimaced. She did not want to tell her mother she no longer had a laptop. It had been in one of the boxes she'd left behind when she stormed off to the bus station after meeting Bruce's pregnant fiancée.

"No. I think I'd rather do research at the library. On a regular-sized computer with lots of desk space to spread out and take notes. Even at college, I preferred working at the library instead of my dorm room or the local Starbucks. I need quiet. I need to focus on the crime at hand." She laughed with what she hoped was sinister glee.

"Okay, dear. That sounds lovely. Be sure to be home in time for dinner. I'm planning a special treat."

"I will." Amber ran upstairs, threw on some clothes, grabbed her backpack, and left.

She headed to the shops and library on Main Street. She loved living in a small town where everything was within walking distance, which was lucky for her since she no longer had a vehicle. Her parents hadn't taken the news of her selling her car very well. Fluffy was almost speechless. Her father was, of course, speechless, but Amber could tell he was furious.

"You sold your car?" Fluffy finally managed to say after a few stops and starts. "Why? You loved that car. You bought it after working all those years at the Hot Spot."

Tears began to gather at the corners of Amber's eyes. She had loved her car. She'd been so proud when she was able to purchase the Honda Civic all by herself.

Bruce had laughed at her when she told him about working for years to save up the money to buy a car. "So, you saved up money to buy this ugly green wreck?"

Amber should have known right then that Bruce was an ass. It was true that her car was a rather unfortunate shade of green, but it had a good heart and never let her down. How could she have let him talk her into selling the Green Flash?

She cried when it drove away, and Bruce laughed again. "Babe. Stop. Why are you crying over that thing? I'll get you something much better one day."

Of course, that never happened.

Now she had no car. No inheritance. And no laptop.

All the way down the street, Amber muttered, "Delete Bruce file, delete Bruce file."

First stop was at the local general store to pick up writing supplies. Amber loved notebooks and mechanical pencils and gel pens. She also decided she needed a journal to keep track of deadlines and goals.

The bell on the door jangled when she stepped into the shop. The clerk looked up and smiled. "Amber? I thought you were off at college. Home for a visit?"

Amber hoped Mrs. Jenkins couldn't see her blush. "Yes. College wasn't working for me. Came home for a reboot. Figure out what I want to do."

Mrs. Jenkins nodded. "Is Scarlet still in law school? She was always so smart."

"Yes, she is," Amber replied brightly, forcing the smile to remain on her face. It never ended. People talking about Scarlet and though they didn't come right out and say it, it was always implied: why are you such a loser?

"Looking for anything in particular?" Mrs. Jenkins continued, hovering.

"Notebooks. Pens, pencils…" Amber walked to the office supplies.

"Help yourself dear. I'm here if you need me."

Amber liked notebooks with lined pages. She also liked spiral notebooks. If she messed up, she could rip the sheet out. In school, she had to use black-and-white composition books, and if the teachers noticed the remnants of a torn page, they gave her the third degree about it.

Settling on five notebooks with floral and nature designs and a matching planner, she then picked up a pack of mechanical pencils, extra lead, a pack of gel pens with different colored ink, and sticky notes. Sticky notes were critical. She paid for her purchases and headed to the library.

I almost threw my coffee cup across the room when the TV news announced they'd found the bodies of the college students. What a shock. Damn hunters.

Could they tell they were killed with the same hammer I'd used in the first crime? I laughed. These were the Westburg police. Sheriff Wallace was too busy strutting around like he owned the county. He couldn't care less about solving crime.

I never expected I'd kill again. I never planned on killing anyone. The first occurred in a blind rage. When it was over, for a moment I didn't know what had happened. My only thought was to cover my tracks. Later, I remembered the thrill that came over me when I watched the car burning. I'd never felt a sensation like that before and I wanted to feel it again.

Killing those last two was like shooting fish in a barrel. So innocent. So eager to help. So completely pathetic. The girl walked around to the back of the car and saw her boyfriend lying in a heap.

"What's wrong with him?" she asked.

"I don't know. He just collapsed. Why don't you check?"

She never saw it coming.

I planned on stuffing them in their car and lighting it on fire. But when the lights of a ranger car passed, I quickly pushed the trunk closed before he returned. Might be someone I knew, and I couldn't risk being found there. Especially not with two bodies in my trunk.

I quickly got in my car and drove off. I decided later that it was good to mix things up. The next time I'd do something completely different.

I was getting that tingly feeling again.

CHAPTER EIGHT

*A*mber *walked confidently through the* door of the Easton town library. Despite not being much of a student, she loved the library. When they were little, Fluffy took them to summer and weekend programs. There was reading, of course, but also drawing—illustrating your favorite character from a book and acting—performing roles from the books they read. That was her favorite part. Scarlet only wanted to read. She didn't enjoy drawing or acting.

Glancing around, Amber noticed several updates to the old library. There was an entire children's room now, with glass doors that kept the noise out of the main library. She located the computer room and selected a workstation in the corner. The large, empty surface of the desk spread out invitingly. She set her notebooks and pens and journal out and jiggled the computer mouse. A message flashed on the screen about entering your library card number. Pulling out her wallet, Amber searched for the card. She couldn't remember the last time she'd used it. Do library cards expire?

Sheepishly she approached the information desk. An older woman stood there, looking intimidating. Recognition struck Amber. This was her old nemesis, Ms. Bolger. Bolgey, as the kids called her, was strict. Strict was too kind. She was mean. She did not like children and delighted in making their lives miserable. Amber had been on Bolgey's shit list ever since she ran through the library screaming. When she tried to explain she was acting out the role of Tarzan swinging through the jungle, Bolgey grabbed her arm, sat her in a corner, and told her not to move until her mother picked her up. Hot tears had poured down Amber's cheeks in anger and embarrassment. No surprise children grew up to commit murder with people like Bolger in the world.

Amber's steps slowed as she approached the desk. She thought maybe she'd go back to the computer and wait until Bolgey went on break. Surely she took breaks? Before she could turn around, the stern librarian looked up, staring at her intensely. A slow smile began to spread across her face. It was not a friendly smile. "Amber Steen? Is that you? To what do I owe the pleasure of a visit from Tarzan?"

Amber forced a smile onto her face in reply. "Ms. Bolger. How lovely to see you. I didn't know you were still working here at the library."

The librarian's face returned to its usual grim mask. "Where would I be but here?"

Apparently, she believed Amber was suggesting she should be retired. That she was old. Bolgey was probably only in her fifties, the same age as her parents. "It's nice to see a familiar face," Amber continued with her frozen smile. "I can't find my library card and wondered if I could get a replacement?"

Ms. Bolger glared at Amber, probably contemplating on what grounds she could refuse to give her a new library card. Looking down, she typed on her keyboard and a hard plastic card, the size and shape of a credit card, popped out of a machine. "We've gone high tech. No more paper," she said as she handed it to Amber. "Let me know if I can help."

"Thanks. I will." Amber turned to the computer room. She forced herself to walk slowly, even though she wanted to run as fast as she could. Bolgey's gaze burned a hole in her back. Sitting down, she turned on the computer again and entered the card number at the prompt.

Time to get to work.

CHAPTER NINE

mber stared at the computer. She had no idea what she was looking for. Newspapers? Trial conscripts? Police reports? Were they all on the internet? Accessible to anyone? She should have asked Scarlet more questions.

Straightening her notebooks and writing instruments again, she waited for inspiration to strike. Maybe start by typing in the name of her friend? Heather Finn? Her fingers hovered over the keys. She felt paralyzed. Not ready to read the story again. When it all happened during her senior year of high school, she read everything she could. And of course, she and all her friends talked about it non-stop. Everyone knew Heather. Everyone knew everyone, which was one of the drawbacks of living in a small town. And this was certainly the first murder/murderer they knew. After the trial ended, Amber put the memories away. Now she was going to bring it all back up again. She loved true crime, but most of the cases she listened to were about strangers but here she was, researching to do a podcast specifically about people she knew. Was she ready for this?

A jarring voice jolted her back to reality. "Do you need some help?"

Amber looked up to see Bolgey looming over her. This was the last thing she needed. "Ummm… no. Just collecting my thoughts." The computer screen was still blank.

"You looked like a deer caught in the headlights, so it occurred to me, maybe you needed assistance." The librarian said, sitting in the seat next to her. This was getting worse and worse. "What are you looking for?"

Without thinking Amber said, "Murder."

"Oh!" Bolgey replied, her face lit up with sudden interest. "Are you looking into the River Road murders? Did you hear they found the bodies—skeletons more likely—of the two college students? I'm sure it's a serial killer. The question is, why did he wait six months between murders? Or maybe he travels around and there are more bodies piled up somewhere. Maybe there's a string of crimes stretching from here to California." Bolgey was off and running, and Amber waited until she ran out of steam.

When Bolgey finally stopped, Amber said, "No. Not the River Road murders, but now that you mention it, don't serial killers follow a pattern? These two crimes don't appear to have anything in common. The first one, the bodies were left in the car, basically in plain sight, and the second, the car was left but the victims were abducted and found miles away, buried in the woods? It doesn't really sound like the same killer. Other than location and two victims, what are the similarities?"

"Maybe the killer was interrupted the first time and had more time the second go round?" Bolgey countered. "Or maybe they wanted to mix it up to confuse the investigators, who now don't know if they are looking at the same killer in both cases."

"Ms. Bolger, I'd never have imagined you'd be interested in such things."

"I love true crime," the older woman said, a huge grin splitting her face. "I listen to it, read it, watch it. It's my passion."

Amber was stunned. Who would have ever imagined the strait-laced Bolgey would be a fan of true crime? "Me too. I'm totally obsessed, too." Amber nodded enthusiastically. Now she had an ally to help her. "But right now, I don't think we know enough about the River Road murders."

"True," Bolgey replied and paused. "I know the mother of one of the first victims. The younger woman, Becky Laurelwood. It's destroyed her not knowing why or what happened."

Amber glanced around conspiratorially, making sure no one could overhear them. The library appeared to be completely empty. "Wow. You know the victim? It's kinda why I'm here. My sister and I are starting a podcast called *The Murderer You Know*, and we're going to be focusing on murderers and victims we know and that our friends and family know. Maybe you could do a guest appearance." As soon as the words were out of her mouth, Amber wondered why the hell she'd confided in her old nemesis.

"Oh, I'd love to. That sounds so cool." The word cool did not sound natural coming out of the librarian's mouth. "What crime are you starting with?"

Too late now, Amber realized. She'd have to spill the beans. "Heather Finn."

"Your friend." Bolgey looked down, shaking her head. "That was a tough one. A complete shock. No one could have ever imagined something like that happening in our town."

Amber nodded, tears pricking the corners of her eyes.

They sat for a few moments, lost in their own memories. Bolgey sat up with a determined look on her face. "No time to waste. You need to get to work."

Amber was galvanized by Bolgey's determination. "Right. You're right. Where do I start?" she blurted out and then felt stupid. This was her podcast. Why was she deferring to Ms. Bolger?

"That depends," Bolgey replied. "What's your set-up? Timeline, so to speak? Backstory? Crime? Evidence? Trial?"

"The plan is to present the cases in two episodes." Amber hoped she sounded confident and in charge. "In the first, we'll discuss the crime. In the second, we'll cover the trial and the outcome. Sentence. Appeals. The legal stuff."

"I like it." The librarian replied. "Hook the listener with the first episode so they'll come back for the outcome of the case."

Amber nodded in agreement. "Exactly. I'll do most of the talking in the first episode, though Scarlet will be there to chime in. She'll take over in the second since she's the lawyer. Well, almost a lawyer."

"Okay, first you need to find all the information you can on the crime. Newspaper articles. For the trial part, you will have to file a FOIA request with the courts to get transcripts."

"FOIA?" Amber asked. "What?

"It means Freedom of Information Act, which was enacted in the sixties to give people access to federal agency records. In this case, we're looking for court records. Police reports. Those sorts of things."

Amber nodded. This was good to know. Maybe Scarlet mentioned something about it, but at the time it went right over her head.

Bolgey was still talking. "Sometimes you can even get autopsy reports. Trial transcripts. Some localities might be more difficult to deal with than others. Our little town should be easier because we don't have much violent crime." Bolgey paused, removing her eyeglasses, looking through the glass to check for dirt. She placed them back on the bridge of her nose and added, "Though I'm not sure if that is true anymore. Crime seems to be on the rise even in our sleepy edge of the world. Look at the River Road murders—though technically, I guess they didn't happen here but in a state park."

"Does River Road even qualify as a state park?" Amber asked. "It's just a scenic road along the river. People claim it only exists to generate revenue since the rangers spend all their time ticketing people for everything from speeding to camping violations."

"True. It is in its own little niche," Bolgey said. "No one seems to want to claim the River Road murders—not the park rangers or the local police. The park starts at the edge of our town and ends in Westburg. So I'm going to call it our crime."

After getting some pointers from Bolgey, Amber began her research in earnest. She Googled Heather's name and read all the newspaper articles she could find. Several pages of her first notebook were quickly filled. Even though she'd read all this back in high school when the crime occurred, she was surprised at how much she'd forgotten.

Before leaving for the day, she also got information on how to file a FOIA request. She decided she'd borrow her mother's car in the morning and drive to the courthouse. Without her laptop, it seemed the quickest way to get the information.

As she walked home, Amber realized she was going to have to get in touch with Bruce. The idea made her sick to her stomach, but she needed her laptop. She could do all the research at the library, however, once they started taping, she'd need her computer to record with Scarlet. It was probably a waste of time. If he'd found it in the boxes she'd left behind, he'd no doubt already sold it to pay rent for his baby-mama. The mantra *delete Bruce, delete Bruce*, played in her head as she walked home.

CHAPTER TEN

"**H**i, mom, I'm home," Amber called as she walked through the front door. She stopped inside the entrance and took a deep breath. The house smelled heavenly. Was that her all-time favorite? Tuna casserole and…? She couldn't quite discern the other smell, but she knew it was something baked and if her mom was making her favorites, they must be lemon bars.

"Hello dear, I'm in the kitchen," Fluffy called.

Of course, her mom was in the kitchen. It was her domain.

Amber set her notebooks on the hall table before heading to the kitchen. "Oh, Mom," she cried when she saw a full tray of lemon bars, "you've outdone yourself."

Reaching for a bar, Amber recoiled when her mom swatted her with a plastic spoon. "Dinner first. Go clean up and be back in fifteen minutes and you can tell your father and me all about your first day as a media star. My daughter, the influiser."

She leaned over and kissed her mom on the cheek. "Influencer, Mom. Remember?" Heading to the hall, she grabbed her notebooks and ran upstairs to her room. She set all her writing paraphernalia on her old desk and flopped down on her bed. Wait until she told her mother about her old nemesis, the dreaded Ms. Bolger, a true crime junkie who was helping her with research. Maybe Bolgey was also a *Law & Order* addict. They should have her over for dinner and Mom and Bolgey could chat about their favorite episode.

The first episode of the podcast was almost written. Tomorrow she'd go to the courthouse. Things were turning around. As Scarlet said, she just needed to find her passion. Who knew she could make a living talking about murder? In truth, she wasn't making any money yet and might never. Still, she could live with her parents forever, which might not be a bad thing.

The aroma of the tuna casserole wafting up the stairs brought another Bruce memory. One day she prepared it for dinner using her mom's recipe. She'd just pulled it out of the oven, piping hot, when Bruce walked into the kitchen and said, "What's that horrible smell?"

"Horrible? What on earth do you mean? It's tuna casserole, one of my all-time favorites."

Without another word, he marched across the kitchen, picked up a dish towel, grabbed the casserole off the stove, walked to the back door, flung the door wide, and tossed the casserole out into the yard where it shattered, scattering shards of glass and tuna all over.

"Leave the door open to get rid of the smell." Bruce snatched a beer out of the fridge and headed to the living room.

Amber felt as shattered as the casserole dish. Why hadn't she packed and left right then?

She repeated her mantra *delete Bruce, delete Bruce*, until her mom called her to dinner. She bounced down the steps with a smile on her face.

Dad was already sitting at the table. He nodded at Amber before turning his attention to his food. Fluffy placed a plate mounded up with the delectable dish in front of Amber. "I know how much you love my tuna casserole." She smiled.

"And lemon bars." Amber grinned at her mother before digging in.

Later in the den, munching on lemon bars, Amber filled her mother in on her day. "You'll never believe who is a huge true crime fan," she said. "Ms. Bolger. That stuffy old librarian. Who'd have ever imagined that? And it's great because she's excited to help and has already given me helpful hints on my research. I'm glad I went to the library to do my work."

"People are full of surprises," her mother replied.

"You remember her, right?" Amber asked. "She was always calling you to complain about me. I almost fainted when I walked in, and she was behind the desk. I assumed she was retired." Amber took another bite of her lemon bar. "She probably isn't even that old, but when I was in elementary school, I considered her ancient."

Fluffy smiled. "Yes, of course I remember her. I do still go to the library. I belong to the book club. And your Aunt Ida is great friends with Ms. B. In fact, we were all in school together. I always thought she liked you. She admired your spunk, but she couldn't let you run amok."

Amber was shocked. "Aunt Ida is friends with Bolgey? Wow. They're so different. Bolgey is all suits and blouses and Ida, is, you know, like jeans and boots."

"Opposites attract," Fluffy said, picking up her knitting.

CHAPTER ELEVEN

W*ith Bolgey's help, Amber was* able to complete the research on their first three murders. She filled out all the FIOA requests and visited the courthouse. She also went to Westburg, where some of the trials took place. She used the information she gathered to write up the episodes. Basically, bullet points to bring up during the podcast while talking with Scarlet. She also included questions about the trials.

One day, while she was finishing up at the library, Bolgey came over and handed her a piece of paper with a web address.

"What's this?" Amber asked, staring at what looked like the library website.

"Since you're spending so much time at the library, maybe you should get a job here. I know you don't have a lot of expenses living at your parents' house, but it's nice to have something to put on your resume when you start looking for a job. A real job. Or if you go back to school." Bolgey smiled. "Of course, once the podcast takes off, you won't have time for a small-town library."

"Wouldn't it be wonderful if I could make a living talking about crime and murder?" Amber grinned.

"It would be, but you're up against a lot of competition. Take this home and if you want to, fill it out. If nothing else, it will give you some pocket money. Your Aunt Ida told me you don't have a car. Always nice for a young person to have a car. Get out. Meet friends."

This was the first time Bolgey mentioned Ida's name. She managed to drop it casually into their conversation. Amber was still mulling over her mother's words about opposites being attracted. Giving Bolgey a stealthy look under her lashes, she wondered if Ida and Ms. Bolger were more than casual acquaintances? More than friends? Ida never married. When Amber was little, she asked her aunt why she didn't have a husband and kids.

Ida had laughed uproariously. "Being married is nice for people like your mother. Domestic sorts. Mothering types. That's not me. I want to be my own person. Don't want anyone telling me what to do, and sometimes husbands feel they can do that." Ida pointed to herself and shook her head with a smile. "Look at me. I'm no beauty queen or Barbie doll. I'm bigger and stronger than most of the men I know. Even in high school, the boys were kinda scared of me. Which suited me just fine."

Was her aunt gay? Amber shook her head. It wasn't any of her business how Ida lived her life or who her friends were or what their relationship was.

After being involved with Bruce, she envied Ida and wished she'd never gotten involved with a man. That wasn't fair, she told herself. Not all men were like Bruce. Very few, in fact. Lots of nice guys who were friends of hers wanted to date her. What was wrong with her that she fell for a totally self-centered ass?

Bruce still has my laptop. They were ready to start recording the podcast, but Amber didn't have a laptop. She couldn't record at the library. She shuddered. *I'm going to have to call Bruce.* Maybe she could threaten him with the police. Or better yet, she could threaten him with Scarlet.

As soon as she got home, right after dinner, she'd fill out the job application and then text Bruce. She thought she might throw up if she heard his voice.

CHAPTER TWELVE

At dinner, Amber proudly told her parents about her job application. "Who'd have ever thought that Bolgey, excuse me, Ms. Bolger, would offer me, of all people, a job at the library?"

"It shows how far you've come." Her mother smiled. "People know you aren't that wild child anymore. You're a mature, responsible adult."

Her father grunted in assent.

Amber winced inwardly. Not quite a hundred percent responsible but working toward it. First step was getting her laptop. She couldn't wait any longer. And she couldn't wait until she got her first paycheck, which might be a month or more. Her parents would loan her the money, but she didn't want to have to explain why she needed a new laptop. And her mother might suggest she use her money from her grandmother. Amber did not want to open the Pandora's box of her inheritance.

In her room, she took her phone out and stared at Bruce's name in the contacts. *Now or never. I won't explode into flames from one text.* If he ignored her, she'd have to go to Plan B. He'd call her names. Did she care? The most likely scenario was he'd deny any knowledge of her laptop or its whereabouts since he'd no doubt already sold it.

She blew out a long breath.

Bruce. I know we didn't part on the best of terms. I was blindsided by the bank taking the farm and meeting your pregnant fiancée.

She paused. Making him feel guilty might work. Maybe there was one ounce of decency left in him.

I left my laptop behind. I need it for my new job and can't purchase a new one since I have no money. Is it in your car?

She decided to lay the guilt on. Why not? He deserved it.

Please let me know asap so I can get it.

Now she considered a little kindness and generosity might go a long way.

Congratulations on your upcoming wedding and baby.

Before she chickened out, she pushed send. Flopping onto her bed, she stared at the ceiling. Now she'd have to wait. Chances were she'd never hear from him. Or he'd send a lame-ass text beginning with "Babe, so sorry" and other bullshit. It had been worth a try. Maybe she could borrow money from Aunt Ida. She wouldn't feel completely humiliated admitting to Ida she'd lost all the money her grandmother left her. Ida was a roll-with-the-punches kind of person. Fluffy wouldn't scream or yell, but the hurt look in her eyes would be worse.

Amber must have dozed off because she startled awake when her phone pinged. A text! Was it Bruce? Other than Scarlet, no one else texted her. Bolting up, she scrambled to find her phone, which was lost in the bedsheets. The screen said *Bruce*. She felt like she might vomit. Nervously, she swiped her screen.

Babe. I miss you. I was so confused when you ran off. That girl was not my fiancée. No way. And that baby is definitely not mine.

Amber rolled her eyes. No surprise he started off calling her Babe and made excuses about the pregnant girl.

I haven't looked in those boxes. I'm living in a dumpy room. I've been too depressed to do anything.

I miss you. I miss our farm. Our life.

OMG! Amber wanted to scream. She just wanted her laptop, not a travelogue of Bruce's misery.

I'll check and let you know.

Amber set the phone down and groaned. How and why did she ever fall in love with someone so utterly useless? An hour later, her phone pinged, and she picked it up. Another text from Bruce.

Good news. I found your laptop. I'll bring it this week. Let's talk. Straighten things out.

There was nothing to straighten out. Did he really think she was dumb enough to fall for his lines again? Probably.

So glad you found my laptop. Don't worry about bringing it. I can come up. What day is good?

Bruce texted back, saying he was more than happy to bring it. He wanted to see her again. Amber said no, don't come. Finally, he said he'd give her a day he'd be available. This was followed by more sloppy, crappy, moany stuff about loving and missing her. Amber ignored it all and insisted he give her a day and a time. She needed her laptop that week.

He responded, *Okay Babe.*

She almost gagged. Thank goodness it was over. She was proud of herself. She didn't cave to Bruce and his apparent desire to resurrect their relationship. She wondered briefly about the pregnant girl. And thought about Bruce living in a room instead of a whole farm. That wouldn't sit well with him. He held a rather high opinion of himself, envisioning himself as the lord of the manor. Now he was lord of a bed-sit.

Tomorrow she'd ask to borrow the car, telling her mom she had to go up to the mountains to collect some things she left. Which was true.

CHAPTER THIRTEEN

*A*mber *checked her phone for* a message from Bruce the minute she woke up. Nothing. She snorted in disgust. How hard was it for him to give her a day to come up? Resolving to call him after lunch if she still hadn't heard anything, she went downstairs for breakfast.

After eating, she used her phone to finish her job application for the library. Her anger at Bruce bubbled up. She needed her laptop. Although I am to blame for storming off and leaving it with him, she thought.

After working for a couple of hours on the podcast, she looked at her watch. It was eleven. There was still nothing from Bruce. She'd call at eleven-thirty, despite not wanting to have an actual conversation with him. He was annoying and manipulative enough on text. She probably couldn't shut him up long enough to arrange a date to come up. Maybe she'd drive up tomorrow. A surprise attack. He'd be completely shocked to see her outside his door—stunned into silence. She could waltz past him, grab her laptop, and be in the car heading home before he recovered enough to speak.

There was only one problem with this plan. She had no idea where he was living. He mentioned a one room dump but didn't give the address. Hmmm.

Who might know where he was? Maybe the ex-fiancée? Amber remembered where she lived. Hopefully that girl would know where Bruce was.

While considering her options, the doorbell rang. Maybe it was the delivery of the microphones and headphones she'd ordered. "I'll get it." Swinging the front door open, she felt the bombs dropping on her. Talk about a sneak attack. Bruce stood in the doorway with a huge smile on his face. There was a box by his feet, which she hoped held her laptop.

"Hey babe. I had nothing better to do, so I thought I'd drive down and deliver this in person. Take you out for lunch. Talk about all the good old times and hopefully convince you to forgive me and take me back." He smiled with what she assumed he believed was an endearing, heartbroken puppy smile. He'd probably spent an hour practicing it in the mirror.

"That is not happening," Amber squeaked. "Give me my things and leave."

"Babe. Why so angry? You know, you're kind of cute when you're mad." Bruce leaned in the door, like he was going for a hug and a kiss to soothe her.

"And if you say *Babe* one more time, I swear I will punch you in the face. As hard as I can," Amber spit out.

Bruce laughed. "Babe..."

Amber hauled off and punched him in the jaw. His head jerked back a bit from the blow, though it didn't look like it had affected him very much. Her brain, meanwhile, exploded with pain signals. Horrible agony radiated from her hand, and sharp screaming sensations shot up and down her arm. She was sure she'd broken her hand, her wrist, and her arm.

Last night, Amber and her dad watched an action movie and nobody winced when they slugged someone. It looked so easy and so satisfying.

Reality hurt. A tortured scream erupted from Amber's lips as she clutched her throbbing hand. Bruce stood there, rubbing his jaw, looking at her, completely mystified. "Babe, what the hell? That kinda hurt."

Babe! He'd said "Babe" again. She wished she had the resilience of the people in the movie so she could punch him again. And again. Suddenly her father was next to her, clutching Bruce by his shirt, wrestling him out the door while uttering incoherent sounds of rage.

Bruce tried to defend himself as he was pushed backwards. "Dude! I didn't do anything. Amber punched me. I didn't touch her."

They disappeared from sight, and Amber heard someone stumbling down the stairs. "You guys are all fucking nuts," Bruce yelled.

The next moment, her father was in the doorway picking up the box, turning to throw it out after Bruce.

"No, Dad!" Amber screeched. "No. That's mine, not his. Don't toss it out." Her father set the box down and slammed the door before enveloping Amber in a bear hug.

Fluffy appeared a moment later. She took one look at Amber's hand, which she held out in front of her, her fingers outstretched. "What on earth?" Fluffy took her into the kitchen to apply first aid. "What were you thinking?" Fluffy shook her head while swathing Amber's hand in an ice wrap. "Punching someone in the jaw? Didn't you realize it would hurt?"

"It always looks easy in the movies," Amber moaned.

"You two are forbidden to watch any more of those silly action movies." Amber's father hung his head, looking embarrassed. "Why was Bruce here? I thought you two broke up?"

"Yes. We did. But he apparently thought we should get back together. I told him I was going up to see him for the few things I'd left there, and he decided to come here and woo me." Amber slumped in her chair and put her head on the table.

"Don't worry, dear. First, I don't think your hand is broken and I don't think Bruce will want to take on you two ever again."

Later, her father carried the box upstairs, and Amber opened it, pulled out her laptop, and lovingly hugged it. She felt like she was whole again.

The next day Amber made it to the library and asked Bolgey about her job application. Bolgey smiled. "It looked great. Quite professional. We can start you in a week or two, after HR completes the paperwork. Part time. Does that sound good?"

Wow. That was going to be great. She'd get paid for hanging out at the library. Best job ever.

CHAPTER FOURTEEN

Two *weeks after Amber emailed* her application, she had a part-time job at the library. The job varied daily since she filled in wherever needed, from sorting and shelving books to checking them out. She was also in charge of the preschool reading hour on Wednesdays.

The best part of the job was that she still had plenty of time to work on the podcast. Amber had written the introductory episode which she and Scarlet would be recording that night. They planned to record once a week. Once they had a dozen episodes recorded, edited, and in the can, they'd blast the debut all over social media.

Amber fiddled with her headphones and cleared her throat for the tenth time. She didn't know why she was so nervous. It wasn't as if they were broadcasting live. Still, she wanted everything to be perfect. Thank goodness she got her laptop back.

Logging into Zoom, Scarlet's face popped up on the screen, her mouth moving without sound. Scarlet was flapping her hands and pointing. Amber looked down and saw the audio symbol at the bottom of the screen was x-ed out. She clicked on it.

"Damn girl." Scarlet said. "I thought you at least knew how to turn on your system."

"Stop. I'm nervous."

"Nothing to be nervous about. You got this. It's just the intro. Not a complete episode."

Amber swallowed. "I know, but we have to hook the audience on this one. I'll have to use my deep and serious voice." She pushed the record button, and a disembodied voice said, "Recording in progress."

PODCAST

Episode One: Introduction

Amber: This is *The Murderer You Know*. Episode One. Coming to you live.

Scarlet: Not exactly live, but still you got us.

Amber: True. Are you ready to talk about murder?

Scarlet: Always. This is going to be good research for my job.

Amber: First, let's introduce ourselves and explain how we ended up here. Basically, I'm a blabbermouth and you're an expert on crime and legal stuff.

Scarlet: How exciting to be called an expert.

Amber: Now we have a mystery for our audience. You are knowledgeable in the world of crime, but does that mean you work in the judicial system or are you a criminal?

Scarlet: Ohhh… good question. We'll let people wonder about it for now. When should we have the big reveal? At the end of this episode?

Amber: Let's wait and see. Right now, I want to ask you, when you are walking down the street or out shopping, do you look at people and think, "OMG, do they have a body in their trunk?"

Scarlet: Yes. Especially if they're buying duct tape and a shovel.

Amber: That's way too obvious. My radar goes up when I see people with tarps in their shopping carts.

Scarlet: I often speculate about people's secrets. Especially people who look like they are trying way too hard to seem normal.

Amber: Me too. I've always been obsessed with true crime and I'm always imagining the worst. Like last night when my dad went in the house and I walked in five minutes later and didn't hear anyone moving around, I immediately thought a murderer had snuck in the back door and killed everyone. It was crazy.

Scarlet: Pretty crazy and a bit paranoid.

Amber: Maybe. But we shall begin by telling the audience about Enrico Fermi and the Fermi problem. Have you heard his murder theory?

Scarlet: No, I don't believe I have.

Amber: Have you heard the statement that most of us walk past thirty-six murderers in our lifetime? It's based on a mathematical equation. That was Fermi's premise. If it's not obvious, he was a mathematician.

Scarlet: Oh no. Are we going to talk about math? That alone might cause people to commit murder.

Amber: I'm horrified by the thought that we are possibly walking past murderers all day long. Might be way more than thirty-six. Does that number make sense to you? That the average person passes by that many murderers in their lifetime? How many would that be? Less than one a year?

Scarlet: Don't tell me you are actually doing math.

Amber: I need a calculator. But back to the question. Do you think that's true?

Scarlet: Remember, I'm not the best example of the average person since I'm in court a lot of the time, so I'm encountering far more criminals than normal people do.

Amber: True, but are you walking by them in a business suit or in a prison jumpsuit?

Scarlet: Wouldn't you like to know? Also, it depends on where you live. If you live in New York City, you walk by more people than if you live in a small town. There are probably lots more murderers in big cities.

Amber: I live in one of those small towns. And even I know murderers. Shocking but true. My mom and dad know murderers and my aunt does too. So, other than in your professional life, do you know any murderers or people who have been murdered?

Scarlet: Sadly yes. However, we must remember it is not the random murderer that we are passing on the street who we need to fear. Most murders, almost eighty percent, are committed by family members or friends of the victim.

Amber: Hence the title of our podcast: *The Murderer You Know*. We will be discussing crimes that were personal. Committed by the people the victim thought they had nothing to fear from.

Scarlet: We are exploring what makes some people snap. What makes them think they can get away with murder, and why they murder the people they know. And supposedly love.

Amber: Our podcast will be a little different from most True Crime podcasts because we are not going after the big names or the sensational crimes absolutely everyone talks about. We are talking about the person next door. The surprise murderer. People we never imagined would ever murder anyone. Also, we won't be naming the names of the perpetrator or the victims.

Scarlet: Since these are small crimes that never made the national news, we don't want to out anyone on the show.

Amber: Join us next week for our first case. We hope this intro has intrigued you and you'll come back. We'd love to hear from you on our socials.

Scarlet: I can't wait.

Amber: And now I will say goodbye to my co-host who might be a criminal, or a judge, or a cop.

Scarlet: Good night.

Amber stopped recording.

"Damn girl," Scarlet hooted. "We did it. Now we put it out into the world and see what happens."

"Yes indeed. I'll see you in a couple of days to record the first episode. My Childhood BFF. And Scarlet, thank you for doing this with me. It means a lot."

"Of course. Anytime."

CHAPTER FIFTEEN

*A*mber squealed when she saw the time. This was her first day running
the children's reading program and she wanted to be early to get everything
set up. Downstairs, she grabbed a granola bar and the lunch Fluffy packed
for her.

"Sit down, breakfast will be ready in a minute," her mom said.

Amber gave her a quick kiss on the cheek. "Sorry mom, I'm running
late."

As Amber turned to leave, the news came on the radio. Fluffy never
turned the TV on during the day, preferring to listen to the local radio
station with all its news about events in their town instead of stories from
all around the world. Her mom planned her day by the weather report
given daily at five minutes after the hour.

A serious voice came over the radio: "We have breaking news. An
abandoned vehicle has been found on River Road and foul play is suspected.
The police aren't releasing much information but dogs and officers are
searching the area. We'll update the story as we learn more."

Amber and her mother stared at each other.

"Not another one," Amber said.

"Serial killer," her mother mouthed to her.

"We'll talk later. I have to go," Amber said, running out the door. As she half jogged to the library, Amber knew Bolgey would be full of the news, speculating on this latest event.

Rushing in the back door, she ran into Bolgey in the staff lunchroom.

"Have you heard the latest?" Bolgey said. "We need to talk."

"Yes. We do. I heard it on the way out the door but haven't heard any details. But right now, I need to get to my program."

"Let's meet at lunch," the librarian suggested.

Amber only nodded as she dashed to the kid's room. The children's program went well, even though Amber had a hard time focusing on fuzzy animals and the lessons they were imparting. She couldn't wait for the program to end so she could sit down with Bolgey and talk about the news.

After the kids left, each clutching a book in hand, Amber put away all the supplies—crayons, drawing paper, and books. Lucky for her, she loved kid's books, reading each character in a different voice to engage the children and make them laugh. It wasn't quite the acting career she once dreamed of, but she enjoyed her job. When everything had been returned to its proper cubby, Amber walked to the lunchroom.

Bolgey was waiting. "You sure took long enough."

"Did you want me to tell the little darlings I had to cut the program short so I could talk about murder?" Amber laughed.

"Of course not," Bolgey replied. "Now sit down. We don't have a lot of time. Our lunch break is almost over."

"Let me grab my sandwich," Amber said.

She sat and unwrapped her tuna sandwich, which was beautifully prepared by her mother. There was also a soda, a bag of chips, and an apple. And of course there was a cookie. "Is there any more news? I only heard they'd found a car on River Road and were searching with dogs."

"Not much. You know how the police are. And the park rangers. I think the Chief Ranger, Rick Richardson, is trying to keep the investigation under the parks' jurisdiction, but Chief Wallace and the Westburg police are horning in, saying they are out of their depth." Bolgey shook her head. "Which is no doubt true. Even our local police are trying to get in on the action. Everyone thinks whoever solves this will be local heroes."

"They will be. I mean, this is crazy. Nothing like this has ever happened here before." Amber took a bite of her sandwich and chewed thoughtfully.

"All we know so far," Bolgey continued, "is they found another car. Empty. Not burned. I'm sure they've identified the owner of the car, but they're saying nothing, and I mean nothing. Maybe they'll have a press conference on the evening news."

"I remember when they tried to pass off the second disappearance as a possible drowning," Amber said. "Now what are they saying since they finally found the bodies? Miles away! How crazy is that? Will they finally admit these events are connected?"

"Could it be the work of one person?" Bolgey said.

"I'm guessing it would have to be two at least," Amber replied. "Working together. Because how could one person control two people while trying to murder them?"

"I'm not sure if they've reached that conclusion yet. Maybe they think it's just all a coincidence," Bolgey said.

Amber swallowed the last bite of her sandwich. "You know what they say—there are no coincidences."

Bolgey nodded.

CHAPTER SIXTEEN

𝒜*mber finished her shift at* the library and headed home. She and Scarlet were recording that night, so she had to get ready. Which, of course, meant first eating another one of her mother's fabulous dinners. It was a good thing she was walking everywhere.

After dinner, Amber and her parents watched the news together. Her mother's favorite investigative reporter, Sandy Foss, stood in front of police headquarters but he had very little information. It appeared the Westburg police had finally muscled the park rangers out of the way since it was the Westburg chief of police, Bob Wallace, at the podium with a dozen microphones in front of him. Chief Wallace was a bull of a man and looked impressive in his pressed gray and blue uniform, complete with lots of stripes, epaulets, and what appeared to be medals.

Standing behind him was the chief park ranger, someone from the state police, and even Easton's local sheriff, Buster Fenster. In comparison to Chief Wallace, Sheriff Fenster seemed a bit rumpled in his khaki uniform.

Chief Wallace announced he had a statement and would not be taking any questions. "We found an abandoned car on River Road this morning.

A jogger reported it. When park rangers arrived, they found no signs of a struggle or any other kind of disturbance. After a preliminary search, the state police brought in their dogs. The canines led us down to the river, but the trail ended there." He glanced at his notes.

"We have identified the owner of the car; however, we will not be divulging that information at this time." He looked around at the officers standing behind him before facing the reporters again. "It is our consensus there is no connection between this event and other incidents on River Road."

Chief Wallace stood back, and the chief park ranger, Richards or Rogers, Amber could not remember his name, stepped forward. "If you were on River Road between last evening and early this morning and were in the vicinity of the Eagle Nest Outlook parking spot, and saw anything, anything at all, a car, a person acting suspiciously, please call the number on your screen." A phone number popped up on the bottom of the TV screen. "We have people standing by to take your call."

"We are coordinating efforts between all the law enforcement agencies that border River Road. Which of course includes my park rangers, the Westburg police, and the Sheriff's department from Easton." Sheriff Fenster stood taller at the mention of his little town.

"The phone lines are open now. Thank you." At that, all the various law enforcement officers turned and walked away while reporters shouted questions after them.

Dad turned the TV off. Fluffy shook her head in disgust. "No connection? Really? Who are they trying to fool?" Dad grunted in what Amber assumed was agreement.

"It is a bit of a coincidence cars are left on River Road, people disappear and are murdered, and yet they want us to think there's no connection." Amber snorted. "I'm not buying it. I guess they don't want to cause a panic. People thinking there's a serial killer loose in our town."

Fluffy agreed. "I don't like that Chief Wallace. I've heard things about him over the years. I think he's as crooked as they come. I wish our own

Sheriff Fenster was in charge. He may not look as spit and polished as Wallace but he's local and a good honest fellow. I think Wallace spends half the police budget on his fancy uniforms."

Amber's phone dinged and she looked down. Scarlet texted saying she'd be ready to record by 7:30. Amber said goodnight to her parents and went up to her room. This was the night they were finally recording their first murder podcast. About her childhood BFF, Heather. Amber was nervous. She closed the door to her room. Making sure the script was close by, she checked her headphones and microphone before logging in. A moment later, Scarlet's face and voice appeared on her computer screen.

"You ready for our first real case?" Scarlet asked.

"Yeah, but have you heard the latest? Another car has been found on River Road and the occupants are missing."

"No," Scarlet gasped.

"At this point, they don't even know if they're dead or maybe got picked up by a friend or if there was more than one occupant in the car. Or if they do know, they're not saying."

"I guess it could be somebody who broke down and walked to a friend's house," Scarlet said hopefully.

"I don't like how this sounds. Something is happening every six months. The first murder, and that definitely was a murder, since the victims were bludgeoned, strangled, and burned, happened a year ago. Six months later those college kids disappeared and of course the police decided drunk college kids went skinny dipping and drowned. Not a murder. Now their bodies, or I should say bones, were found, which was a complete fluke. What are the chances of someone stumbling over their remains in the woods?"

"Have they said how they died?" Scarlet asked.

"Not really. It appeared they were possibly, maybe, hit on the head. Who knows what actually killed them."

"Damn."

"The police say there is nothing linking the incidents."

"That sounds like total crap," Scarlet said.

"I agree. It's too much of a coincidence."

"And there are no such thing as coincidences," Scarlet said.

They both laughed. "Truth."

"It's obvious they think they're related because they have this huge task force made up of the park rangers, state police, Chief Wallace from Westburg, and even our own sheriff."

"If Buster Fenster is on the case, they'll crack it soon," Scarlet said, rolling her eyes.

"For sure." Amber laughed.

"We better get to recording before we run out of time," Scarlet said. "Turn on the recording and let's start."

CHAPTER SEVENTEEN

The robotic voice said, "Recording in Progress," and Amber's pre-recorded voice intoned, "This is *The Murderer You Know*, coming to you with our first full episode and our first murder."

PODCAST

Episode Two: Your Childhood BFF

Amber: Welcome back. As promised, this story is about a murderer we both knew. It was a case that rocked our small town. This episode is called *Your Childhood BFF*.

Scarlet: A few years ago, the 911 dispatcher received a call saying there'd been an accident, and they needed to send an ambulance to a certain address. The dispatcher tried to ask more questions, but the caller just repeated they needed to get there as quickly as possible before hanging up.

Amber: The police, fire, and ambulance were dispatched. The police arrived first and saw the door to the garage was open. A young woman sat there calmly smoking a cigarette. She appeared to be covered in blood.

Scarlet: The police asked what happened and the young woman said, "My mom's in the bedroom." An officer asked if her mother was injured. The young woman nodded and continued smoking. The police entered the house and in one of the back bedrooms, the police found an older woman on the floor.

Amber: The dead woman was the mother of the young woman who called 911. That young woman was my best friend. My BFF. We had been so close. Did everything together. Dance. Gymnastics. Sleepovers.

Scarlet: It must have been a terrible shock to find out your friend had murdered her mother.

Amber: Yes, it was. The murder was shocking to all of us at school—everyone in the community.

Scarlet: But we need to get back to the crime. The police arrived, and they found an older woman dead.

Amber: The report said there was blood everywhere, though they called it a red substance, consistent with blood. Why do they do that? Can't they just say blood?

Scarlet: Because saying it's blood is a legal conclusion or a factual conclusion. At this point, it looks like blood, but it hasn't been conclusively determined yet through forensics.

Amber: I don't want to give anything away; however, you're sounding pretty legal. Are you possibly a police officer?

Scarlet: You'll have to wait until the big reveal. In the police's defense, they can report what they see but they can't make a conclusion, like saying it's blood. They can only say it appears to be blood.

Amber: Got it. And I'm really leaning toward you being on the side of law and order.

Scarlet: I'm happy to find out you think I'm on the right side of the law. So, what else did the police find besides a body and lots of blood?

Amber: Once they found the body, they probably had to wait for the detectives and the medical examiner. After taking pictures and doing everything they needed to do, they moved the body and found a large butcher knife underneath the victim.

Scarlet: I'm guessing the knife was the murder weapon.

Amber: I'm sure they assumed it was, but they couldn't say for sure. There was lots of forensic evidence to collect. There were tons of bloody paper towels in the trash. There was also a weird scene in the bathroom. The sink was smeared with blood, as if someone tried to wipe the surface with a towel but only managed to make a bigger mess.

While they were searching, they kept hearing the dryer stopping and starting, so they checked it out and found clothes and towels in the dryer. Apparently, they'd been washed and were in the process of being dried.

Scarlet: So, it was a mixed scene. Blood everywhere but some signs of attempts to clean up?

Amber: Yes. Later, when they got the body to the medical examiner, a whole new level of hell was discovered. The older woman was covered in bruises and cuts, many small and partially healed but others deep and wrapped in bandages. It appeared abuse had been going on for a long time.

Scarlet: That is horrific.

Amber: At some point, one of the detectives returned to the garage, read the young woman her Miranda rights, and told her they'd be taking her to the police station. She didn't react, just stood up, allowing the police to cuff her and drive her to the station.

Scarlet: At the station, the police asked if she wanted a lawyer, and she said no. Then they asked her what happened. She said she and her mom argued constantly because her mom stayed in bed all day and did nothing. She didn't even cook. The young girl said she was exhausted trying to take care of everything. Remember, this girl was still in high school.

Amber: She also said she was worried about her mom's mental and physical well-being, which is surprising since it certainly appeared she'd been hurting her mom for some time based on all the bruises and cuts.

Scarlet: I know. Doesn't make any sense. She told the police before she left for school that morning, she'd given her mom some tasks to complete, but when she got home in the afternoon, her mom was still in bed and, of course, there was no dinner. She said she lost it and started yelling at her mom.

Amber: Did she explain about the knife?

Scarlet: She claimed she'd started making dinner and went into her mom's room and began 'poking' her mom with the knife. She claimed she never meant to hurt her. She was only trying to get her mom's attention. At some point, one of the 'pokes' went into her left chest. This poke was two inches deep and severed her aorta. And her mother died.

Amber: So, she's claiming she snapped and started poking her mom with the knife to make a point? To get her attention? Still, it doesn't explain the bruises and bandages all over her body.

Scarlet: It's horrifying to imagine that this went on for… days? Weeks? Months? Her mom had bandages covering cuts all over her body. And if that wasn't bad enough, she had seven rib fractures in various stages of healing.

Amber: At some point during the interview, she cracked. She began to sob as if she finally grasped what happened. What she'd done. It was like she was in denial and suddenly the fog lifted.

Scarlet: You have to wonder what turned this basically normal kid into someone who tortures and kills their mother.

Amber: I remember her when we were little as the sweetest kid. She was happy and so full of joy. Even my mom described her as a little ray of sunshine. How did she become this person? I couldn't wrap my head around it.

Scarlet: It's hard to imagine that little girl grew up to commit murder.

Amber: I felt so guilty at the time. I never asked her what the hell was going on. Why didn't I say anything after she stopped going to dance and gymnastics? Or when she started hanging out with the wrong crowd? I just let her drift away.

Scarlet: It's easy to see what we should have done when we're looking backwards.

Amber: Exactly. Everyone felt they should have done something. Should have noticed. All the what-if's and if-onlys. It's a normal human reaction. We beat ourselves up for what we should have done.

Scarlet: On next week's episode, we'll discuss the trial.

Amber: It doesn't seem to be much of a cliff hanger since BFF confessed.

Scarlet: You never know. Even though this seems cut and dried, even if people confess, they still get a lawyer. Once a defense attorney gets the case, it's a whole new ball game.

Amber: I'm guessing there might be some surprises. Our listeners will have to come back next week to find out. When we talk about the trial and the verdict.

Amber gave the closing byline for the show and stopped recording.

She laid her head on the table and let out a big sigh. "Wow, that was really emotional. Researching brought back all the memories I tried to bury and forget."

"I bet," Scarlet said. "It was a great episode and a good place to stop because it will make people want to listen to find out what happened. I want to find out! Since I was already off at college, I wasn't as deeply affected by this as you were. Didn't even know about Mom and BFF's mom being friends."

"Do you think it went well? Of course, I'll listen and clean it up. I say let's not wait until we have a bunch of recordings. Let's drop the intro episode and this one the week after. If we record once or twice a week, we should be able to keep up. I'm excited and don't want to wait."

"I can understand that," Scarlet replied. "Let's go for it. Hopefully, the world will be as excited as we are, and we'll have a huge following soon."

"Love you, Scarlet. Thank you. And I'm going to start keeping track of the River Road murders. They're getting way too creepy."

"I agree. Something weird is going on, and either the police are lying to us or there really is no connection. As a Murder Podcaster, what is your professional opinion?" Scarlet laughed.

"I seriously don't know what to think. Sometimes I think the crimes are completely unrelated. Hell, we don't even know any details on this last one. Could be a simple explanation. Maybe someone's car broke down and they walked home?"

"But if that's what happened, why did they have a press conference?" Scarlet asked. "Why didn't they simply say: 'Nobody panic. Nothing's going on.'"

"That's why I want to write it all down. I'm going revisit the first crime and dig up everything I can. When it's solved, we'll be ready."

Talk about shock. When I heard the news on the radio about the latest murders, I almost ran off the road. What the hell was going on? I hadn't killed anyone. Was thinking about it but hadn't gotten around to it. Someone appeared to be horning in on my murders. A copycat killer? Perhaps a personal murder and they thought they'd confuse things by convincing the police it was part of the crime spree on River Road. I couldn't decide if I should be angry or proud.

Later, after I watched the press conference, I couldn't stop laughing. Apparently, the Keystone Cops were in charge of the investigation. I felt bolstered by their ineptitude.

When they said there didn't appear to be a connection between the crimes, they were right, but I doubt they knew that. They're trying to stop mass hysteria from sweeping the towns of Easton and Westburg. "Serial killer on the loose," the mob would scream.

I could go on killing people for years before they connected the dots. Especially if there's another killer lurking out there. Wonder how I might find out who that clever person is. Maybe we could work together.

CHAPTER EIGHTEEN

Amber couldn't wait to get to the library the next day and talk to Bolgey. She wanted to tell her she and Scarlet had recorded the first official murder podcast. They decided not to wait to launch it, hoping to do it next week after the second episode was recorded.

She knew the librarian would be all worked up about the latest events and the police press conference. She was not surprised to find Bolgey waiting by the door for her to arrive. The librarian started talking the minute Amber walked in.

"Hold on," Amber said, heading to the breakroom. "Let me put my lunch in the fridge and I'll be right back out."

Bolgey could not contain herself and followed Amber to the break room.

"Did you see the press conference?" she asked.

"Yes. Watched it with mom and dad."

"How did you feel about it? I don't think they're telling us the whole story. Even on the news this morning, there is nothing about the owner of the car. Of course, the internet is blowing up with theories."

"I agree. It was seriously the strangest event. Like we're all gathered here but there's really nothing going on."

"They're going to have to tell us about the car soon," Bolgey said. "People are panicking. Some say they need to close down River Road."

"I hope they don't do that. It's really the only good way to get from here to Westburg. Maybe just close it after dark or have more patrols?"

Bolgey's watch dinged, and she glanced down at her wrist. "Let's check the news online."

Luckily, there were no patrons in the library, and Amber's shift didn't start for an hour. Amber pulled up her phone and scrolled through the local news app while standing at the open door, keeping an eye out for anyone coming in.

The headline read: *Breaking News: abandoned car on River Road identified. Police have identified the owner of the car as a seventeen-year-old high school student. He was giving his brother's girlfriend a ride home after a family cookout. The body of the boy has been found along the bank of the river. The young girl has not been found yet. The police are searching the area. It appears they may be speculating she's in the water. A cause of death for the boy hasn't been released.*

The door of the library opened and Amber swiped to close the app. Both women exited the breakroom and went to their duty stations to get ready for the day.

All day long it was all anyone who came in talked about. Even young mothers, after dropping their children off for the reading programs, gathered to gossip. "Another car. Another body. Another murder."

Details floated through Amber's mind all day. Could this be the work of a serial killer or an odd coincidence? The first killing appeared to be very personal. The other two did not appear to have anything in common with each other or with the first crime.

The only similarity was a car was involved. Were they parked, and the killer snuck up on them? Did they know their killer (or killers) and were meeting them on River Road for some reason? Rumors had started flying that the young boy, who was now identified as Kyle Phillips, was a suspected drug supplier at the high school.

But Amber wasn't sure. Some people thought he might have sold marijuana but he wasn't a hard-core drug dealer. Even so, did someone text him and ask him to meet them to buy drugs? Was his brother's girlfriend an accidental victim of a drug deal gone wrong?

Around four o'clock, Amber got a notification on her phone. A young girl's body had been found floating in the river, entangled in some dead trees along the bank. A cause of death was not released.

Amber paid attention to the patron's whispers. While most continued to believe the first murder was a crime of passion, since it involved bludgeoning and strangling, others argued it was the work of a crazed psycho. In the second crime, no one knew how the victims were killed. One young mother gossiped to another that the bodies had been burned before they were buried in the shallow grave. Also, why were they taken and buried so far away? That was nothing like the first crime. There wasn't enough information on the latest murder since the police hadn't even said how the victims were killed. It might have involved drugs, which didn't seem to have figured in the first two murders. The only similarity was there were two people in each case, their cars were abandoned, and the crimes took place six months apart.

At five o'clock, Bolgey was happy to shoo everyone out and lock the door. "That was exhausting."

"It's not going to get any better. Do you suppose our illustrious task force will give another press conference tonight?"

Bolgey rolled her eyes. "I think they have to."

Walking home, Amber realized she never got to talk to Bolgey about the podcast.

CHAPTER NINETEEN

There was not another press conference that evening. The next day an article appeared in the Daily Blatt castigating, in the nicest possible way, the local police and their inefficiency. Fluffy read the article to Amber after dinner while her father listened. After finishing, Fluffy folded the newspaper with a resounding snap, which Amber found amusing. Her mother was not going to get her news on a phone, ever.

"I couldn't agree more with Duncan Abbott," Fluffy said. "He's a sharp young reporter and is always one step ahead of the police."

"Where does he get his information? The police have been pretty tight-lipped about the latest crime."

"Reporters have their sources," Fluffy said.

Amber was completely baffled by her mother's seeming knowledge of murder, police work, and reporting.

The next morning at the library, Amber asked Bolgey if she'd read the article.

"Of course. I enjoy Duncan's writing. He always knows what's going on. Behind the scenes, so to speak."

"Don't you wonder where he gets his information?" Amber asked. "He might be a suspect. Don't you think?"

Bolgey started to laugh but stopped and looked at Amber. "You know, you could be right. He's in a perfect job to control the narrative of the story, and he's definitely hanging the police out to dry. I like your thinking. If this was a murder mystery, who better than the ace reporter, who is actually creating the news by murdering people. If he's not caught, he could win a Pulitzer."

"Unfortunately, writing about the River Road murders is not going to lead to fame and fortune. Does anyone pay attention to crimes in small towns? They're more interested in rich and famous people who get murdered."

"We shall see." Bolgey nodded.

A brief article had been posted saying the latest victims were shot. The boy, Kyle, was shot once in the back and then in the back of the head as if he'd been fleeing the killer. The young girl, Brittany Brewster, was shot once in the chest. She must have been facing the killer. Was she shot first and Kyle then tried to run away? Both bodies were dragged to the river as if the killer hoped they might float away and never be found. The police were strangely silent, offering no new information. Once again, Amber wasn't able to talk to Bolgey about the podcast.

When she got home after work, Fluffy was in a state. "We have to eat quickly. There's going to be another press conference at six-thirty, and we don't want to miss it."

Her father appeared to be annoyed, but he picked up the pace of his eating. This is totally consuming everyone, Amber thought. No one could stop talking about what was going on. Hopefully the press conference would answer some questions and people could get back to their normal lives.

They gathered in the living room at 6:25, and Fluffy turned on the TV. "We interrupt our regularly scheduled broadcast for a special announcement."

The same officials who'd been at the last press conference stood in a line facing the cameras, with one difference. Chief Wallace of Westburg had been shuffled to the back line, standing between the Chief Park Ranger and Sheriff Fenster, who appeared even more rumpled next to Chief Wallace. Now a different man stood at the podium in front of the bank of microphones, staring at the camera. He wore a dark suit and exuded an air of professionalism, especially next to the local law enforcement.

He cleared his throat and began to speak. "Good evening. I am agent Marcus Devereaux with the FBI. Our agency has been called in to investigate a series of crimes. A car was found several days ago on River Road. It appeared to be abandoned. The doors were left open, and the radio was still on.

"When local police identified the owner of the car, they contacted his parents, who said their son should have been home since he had school that day. He'd driven his brother's girlfriend home after a party, and the parents assumed he'd returned. When they didn't see his car in the morning, they thought he'd already left for school."

Agent Devereaux briefly scanned his notes before looking up. "The young girl's parents reported their daughter missing when she failed to return home by her curfew." His jaw tightened. "But since there was no evidence of foul play, local law enforcement didn't respond." He glanced down, apparently not wanting to throw anyone under the bus, though obviously he was not happy with the men standing behind him. The only sign of his anger was his hands gripping the sides of the podium.

Chief Wallace stared at his feet, looking uncomfortable. The Chief Park Ranger rocked back and forth as if he wanted to bolt. Sheriff Fenster stood there with a benign expression on his face.

Agent Devereaux stared into the camera with a steely gleam in his eye. "I know there has been much speculation about whether these three events on River Road were committed by the same person or persons. What I, and my team, will be doing is going back to the first crime and going over everything with a fine-tooth comb."

Amber felt anger radiating off the agent. He began to turn toward the line of men behind him but stopped and turned back to look in the cameras. "Crucial evidence might have been lost in the first case, since the rangers who came upon the crime had never been confronted with a murder scene before. Possible DNA evidence was lost when they removed the bodies and car before a thorough investigation had been completed."

The Chief Ranger looked like he might faint or throw up.

"Much the same happened in the second case because…" he paused, clearly not wanting to name names or point fingers, "it was thought the missing college students had wandered down to the river and drowned or that they were sleeping off a hangover at a friend's house."

Chief Wallace looked stricken. He was such an ass. Every election he swaggered around town touting his years of experience and attributing the low crime in Westburg to his extensive law enforcement knowledge.

Sheriff Buster Fenster, known affectionately as Busted Window since his name in German meant Window, stood proudly representing Easton. He'd dodged a bullet by being forced into the background by Chief Wallace and his buddy, Ranger Rick, who wouldn't let someone as incompetent as Sheriff Buster anywhere near a real crime scene.

The FBI agent continued. "I know all of you have a lot of questions, however currently, I have no answers. Are the murders connected? What connects them?" He stared at the camera. He was good at creating dramatic effect. Amber thought she'd have to use that in her podcast.

"At this point, we don't know. As I stated previously, we will be going back to the first murder and start digging through every report, every piece of evidence and *every*," he emphasized every, "phone call received. We will follow up on all of them, no matter how insignificant they appear."

Amber believed he was addressing Chief Wallace, since the Chief hadn't been very good at follow-up or follow-through.

"We've set up an office here in Westburg. We will also have an agent in Easton. If you remember anything about any of these crimes, no matter how insignificant, call the number at the bottom of your screen. If you saw a light, heard a noise, saw a car. It doesn't matter. Call and tell us. Crimes are often solved because someone calls with some tiny little tidbit, which turns out to be the very last piece of the puzzle needed to solve the crime."

He began collecting his papers. "I know these are small communities and the citizens are used to dealing directly with the local police," he almost sneered when he said local police. "However, direct communication with the task force is best. We will, of course, continue to use the expertise and experience of local law enforcement." Amber felt it killed him to have to say those words.

He turned and walked away as reporters stood, waving their hands, firing questions at him. As Agent Devereaux strode away, the chastened figures of the local police slunk behind him.

Amber's dad turned off the TV. Fluffy turned to Amber. "I like him. I really do. He instills confidence. I've never thought much of Chief Wallace. He's more of a politician than a policeman." The Great Silence grunted his agreement as he walked out of the room.

I flicked the TV off and stared at the blank screen. The FBI is taking over the investigation. Should I be worried?

No. I laughed. They might look great in their business suits, and they certainly put local law enforcement to shame, but even if they took over from Tweedledee and Tweedledum, they wouldn't be able to solve these crimes.

Not being one to brag but no one would be able to see or figure out the connection or the pattern. Because there wasn't one. Will they even figure out there were two killers? They might determine this latest crime was committed by someone else, or maybe they'd simply conclude that none of the murders are linked.

Still, I might want to lay low for a while. That might confuse them even more. On the other hand, maybe I should jump in with a murder of my own. Throw them for a loop. Break the pattern. Well, not break my pattern. Couldn't include that copycat killer in my crimes.

Decisions… decisions.

CHAPTER TWENTY

As soon as Amber closed her bedroom door, she called Scarlet. Her sister picked up after the first ring.

"Hey there. I've been waiting for you to call. What did Bolgey think of us dropping the podcast next week instead of waiting?"

Flopping back on the bed, Amber closed her eyes. "I never got to discuss it with her. The library was a swarm of rumor and conjecture about the murders. Everyone has a different idea. One killer, two killers. Serial killer, no connection. Personal, random acts of violence."

"Sounds like everyone is really concerned."

"Probably because the police seem completely incompetent," Amber said. "An article in the local paper basically said that."

"How can you say that? Sheriff Busted Window is on the case." Scarlet laughed.

"Not anymore, and Chief Wallace has also been kicked to the curb."

"What?"

Amber sat up. "Yes, at the press conference tonight, a rather hunky… is it okay to say hunky about an FBI agent? Anyway, the FBI has taken over the three cases. This agent Devereaux, I love his name, so French sounding, so sexy…."

"Can you control your hormones long enough to tell me what happened?" Scarlet said.

"Sorry. Basically, the FBI guy implied the local police messed everything up. Though I doubt he was including poor Sheriff Fenster in that assessment, since he'd been pushed to the side by Chief Wallace and the Chief Ranger, Richards or Rogers…" Amber paused halfway through her thought. "I guess I need to get the correct name for the Chief Ranger if I'm going to be keeping a diary of the case."

"Back to the FBI, please. I'm confused by all your side trips."

"The FBI is taking over all three cases. They implied they were mishandled from the start. Said evidence had been destroyed. The scenes were not preserved. All kinds of stuff along those lines. They plan to go back to the first murders and start from the beginning. Fresh eyes. The usual."

"Wow. What are the chances they'll actually find anything? The first murders happened like a year ago, right?" Scarlet said.

"Yeah, but they have all kinds of things at their disposal, including profilers and high-tech crime equipment and computer programs."

"I wonder if the murderer or murderers are worried now the FBI is taking over."

Amber nodded slowly, even though Scarlet couldn't see her. "I would be."

"Me too. However, right now we need to get on with our podcast. Part Two of My Childhood BFF. Fire up your computer and get your headphones on. Time to get to work."

"Who made you the boss?" Amber teased.

"Someone must keep us on task and that is apparently me even though I'm in law school and already have ten zillion things to do, study, read, write papers, take tests, the list is endless. Not to mention, I have no time for hunky FBI agents."

"He's so dreamy." Amber sighed.

"Too old for you. If he's leading the investigation, he's at least in his mid-thirties."

"Maybe I need an older man…" Amber said.

"You don't need an older man or any man. You need to get to recording."

"Damn. Sometimes you are no fun at all, but I guess it's why you made all As in school. Old Nose to the Grindstone they used to call you."

"No one called me that. They called me hard-working and successful."

Amber was glad Scarlet couldn't see her expression because sometimes she still got the tiniest bit annoyed with her successful sister. "Okay, hanging up now. See you on air."

Amber put her headphones on and logged into Zoom. She checked her microphone and a minute later Scarlet's face popped up on the screen.

Amber pushed a button, and the robotic voice said, "Recording in session."

PODCAST

EPISODE 3: YOUR CHILDHOOD BFF

Amber: Welcome back fans. We hope we have some fans out there already. Last week we talked about my childhood BFF who murdered her mother. Brutally. The autopsy revealed long-term abuse of the older woman by her daughter.

Scarlet: Now to the evidence and the trial.

Amber: If I may interject. Since we are talking about evidence and the trial, I think it is time to let our listeners in on your real identity. My co-host is not a criminal or a cop or a judge. She's a lawyer.

Scarlet: Some people think lawyers are almost as bad as criminals.

Amber: Maybe because we only deal with lawyers during the worst times? Or maybe we get mad at them for defending the worst people ever.

Scarlet: Innocent until proven guilty. Remember those words.

Amber: If you say so, Lawyer. Now back to the crime. At the police station during questioning, BFF broke down. Once she realized what she'd done, she confessed and said she wanted to stay in jail, deserved to stay in jail, and didn't want a trial.

Scarlet: Nevertheless, they appointed BFF a lawyer because everyone is entitled to a defense. No doubt her legal team worried about the death penalty or, at the least, life in prison for her. At that time the death penalty was still an option. They sometimes liked to dangle that over the accused to get a confession.

Amber: They didn't need to threaten her with that since she happily, or at least willingly, confessed. Her court-appointed lawyer got a psychiatrist to evaluate her. A lot of awful information came out, though not all the details were released to the public.

Scarlet: Suffice it to say, poor BFF had some appalling things happen to her. Her lawyer said she'd experienced a crushing amount of trauma in her childhood, starting with the death of her beloved father. There were rumors about sexual abuse. This was one of the reasons BFF dropped out of all her activities and turned to drugs. If her mom hadn't been so totally wrapped up in grief, she might have noticed something.

Amber: After her father's death, BFF's mom started withdrawing from daily activities, leaving BFF with all the household chores. At the same time, BFF suffered from massive depression, started cutting herself, became anorexic, and attempted suicide. She coped by disassociating herself and repressing the terrible memories.

Her lawyer said she suffered from a serious mental illness and in the end, she couldn't resist the impulse to stab her mother.

Scarlet: Oh yes. The old irresistible impulse.

Amber: Even though she loved her mom and didn't want to hurt her, she couldn't stop herself. Her lawyer stated this set of circumstances met the qualifications for insanity as defined by the State. My question for you, Lawyer, what are the requirements for this test and who decides if a person meets the definition of mentally incompetent and unable to stand trial?

Scarlet: I haven't done a lot of work with NGRI cases, which means Not Guilty by Reason of Insanity. But generally the defense makes a request to the court for an evaluation to determine sanity at the time of the offense and competency to stand trial. Once the request is made, it's usually granted by the court and the court assigns a psychiatrist/psychologist to evaluate the person.

I'm sure all this lawyer talk has people rolling their eyes but the long and the short of it is, the evaluation determines if the person suffered from mental disease at the time of the crime and irresistible impulse is considered an insanity defense, meaning the person is totally deprived of the mental power to control or restrain their actions.

Amber: So, they are saying she had a disease? A mental illness? I have to say, I feel so many times in our country mental diseases are not respected or given the same weight as physical disease. Most people don't get any kind of treatment. In this case, it appears they were willing to let a professional decide if she was competent.

Scarlet: They had no choice. That's the law. Both the State and the Defense can get their own mental health professionals to evaluate the perp. Often these health experts don't agree, and you have competing evaluations.

Amber: From what I read, that's what happened in this case. Two psychiatrists interviewed and evaluated her. In BFF's case, the defense expert concluded she suffered from mental illness, which resulted in a breakdown leading to an irresistible impulse to murder her mother. The State's expert said while she suffered from major depression and PTSD, he did not agree she was insane at the time of the crime. I am quoting what he said: "While I have no doubt she suffered from severe emotional distress, and probably did not intend to kill her mother, I'd be hard pressed to say she was driven by irresistible impulses."

This expert added she admitted to drinking that night, which can disinhibit impulse. He concluded by saying he did not believe that her mental condition robbed her of the ability to control her actions. Or robbed her of the knowledge of right and wrong.

Amber: Can you elaborate on this? Since the two experts did not agree, what did the court do?

Scarlet: It would come down to cross-examination and how much time each of these experts spent with her. Both the Defense and the State have the chance to put up their expert and present their case.

Amber: The State planned on charging her with first degree murder. The Defense stuck to their theory of not guilty by reason of insanity, saying she was traumatized and not in her right mind when the murder occurred. If they had convicted her of that, what would have happened?

Scarlet: The concept of not guilty by reason of insanity recognizes people can't be held responsible if they are mentally ill at the time of the crime. At the same time, you can't just let them go. So, if they are found guilty, they can either be committed to a mental facility or they can be conditionally released with supervision. If it is determined at some point they have recovered, they can be released, but the State can jump in and say no, we don't agree.

Amber: I have to say, even though I might sound like a total jerk, I'm wondering about all the old bruises and broken ribs. How did the defense explain that away? This does not appear to be a moment of someone snapping.

Scarlet: True. However, she could have been in a spiraling downward dive toward the final moment of irresistible impulse.

Amber: Good point. Now, I want to add some of the other things we didn't include.

Scarlet: Such as?

Amber: Some creepy sidebars. The medical examiner said it appeared the victim had been dead for a couple of hours before the police arrived. But they didn't do any of the basic tests to determine time of death. Maybe because BFF confessed?

Also, one of the assumptions of irresistible impulse is the perpetrator has no idea what they are doing. However, evidence suggests she did know she'd done something wrong. She cleaned up. Wiped up blood. Did laundry. So, the time of death and how much time she spent cleaning up before she called 911 is totally relevant.

They also asked BFF if she attempted CPR, and she told them she didn't know how, so she immediately called 911. But it's obvious she didn't call right away.

Scarlet: I see what you mean. This evidence certainly refutes the Defense's theory. Plus, the old bruises, broken bones, etc. indicate ongoing, long-term abuse.

Domestic abuse takes many forms, and this is domestic violence. There is an adult protective service, and you can call them if you suspect abuse. We are all aware of child abuse and teachers and other caregivers take classes on how to spot and help abused children, but abuse of the elderly often goes unnoticed and unreported.

Amber: Even though this woman's sister and friend were worried, they didn't want to call the authorities and report their suspicions because they didn't want to embarrass her. How much better would it have been for everyone if they had? If only one person had called. This is not the outcome anyone wanted, including my childhood BFF.

Scarlet: I'm sure at this point everyone is dying to know the outcome of the trial. Did the Defense win with Not Guilty by reason of insanity? Were they able to prove she was incapacitated and acted on irresistible impulse?

Amber: It never got to trial. At least not a full jury trial. The Defense planned on going with the NGRI defense, but the prosecutors said, not only no, but hell no. They brought up all the previous abuse and the fact she tried to clean up, which proved she knew right from wrong. They told her lawyers they were going all out for first degree murder, which is a sentence of life imprisonment without parole. They offered her a plea to second degree, which carries a sentence of five to forty years. They said if she pled to that, they'd give her a twenty-year sentence and she'd be out by the time she turned forty.

Scarlet: Tough choice, but her case wasn't a slam dunk. You never really know how a jury will go. Sympathy for her because of the trauma she suffered or completely horrified and appalled by her treatment of her mother. She could have ended up with life in prison.

Amber: Her lawyers laid it all out and told her it was her call. She's the one who decided to take the twenty years.

Scarlet: What a first episode. It was a tough one. There are no winners and more than one victim. BFF's mother lost her life, but BFF did too. She'll never be able to live a normal life. Plus, she has to live every day knowing she killed her own mother.

Amber: I know. Definitely no winners here. But there are never any winners in these cases. Just tragedy.

Scarlet: A shocking case, which just goes to prove that the most unlikely person can commit murder under certain circumstances.

Amber: I guess that is true. We should never be surprised.

Join us next week for another episode of The Murderer You Know, where we will talk about another case we personally experienced. Check us out on social media. Until next time…"

Amber clicked the record button off. "Wow, I feel like I lived this whole awful thing again."

"Try to get a good night's sleep," Scarlet said. "Hopefully, we can drop our intro soon. Talk to Bolgey. She's quite tech savvy."

Amber laughed. "Certainly way more than me, which is embarrassing."

CHAPTER TWENTY-ONE

Amber arrived at the library thirty minutes before her shift began. She needed to talk to Bolgey about getting the website and all the other social media in place. If they promoted the podcast for at least a week before the launch, they'd hopefully drum up interest for the Intro episode.

This is where Bolgey would be instrumental. She had the knowledge and the time to do it. Amber had an Instagram page, though honestly she didn't keep up with it. Scarlet didn't even have one because she claimed she had no time for social things.

Amber found Bolgey in the kitchen pouring herself a huge mug of coffee. When she heard the door open, the librarian swung around and immediately started talking, "OMG, did you see the press conference last night? The FBI is taking over?"

Forcing a smile on her face, Amber said, "I know. Quite the turn of events for our little neck of the woods." Bolgey started up again, and Amber held up her hand. "I know everyone wants to talk about the River Road murders, but right now, I need to talk about the podcast."

Bolgey's face clouded over, and she sat down with her warm mug gripped between her hands. "What's up? Nothing wrong, I hope?"

"Nothing's wrong. It's all good. We've recorded the intro and the two episodes about Heather, and we decided to drop the intro next week. This gives us a three-week cushion and we think we can keep up with the recordings by taping each week. This is where you come up in, our social media wiz."

Bolgey nodded slowly. "Actually, that's not a bad idea. No point in waiting. The world of True Crime is only getting more crowded. We need to claim our niche and our audience. However, remember, we don't have a logo or theme music yet."

"Oh sh… shoot," Amber said. "Wasn't Ida working on both of those? What's the holdup?"

"Ida's almost done, but she didn't know there was a rush since we were talking about waiting a few months before we introduced our podcast to the world," Bolgey said.

Amber grimaced. "I'll call her and tell her we want to speed up our debut."

"Have you thought about whether to use your real names? List them on social media? Have it so people can contact you? Check you out?"

"Scarlet and I discussed it. She doesn't want anyone at law school to know she's doing a murder podcast. They might frown on her giving legal opinions over the airways. You know what a goodie-two-shoes she is." Amber rolled her eyes. "We're going to be 'the Host' and 'the Lawyer'. And if we have guests, we'll give them clever pseudonyms."

Amber grinned. "Do you want to be listed on the podcast? Maybe 'Social Media Wiz'?"

The librarian laughed. "No. Let our adoring public assume you guys are doing it all. Don't muddy the waters with other pseudonyms."

"I'm having business cards made up to hand out with my name and email and the title 'True Crime Podcaster'. I'll hand them out and say I know the hosts of this fabulous new podcast and would like to chat about possibly including them on the show. That way, if I want to interview someone about a crime, I'll look more official," Amber said.

"That's a great idea. Might open doors."

"Speaking of names and pseudonyms, I'm almost embarrassed to say I have no idea what your first name is. Since we are now partners in crime." Amber laughed wickedly. "Maybe we should be on a first name basis?" Bolgey's name tag read *M. Bolger*. "I know your first name starts with an 'M', but there are a lot of names starting with M. Mary, Maggie, Martha…"

Bolgey laughed. "You'll never guess! Ha. It's pretty old-fashioned. My name is Maxine. What was my mother thinking? I go by Max. Always have. In school, I would have killed anyone who called me Maxine."

"Max?" Amber tilted her head and looked at the librarian. "I like it. It suits you. And I'm glad I can now call you by your proper name."

"You mean instead of that nickname? Bulgey? Bolgey? Bogey?"

Amber blushed and looked down. "Sorry," she managed to squeak out. Changing the subject quickly, she said, "Scarlet will be down this weekend. Why don't you come over Saturday night for dinner? I'll invite Ida, after telling her she needs to finish the logo and the theme music. We can talk about dropping the first episode and where to go from there. Do we drop at midnight? What day of the week? You know, all the nitty-gritty details."

"Thanks. It's always nice to see Ida and your mother, Fluffy." Max laughed. "Another nickname."

"I didn't give her that one," Amber said in her own defense.

"It's the perfect nickname for her. What time should I come over?"

"Six. We can eat first and talk after."

"Sounds like a plan. We can also talk about the River Road murders. I believe eventually you're going to end up doing several episodes on those crimes during your podcast."

"If they catch the guy," Amber replied.

"Even if they don't," Max said before turning to unlock the doors for the day.

At the end of her shift, Amber headed home. As soon as she got there, she'd have to tell her mother to expect company for dinner Saturday night. Mom won't mind, Amber thought. She loves cooking.

CHAPTER TWENTY-TWO

At home Amber tracked her mother down to the kitchen and asked her if it would be all right to have people over for dinner Saturday. "We need to get everyone together to talk about next steps and everyone's roles to make sure we are ready to go."

"Fine with me." Amber's mom smiled. "It's always more fun to cook for a crowd. The more the merrier, I always say."

"Scarlet and I are the hosts, you're our cheerleader and possible guest host. Same for Ida, and Max is doing all the social media stuff.

"Max? Getting quite friendly, are we? First name basis and all," Amber's mom said.

"Seriously Mom," Amber huffed. "I work at the library. We are work colleagues. She's helping with the podcast and it's time for me to stop calling her Ms. Bolger to her face and Bolgey behind her back. I'm no longer that seven-year-old kid running screaming through the library. I am a responsible adult."

Fluffy smiled at her. "So, you are. And I do prefer Max to Bolgey. I'm sure she does too."

Amber blushed. "She knew I was calling her some atrocious nickname behind her back. It was so embarrassing to be found out."

"Well, we shall let bygones be bygones. Now we are all partners in murder." Fluffy laughed. "More importantly, what should I cook?"

"You decide, Mom. I know whatever you make will be delicious. I need to call Aunt Ida and invite her over."

Amber turned to leave, but her mother stopped her. "Do you think we'll have time to discuss all the latest on the River Road murders? It's getting more and more exciting with the FBI taking over."

Feeling a bit of frustration, Amber forced a smile onto her face. "If we have time. We really need to talk about getting the podcast up and running. No one besides Scarlet and I have listened to the episodes we've recorded yet, and we want to be sure we're on the right track. Might have to save River Road for another dinner."

Fluffy got quite excited. "Let's start the Saturday night Murder Mystery dinner. We can get together every week and talk about murder."

"Sure Mom. Great idea." Amber was beginning to worry about her mother's seemingly endless enthusiasm for murder.

A few minutes later, she was on the phone with her aunt. "Hey, Ida. I want to get the podcast gang together this Saturday, since Scarlet and I have recorded our first three episodes. We want to let everyone listen to them because we hope to start dropping them next week." Every time Amber said "dropping" she felt like a real podcaster.

"Sounds good," Ida responded.

"Scarlet is coming down this weekend, and I invited Max over too. She's been incredibly helpful with the podcast. Technical things which I don't know anything about, and Scarlet doesn't have time for."

"Max? Well, aren't you two getting chummy."

Amber's blood pressure shot up. Why was everyone making such a big deal about her being on a first name basis with Max?

Forcing herself to respond in a calm, even tone, she said, "Yes. It seemed silly to still be calling her Ms. Bolger, considering we are now colleagues at the library and on the podcast."

"Quite true. You are entering the adult work world," Ida said.

"I hate to put any pressure on you, but could you possibly finish the logo and theme music? We're going to have dinner at six and talk after."

"I'd never, ever turn down an invitation for dinner at your mom's. See you Saturday."

After hanging up, Amber immediately called Scarlet. "You're still coming down this weekend, I hope? I've got the whole murder podcast crew lined up for dinner on Saturday night."

"Okay. I'll get there Friday afternoon, and we can listen to all our podcasts first and see if they need tweaking."

"I did a little editing already. They have this audio editing program that removes all the ums and errs and other little annoying habits we have when we talk. I've already cleaned up the podcasts a bit."

"Glad to hear that. I was worried about those because I know I'm guilty of those little quirks. Where did you find out about it?"

"Bolgey told me. She knows about all those things. By the way, we are now on a first name basis with Bolgey. It just made sense since we're all work colleagues. Her name is Maxine, which doesn't suit her at all, but she said she's always gone by Max and that does."

"I agree. With both. That we need to be on a first name basis and that Max suits her."

"Can't wait to see you Friday and can't wait to see what everyone thinks of the first three episodes. If we're ready to go, we can start getting our name out in the world."

"Can't wait to hear it all." Scarlet laughed. "See you Saturday. Hopefully Mom has a stash of fresh cookies."

"Are you kidding? Has Fluffy ever run out of cookies?"

CHAPTER TWENTY-THREE

*A*mber and Scarlet *worked on t*heir nails while their podcasts played. If they heard something they thought needed changing, they'd stop the recording and write a quick note before continuing. It took over two hours. The first episode was only thirty minutes, and the other two were around forty. Fluffy, Ida, and Max had also been sent copies to listen to and make comments.

When the last word was said, Amber flopped back on the bed. "Oh, my… I am completely exhausted. From now on, we listen and edit as we record. This was a bit much."

"I agree," Scarlet said, waving her hands in the air to dry her nails. "I hope everyone else got through them."

"They can listen tonight and tomorrow. They don't have to do a marathon like we did." Amber laughed.

"True. If everyone says we're hitting the right tone with our podcast and keeping it interesting, what crime should we do next?"

"I've been thinking about that." Amber blew on her nails. "We want to keep the momentum going. We need a story just as good as the BFF Killer."

"Oh Lord, you're not going to call it that, are you?"

"No. We'll probably stick with Your Childhood BFF."

"How about the one involving my high school friend who was murdered in a drug deal gone wrong? Don't drug deals always go wrong? Why do people get involved in drug deals?" Scarlet shook her head.

"Cause drugs kill," Amber said solemnly. "We could both talk about all the friends we've lost to drugs. Overdoses mostly and occasionally in drug deals gone wrong. Though it wasn't really a drug deal, remember? The guy, who you also knew—"

Scarlet interrupted. "Knew is a bit of an overstatement. We went to school together, along with the victim, but he was several years ahead. I knew his name, like if someone said have you seen Joe Blow around, I'd know who they were talking about, though we weren't friends. I was friends with the victim. We double-dated for junior prom."

"Wow. I'd forgotten that."

"And I wouldn't call it a drug deal gone wrong. Joe Blow went there specifically to rob Prom Girl. To steal her money and her drugs. She sold a little pot on the side."

"I guess we're doing another two-parter. The crime and the trial."

"Of course. The set up and the conclusion," Scarlet said.

"Well, we know Joe Blow was caught and charged or we wouldn't be doing this crime on our podcast," Amber said.

"True. He was charged with all kinds of things," Scarlet replied.

"I always find it odd murderers aren't simply charged with murder. Instead, they dump all kinds of charges on them from jaywalking to first degree murder."

Scarlet laughed. "Methinks you are exaggerating a tad but the reason they pile the charges up is to convince the defendant and his or her lawyers that the prosecution has a very strong case and they're going to get you one way or another, so you better just take the plea. The Commonwealth of Virginia loves a plea. Cut to the chase."

"Just like our last case. So, let's see if Joe Blow took the plea."

Amber studied her nails for a moment. "I really hope the others listened to the podcasts."

"Why wouldn't they?" Scarlet asked.

"Everyone is so totally obsessed with the River Road murders. That's all they want to talk about. I get to work, and Max says, 'Have you heard the latest.' I get home and tell Mom everyone's coming over to talk about the podcast and her only comment is, 'Can we talk about the River Road murders too?' It's frustrating."

"I understand. But let's face it, this is the biggest, most mysterious crime wave to hit our little town, or towns, since I should include Westburg, in forever. Nothing like this has ever happened."

"I know that," Amber snapped, "and they all want us to put it on our podcast, but we don't know anything about these crimes. Our show is about murderers we know, not mysterious serial killers. However, I am starting to make notes about what's going on in case one day they solve the crimes, and we can be the first to report on it."

"Good idea. Meanwhile, don't let Mom and Max get you down. They're interested in our podcast too."

CHAPTER TWENTY-FOUR

Ida and Max arrived at the Steen's promptly at 6:00. Amber glanced out the door and only saw one car in the driveway. "You guys come together?" she asked as she shut the door behind them.

"Max said she'd swing by and pick me up and I said sure. This way I get to drink," Ida said, laughing.

Amber rolled her eyes. Ida knew the strongest beverage served at her parent's house was black coffee.

"Dinner's ready," Fluffy called from the kitchen. "Go into the dining room and grab a seat."

The Great Silence was already seated at the head of the table. Amber knew he was a creature of habit and liked his meals served at the same time every evening. He nodded at Ida and grunted at Max in what Amber assumed was a warm welcome. She knew they'd all grown up in Easton and gone to school together, though Max and Ida were a few years older.

Fluffy and Scarlet came out carrying platters and bowls and casseroles steaming and smelling delicious. A second trip was required, and Amber jumped in to help. After all the food was on the table, a quick thank you was said to a kind and benevolent God, and then dishes were passed around. Conversation lagged as everyone piled food on their plate, while complimenting Fluffy for yet another masterpiece. Her mom blushed and held up her hand as if to deflect all the praise, but Amber knew she secretly ate it up.

As they soaked up the last bit of dinner with their biscuits, Ida finally spoke. "So, what's the plan for this evening?"

"Did you all listen to our first three episodes?" Amber asked.

Their father got up and made appreciative noises in his wife's direction before going into the den and shutting the door. They could hear the TV being turned on to a football game.

"Yes, we all did, except your dad, of course, which is why he left."

"So?" Scarlet glanced nervously at Amber. "What did you think?"

"I enjoyed them. Loved the intro," Ida started. "It was fun and intriguing. The case was, of course, sad and terrible, but I thought you handled it well."

Max agreed.

Fluffy added, "It made me sad all over again that I didn't do more at the time. Didn't check in with Mrs. Finn. Sadly, I assumed she was okay."

They all nodded solemnly.

"The software I suggested really helped with the ums and ahs that we all say," Max said. "People get annoyed listening to those. It's unprofessional. I'm glad you were able to use the program."

"I agree. First time I listened was before I ran the program, and I literally cringed at all of those. It's much better now."

"Now we want to launch the podcast," Amber said. "Originally we talked about waiting until we had twelve episodes done, which would be about three months' worth—"

Scarlet broke in, "Then we decided why wait? The sooner we get out into the world, the sooner people will start listening and talking and sharing."

"And the sooner you will be the next million-dollar influencer," Fluffy smiled.

Thank God Fluffy finally got the word right, Amber thought. "We're not influencers, Mom, but hopefully the next hot million-dollar podcasters."

"This next step is where Max is really going to help. She knows all about social media from doing the library's Facebook and Instagram and public posts, so she's going to do all that for us." Amber smiled at Max. "Thank goodness because Scarlet doesn't have the time, and I am a complete techno-dolt."

Everyone looked at Max expectantly.

Max cleared her throat and sat up straighter. "We'll drop our episodes on Thursdays. People can listen in the car on the way or coming home from work, or if they don't have time, they can catch up on the weekend."

"I like that plan," Ida said. "And I want everyone to know I haven't been slacking either. Back in the day, I did a little art, and I came up with a logo." She held up a circular drawing of two arms with hands shaking. A snake coiled around one of the arms and appeared about to sink its fangs into the arm of the other person. The title, *The Murderer You Know*, appeared below in italicized capital letters. "What do you think?"

"Oh, my goodness, I totally love it," Amber squealed.

"Very cool," Scarlet added.

"And now for the theme music," Ida said, pulling out her phone. They could hear Amber's voice echoing in the background saying "This is *The Murderer You Know*," while eerie music played with a thumping back beat. "I read one time what made the theme music in the *Jaws* movie so terrifying was it mimicked the beating of a human heart. Increasing in fear." Ida said as she turned the phone off.

"I love it," Fluffy said enthusiastically.

They all suppressed their laughter since Fluffy appeared to be the last person on earth to be excited about murder or scary music.

"The music and logo are so cool, Aunt Ida," Amber gushed. "Where did you get the music?"

"One of my customers is in a band and I talked to him about needing theme music for a podcast. I told him it had to be scary and intriguing. I think he nailed it. Plus, he did it for free, 'cause I do such good work on his truck." Ida smiled.

"So, this is what I've done," Max broke in. "I've set up a website for us where people can ask questions, talk about murderers they know, basically whatever they want. We'll have a Facebook page, Instagram, and a BlueSky account. I've signed up for a platform to host all the streaming services."

"Is that expensive?" Amber said, concerned. She certainly didn't have any money and neither did Scarlet.

"No, not really. Still, I suggest we don't drop the first episode next week because we need to promote it first, by doing a week's worth of Facebook ads with teasers. I've also ordered some inexpensive giveaways—stickers, magnets, mugs. We'll tell listeners the first twenty people to like us will receive a prize. We'll post everywhere and get people interested. Since everyone is on social media, we can like and share everything that's posted on the official *Murderer You Know* page."

Scarlet and Amber stared at their mother. "Everyone? You have a Facebook page, Mom?"

Fluffy nodded sheepishly.

"And you haven't friended us?"

"I don't even use my real name. It's just an old lady book club group." She laughed. "Ida and Max are members too."

"Actually, it's perfect," Ida jumped in. "Since we read lots of mysteries, we can post that we listened to this new podcast, and everyone needs to check it out."

"Yes," Scarlet nodded. "Remember, since we aren't using our real names, we can all like and share and say great podcast, with great hosts." She grinned at Amber. "Give it a listen."

"Some people will recognize our voices and if they contact us, we'll admit it's us but ask them to keep the secret," Amber said.

"So, let's start writing on the calendar when we will start the media blitz, drop the first episode…" Max continued as Amber took notes.

CHAPTER TWENTY-FIVE

Amber slumped in her chair and let out a long breath. "OMG. I'm exhausted. You guys have way too much energy."

The older ladies laughed. Fluffy jumped up. "Time for dessert. Let's go into the living room and relax."

In the living room, Fluffy brought out a tray of plates, each with a slice of rhubarb pie and whipped cream. "Coffee is brewing," she added as she handed the plates around.

"What episode are you going to do next?" Max asked before forking a huge piece of pie into her mouth.

"Sticking with the theme, we decided to do my high school friend, who got pregnant, dropped out of school, and started selling drugs. Then when she was trying to turn her life around, tragedy struck," Scarlet replied, licking whipped cream off her fork.

"Yes. Another local tragedy," Fluffy said, pouring coffee for everyone.

"We plan to call it, 'Drugs Kill—in Many Ways,'" Amber said.

"Sad but true," Ida agreed.

They sat quietly, enjoying their pie. When they were done, Fluffy picked up the plates and carried them to the kitchen. Amber knew she should help her mom, but she didn't think she could get out of her chair.

When Fluffy came back, Max said, "You have outdone yourself, Madge."

Amber blinked. She almost forgot that her mother had a real name since no one ever used it. Their father, of course, never called her anything. Ida called her Sis. She and Scarlet called her Mom or Fluffy. Why on earth did her grandmother name her daughters Madge and Ida? Those names certainly didn't come from some steamy romance novel. And not from the Bible either, as far as Amber could remember. Maybe after some old maid great aunts? Awful names.

Madge/Mom/Fluffy sat down. "I love to make everyone happy."

"And you most certainly did," Ida added.

"Now let's talk about the FBI and the River Road murders," Max said almost gleefully. "What do you all think of the FBI taking over? They must think it's a serial killer or they wouldn't get involved."

"Some local bigwigs probably called the governor all hysterical and got him to call in the FBI," Fluffy said.

Ida jumped in, "No doubt, you're right. They want to catch the killer, or killers, before they strike again. If they stick to their pattern, the FBI only has six months to catch them."

"True." Amber nodded. "I am very impressed by Agent Devereaux. He gives off such an aura of competence."

"In truth," Scarlet said, "our Amber has the hots for the FBI agent."

Amber blushed down to her toes while everyone laughed. "I do not," she protested. "I mean, he's handsome and all …"

She couldn't finish her sentence because all the others were teasing her.

"Okay, okay, enough. Let's move on," Amber snapped. The others wiped the tears from their eyes and tried to look serious.

"Are you going to do an episode on the River Road murders?" Fluffy asked.

"No. Because our show is *The Murderer You Know*, and no one knows who this murderer is," Amber said. "However, like the FBI, I'm going back to the beginning and making extensive notes in case it's solved, and we'll be in position to be the first podcast to jump on it. After all, this is happening in our own backyard."

"It's terrifying to imagine we have a serial killer in our town," Fluffy added.

"Please don't claim the serial killer for Easton yet. They could just as easily live in Westburg. It's more likely they're from there. For one thing, Westburg is a lot bigger. Not as much sense of decency as our little town," Ida added, looking quite proud to be throwing Westburg's population under the bus. "They have the college, and you know that adds another element. Who knows what some crazy student could be up to?"

"I've always been a little suspicious of Chief Wallace. It's not like he's any good at his job, but he keeps getting re-elected," Max said.

"It's not a crime to be re-elected," Scarlet said. "It might mean he does a fine job, or at least the citizens think he's competent?"

Max snorted, making her thoughts about it known.

"Lots of people assume the killer is a policeman or a ranger or someone who is pretending to be in law enforcement. They drive along River Road at night and when they spot two people in a car, they put one of those fake flashing light things on their roof and pull them over. You're going to pull over if you think the police are behind you," Amber said.

"Yeah, there are all these theories in chat groups on the internet," Max said. "So much speculation. Some people say it's one killer, others say it's two working together, and others think the murders aren't even related. First crime was a crime of passion. Old boyfriend or something. Second one a random crazed killer, and the latest was drug related."

"We shouldn't limit ourselves to thinking the killer is a man. Could be a woman," Max said.

"That's a shocking thought, but you're right," Fluffy said. "It's a new world and women can kill as easily as men."

They sat quietly, considering what might be the most likely scenario.

"Unfortunately, we don't have much to go on. Personally, I believe it's one killer and they're mixing it up to keep everyone, especially the police, off balance," Amber said.

"I've heard the theory that only one of the crimes was the real crime," Ida said. "In only one did the killer know the victims and specifically target them. And the rest are copy-cat killings to muddy the waters. If anyone could figure out which is the real crime, they'd be halfway to solving it."

"Oh," Fluffy said, "like the Tylenol murders."

Amber and Scarlet stared at their mom, having no idea what she was talking about.

"Sorry dears. This happened way before you two were born. Ida and Max remember." They both nodded and Fluffy continued. "Back in the eighties, people in Chicago began dropping dead unexpectedly. About six or seven people died. The police traced it to a poison that had been put in Tylenol capsules. Everyone became completely hysterical, convinced a madman was opening Tylenol bottles and filling the capsules with poison before putting them back on the shelf. They even considered it might be someone in the factory putting poisoned capsules in bottles. But the police thought it wasn't a crazed killer, that the murderer wanted to kill someone and really didn't care how many other people died as long as they got that person."

"Did they catch them?" Amber and Scarlet asked in unison.

"No, they never did. They had a couple of suspects, but no real proof. All the bottles of Tylenol were removed from the shelves, safety measures were instituted, and the deaths stopped. The killer probably only ever put poison capsules in a dozen bottles." Fluffy paused. "I know people who have never taken a Tylenol capsule since."

"Wow. How completely awful. To kill a bunch of people to get rid of one person. You have to be pretty cold and calculating," Amber said.

"Kind of like the River Road killer, if only one of the crimes is the real murder. Or the deliberate murder? Planned murder? What am I trying to say?" Scarlet babbled.

Max put her hands up to get everyone's attention. "I have heard there is going to be a memorial at the site of the first murder for the first anniversary of the crime. It's going to be in two weeks. I suggest we all attend the memorial and make notes of who's there. They say the murderer always returns to the scene of the crime."

"Max, what a fabulous idea," Amber said. "Count me in."

"Sorry, I can't be there. I'd love to, but I'll be at school. We're doing a mock trial that weekend," Scarlet said.

"We can go in pairs," Max suggested. "I actually know the family, well the mother, of one of the victims, so it's logical I'd be there to offer my condolences. I can say Amber is my niece."

"Should we really make up a story to explain why we're there?" Ida asked. "We don't want people wondering why we're lying."

"You're right," Max grimaced. "I'll drive separately and you three can go together. You can mill around in the background. There will probably be a lot of people there. Everyone should make notes of who they see besides the immediate family. Though we should make notes on them too." Max laughed. "Make notes on everyone, including the police and rangers, reporters, photographers. You might get lucky, Amber, and Agent Dreamboat will be there."

Amber blushed furiously again. "I am not interested in him. After Bruce, I have sworn off handsome men. Actually, all men."

The more I thought about it, the more I realized I shouldn't be so arrogant and dismiss the FBI as another bunch of bozos. They're not only a lot smarter than the local law enforcement, they have more resources at their disposal. Who knows what they might turn up from the first murder.

They will look at everyone and everything again. No one will be safe, no matter their position or occupation. They'll dig deep and find connections the local police glossed over in their haste to clean up the scene for the tourists driving on River Road. Westburg relies on those tourists, since the only other source of income is the local college. Easton relies mostly on farming and fishing.

I'd written the number down Agent Devereaux had given out, asking for information. Maybe I could use that to my advantage. I could call and point fingers at likely suspects. Or even unlikely suspects, keep them from finding the connections. Finding anything personal about the murders. In the meantime, I'll stay low. Off the radar. No murders. I know the FBI wants to solve the crimes before the killer, me, strikes again. They think they have six months. Fools.

Also, I need to figure out how best to handle the copycat crime. The FBI might quickly figure out that the recent murder doesn't fit the pattern. Well, none of them fit a pattern. Still, the gun to me is a giveaway. Of course, that only might be because I know I didn't commit that crime.

Another option might be to commit a murder right now. I planned on doing another one anyway. Stick with my six months. I'm getting that itchy feeling. If I did one now, it would seem like a break in the pattern, though in reality it isn't. The copycat just gummed up the timeline.

First, there's the memorial to attend. Need to put a good face on.

Convince everyone I'm not involved.

I am working toward solving the murders, not committing them. What a joke.

CHAPTER TWENTY-SIX

The next week flew by. Everyone stayed busy with their assigned tasks. Max set up all the social media accounts, posted Facebook ads, and dropped the new logo with the teaser about walking by murderers and how much more common they were than anyone imagined. "Even in small towns," a deep voice intoned on a reel she created.

Amber wrote up episodes four and five, which she and Scarlet planned to record over the weekend. And the memorial service would be held the following weekend. She ordered her business cards and hoped to be able to talk to some of the people at the memorial. Reporters. Police. Maybe even some of the family members. Max could introduce her. Maybe to the sister. Not to the mother, since Max said she was still devastated by the loss of her daughter.

The introductory episode would be dropped the Thursday after the memorial. Amber felt like a real true crime reporter, especially with all the notes she'd written on the River Road murders. After looking up all the information on the first crime, she agreed with Agent Devereaux that the investigation had been sloppy.

After they found the burned-out car with the two bodies inside, the rangers called an ambulance to take away the victims. And even though it couldn't be more obvious they hadn't died in a car crash, very few photos were taken of the scene. The Park Rangers then towed the car to their maintenance facility, where it sat for several days. There was a rumor that the park rangers had written it off as a murder-suicide and didn't think any more needed to be done. Finally, the Westburg police sent over a forensics team, which only happened because the mother of the younger girl raised hell about the lack of progress in the investigation. By then it might have been too little too late.

Amber looked up the names of the victims. Becky Laurelwood was the younger of the two. She grew up in Westburg, graduated from Westburg High, and attended Westburg College. Even though she could have lived at home, she insisted on living on campus. By all reports she was a straight-A student (another Scarlet, Amber rolled her eyes), ran track on the college team, and studied finance and international business. She would have graduated that year. Her parents were well known in the community. Her father a respected doctor and her mother a society lady who served on every committee, deemed important by those who decided such things. They were completely crushed by the unexpected death of their daughter in an apparent murder. Becky's one sibling, an older sister Suzanne, was unmarried and worked in Westburg as a sales manager for a small company.

The name of the other woman in the car was Annie Forst. She was several years older than Becky and worked as a stockbroker for an investment firm in Westburg. She'd only moved to Westburg a year before the murders. Originally from Pennsylvania, she joined the army after graduating from college. From all accounts, she'd done well but left after five years. Maybe she'd only stayed long enough to fulfill her commitment. No one knew why she moved to Westburg, since she didn't have any friends or family in the area. In fact, no one knew much about her at all. Her co-workers said she worked hard but kept to herself. She made no close friends and didn't share much about her past. When the police contacted her family, they were shocked and saddened by the news but had little to add. They didn't even come down to make arrangements but decided to have her cremated and shipped home.

So, was this the "real" crime? Amber wondered. What reason did anyone have to kill these two? One theory involved a jilted lover. However, according to Becky's friends she broke up with her high school boyfriend when he went to an out-of-state college, and while she dated several guys at college, there hadn't been any serious relationships.

Annie's co-workers said they never saw her with a guy, and she never talked about dating. Her family added she'd always been quite career focused and didn't have time for relationships. Local online chat groups speculated that she had quit the army because of a broken heart. Though none of her former fellow soldiers confirmed that, they didn't deny it either. Amber thought it strange that no one seemed willing to talk about her.

How did these two meet and what did they have in common? Maybe Annie mentored the younger girl? Giving her advice about possible careers in the exciting world of finance. It made sense, but no one had any information about how they became friends. Chance meeting? A mutual friend?

Amber felt that question needed to be answered before the mystery could be solved.

CHAPTER TWENTY-SEVEN

Amber dialed into the Zoom account and waited for Scarlet to appear on the screen.

"There you are," Amber said. "I started to worry you wouldn't show up."

"Sorry, the life of a law school student. I was at the library doing research and had to run back to my room."

"Tonight is our episode on *The Evil of Drugs*."

"Aren't we going to call this episode *Drugs Kill—In More Ways than One*?" Scarlet said.

"Okay. Sure. Let's get started."

Amber pushed a button, and the robotic voice stated, "recording in session", then the theme music and intro played.

PODCAST

Episode 4: Drugs Kill

Amber: Welcome back to *The Murderer You Know*, once again bringing you an episode of murders close to home. Well, close to our home but I think everyone has probably experienced similar things in their towns.

Scarlet: Last week we did the Host's childhood BFF, and this week we'll be covering a story about my high school friend. This story took place a few years after I left for college. We were close in high school and even double dated for junior prom. Then she got pregnant and dropped out in her senior year. I lost touch with her. One of those sad facts. You don't see people every day and they fade from sight and mind.

Amber: It makes me mad when I hear about girls having to drop out of high school because they got pregnant. You never hear of guys dropping out because they got their girlfriends pregnant.

Scarlet: It was quite the scandal at the time. Apparently, the star quarterback of the football team was the father of her baby. And you're right. He didn't drop out. Can't be losing the star.

Amber: Not like our team ever wins anyway.

Scarlet: And after everyone snickered and gossiped about what happened, the furor died down. And sadly, like you, I didn't check on my former friend. I moved on with my plans for the future.

Amber: Did you know the assailants in this case… is that a good word? Assailants? Perpetrators?

Scarlet: They perpetrated the crime, and they assailed the victims… so either is okay

Amber: Okay Lawyer, pick your term and tell the story.

Scarlet: I didn't know the perpetrator. I knew of him. I knew his reputation. Maybe he had some redeeming qualities, but I doubt it based on what he did. And I definitely didn't know his so-called friends who helped him.

Amber: If people perpetrate a crime and assault people, I'm going with no redeeming qualities.

Scarlet: Agree. But have you heard the saying every human being has value?

Amber: Sounds like a bunch of hokey philosophical BS to me. Some people are shit. Look at Hitler.

Scarlet: Luckily, we aren't talking about him. Thank goodness. Let's start by looking at the victims.

Amber: Oh, no. There was more than one victim. Two? Or more?

Scarlet: Two, which is enough. A quick aside, in the newspaper and television news reports these two were described as roommates but they were a couple.

Amber: So, we have a couple.

Scarlet: My former friend, who I will call Prom girl, worked at the cell phone store and everyone described her as kind and caring. A wonderful mom to her little daughter. She didn't have a criminal record other than a speeding ticket. It appeared she'd slowly begun pulling her life back together. Her girlfriend, who we'll call Friend, was several years older. A college graduate, who encouraged Prom Girl to go back to school for her GED. People described Friend as genuine and a person who loved her family.

Amber: Sounds like two really nice women.

Scarlet: Which brings us to the night of December 11th. According to interviews, Friend's mom came over to plan the family Christmas get together. When the mom left, they hugged and said, "I love you" as they parted. It almost makes me cry, but at least they got to say goodbye. You never know when you might be saying your last goodbyes to someone you love.

Amber: This is not sounding good.

Scarlet: Well, this is The Murderer You Know, so you can assume things are going to go bad.

Amber: True. But I'm always hoping for a happy ending.

Scarlet: At 10:07 that same night, 911 dispatchers received a call about shots fired at a residence. The deputies arrived by 10:15 and found two victims with gunshot wounds to the back of their heads. Friend was pronounced dead at the scene. Prom Girl was still alive. They airlifted her to a hospital in a bigger town.

Amber: Sounds serious if they airlifted her.

Scarlet: Sadly, Prom Girl died the next day from her injuries.

Amber: Sad. This is sounding rather personal. The perpetrator had to be right up on them to shoot them in the back of the head.

Scarlet: Let's wait until we get the details of the crime before we jump to judgement. The perpetrator, or should I say, alleged perpetrator like they always do on the news...

Amber: No, forget that. No pussy footing around. We know he did it.

Scarlet: A bit of background. Bad Dude was twenty-seven years old. Not much of a student; he failed several times, which explains why he was still in high school with us. On the night of the murder, he convinced a twenty-year-old girl to drive him to the women's house to buy some weed.

Amber: They sold weed? I thought you said Prom Girl didn't have a criminal record? Isn't selling pot against the law?

Scarlet: Yes, technically, but I guess she'd never been busted, and a lot of police just turn a blind eye to that kind of thing. There are more serious crimes to worry about.

Amber: Like murder?

Scarlet: Exactly. Anyway, this whole thing becomes more convoluted. In addition to this young girl who was driving the car, a twenty-five-year-old man joined them. He had been invited along because he had a gun. These two, who were in the car, one acting as the driver and the other hanging out, appeared to think this was a good plan. Just go get some weed. With a gun.

Amber: Why did they need a gun if they were going to buy the stuff?

Scarlet: A good question that no one seemed to consider. On the other hand, maybe Bad Dude was planning on robbing them from the get-go but didn't tell his friends that was his plan.

Amber: They should have been smart enough to figure it out.

Scarlet: My experience is criminals aren't that smart. In their defense, they weren't criminals yet.

Back to the events of the crime. Turns out the women had video cameras inside and outside of their house. The video the police found after the murders shows Bad Dude arriving at the house, knocking on the door, coming inside, and arguing with the two women before storming off. Unfortunately, the tapes had no audio, so the police could only assume they argued about drugs. He wanted some. They didn't want to sell him any. Who knows. Next it shows him going to the car and talking to his two friends. The guy in the back seat handed him the gun and three bullets. Bad Dude took the bullets and loaded the gun.

Amber: Only three bullets? That's all? Maybe he didn't think he'd need them?

Maybe he only meant to scare the women? Or maybe he meant to shoot them in the back of the head and one bullet would be enough for each one.

Scarlet: Only he knows what his plan was at this point. The video shows him going back to the house, knocking and then forcing his way inside. The camera shows him threatening them with the gun and marching them down the hall to their bedroom. Maybe he still only planned on robbing them?

The women stood with their backs to him and then the camera shows two muzzle flashes from the gun. The women collapse and he steps over them, as if they are nothing, removes a safe and a bag from the closet, and returns to the car, and the three of them drive off.

Amber: I'm almost afraid to ask how much money they had in the safe. Though no amount of money is worth the lives of two people. Two people who had their whole lives in front of them. One who had a child. Who had families who loved them. Friends who loved them. One deed sends such a traumatic ripple through a community, destroying so many lives.

Scarlet: And in addition to the crime being recorded, turns out someone else was there, hiding in a closet.

Amber: Who?

Scarlet: You and our listeners will have to come back next week to find out.

Amber pushed the button to stop the recording. "Oh wow, Scarlet. Good job. Way to leave us dangling in the wind. I'm absolutely coming back next week to find out."

Scarlet laughed. "Duh. You're the host. You have to come back, and I hope our listeners will be on pins and needles until the exciting conclusion."

"You were more hosty on this episode, but I guess it's because you knew these people. Or at least one of these people."

"True. So, are you all going to the River Road murder memorial tomorrow? Have you figured out your roles? Who will be related to who? Why you are there?"

Amber laughed. "I don't know why Bolg—Max thought we needed to define our relationships. I'm sure there will be a lot of people there. Some who knew the victims, some who know the family, curiosity seekers, press, police. I don't feel we need to explain why we're there."

"Yeah, it's odd she wanted to come up with some strange story explaining your presence. Half of Easton and Westburg will probably be there."

Amber said, "Maybe she's uncomfortable because she knows the family and will want to talk to the mom and offer condolences and doesn't want to say, 'oh by the way, this is my friend's niece, and she does a murder podcast and wants to talk about the terrible tragic death of your daughter.' Awkward!"

"True. Are you going to let people know you're a podcaster?"

"Yes. I had some cards printed up already. They say 'True Crime Podcaster' with my name, number, and email. I didn't want to go all out and name our podcast yet. I think handing a card to the mom and/or sister with the words, *The Murderer You Know* on them might be a little off-putting."

"So, you're planning on talking to them?"

"Probably not the mom. I might talk to the sister if the moment seems right and explain I'm following the crimes closely and might possibly do a story on it in the future. Make it vague."

"Vague is good. I know it's been a year, and their grief is probably not quite so raw but every time another incident happens it must really be upsetting to know this monster is still out there. Of course, that only applies if it is the same killer."

"I wonder what they think happened," Amber said. "Do they think it's some psycho serial killer and their daughter fell victim to him and he's still out there? Or do they think someone, maybe someone they know, killed their daughter and the rest of the murders/disappearances are just coincidences? I'd love to ask them."

"I suggest you don't," Scarlet warned. "At least not the first time you meet them. Maybe you'll be able to talk to them another time. Hopefully, your hot FBI guy will get to the bottom of it." Scarlet hooted. "Are you planning on giving him a card and telling him to call if he needs advice?"

Amber blushed again, which she did a lot of when he was mentioned. "No. I do not plan to give him a card or suggest he contact me. However, I do want to talk to the reporter Mom and Max think so highly of. It's rather suspicious he seems to be one step ahead of the police. Duncan Abbott. I'll give him a card."

"Great idea. If he's the killer, he'll certainly know who to kill next!" Scarlet laughed.

"I have to touch base with people. Maybe find some friendly talkative police or rangers."

"Good idea. Bat your eyelashes at them. Use your feminine wiles."

"I plan to use my brains, not my so-called feminine wiles."

"Use what you gotta use."

"Okay, thanks for the advice. I'll call you tomorrow and let you know how it went. Maybe the killer will fall down and confess faced with my sheer overwhelming personality, brain power and of course, my feminine wiles."

Scarlet snickered. "We can hope. But don't call tomorrow. I've got the mock trial and we all go out afterwards, have a drink and lick our wounds. I'll call you Sunday."

CHAPTER TWENTY-EIGHT

Amber, Ida, and Fluffy planned to drive together to the memorial. Max said she'd meet them there. Amber couldn't decide what to wear. Obviously, nothing as casual as jeans, but should she wear black? Maybe a modest blouse and skirt? A plain dress? She'd never been to a memorial for a murder victim before and had no idea what the proper attire might be.

Standing in front of her closet, staring blankly, Amber heard her mother in the doorway. "We have to leave in thirty minutes, so you need to get ready. Wear your simple black dress."

I should have asked Mom, Amber realized, yanking her black dress out of the closet. Her mom knew what was proper. She quickly put on her black dress and black flats. In the bathroom, she combed her hair. She stared at her reflection. Not bad looking. Maybe a little mascara and blush. A few batted eyelashes might get some answers from the men there. She wanted to talk to the reporter and maybe find one of the rangers who had been first on the scene. But which scene did she mean? The first murder or the next two?

"Amber, we have to go." Fluffy's voice floated up the stairs, snapping

Amber out of her daze. Quickly applying lip gloss, she smacked her lips and headed downstairs.

Sitting in the car, Amber stared out the window as Fluffy turned on the entrance to River Road. The silence became awkward. Ida cleared her throat and said, "I wonder if there will be a big crowd or just family and friends."

"I'm guessing a big crowd. This kind of thing brings people out. Some feel sorry for the family. Others because it's ghoulish and they think, or possibly hope, something might happen. Of course, there will be tons of police, some probably in plainclothes, trying to blend in."

Ida turned to stare at her sister. "What are you talking about?"

"The murderer always returns to the scene of the crime. The police know that, so they'll be looking at everyone, identifying them and making notes."

"Did you learn that from *Law and Order*?" Amber snickered.

"Yes, I did, young lady. There is a lot of good information on that show. You should watch it."

"Pay attention, there's a ranger waving at us and pointing," Ida said.

Fluffy slowed down as they approached the ranger and stopped. "Yes?" she asked with a bright smile.

"We're having people park here," the young man responded. "It's a short walk to where they're holding the memorial."

"Thank you," Fluffy said and followed his directions to the parking area. Dozens of cars were already parked. As they got out, they noticed a long line of cars on River Road following them into the parking space.

"I wonder if Max is here," Amber said as they walked toward the overlook where the burned vehicle had been found, pushed almost off the edge into the river.

Butterflies erupted in Amber's stomach. Who was she to approach all these people, handing out cards and asking questions? She sucked in a huge breath and let it out slowly. All those acting classes and roles she'd played would come in handy today. She had to think of it as simply another role. In this scene, she'd be acting the part of the savvy investigative reporter. "I can do it," she muttered.

Her mother turned around with a look of concern. "Are you talking to yourself? I hope you're not going to faint and cause a scene. That would probably upset the family."

"No, Mom. Not fainting. Giving myself a pep talk."

Ida grinned at her and gave her a thumbs up.

As they got closer, Amber noticed the Channel 9 News van. The Tide was her parent's favorite local news show and Sandy Foss, their favorite investigative reporter. "Mom, Channel 9 is here," Amber said.

"Oh, my goodness. I wonder if Sandy Foss is here. It would be so amazing to see him in person," her mother gushed.

Amber had never understood her mother's obsession with Sandy, a rather lumpy individual. But his suits were immaculately tailored and his sandy hair was brushed into a high wave. He did have nice hair. Maybe that was his intention, to look rather unimpressive before he asked the right question to skewer the person he was interviewing. Amber grudgingly admitted he was a good interviewer.

Her mother was practically jumping up and down, looking all around, trying to spot the reporter and his cameraman. "Do you see him?"

Ida put a calming hand on her sister. "I'm sure we'll see him. He'll probably be front and center filming the memorial and then you can see him on the news tonight."

That calmed Fluffy down and they proceeded to the area where everyone seemed to be gathering.

As more and more people arrived, Amber worried they might not be able to find Max in the crush. Large groups gathered around a podium with a microphone. A huge memorial wreath had been placed in front of the podium. To the left stood Chief Wallace and Ranger Rick. Amber kicked herself. She really needed to find out that man's name. Sheriff Fenster and a few Easton deputies stood with the other police, though it was apparent they were being ignored.

As expected, Sandy Foss and his cameraman were well placed to film the entire event. Her mom squeezed her hand and pointed to the reporter. "Yes Mom. I see him." Amber squeezed her mom's hand back.

Farther in the background, Amber saw a group of men in dark suits. This had to be the FBI. She spotted Agent Devereaux, trying to look unobtrusive. Her heart did a little flip. He was even better looking in person. Maybe she would try to talk to him.

The other agents scanned the crowd, chatting quietly, obviously checking out the attendees to look for that one person who didn't quite fit. The one who might possibly have come to see the turmoil they created.

To the right of the podium, a priest was talking to an older woman and man. Amber thought they must be Becky Laurelwood's parents. A younger woman stood several feet away from the parents. No doubt, this was Suzanne, Becky's sister.

Scores of people walked to the site on the riverbank from the parking area. Amber glanced at her watch. The memorial was supposed to start in ten minutes. The presence of a podium indicated speeches were going to be given. But by whom? Maybe the priest would say a few words and then flowers would be thrown in the river. Amber had spotted several buckets filled with pink and white carnations behind the podium, closer to the river's edge.

Amber leaned over and whispered in her mom's ear. "What do you suppose is going to happen? Speeches? Prayers? Do you think the parents will say anything?"

"Yes, to all of that," Fluffy answered, glancing around. "I don't think all these people are friends of the family." She seemed rather indignant about strangers showing up.

"Mom," Amber said, "we're not friends of the family either. We're..." Amber didn't know what they were. Curiosity seekers might be the nicest way to describe them.

Fluffy started to speak, apparently to defend their right to be there, when Max suddenly popped up. "Oh good. You're all here. From what I've been able to gather, the priest will speak first, then I think Mr. and Mrs.

Laurelwood will say a few words, then the police are going to ask for the public's help in solving the crime. Again. Afterwards, we'll be invited to toss flowers into the river and then there will be an opportunity to talk to the family. That's when you come in, Amber. I'll introduce you, and while we're chatting with the parents, maybe you could talk to Suzanne. Give her a card. Tell her you're looking into the murder as a True Crime Reporter. Tell her you'd like to chat with her sometime, though you know how hard this must still be…"

"Thanks Max. I can handle it. I won't be pushy."

Max looked a little embarrassed. "I'm sorry. I'm nervous. I know you'll do a good job."

"I might even be able to talk to Sandy Foss," Amber said. "Give him a card but he's like a big-time reporter. He probably won't be interested. After that I'm hoping to talk to that newspaper reporter who seems to always have the scoop on what's happening. Duncan Abbott. Can you point him out to me?"

Max looked around. "That's him. Under that tall pine tree to the left of Chief Wallace and company."

Amber glanced in the direction Max had indicated. He appeared young, with shaggy light brown hair and glasses. Ordinary. Maybe that was a plus in the newspaper business. Better to be able to fade into the background. Not be memorable in the least. She definitely needed to hand him a card and ask to chat later.

"I also want to try and track down the park rangers who were first on the scene and maybe even talk to Chief Wallace."

"Good luck talking to the Chief. If you aren't someone important or a big campaign donor, he'll probably brush you off."

"I have to try."

"I admire your persistence," Max said.

The ceremony went as predicted. The priest spoke and said some prayers he must have assumed would be soothing and relieve some of the grief of the parents. Though how did one get over the loss of a child? And how could Becky's parents accept her murder as part of God's plan?

At one point Amber whispered to Max, "Isn't anyone going to say anything about the other victim? Annie? There were two people murdered."

Max leaned over and whispered back, "Her family was invited to participate. They declined."

Mr. Laurelwood stepped to the podium. He only said a few words, asking for help from the public. Amber was surprised that he appeared quite calm. Not emotional at all when talking about his murdered daughter. The older sister stood in the background, partially obscured by a tree branch. For some reason Amber felt that Suzanne did not care much for her father. There was an odd expression of… disdain? disgust?… on her face as he spoke. Her posture was stiff and her face rigid. When Mrs. Laurelwood moved up to the podium, Suzanne quickly stepped up, standing close beside her. Mrs. Laurelwood gripped the podium as if she needed it for strength. Deep, dark lines etched her face as if someone had drawn on it with a marker. This is what grief does, Amber thought.

Closing her eyes, Mrs. Laurelwood swayed for a moment. Suzanne put her arm out to steady her mother. Mrs. Laurelwood barely acknowledged her. She sighed deeply and began to speak about how terrible it was to lose a child and that until she knew why someone had murdered her daughter and taken her away, she would never be completely at rest or able to heal.

Amber watched Suzanne as her mother spoke. She had dropped her hand and no longer reached out to her mother. The family dynamic was odd, as if the death of Becky had separated, rather than united them. Suzanne did not speak, which didn't surprise Amber.

After the parents, Chief Wallace stepped to the microphone and said a few words about needing help from the public to solve this terrible crime, adding once again if anyone had any information to please contact the FBI at the number they had given out. Cards were handed to the crowd with the number printed in big bold black letters in case people didn't remember. Agent Devereaux did not speak, which broke Amber's heart a little. She was still considering whether she might try to talk to him at the end of the ceremony.

The priest stepped back to the podium, inviting the crowd to come forward to pick up a carnation to throw over the bank into the river. As people returned from the riverbank, they milled around, talking. Amber tried to decide who to approach. She was worried about everyone leaving before she had a chance to corner them and hand out her cards.

She saw Chief Wallace walking toward her with his posse following behind. Amber hurried over to him. "Chief Wallace," she began. He stopped and looked at her. Determining she was no one of importance, he tried to brush past her. "Excuse me," Amber said, holding a card out to him. "I'm…" He snatched her card out of her hand, stared at it before shoving it into his pocket. Then he pushed her aside as he strode by.

"Wow," she huffed out to his retreating back. One of his deputies stopped to make sure she hadn't been injured by the Chief's abrupt departure.

"Are you all right, Miss?" he inquired, offering her his hand.

"What an incredibly rude man," Amber replied.

The deputy was good-looking, with silky blonde hair and deep blue eyes. He blushed. "The Chief can be a little brusque when he has a lot on his mind."

"That wasn't brusque, that was rude," Amber declared. "I wanted to make an appointment with him. I'm a podcaster and I'd like to interview him about the murders."

The deputy turned a deeper shade of red. "Oh, if you're a member of the press, don't even bother. He hates the press and refuses to talk to them."

"I'm not exactly the press. I do a podcast about True Crime and I'm doing an episode about local murders." Amber winced inwardly. She felt a little awkward lying to this very nice person. "I'd like to be able to quote the chief investigator, since your department was first on the scene." She flashed him a brilliant smile. Scarlet would be so happy to find out she was using her feminine wiles.

"Yes, we were. Well, the park rangers were the first, but they aren't real policemen like we are." His chest swelled with pride.

"Maybe I could talk to you, Officer…?"

"Talley. John Talley. So, pleased to make your acquaintance, Miss…?"

Amber thrust out her hand. "Amber. Amber Steen. Let me give you my card. Please call and let me know when we might chat. If that would be all right with you?" She smiled again, embarrassed by her behavior. "Actually, let me give you several and you can pass them to your fellow officers. You know, in case someone has something they want to share."

He glanced briefly at the cards before putting them in his breast pocket. "I'll be sure to do that. This has been such a terrible thing to happen to our community. I only wish I could have done more."

Amber nodded. Suddenly Officer Talley remembered his duty. "I have to catch up with the Chief and the others or I'll miss my ride." He laughed but it seemed forced.

Amber watched him trot after the rest of the Westburg police force and climb into a car. "Hmm… my first conquest… I mean contact." She saw the retreating backs of the FBI agents and sighed. No chance to talk to Agent Devereaux.

She spotted Sheriff Fenster standing with a few of the Easton police. He saw all the other law enforcement officers leave and nodded to his group to indicate they should follow suit. She had always liked Sheriff Fenster. He was a decent man who tried to be fair with anyone who stumbled and fell outside the law, especially young, first offenders.

As he passed by, she stopped him. "Hello Sheriff Fenster, my name is Amber Steen." She held out her hand.

He stopped and smiled at her. "Steen? Any relation to Madge and Bob Steen?"

"Yes. They're my parents."

"Wonderful people. Just wonderful," Sheriff Fenster said, shaking Amber's hand. "How can I help you, young lady?"

"Well, I have a true crime podcast and I'm thinking of doing an episode on the River Road Murders since they are so close to home." She held out one of her cards. "I'm trying to talk to all the key players in the investigation—the police, the FBI, the rangers."

Sheriff Fenster took her card and, after looking at it, put it in his breast pocket. "That's kind of you to call me a key player." He looked at his deputies. "Did you know we were key players?" The deputies smiled and chuckled. "Sadly, we've been kept on the sidelines by Chief Wallace and Chief Ranger Richardson. But drop by any time and we can chat. And please give your parents my regards." He tipped his hat to her and, followed by his deputies, walked to his car.

What a nice man, Amber thought. Such a contrast to that awful Chief Wallace.

Amber spotted Max with her mom and Ida, talking to Mrs. Laurelwood. Once again Suzanne was close, almost as if she was trying to protect her mother. Sadly, it was too late. The worst had already happened to the woman. Amber walked over.

Max turned as Amber approached. "Hello Amber." She pretended to be surprised to see Amber at the memorial. It was a little too much cloak and dagger for Amber. Turning to Mrs. Laurelwood, Max introduced her. "This is one of my newest employees at the library, Amber Steen. I went to school with her mother and aunt." Max held out her arm to introduce Ida and Fluffy.

Amber put out her hand. "I am so very sorry about your daughter. I can't even imagine what you've gone through."

Mrs. Laurelwood took Amber's hand and gave it one very limp shake. Ida and Fluffy murmured their condolences as well. Mrs. Laurelwood turned her attention to Max, and they continued to talk. Amber moved closer to Suzanne. "I am sure you're devastated as well. People don't really understand how close sisters are. I have an older sister, and I wouldn't be able to survive if anything happened to her."

For a moment, Amber thought she saw a look of total disgust flit across Suzanne's face. It was only an instant and Amber assumed she must have imagined it, because Suzanne now smiled sadly at her. "Yes, people don't realize how hard this has been for me as well. I've lost my childhood companion. My best friend. And I have to be there for my parents in their all-consuming grief." Amber felt a flare of anger radiating off Suzanne. What was she angry about? The loss of her sister? Or something to do with her parents?

"So, why are you here?" Suzanne fixed Amber with a probing stare.

Awkward. Amber froze for a moment. "I came with my mother and aunt. The entire community is horrified by what happened, and we wanted to show your family our support," she stammered.

Suzanne's stiff posture relaxed a bit. "Yes. It is shocking. More so when it's a family member."

"I can't even imagine." Amber took a deep breath and let it out slowly. It was now or never. "Also, I do a true crime podcast, and I know this is probably not the right time or place, but I would love to talk to you about that very thing. The devastation caused by crime. People often don't realize the ripple effect murder has on families."

Suzanne's eyes narrowed as she continued to look straight into Amber's eyes. Amber couldn't decide if she was furious or curious.

"You certainly don't have to answer me now. Here's my card. Think about it and let me know." Amber tried to look serious and concerned. She decided a smile would not be in order.

Suzanne took Amber's card and stared at it before putting it in her purse. At least she hadn't thrown it in Amber's face. She gave Amber a brief nod before turning back to her mother.

CHAPTER TWENTY-NINE

*A**mber walked away on shaky** legs.* She didn't know how she had pulled that off without fainting. "Deep breaths, deep breaths," she mumbled as she headed to the other side of the field. As she approached the spot where Sandy Foss had been, she spotted the Channel 9 News van pulling up. The reporter and cameraman were walking toward it. Amber broke into a jog and caught up to Sandy as he climbed into the van.

"Hello. I was hoping to chat with you," she blurted out. "I'm a true crime podcaster and would love to talk to you about the murders. Here's my card."

Sandy looked at the card before glancing up at Amber.

"My mother's a huge fan of yours." Amber grinned.

Sandy grinned back and waved the card at her. "Give your mother my regards." The door slammed and the van pulled off.

Letting out a huge sigh of relief, Amber looked for Duncan Abbott. She felt sure he'd still be around. He'd probably be among the last to leave.

She finally spotted him standing on the bank, peering into the river. What was he thinking? Was he trying to get into the head of the murderer, or, she thought wickedly, was he the murderer returning to the scene of the crime?

"Mr. Abbott?"

He turned and looked at her. "Yes?"

"My name is Amber Steen. I'm a true crime podcaster." She held out one of her cards to him. He took it and stared down at it as if all the answers to life's questions could be found on it.

Glancing up, he smiled. "Charming. What exactly is a true crime podcaster?"

She tried to pull herself up and look haughty. "Isn't it rather obvious? I have a podcast, and I discuss true crime. Of course, I'm quite interested in the River Road murders. There are so many questions. And now the FBI is involved."

"It is quite an interesting series of events. Are you local?"

"Yes. I only talk about crimes that take place in this area. Mostly I discuss murders I am somewhat involved with because I knew the murderer or the victim or both."

"I'm intrigued. Most people don't know anyone who's been the victim of a crime, and you know an entire cast of murderers? Sounds like you might be more involved in these crimes than you let on."

He grinned at her, tilting his head to the side as if considering her as a suspect. His mop of hair fell over his glasses. He was cute up close. Focus, she thought.

"You seem to know a lot about these murders too. Perhaps you're the murderer."

"Touché!" Duncan laughed. "I have been accused of that. We definitely need to talk, if for no other reason than to eliminate each other as suspects. However, I'm working right now and need to get back to it." He glanced down at the card again. "I'll give you a call, Miss Steen, and we can set up a time and place to chat."

"Amber," Amber replied.

"While you're here, you might want to talk to Ranger Joshua Renn, the first person on the scene of the murder. In a strange turn of events, he was also first on scene of the other two incidents." The reporter looked around.

"That's him over there. That kind of tall, awkward guy in the ranger uniform."

Amber glanced over and spotted the ranger he was referring to. "Thank you, Mr. Abbott."

"Duncan," he said. With a smile, he turned and melted into the crowd.

Amber watched him go. He was just arrogant enough to be a murderer who wrote articles about his own crimes. Laughing all the way to the bank. She already had three people she hoped would call and talk to her. She still wasn't sure if she'd ever hear from Suzanne. And now for the final piece of the puzzle. The ranger who found the bodies.

Ranger Renn stood talking to a group of his fellow rangers, laughing and punching them playfully. Amber instantly disliked him. It was no way to behave at a memorial service. She glanced around quickly to see if Becky's parents were nearby. Luckily, they were on the far side of the clearing, talking to the priest and another man in a suit. Probably a local politician.

Amber stood quietly a few feet behind Ranger Renn until one of the other rangers noticed her and tried to shut Renn up. At least this man appeared to be embarrassed by their behavior. The ranger nodded in her direction and Renn turned around. He looked her up and down and grinned.

Bile rose in Amber's throat. This guy was another Bruce. Full of himself and thinking he was God's gift to women. Even though she needed to talk to him, she didn't want to. Holding out her hand, Amber introduced herself. "Hi, I'm Amber Steen. I do a true crime podcast, and I was told you were the ranger who found the victims of the first murder."

Renn took her hand and squeezed it, running his thumb over the back of her hand. Amber remembered punching Bruce. This guy deserved a punch even more. Forcing her smile to remain on her lips, Amber extricated her hand. She pulled a card from her pocket and handed it to him.

Amber hoped the other rangers would leave. She didn't want an audience, but they edged closer, trying to find out what was going on. Renn, sensing their presence, turned. "Dudes, back off. This lady wants to talk to me." The group collectively drifted away.

"This isn't the best time or place to talk, what with the parents standing right there," Amber nodded toward Becky's parents. "I'm wondering if you could call me, and we could set up an appointment. I'm fleshing out the story. I'm planning on talking to the press, the police, and maybe the FBI."

The ranger's lips curled in disdain. "Damn FBI. Think they know everything. We did a good job here. We just don't have all their fancy equipment. Profilers and all that crap. People hear FBI and act like they're the saviors of the universe. They don't know shit."

Amber attempted to hide her disgust. He was the first person involved with the crime who was completely off putting. He didn't appreciate that real people with real families had been murdered under his nose. It would be perfect if he was the murderer because he was so completely despicable.

"It's exactly why I came to you first. The FBI is way down my list. You were there. You saw things. Maybe you caught a glimpse of the murderer? I'm sure you have a theory about who is perpetuating these crimes."

"You bet I do. Course, no one is going to listen to some lowly park ranger." He sneered. "I was there. You can't imagine what it was like to walk up to that car. Man, like a scene out of a horror movie. The blood…"

Amber interrupted. "Wasn't the car burned? I didn't realize there was a lot of blood outside the car?"

Renn looked uneasy. Amber thought he realized he'd been caught in a lie. Or at least an embellishment of the truth. No doubt, he'd been making himself popular at the local bar, telling his gory story over and over. Adding tidbits to make it more exciting. By the time the FBI interviewed him, he probably couldn't remember what really happened.

"How awful for you. I'm sorry, but I need to go. I caught a ride with friends, and they're leaving. Please call. We need to talk." Amber smiled at him with what she hoped looked like a sincere smile instead of a disgusted sneer.

Before she got away from him, he smiled back and said, "Sure thing, babe. Can't wait."

Her blood ran hot with rage. "Babe." He actually called her babe. It was Bruce all over again.

CHAPTER THIRTY

Amber caught up with her mom and Ida on the edge of the woods.

"There you are," her mom said. "Have you accomplished everything you hoped to? Interrogated all the suspects? Solved the crimes?"

"More importantly," Ida interrupted, "were you able to get a date with Agent Devereaux?"

Amber knew her mom and aunt were teasing, so she tried not to get upset. "No, Ida, I didn't get a date with Agent Devereaux. I didn't even get close to him. He left right after the speeches, which surprised me. I talked to some people who I hope will call me back."

Ida's phone rang, and she answered it. "Yeah." She paused. "Okay. Us too. We're almost to the car. See you at the house."

She disconnected and looked at Fluffy and Amber. "That was Max. She's leaving and suggested we meet at the house to compare notes."

"Good idea," Amber said. They drove in silence.

When they got home, Amber ran straight upstairs.

"Where are you going? Max should be here any minute," Ida called.

"I have to get out of this dress and these shoes. I'm so uncomfortable. I want to get my sweats on. I need to be comfy to think."

Once in her room, Amber pushed her door shut. She kicked her shoes into the closet and yanked her dress over her head, tossing it on the bed. She picked up her sweats and shoved her feet into her slippers.

On the way to the den, Amber took a detour by the kitchen, poured a glass of milk, and grabbed several cookies from the jar. Ida and Fluffy were already in the den. Amber flopped down in a chair and gulped half her milk before starting on the cookies.

Fluffy appeared to be about to say something when the front door opened, and they heard Max call out. "Hello? Where is everyone?"

"We're in the den," Ida called.

Fluffy stood. "Excuse me while I fix a tray of refreshments. Then we can talk."

Amber winced in embarrassment. She really hadn't considered anyone else when she grabbed her snack.

Max walked into the den and collapsed onto the couch. "What an emotional, draining day." She kicked her shoes off and splayed out, staring at the ceiling.

"Don't worry, Madge is getting food and drink to fortify us," Ida said.

"Thank goodness," Max responded. "I need something cold to drink and something sweet to eat."

"You've come to the right place," Fluffy called out as she returned with a huge tray loaded with sandwiches, cookies, milk, and iced tea. She set the tray down on the coffee table. "I'll be back in a sec with plates and napkins."

After a few minutes restoring their souls, everyone felt much better.

Max brushed some crumbs off her fingers and lap and wiped her lips with a napkin. "So, who wants to go first? What did anyone discover?"

Ida and Fluffy looked at each other before looking at Max and Amber. "Not much," Ida said. "We circulated and tried to overhear people's conversations. Most people seemed happy that the FBI had taken over the investigations. There was a lot of conversation about whether the crimes were related, but there didn't seem to be any consensus."

Max agreed. "I heard most of the same things. Mrs. Laurelwood didn't seem to care if the crime was committed by a serial killer or if it was a random act of violence. In her mind, the only crime worth pursuing or talking about is the death of her daughter." Max paused. "I guess I can understand, but it's a bit odd she doesn't appear to have much sympathy for the other grieving families. She didn't even mention the other woman who was in the car and murdered along with Becky. She hardly acknowledges there was another victim. It's almost as if their grief isn't equal to hers." Max appeared to be struggling with what she wanted to say. "I guess she still can't fathom what happened. Murder happens to other people. Not people of their class."

"It must have been such a complete shock," Ida said. "Who expects that someone they know and love will be murdered?"

Max nodded. "I wanted to talk to a few other people, including Duncan Abbott, but I lost track of him in the crowd. What about you, Amber? Did you touch base with everyone you wanted to?" Max grinned. "Like Agent Devereaux?"

Amber felt a little angry. She'd worked hard today, connecting with several possible suspects, or if not suspects, good witnesses. "Let's drop the whole Agent D. thing."

"Okay." Max put her hands up. "I'm sorry. Who did you talk to? What did you find out?"

"First, I managed to get my cards in the hands of several key people, the first being Chief Wallace as he stormed past me. I'm sure he threw it away the minute he got to his car. What a complete jerk. Probably wanted to beat a hasty retreat in case someone from the press tried to talk to him.

"After Chief Wallace almost knocked me down, one of the Westburg deputies helped me regain my balance. He was really nice, and I gave him a bunch of cards and asked him to call me."

"It's good to have an 'in' at the Westburg police department. There's still a chance that these murders were committed by someone in law enforcement," Ida said. "They have the means and opportunity."

"I heard a lot of people suggesting Chief Wallace was involved. I don't think anyone is a fan of his." Max grimaced. "In fact, people were grumbling about him and suggesting he and Chief Ranger Richardson had some shady dealings going on and the victims were in the wrong place at the wrong time."

"Interesting," Ida said. "That actually makes a lot of sense."

"That's one of the reasons everyone is glad the FBI is involved. Some people think that the governor requested their assistance because he's heard rumors that Wallace is a dirty cop."

They sat quietly digesting that news.

"Whoever it is, I keep asking myself, what's the motive?" Ida said.

Before Amber could respond, Fluffy jumped in. "Serial killer. They don't need a motive. They like to kill."

Everyone stared at Fluffy. She had a point. Some people did like to kill, but was that really what was going on here?

"Who did you talk to next?" Max asked.

Amber took up her narrative again. "I talked to Sheriff Fenster. What a contrast to that jerk, Wallace. Apparently he knows you and Dad and asked me to pass on his regards to you. He was so nice. Said he didn't know much of anything but would be happy to talk to me anytime I wanted."

"Buster is a very nice fellow," Fluffy said. "Maybe not the sharpest crayon in the box but a good decent person. We all went to school together."

"You're right. Probably why Easton has such a low crime rate. No one wants to hurt his feelings by behaving badly," Ida said.

Max laughed.

"I'm kinda joking but I think his integrity really sets a tone for the town."

"Then I joined you guys and met Mrs. Laurelwood." Amber paused. "I don't know how you all feel but I got the impression something is a little off in that family. The other daughter, Suzanne, doesn't appear to like her father much. Did you all notice when he gave his speech, she stood in the shadows? With a kind of weird expression on her face? When her mom stepped up, Suzanne tried to help her, and her mom practically shook her off as if she didn't want her around."

"I noticed that too," Fluffy said. "I feel sorry for her. It's as if their world was all wrapped up in Becky, and even though she's gone, they still don't notice Suzanne."

"I agree," Max said. "Suzanne is one of those girls who kind of coasted along. Grades were okay. No sports or other activities. No articles in the paper. Has a good, but not exciting job. Then Becky comes along and was always in the paper for something—track, scholarships, space camp. The list goes on. I'm willing to bet that Mrs. Laurelwood has a scrapbook or two with every one of Becky's newspaper articles in it. Suzanne will never fill the void."

"And the father is…" Amber said. "I don't know. Cold? When he spoke about Becky, it was like he was giving a report at a stock meeting."

They sat quietly for a few minutes, thinking about families and how different they all were.

Max finally broke the silence. "I saw you talking to Suzanne."

"Yes, and I can only describe it as awkward. She's not very…" Amber struggled to find the right word. "…easy. I felt a lot of different emotions there. Anger. Sorrow. Maybe jealousy. But I gave her my card, and she didn't tear it up or spit in my face, so hopefully I'll hear from her."

"Oh, that must have been tough. Good for you. Anyone else?" Max asked.

"After Suzanne I caught up with Sandy Foss. I told him my mom was a huge fan and he smiled and took my card. Thanks, Mom. He probably wouldn't have responded if I hadn't said that."

"How exciting," Fluffy gushed. "I wish I'd been able to meet him. We'll have to watch his report on the news tonight."

"Don't get too excited Mom," Amber said with a laugh. "He could be one of our suspects."

Fluffy looked outraged at the suggestion. "Don't be ridiculous."

"Then I found Duncan Abbott on the riverbank looking at the flowers floating in the water." Amber paused, considering the man with the shaggy hair. "He's a really interesting guy. I liked him, but I could definitely see him as the murderer." She laughed. "He's smart enough and a bit full of himself. Probably tired of writing for the local rag and hopes this might propel him to a bigger scene."

"Would someone murder people to advance their careers?" Ida asked.

"People kill for all kinds of reasons. Love. Hate, which is the flip side of love. Jealousy. Rage. Greed. The list goes on." Fluffy said, once again assuming the mantle of an expert on murder. "So why not ego?"

"True." Max agreed.

"Which is why Sandy can't be dismissed," Amber said. Her mom shot her a dirty look.

"Duncan and I joked around a bit. I gave him my card. I feel sure he'll call me back," Amber said.

"Good," Max said.

"Finally, I talked to the park ranger who was first on the scene of all three murders. It's a bit too much of a coincidence for me," Amber said. "He really gave me the creeps. He seemed much more concerned about being recognized for what he'd done than what the families suffered. He has my vote for being the murderer. In fact, I hope it's him."

The others all hooted with laughter.

"He's such a sleaze. I'm not looking forward to seeing him again. And if we do meet up, it will be in a crowded place in broad daylight. He's one of those guys who thinks he's all that. He reminded me so much of Bruce. He even called me 'babe'." Amber shuddered and shook her head as if she had eaten something sour. "Ick."

"I agree. Let's hope it's him," Ida said and they all laughed.

Watching the news later with her parents, Amber thought, once again, Sandy Foss did a good job as the concerned reporter. He stood by the riverbank with the podium in the background. The camera panned to show the carnations floating in the river. "We are here to commemorate a sad anniversary. One year ago, two young women were found dead at this exact spot." He went on to update the events of the past year and the FBI joining in the search for the killer. He brushed his hair back and signed off with his signature wave.

"Oh, I do hope he calls you, Amber," her mother gushed.

That was certainly interesting. Everyone acting so concerned, so polite... so civilized, while at the same time everyone was eyeing everyone else to see who was acting nervous, odd, or should I say—guilty. I was doing the same since I was looking for the Copycat killer.

It surprised me when Agent Devereaux left early, but there were probably a dozen FBI agents dressed in ordinary civilian clothes, hanging around, mingling with the crowd. There might have been as many police as mourners there.

Those cards were a good idea. I stared at the card in my hand and turned it over.

Amber Steen

True Crime Podcaster

I smirked. Sweet innocent Amber. She has no idea what she's getting into. She thinks she can smile at everyone with those big innocent doe eyes, and we'll all confess. Silly girl. Does she have any idea she spoke with at least one murderer today—me—and possibly two, the Copycat, since no doubt he or she was there? I looked for them but they might appear as ordinary as me.

Yes. I hope all her suspects give her a call to set up meetings. Muddy the waters. What would little Miss Innocent do if she ever came face to face with a real killer? She might soon find out. I have to add her to my list, though I'll have to find her a partner. Need to stick to the pattern. Two at a time.

CHAPTER THIRTY-ONE

The next morning, Amber waited to hear from Scarlet. She finally gave up and called a little before lunch.

"I've been waiting for hours to hear from you," Amber sniffed. "I assumed you'd be dying to hear about the memorial."

"Please…" Scarlet spoke in a low voice. "Don't talk so loud. My head is pounding. We celebrated a bit too much last night since we won the Mock Trial competition."

"Must be nice to be partying out with your friends while I'm hanging out with Mom, Ida, and Max."

"Yes. It was fun. Probably the first time I've let my hair down with my fellow students. It's a bit of a cut-throat atmosphere in law school."

"Sounds like you maybe went a little overboard."

"Agreed," Scarlet said in a pained tone. "I haven't had more than one glass of wine in years and last night… I don't remember how many… was it glasses or bottles…?"

"Doesn't sound like you're up for recording," Amber said, trying hard to be sympathetic and failing.

"Give me a couple of hours. A hot shower and something to eat will bring me back to the land of the living."

"Hopefully," Amber replied before disconnecting.

Bored and feeling at loose ends, Amber wandered down to the kitchen, where she knew she'd find her mother. And probably a plate of cookies.

Fluffy looked up from a mixing bowl. She wiped her hands on her apron. "Hi there. Aren't you and Scarlet recording today?"

Amber decided not to reveal Scarlet's hangover to their mom. "We are, but probably later. Scarlet slept in late because she and her team won the Mock Trial. She needed to get prepared before we start."

"Oh, how exciting her team won. I'm sure she's thrilled."

More hungover than thrilled, Amber thought. "Oh, yes. No doubt. When she calls later, don't tell her I told you already. I'm sure she'll want to tell you all about it herself."

"Of course. Have you had lunch yet?"

Amber laughed. "No, which is why I'm skulking around the kitchen. Is there anything planned, or should I help myself to leftovers?" There were always wonderful leftovers in the fridge.

"Leftovers are a good idea. I'm working on dinner."

Staring in the fridge, Amber saw numerous labeled containers. Her mother kept everything in the kitchen organized. Even leftovers. Amber pulled each container out and read the labels. "Yes!" she murmured when she found the lasagna. Her mother's lasagna was one of her favorites and always got better after a few days.

"I'm going to finish off the leftover lasagna, if it's all right," Amber said as she stood up.

"Perfect." Her mother continued to mix and add ingredients to a huge bowl.

Amber popped the leftovers into the microwave and took the steaming plate to the den to eat. After finishing the lasagna, Amber took her plate to the kitchen, rinsed it off, and put it in the dishwasher. Her mom did expect everyone to take care of their own dirty dishes.

Wandering to her bedroom, Amber went over her notes for the second half of their current episode. She wasn't stressed about getting the episode recorded, but for some reason she felt antsy and discombobulated. There was too much going on. The Podcast and the River Road Murders. Not to mention her job at the library, which luckily wasn't very demanding.

Amber must have dozed off because her cell phone tone startled her awake. "Hello," she said, as she snatched up the phone.

"Hello," Scarlet replied.

"You sound better."

"I feel better," Scarlet said. "Amazing what a hot shower, short nap, and some greasy food can do for the soul. I seriously never want to drink again."

Amber laughed. "Good plan. Also, congrats on the win. You need to call Mom and Dad and tell them. They'll be so proud."

"Good idea. I'll do that right now and call you back."

Amber waited about ten minutes before she fired up the computer and logged into Zoom.

A moment later, she saw Scarlet trying to log in and she accepted the request. As soon as Scarlet said hello, Amber pushed the record button.

THE PODCAST
Episode Five: Drugs Kill

Amber: Welcome back everyone. This is *The Murderer You Know*. Today we are doing part two of *Drugs Kill in Many Ways*.

Scarlet: Sad, but true.

Amber: At the end of our last episode, we mentioned there was a witness to this crime, and this is the person who called 911. Before we get to that, we need to go over some other details of the crime.

Scarlet: Yes. This is one of those unbelievable crimes, with several perpetrators and two victims. What were the people in the car thinking when Bad Dude returned to the house with the gun? Did they know Bad Dude intended to kill these women? Did they think he only planned to scare the women into handing over all the goods?

Amber: It's hard to comprehend that they sat there and went along with what happened. Stupid One, the guy who brought the gun, said he heard the gunshots. A few moments later Bad Dude returned to the car carrying a safe and a huge bag of pot. Stupid Two, Driver Girl, took off.

Scarlet: Don't forget Bad Dude knew these women. They were supposedly his friends, and yet it didn't stop him from murdering them in cold blood.

Amber: Statistics show most people are murdered by people they know. We are all afraid of the boogeyman in the dark, when in truth, most violent crimes are committed by family and friends, not by strangers.

Scarlet: It is usually the murderer you know.

Amber: A scary, depressing thought.

Scarlet: Did he plan the murder, or did things spiral out of control and in the heat of the moment he lost it? What does the evidence show? Did he take the gun to scare them, or did he plan to kill them? Maybe he thought they wouldn't call the police and say their drugs and money were stolen, but he suddenly panicked? Did they say something that set him off?

Amber: It's too bad the video didn't have any audio. We'll never know what was said. The video only shows a heated argument broke out.

Scarlet: If he snapped when he first went into the house, he could have used that to explain or to defend himself. However, he left and walked out to the car to get the gun, which would be considered a cooling-off period. Legally, an act committed in the heat of passion can be viewed as a mitigating circumstance. Once he walked out to the car, he could have simply driven away. So, heat of passion is no longer a mitigator.

Amber: Once he got the gun and went back in, he must have decided to kill them. He told his two accomplices he killed them because they were going to call 911.

Scarlet: After they left the crime scene, they drove to his house to divvy up the money. There was a total of $17,000 in the safe. That was what a life was worth to him. $8,500 per person.

Bad Dude took the lion's share since he committed the murders. The other two got $3,500 each. I am appalled they were willing to kill someone for that pitiful amount, although sad to say people have been murdered for less.

Amber: What happened next? Who was the witness you mentioned?

Scarlet: During the entire episode, Prom Girl's young daughter was hiding in the hall closet. This little girl was so brave. As soon as Bad Dude left, she came out of the closet and called 911.

First responders were on the scene in minutes. Sadly, they couldn't save either of the women. The police started collecting evidence immediately, and they quickly focused in on Bad Dude.

Amber: How did they narrow in on him?

Scarlet: I think the little girl told them about the video. Maybe she recognized his voice, or maybe her mother said his name.

Amber: I remember the next day people were phoning the police with tips and that was enough to arrest him.

Scarlet: Yes, the old "person of interest" or what do the English say, "he's helping us with our inquiries." At the scene, DNA swabs and fingerprints were taken. They had the video evidence. Bad Dude was arrested only two days after the crime.

Amber: What a complete idiot. He commits a murder and leaves his fingerprints and DNA all over the house and was also caught on video. Surely, he knew his fingerprints were on file?

Scarlet: It's hard to imagine he expected he'd get away with it. After he was arrested, he was charged with two counts of First-Degree Murder and one count of Use of a Firearm in the Commission of a Felony. He pled not guilty.

Amber: I wonder what his defense was? "I didn't know the gun was loaded?"

Scarlet: No surprise, the jury found him guilty. The judge sentenced him to fifty years for each count of First-Degree Murder, thirty years for robbery, and eight years for use of a firearm, which gave him a total sentence of eighty-eight years. He is never getting out unless he somehow makes geriatric parole, which will be a long, long time from now.

Amber: What happened to his accomplices?

Scarlet: They were also quickly arrested. In their case, there was no physical evidence to link them, but the police tip line received many calls. The young woman who drove the car turned out to be Bad Dude's girlfriend, which explains her involvement to a degree. The police arrested her two days after Bad Dude. The guy who brought the gun and sat in the back seat was the last to be arrested.

Don't know if Bad Dude or Girlfriend sold him out.

Amber: What were they charged with?

Scarlet: The girlfriend, AKA the driver, was charged with two counts of First-Degree murder along with use of a firearm in the commission of a felony. She pled guilty to all counts.

The dumb guy who went for a ride along and brought the gun also pled guilty. He was charged with felony accessory after the fact. And only because he disposed of the last bullet after the murder. Odd, he brought four bullets, but Bad Dude only took and used three.

Amber: That is odd. Bad Dude tried for a not guilty plea, but the other two completely folded and confessed. Maybe Driver Girl believed she wouldn't get much time since she was outside in the car. Would the DA have to prove she knew what was going to happen? That Bad Dude intended to rob and possibly murder these women?

Scarlet: If she thought that at first, her lawyer would have informed her that it didn't make a difference. To be charged as a co-conspirator, you don't need to walk in the door or commit the crime. The prosecutors only have to prove she knew he had a gun, and she knew he planned to rob them. Which is why it's incredibly stupid to participate in a crime where a gun is involved. Even if you're only sitting out in the car waiting, you'll be charged with the same crimes as the person who pulls the trigger. There's something called reasonable and probable consequences and if a gun is involved, one of the probable consequences is someone will get shot.

Amber: I guess since she pled guilty, she was sentenced quickly.

Scarlet: Yes. She got twenty-three years in prison. Ten years for each murder and three years for use of firearm in the commission of a crime.

Amber: And Gun Boy?

Scarlet: Gun boy received a sentence of five years for each murder and four years as an accessory after the fact. So fourteen years total.

Amber: I'm shocked that's all they charged him with. He brought the gun with him and gave it to Bad Dude.

Scarlet: I agree. But it's different levels of horror. Handing a gun to someone is not the same as cold-blooded murder.

Amber: Do you suppose their sentences were lighter because they pled guilty?

Scarlet: Possibly. The prosecution likes a plea. They probably said, "we'll go after you hot and heavy in a trial.". And one of the other reasons they prefer a plea is you never know about juries. It's always a crap shoot.

Amber: All those lives ruined. The victims. Their families. And those stupid young people who participated in the crime will spend years in prison. Do they ask themselves why they went along with Bad Dude? Do they kick themselves about their wasted lives? Do they feel remorse for the lives that were taken? Girlfriend will be forty when she gets out.

I wonder about Bad Dude too. Does he feel remorse? Does he think about what a dumb decision he made? He was the only one who could have changed the outcome. Did he ever give a thought to taking away the lives of these women? And for what? $17,000 he never got to spend.

Scarlet: I can't stop thinking about that little girl in the closet who heard what happened to her mother. I can't imagine what might have happened if Bad Dude found her. Would he have killed her too?

Amber: OMG, it's too awful to consider. Maybe if he knew she was there, he might not have done what he did. Maybe he would have had a small spark of humanity.

Scarlet: The thing to be learned from this is: don't do drugs. Don't sell drugs. Don't buy drugs. Don't have anything to do with drugs. Drugs kill.

Amber: So true, and consider that all actions have consequences. Remember that before you do something stupid.

Thank you for joining us. We hope you enjoyed the show… and until next time we are…

After the credits and theme music played, Amber stopped recording. "Another tough one."

"Yes indeed, but we knew it wasn't going to be easy. We are talking about murder. On that note, tell me about the memorial service. Have you found your suspect?"

Amber laughed. "Maybe."

CHAPTER THIRTY-TWO

"*I don't feel I can* talk without cookies to revive me, but I know Mom won't let me eat any before dinner."

"Oh, poor you. None of Mom's cookies to sustain you. I'm so jealous you can sneak down and munch all you want. I have nothing!" Scarlet moaned, "Just awful store-bought boxed cookies here."

"All right, stop feeling sorry for yourself. Back to business. I'll give you a quick rundown of the memorial." Amber gave Scarlet a synopsis of who she encountered. "I almost knocked myself out batting my eyes and using my feminine wiles. You should be proud."

Scarlet laughed.

"Let's see. I talked to Chief Wallace, who's a total pig, one of his deputies, Sheriff Fenster, and the ranger who found the bodies. Don't know if it's likely but it would be nice if the murderer turned out to be either Chief Wallace or the ranger. He was kind of a creep. Reminded me of Bruce. I could see him committing the crimes to feel important. Walking up to the cars, shining a flashlight in the occupants' faces, telling them to get out. Feeling all powerful and in charge."

"Sounds like a piece of work. Any other suspects among the people you met?" Scarlet joked.

"Something is a bit off in the Laurelwood family. There's a lot of emotional undercurrents going on. If the father had been the victim, I'd immediately suspect the mother and the sister. However, I can't imagine any of them killing the family star, Becky."

"I don't know these people at all. The only possible scenario is the older sister killed the younger out of jealousy," Scarlet said.

"I can understand that as the lesser achieving sister," Amber joked.

Scarlet snorted. "I might have to take you out because you are annoying."

"I hope Suzanne calls me. She might be the key. She could answer a lot of questions, if she's willing."

"Did you meet anyone besides the cops and the family?" Scarlet asked.

"Sandy Foss," Amber said in a deep voice, "…Channel 9 News, reporting."

Scarlet laughed.

"A brief encounter. He seriously almost slammed the van door in my face until I told him Mom was a big fan." Amber laughed. "That stopped him, and he took my card. And gave me a big smile."

"Mom must have been thrilled you actually spoke to him, live and in person," Scarlet said.

"Yes, and thrilled he said to tell her hello. We watched his news report later. I have to admit he does a fine job. Gets that right level of concern on his face. Knits his brow and puts a grave expression on."

"Are you seriously considering him as a suspect?" Scarlet asked.

"Not really, but you have to keep an open mind." Amber paused. "Speaking of which, I'm beginning to doubt that the murders were even committed by the same person. There's nothing to connect them. The victims were killed in different ways. Their bodies burned in a car or dragged off and hidden in the woods. And in this latest murder, they said it looked like the murderer tried to dispose of the bodies by dumping them in the river."

"Interesting," Scarlet said.

"The latest murder popped in my brain while we were doing our podcast. Supposedly, the boy in the most recent murder dealt drugs. Not big time, but what if someone murdered him for his drugs and his money? The poor girl was in the wrong place at the wrong time. The murderer figured the police would think it was the serial killer and he'd be home free."

"Damn. Good thinking. I like it," Scarlet said. "Maybe you're right and we have three murderers, not a serial killer. And it's a coincidence they're all happening now."

"Mom will be devastated. She has her heart set on a serial killer!" The girls laughed uproariously at their mother's obsession with murder.

"So, if the third murder was a drug deal gone wrong, like our podcast, or a murder for drugs and money, what are your theories on the other two? Who killed them and why?" Scarlet asked.

"I'm kicking it around. I'm leaning toward jealousy in the first one. Becky was popular. She could have broken some guy's heart, even though everyone claims she wasn't dating anyone. Or she got a scholarship or something another girl wanted? Won a race? Cheated on a test?"

"It's so odd no one talks about the other victim. Annie? There could be some psycho in her past," Scarlet said.

"You're right," Amber replied. "Poor Annie. She didn't even get a passing mention at the memorial today. She's definitely the forgotten victim. But what if she was the intended target? If Suzanne ever calls me, I can ask her if she knew Annie."

"Oh, my head hurts," Scarlet moaned. "I don't know how the police do it. Come up with all the different scenarios. Chase down the leads. Eliminate suspects. Much easier to be the prosecutor and take the case to trial."

"So much easier to be presented with all the evidence nicely tied up for you," Amber said.

Scarlet snorted. "It's not quite that easy. So, you think jealousy in the first case, drugs in the third, what about the college kids?"

"Now my head hurts." Amber laughed. "No clue other than the same idea as with Becky—someone hated one of them or was jealous of them? Or we go back and say, a serial killer did the first two, but it was drugs and robbery in the third and not the same killer."

"Sounds like your theories are falling apart." Scarlet chuckled. "Did you meet anyone else of interest?"

"I forgot to mention Duncan Abbott, the reporter. I liked him. He's a bit snarky and arrogant but that's probably because he's a fantastic reporter and has been on top of these stories from the start. Both Max and Mom love his writing. And he's always breaking news before we hear from the police."

"So…" Scarlet prompted, "just an interesting guy or possibly a suspect?"

"I'm putting him in the suspect category. He actually kinda joked about it. I'm looking forward to talking to him again." Amber thought about that soft brown hair falling over his glasses.

"And FBI hottie? Did you talk to him?"

"No. He left almost immediately but I had the feeling that plainclothes agents were all over the place. Oops… got to go. Mom's calling. It's dinner time."

"I hate you," Scarlet said and hung up.

CHAPTER THIRTY-THREE

The next day, Amber did not have to work. She felt restless. Unfocused. Unmotivated. She wandered down to the kitchen and found her mother busy creating some kind of masterpiece. It became clear to Amber her mother didn't want her in the kitchen, so she grabbed a banana and headed upstairs to get dressed.

She had plenty to do. There were two projects requiring her attention. She wanted to do a deep dive into the college students who disappeared and were recently found. What was their story? Did someone want one or both of them dead?

And she needed to write up the next episodes for the podcast. These were cases where their mom and Ida knew the victims. And the perpetrators. Amber titled one *The Romeo and Juliet Murders*, since it involved a case with star-crossed lovers, though unlike Romeo and Juliet, they didn't plan on killing themselves. They planned to take out her parents and live happily ever after. Mom would appear as a guest on that episode since she'd been friends with one of the victims.

The second one, tentatively titled *Greed Gone Wrong*, had Ida as a guest since she'd worked with both the murderer and the victim.

First, Amber needed coffee. Since she hadn't been able to get into the kitchen at home, she decided to go to The Nook Café on Main Street. Their baked goods were amazing—not that she'd ever dare say that to her mom.

Amber grabbed her jacket as she headed out the door. This time of year, one never knew about the weather.

She hummed as she walked along the sidewalk, contemplating which task she should do first when she got home. The podcast was the more pressing; however, after the memorial she had become obsessed with the River Road murders. She needed to start calling people she gave cards to if she didn't hear from anyone soon. She wouldn't call Suzanne. Handing over her card had been awkward, and she didn't want to reach out again. She hoped Suzanne would call her. There were questions only Suzanne could answer and possibly clarify. Amber needed to know more about Annie Forst and wanted to ask Suzanne if she knew how her sister, Becky, and Annie met.

A car slowly cruised along the road, as if stalking Amber. A jolt shot through her body. "Oh no. Did I rile up the murderer at the memorial and now they're going to kill me?" She didn't turn to look at the car, comforting herself that she probably wouldn't be murdered in broad daylight. Another thought occurred to her. "I could be abducted at gunpoint and murdered."

Walking faster, Amber hoped she could get to The Nook before she was confronted. The car engine revved, and out of the corner of her eye she could see the car pull parallel with her.

"Hey babe," a voice called out.

For a moment Amber thought Bruce had returned before realizing this was not Bruce's voice. She stopped and bent down to look in the window. Joshua Renn, the ranger who proudly bragged about finding the bodies, smiled back.

Forcing herself to smile, she said, "Oh, hi Joshua. Didn't expect to see you. I assumed you'd call first."

"Well, you know what they say babe, strike while the iron is hot." He laughed. His laugh was shrill and annoying, like a donkey braying.

Amber wasn't sure how that metaphor or cliché or whatever it was, had anything to do with anything, so she smiled weakly. "Nice to see you again."

"Hop in. Let's go for a ride." Joshua revved his engine. Why do men of low intelligence always think women are attracted by the sounds of loud machines? There was no way in hell she was getting in his car.

"I'm going to The Nook for breakfast. Why don't you meet me there? You know where it is?" Amber said.

"Yeah, I know but jump in and I'll drive you."

"Thanks, but I prefer to walk. Build up my appetite, you know."

He looked annoyed but with a wave, he put the car in gear and drove up the street.

At least we'll be in a public place, she thought. It was unfortunate that of all the people and the potential witnesses, Renn was the first to get in touch, the very last person she wanted to be with. He gave her the creeps.

Pushing the door of the café open, Amber spotted Joshua sprawled out in a booth. Forcing herself to smile, she slipped into the seat across from him.

"I already ordered coffee and OJ for us both. You look like a girl that drinks orange juice. Healthy, you know."

Amber smiled and nodded, staring at the menu. She did like orange juice, but she didn't like this guy ordering for her. He was already trying to gain an advantage.

They both focused on the menu for a few minutes. The waitress brought coffee and juice and asked if they were ready to order. "Sure," Joshua jumped in, "I'll have the Mariner's Breakfast Sampler."

Amber knew the sampler included everything from eggs to pancakes to biscuits and meat. It was more food than any person should eat at one meal. Possibly more than a person should eat in a day.

"Do you want that with bacon or sausage?" the waitress asked.

"Can I have both?" Joshua asked and winked at Amber, who wondered what the wink was supposed to convey. Maybe that he didn't care if he was clogging up his arteries for a potential future heart attack.

"Of course," the waitress replied cheerfully. "And for you?"

Amber felt she should order something super healthy to shame him. Yogurt and granola? Or a fruit smoothie? Oatmeal? That was healthy, wasn't it? She didn't eat oatmeal, but it sounded like a perfect choice.

"Ummm…" she started, staring at the menu.

"We just pulled almond croissants out of the oven," the waitress suggested. "And cinnamon date scones." The waitress's voice took on a seductive tone. Amber felt like she was being wooed by a siren, luring her to her death. Dates were healthy, weren't they?

"Maybe I'll try one of each?"

"Good choice," she said.

Amber forced herself to smile at Joshua. Her lips wanted to curl into a sneer. "I'm glad to see you, but I'm surprised you showed up here. In Easton." She wanted to add, stalking me.

"Yeah. I have the day off, so I figured I'd pop over. You know, and help you with your podcast. I mean, that's so cool and all. I'll have to listen to it when it comes out. Will I actually be on it—like recorded? A guest?"

"Interesting idea. I haven't thought the whole thing through yet. I'm just gathering information right now. A recording of some of the key players, such as yourself, might work. I have a friend who is helping me to write the episodes. I'll run it by her."

Renn started looking around the café. Amber thought he didn't have a long attention span. Trying to look official, she yanked a notepad and pen out of her backpack. "Let's start with the first murder. Tell me what you discovered."

His face lit up. He beamed at her. This was what he'd come for. To spread his moment in the spotlight across the airwaves and into the ears of the public.

"You know, it was an ordinary morning. I'm usually on the early shift, driving along, looking for anything out of place. Sometimes we get dumb kids who camp out in the park and I gotta roust them out. Sometimes couples fall asleep in their cars after a night of you know what. If you know what I mean." He leered and winked.

Amber nodded to indicate she knew what he was referring to.

"So, I'm driving along, and I see smoke down by the riverbank. Not a lot. Maybe a campfire dying out but I gotta check that kind of stuff 'cause if the woods catch fire, it could be a big mess. Know what I mean?"

Amber nodded again. At this pace, it could take all day to hear the story.

"So, I parked my car in the small parking area there and walked down to where the smoke seemed to be coming from. Man, when I saw that car, I couldn't wrap my head around it at first. It was already a smoldering wreck. Must have burned all night. And naturally, the first thing you think is there's been a car accident but there wasn't another car, and it hadn't crashed into a tree, so what made it burst into flames? Like spontaneous combustion or something?"

The waitress arrived with the Mariner's Breakfast Sampler. She appeared to struggle under the weight of the over-filled platter. She set it down with a thump in front of Renn. "Damn, look at all that." He grinned at Amber.

"Yes, indeed. Look at it," Amber replied.

A moment later, the waitress placed a plate in front of Amber with two delicious looking pastries on it. The aroma of spices and fruit wafted up. Amber breathed deeply. This was heaven. Or a close approximation.

For the next fifteen minutes they concentrated on their food. Amber tried not to stare in amazement at how quickly the ranger shoveled food into his mouth. He didn't appear to pause to chew.

They finished at the same time. Amber wanted to lick the last crumbs off her plate but restrained herself. Renn fell back in his seat and grabbed his stomach. "I can't believe I ate the whole thing," he moaned and then laughed. Amber couldn't believe it either. The waitress took their plates, and they turned their attention to their coffee.

"You found the car burned out and still smoldering?"

"Yeah. I walked around, still trying to figure out what happened. When the wind blew the smoke toward me, I thought I'd puke. I could smell roasted flesh."

Amber almost gagged. "Really?"

"That's when I noticed the bodies in the car. One in the front and one in the back seat. All twisted up. Man, I hope they were dead before the fire. I took off to my car and called it in. More rangers came. An ambulance showed up, which seemed kinda funny because the people in that car didn't need to go to the hospital, know what I mean? But I guess that's how they transport dead bodies?" He said this last piece as a question.

"When they removed the bodies, I couldn't watch. Our wrecker hauled the car off to the maintenance shop. And that's the last time I saw it."

"So, Agent Devereaux was right. You all moved the car before a forensics team looked over the scene."

Amber realized at once she shouldn't have said that. Renn erupted in anger. "Easy for them to say. They're looking at the whole thing in hindsight. No one at the scene thought for a moment there'd been a murder. Just some kind of weird accident."

Remembering Renn's comment about "all the blood and gore", Amber almost confronted him about that. She bit her tongue. She needed this guy to talk to her. He seemed to be telling the truth.

"I can see that. Who, indeed, would have believed it was murder?"

They continued talking. The waitress brought a whole pot of coffee and set it on the table. Amber smiled up at her.

As soon as the waitress walked away, Amber said, "I remember hearing a rumor about the first one being a murder-suicide. I guess that would explain what happened."

Renn shook his head. "Yeah, someone came up with that idea because we couldn't figure out what happened. Seemed reasonable. But once the autopsy was done, the coroner figured out they were both hit on the head with a blunt object and were dead before the fire was started. No smoke in the lungs or something."

"It's amazing what they can figure out these days. It's a wonder anyone ever gets away with a crime," Amber said.

"Yeah. True." Renn nodded.

"Tell me about the second car. The college students."

Renn looked up as if trying to remember the details. "Again, I was on early shift and while cruising along, I seen this car parked in one of the scenic overlooks. I probably woulda kept going but the doors were open, which looked kinda strange. Plus, it was early, so they must have been there all night. Or maybe they drove out to see the sunrise." Renn shrugged. "People do weird things."

Amber nodded. She didn't say anything because she didn't want to interrupt him.

"So, I pulled over and walked up to the car. Like I said, the doors were open, and the radio on. I looked around and saw a blanket spread out on the grass. I walked around and called out. No one answered. Finally, I called it in. The dispatcher said one of the other rangers reported seeing a car parked there the night before. They saw lights but then they saw a car pull away and figured they'd left.

"I told them I couldn't find no one. Then the car battery died. Or at least I assumed that 'cause the radio went off. Other rangers showed up. We found the registration, which showed the car belonged to a twenty-year-old guy. In the back seat, we found his wallet with his driver's license and college ID and on the floor, we found a purse with a couple of bucks in the wallet and another student ID. Picture showed a girl."

Renn paused and took a swig of coffee. He stared off into space as if trying to remember the scene exactly.

"No one ever imagined this was a second murder. Everyone figured these kids went for a midnight swim and got carried away by the current. Or maybe went to a friend's house and were sleeping it off somewhere. Though the car radio being left on was weird. Maybe they were really drunk?

"We called a tow truck and hauled the car to the maintenance shop. One of the supervisors finally tracked down a phone number and called, and all hell broke loose… hysterical parents."

Renn appeared momentarily overwhelmed. "We called the Westburg police. After a preliminary search, the State Police brought dogs out. The dogs kinda walked around next to the car. They didn't go down to the river. Like the kids never left the parking lot. The State Police came in and dragged the river, but nothing was ever found. Not even a shoe."

"So even though the dogs didn't pick up a scent, most people still considered it was a tragic accident, right?" Amber asked. "Until the bones were found."

"Yeah. Another shocker. I was sure they'd drowned or got picked up by a friend or ran off together. Once they tested the bones, we knew."

"Do you think it's the same killer as the first crime? The MOs are so different."

"Yeah, we talk about it at the ranger station all the time. Everyone has a different opinion."

"And the latest crime? The third murder."

"That morning, a jogger called dispatch and said he saw a car off the road in the grass, kinda hidden by the trees. Once again, I'm the lucky guy on the early shift, and as I drove to the spot, I knew I was going to find something bad. When I saw the car, it was that déjà vu shit all over again. Doors open. Radio on." Renn looked stricken.

"But this time the scene had a different feel. There were signs of a struggle though there were no bodies at first. Later the police found the boy's body. Shot. It looked like maybe the killer had dragged him down to the river. And the girl was found in the river. Maybe the killer hoped they'd be carried off by the current and never found. Like the second couple. Let the fish and the crabs take care of the evidence," Renn said.

Amber grimaced. "And a different weapon was used this time. A gun. Makes you wonder if it's the same killer. Or maybe they're smart enough to mix things up and keep everyone guessing."

Renn ran his hand through his hair. He looked a little nervous. Maybe being first on the scene had taken a toll on him, which he tried to cover up by acting unmoved by what he'd seen. "I got no idea how many killers are out there. I hope they catch this wack-job." He paused. "Or wack-jobs."

"You've given me so much to think about." Amber closed her notebook and slipped it into her bag. "I'll be in touch. It might be cool to have you on the podcast to talk about what you saw." She stood up.

"Hey, you don't need to leave. We can keep talking. Go for a ride."

Amber hoped he didn't notice the look of horror on her face. "Great idea, but it will have to be another time." She glanced at her watch. "I need to get to work," she lied. "And I really want to write all this down before I forget any details. This podcast is going to take up several episodes. Your information will take up an entire episode."

He smiled. "Yeah. Remember, I was first on the scene."

She thanked him for his time, thinking, yes first on all the scenes. How very coincidental, reminding herself there are no coincidences in murder.

CHAPTER THIRTY-FOUR

Renn took off. Amber smiled and waved until he drove out of sight. No surprise, he'd stuck her with the check for their breakfast. I suppose he assumes I'm some big-time podcaster, and I have an expense account, she thought. Clutching a box of assorted pastries to her chest, Amber headed home.

Walking in the front door, Amber called out, "Mom, I'm home." She heard her mom answer from the kitchen.

Running up the stairs to her room, Amber closed the door and jammed the pastries in the bottom drawer of her dresser. It was ridiculous. No doubt they'd be stale by the morning. Amber bought them because she felt she owed The Nook a little extra for taking up a booth for the entire morning. Still, she didn't want her mom to know she'd bought outside sweets. If they were still good in the morning, she could take them to the library. She was on the early shift, and if she put them out in the break room they'd be gone in an instant.

She flopped on the bed and stared at the ceiling. She couldn't decide if she should write up all the notes from what Renn told her about the murder scenes, research the college couple in depth to find out what hidden secrets they harbored, or start writing up the *Romeo and Juliet* episodes for the podcast. She realized with a mixture of anticipation and dread the intro for the podcast was launching in three days. Would anyone listen? Would they get even one "like"? Max claimed she'd created buzz on all the social media platforms but that didn't mean anyone would actually click on it and listen.

"We're giving away cool merch," Max had said, "which will draw people in. Everyone wants something for nothing." The word "merch" sounded weird coming from Max.

Amber knew she didn't need to jump on the next episodes because after the intro aired, they had four other episodes in the can, ready to be downloaded for their adoring public. A month-long grace period. Still, she didn't want to become lazy or complacent.

Rolling over, she propped herself up with a half dozen pillows, snuggled in, and picked up her laptop. First things first. She needed to type up all the things Renn said. He was less annoying one-on-one than he'd been at the memorial, she admitted. No doubt his macho man persona was meant to impress the boys. He completely dropped all references to blood and gore at the first murder scene, admitting at the time he thought it was a terrible accident which was why they hadn't preserved the scene.

Now Amber understood why the second abandoned car didn't set off any alarm bells in anyone's head. The doors left open, the radio on, and the blanket on the grass convinced the police the young couple went for a swim and drowned. It was a logical conclusion until their bones were found.

In this recent murder there was another completely different MO. In the first crime there was a fire. Why? Maybe trying to cover up how the women were murdered? Get rid of DNA? The second crime the victims were abducted, and the pathologist could only say the victims were possibly killed with a blunt instrument. Finally, in the third case, the victims were shot, and their bodies dragged to the river. The murderer probably hoped they'd be swept far away. What Amber found to be the most interesting aspect was in this case the doors were also left open and the radio on. Did the murderer plan to take them away and hide their bodies but something interrupted them? And the use of a gun? That was completely different.

What was the connection? What linked these crimes together, or were they all random acts of violence? She remembered what her mother said about the Tylenol murders. Only one person was the target. The other victims were collateral damage. Who was the target in the River Road murders?

Leaning back on her pillows, she shut her eyes, trying to sort it all out. A moment later, her mom opened the door and called her name. "Time for dinner, sleepy head. I've been calling you for the last fifteen minutes."

Amber rubbed her eyes. She felt heavy and disoriented. Looking at her watch, she saw it was almost six o'clock. She sat up with a jerk. "Oh, my goodness. I must have fallen asleep."

Her mom laughed. "Well, obviously. What wore you out?"

Rolling off the bed, Amber stood up and stretched. "I went to The Nook for coffee this morning and that ranger, Joshua Renn, the one who was first at all the scenes, showed up."

"Oh dear. I hope nothing bad happened. You said he gave you the creeps."

Amber laughed. "Yeah, he is kind of a jerk. Surprisingly he behaved much better today. He told me what he found at each of the crime scenes, and I can now see why murder didn't jump out to any of the investigators. Especially the second crime when all they found was a car."

"I guess that's true," Fluffy admitted, "though a lot of people thought it was too much of a coincidence."

"Mostly in hindsight after the bodies were found, right? Did anyone think they'd been murdered until then?"

"Hmmm…maybe not."

"I came back to type up all my notes and I must have fallen asleep. It's emotionally exhausting."

"I can certainly understand. How did that ranger show up at The Nook at the same time you did?"

"He drove to our house and saw me walking down the road, cruised up next to me, and asked if I wanted to go for a ride."

"I hope you didn't get in his car," Fluffy said in alarm.

"No. Don't worry, I would never do that. Even though he seemed less of a toad today, there's still something about him that sets my danger radar off. Beep, beep, beep."

Her mother's efforts in the kitchen had been worth having to leave the house to find breakfast and coffee elsewhere. And since it also led to the chance encounter with Renn, it was a win-win.

Fluffy was always experimenting with new recipes, and tonight she served an incredible Asian-fusion dish with a variety of vegetables, many of which Amber didn't recognize. The flavors exploded in each bite. Sometimes spicy, sometimes sweet. Her mother made her father a steak and served him a tiny portion of rice and vegetables.

As Amber helped her mom clean up, she thanked her for dinner. "You know I'm no gourmet but that was amazing, mom."

"I'm glad you're home, honey. Your dad could eat a steak and baked potato every single night of his life. It's nice to have someone to experiment on who's willing to try new things."

"If you're able, I'm willing," Amber said.

They made tea and walked out into the living room to chat.

"The podcast is starting this week," her mom said. "Are you nervous?"

"Yes! I feel like I've invested a lot into this. I don't mean money, but all my emotions, my hopes, and dreams for the future. I don't care if I don't make a million dollars; I hope people listen, more than one person, and they enjoy it, so we can build a following."

"Honestly, Well, I know nothing about this kind of stuff. Seems like a crazy world where people can talk and become famous. I'm rooting for you, honey. Whatever you want and need out of this, I hope you get it."

"Thanks Mom. You're the best. Even if it doesn't take off, I've still got you and Dad, and Ida and Max, and of course, the best sister in the world, Scarlet. So, if nothing else, I'll be happy to live with you forever, eat your wonderful food, and work at the library."

"Not a bad life." Fluffy laughed.

"Not at all. Are you ready for your podcast debut? *Romeo and Juliet Part 1?* Are you okay with talking about your friend and what happened to her?"

"Yes. I think I am. I'll pretend I'm on an episode of *Law & Order.*"

They both burst into laughter.

"Though I have to say I'm not sure I like the title."

"No?" Amber asked. "Why not?"

"It romanticizes the murderers. They were horrible people not young lovers. Well, they were young, but incredibly stupid and horrible."

Amber considered what her mom said. "You have a point. I wanted to use that quote from the beginning of *Romeo and Juliet.* You know about the tale of woe? But I'll see what Scarlet thinks."

Later, Amber called Scarlet. "Hope you're not too busy and have time to chat."

"For you always."

"Wanted to catch you up on things. I got my first response to handing out my cards at the memorial. Ranger Renn practically showed up at the house this morning. He wanted to take me for a drive and chat."

"I hope you didn't get in the car with him." Scarlet sounded concerned.

"No, of course not. We had coffee at The Nook." Amber filled Scarlet in on everything Renn told her about the murders.

"Do you still think it's weird he was first at the scene at all the crimes?"

"Yes. Remember, there are no coincidences!" Amber said. "On the other hand, maybe they have a small staff and he's the morning guy. I was curious when he mentioned the night before he found the college kid's car, another ranger said he saw a light, like a car light in that spot. Could it have been the murderer?"

"Maybe? Wonder what might have happened if he'd taken the time to investigate?"

"In other more personal news, our intro launches Thursday. I am on pins and needles. I feel like I might throw up," Amber said.

"Calm down. Sometimes it takes a while to build an audience for a new podcast. It will happen. Are we still recording with Mom this weekend?"

"Yes. She's excited about it. Living the dream of doing a live *Law & Order* episode."

"Okay. How many times do you think mom will mention her extensive investigative experience from watching every episode at least three times?" Scarlet chuckled. "See you Saturday to record."

"Oh, wait a second. Mom wants to change the title of the episode," Amber said.

"Why?" Scarlet asked.

"She thinks it makes the kids like some kind of misguided, star-crossed lovers instead of depraved killers."

"She has a point. Think about something else."

"How about The Depraved Killer murders?" Amber laughed.

"That would be a no. Since it is mom's episode, we should ask her if she has a suggestion."

"Good idea. Good night."

I looked over the list of "potential" suspects in the River Road murders. I decided to start mailing notes to the FBI, throwing each and every one of these people under the bus. Or at least under the scrutiny of the investigators.

I need to be sure I hadn't forgotten anyone or their possible motives for committing the crimes.

Chief Robert Wallace of the Westburg Police Department: A corrupt cop who runs the Westburg Police like his own little fiefdom. Annie Forst was helping him cook the books and she had to go. Becky was collateral damage.

Chief Ranger Rick Richardson: Wallace's right-hand man. Wallace calls the shots, and Richardson carries out the deed.

Deputy John Talley: Has had a crush on Becky since middle school. She broke his heart for the last time.

Ranger Joshua Renn: He wasn't first to find the bodies. He was the one who killed them and covered up by "claiming" to have stumbled on the scenes. He's a serial rapist. He burned the first bodies to cover up the evidence of his crime. And he buried the other girl and threw the body of the third in the river to wash away the evidence.

Sheriff Fenster: That sweet dumb act hides a brilliant mind. He's overseen drugs and gun running up and down the Eastern seaboard for years. It all passes right through Easton, and he gets a cut. The young drug dealer tried to double cross him, which was a huge mistake.

Duncan Abbott: How does he know so much? Because he is the killer and has been one step ahead of everyone since the get-go. He's a brilliant psychopath who enjoys killing and the power it gives him over others.

Sandy Foss: Years of interviewing the worst kinds of criminals have twisted his mind into figuring out the perfect crime. Now he's committed three.

Arthur Laurelwood: Father of the first victim. He'd been abusing her for years and she finally told him she was going to the police.

Helene Laurelwood: Jealous of her beautiful, accomplished youngest daughter, she decided to eliminate the competition.

Suzanne Laurelwood: Jealousy of her younger sister finally spilled over in a murderous rage. And once she started, she decided to cover her tracks by killing others.

Maxine Bolger: Librarian by day, crime obsessed murderer by night. A lonely and bitter old woman who takes out her anger on others who are happier and more successful than she will ever be.

Ida Steen: Her little garage is a front for a chop shop. She had to eliminate Annie Forst, who knew too much.

Madge Steen: Her appearance as the sweet apron-wearing mom is the perfect disguise for a crime obsessed murderer. She just can't stop.

Amber Steen: A girl competing against her older sister, the star of the family. Supposedly starting a murder podcast to jumpstart a career. What better way than to commit a series of crimes on her own doorstep to include them in her podcast.

I read the list over one more time. I believe I've included most of the logical suspects. Did it matter to me if most, if not all, of the people on the list will be devastated by being accused? That would be a no. I am more concerned perhaps I haven't included enough suspects. But I've only just started. More names can be added.

The copycat killer might be on this list. These seem to be the logical suspects for that killing as well but maybe I'm totally off target. I feel sure that the copycat was at the memorial. Standing next to me. Acting like a concerned citizen. I'd love to know who the copycat is.

Some people might think it was foolish to include myself on the list of suspects, but Agent Devereaux and his little FBI cohorts might notice the omission of my name and wonder why. After all, I'm just as likely to have done this as the next person.

CHAPTER THIRTY-FIVE

The next morning, Amber got up earlier than usual. She wanted to fill Max in on her talk with Joshua Renn. Max might have some valuable insights. She got dressed quickly, grabbed the box of pastries out of her drawer, and stuffed them in her bookbag before heading downstairs.

In the kitchen, she grabbed a thermal cup to fill with coffee. Her mom walked in as she was adding cream and sugar. Amber put the lid on the cup and pushed it down to make sure it was secure.

"You're up early. Why are you filling a to-go cup?" Her mom opened the refrigerator door and pulled the egg carton out. "I was about to start breakfast. Would you like eggs or cereal this morning?"

"Neither. Thanks. I want to get to work early and talk to Max. And then I plan on researching the second murder."

"You need a good breakfast to fuel your brain."

"I'll be fine, Mom. Thanks." Amber leaned over and kissed her mom's cheek as she headed out the side door.

Amber arrived at the library right behind the maintenance person, who was happy to let her in. Heading into the breakroom, she turned on the lights and started the coffee so it would be ready when the rest of the staff arrived. Then she opened the box of pastries and looked over them carefully before picking out a yummy-looking scone, or maybe it was a crumpet, filled with berries and drizzled with honey.

Putting her feet up on a chair, Amber leaned back and bit into the pastry. Still as good as yesterday. No one will know they're a day old. She'd just finished the last of her coffee when the door opened and all the lights flicked on.

"Hello," a voice called out, "who's here?"

"It's me, Max. I'm in the breakroom."

Max popped in a moment later. "Aren't you the early bird this morning?"

"I wanted to have time to tell you about my interesting encounter yesterday." Max raised an eyebrow. "I had breakfast with that ranger I met at the memorial. Joshua Renn."

Max plopped down in the seat next to Amber. "No. Tell all."

Amber did. When she finished, she took a deep breath and asked, "What do you think about his story?"

"He's either the unluckiest guy in the world or the smartest murderer in the world," Max said.

"My thought exactly. But which is it?"

"What kind of vibe did you get from him? Innocent or guilty?"

"Mostly creepy. I wouldn't want to be alone with him anywhere, but maybe it's because he reminds me of Bruce."

Max laughed. "That could certainly be true. I'd like to meet him and see what kind of vibe I get."

"Maybe I should invite him over to Mom's house for dinner and afterwards we can all interrogate him."

"I love it." Max chuckled. "But maybe not."

"I've written detailed notes of everything he told me. As I talk to more of the witnesses-slash-suspects, we might get a clearer picture of who was where and when. We know he was right there. Johnny on the spot at all the murders. He could certainly have done them, but what's his motive?"

"That's the main question. What is the motive?" Max said, shaking her head. "He could have murdered them in the middle of the night and then came back and 'found' them? The car was smoldering when he showed up, indicating it had been set on fire hours before. Plus, as a ranger, he'd know the rangers' schedules and when they'd be passing by on patrol. He'd know his window of opportunity."

"Let's do one of those murder boards the next time we're at your house. You know, with the photos of the victims and the suspects. Your mom will love it. It's so *Law & Order*."

"What a brilliant idea. It will help us organize the crimes and Mom *will* love it."

Max noticed the box of pastries and looked them over carefully. "Pastries from The Nook? Yum. Sugar and fat are good for the brain cells." She smiled, pulling out a huge cinnamon glazed bun.

Amber poured another cup of coffee and sat while Max ate. "I'm hoping it will be a quiet day because I want to research the college kids."

"Start with the newspaper stories," Max suggested. "Read them in chronological order. First the stories when they disappeared and work forward."

They walked to the computers and turned them all on for the day. "I'll sit at this middle one, that way I can jump up when the library opens. I'll try to work on my breaks and lunch," Amber said.

An hour later, as Max was unlocking the front doors, Amber was organizing dozens of pages she'd printed from the newspaper stories she'd found.

"Looks like you got a lot of information," Max said as she walked by.

"Yes. I am so embarrassed to admit I didn't even know these kid's names. Everyone has referred to them as the 'college students'. Me included. Now I know who they are. It's a sad story. I wonder if we'll be doing a memorial service for them in six months."

Max nodded somberly and continued to her office.

Amber pulled out her notebook and started taking notes from the newspaper articles. Most of the early information was useless. Their disappearance was hardly front-page news since no one, not even the police, thought they were murdered. Not until their bones were found and everyone was left with egg on their faces.

The girl, Jenna Frankel, was an eighteen-year-old freshman at Westburg College. She wasn't local, having grown up in the capital city, Richmond, which was less than sixty miles away. From all reports, she was a wonderful person, but isn't that what they always say about people after they die? Especially if they died too young and were the victim of a crime.

She attended public school. Made good grades. Nothing about her high school career was remarkable. She didn't do sports or drama or choir. Everyone described her as a sweet, pleasant girl. There were interviews with her parents after she disappeared, and of course, they were devastated, thinking their daughter died in a foolish accident. When the bones were found, they only made a short statement to the press stating they were grateful they'd finally be able to bury their daughter.

Amber wondered why she decided to attend Westburg College. It was a small, liberal arts college with a fairly good reputation, but at least a half dozen other schools in Virginia met those criteria. If she'd chosen a different school, she'd still be alive.

The boy, Alex Spargo, was a sophomore. He'd just turned twenty. He was a local, having grown up in Westburg. The school required freshmen to live on campus, so he lived in the dorm his first year. The next year he moved into a frat house close to campus. He'd met Jenna at a party at the Frat and this was basically their second date. The frat house was the last place Jenna and Alex were seen alive.

According to the witnesses who were interviewed a few days later, Alex told one of his frat buddies they were going for a drive on River Road. River Road was considered a romantic spot to easily seduce a date with the view of the moon over the river.

Of course, no one could remember exactly what time Alex and Jenna left on that fateful drive. The police assumed everyone at the party was blind drunk and their memories were fuzzy at best.

Amber stared at her notes. Two completely ordinary kids. Their whole lives in front of them. When their bodies were discovered four months and miles away, the police went back and interviewed everyone again. Their parents. Their high school friends. Their college friends. Jenna's roommate and Alex's frat buddies. No one could come up with any reason why someone would have singled out these two. Again, the theory of jealous former boyfriends or girlfriends was pursued, but neither dated much. And they weren't even a couple. This was their second date, only if their initial meeting at a frat party was a first date.

Maybe this was when the police began to think there was a crazed killer on River Road and they tried to downplay it so they didn't cause panic.

Amber couldn't see a link to the first murder, either. While Becky was also a student at Westburg college, there wasn't any evidence she'd ever crossed paths with either of these two.

Later, Amber and Max sat in the break room eating their lunch.

"Did you find out anything about those kids that helped clarify things? Is there any connection with the first murder?"

"Absolutely nothing. The only connection was Becky and the boy Alex both grew up in Westburg and both attended Westburg College. But that's it. Seems unlikely their paths crossed. Different neighborhoods, different friends, different churches, different high schools, different interests. And the girl, Jenna, was from Richmond. She'd come to Westburg to attend college. No connections to Becky and hardly any connection to Alex."

"A big dead end."

"Yeah. If Mom is right and the murders are really about killing one particular person and the other murders are a smoke screen, I'm going back to Becky and Annie being the intended targets. I really need to find out more about Annie, but no one is talking. Maybe I could go and see her family?"

"You think they'd talk to you when they haven't talked to anyone?"

Amber let out a huge sigh. "No. Probably not."

They sat quietly, each lost in thought.

"I hope Suzanne will call me and be willing to talk. She's the only one who possibly knows anything about Annie."

CHAPTER THIRTY-SIX

Fluffy planned a dinner for the "murder crew" on Thursday night so Max could report to them on how the launch of the podcast went. Scarlet called Amber a few times and asked if Max had shared anything with her.

"No. She's keeping it a tight secret until we get together tonight."

"Did you listen?" Scarlet asked.

"Yes. And you?"

"Yes. We sounded good. Professional. Knowledgeable." Scarlet laughed. "Captivating."

"We managed all that in our intro?" Amber laughed too. "I'm hoping we made it sound intriguing, so people will come back or tell their friends and things will start snowballing."

"Remember, Max said it might take a while to build an audience."

"At this point, I'd be happy to find out ten people listened," Amber said.

"Don't be so negative," Scarlet said. "Call me after you get the news."

"We could Facetime you. That way you'd get the news at the same time I do."

"Great idea. Text me and let me know when you'll call. I might be at the library studying so I'll have to go somewhere I can listen."

"Okay."

The day dragged by. Amber kept checking the clock every ten minutes. Finally, it was time to go home. Max walked around, locking the doors while Amber turned off the lights. They walked out the door together and Max gave the door one last yank to make sure it was secure.

"Now, we'll head to your house for an amazing meal," Max said with a grin.

"You're seriously not going to tell me?" Amber whined.

"We're all in this together, sweetie. Wouldn't be fair."

Ida was already at the house when they arrived. She was helping set the table while Fluffy put the finishing touches on dinner. Amber's dad came in from the garage and sat down.

"Hey, Dad." Amber said, stooping to kiss him on the cheek. He made his usual indecipherable sounds, smiling up at her and patting her on the cheek.

"It's your favorite, Bob," her mom said, carrying out a huge platter of steak. Dishes of roasted potatoes and fresh green beans were also placed on the table. Her dad grunted in appreciation and speared a slab of steak onto his plate.

When Amber started to speak, her mother silenced her with a look. "Grace first. We have a lot to be thankful for and a lot we're praying for."

Amber noticed Max and Ida stifling laughs as they looked down, their hands pressed together in prayer.

Plates were passed around and filled. General conversation filled the air. They were not going to talk about the podcast until after dinner.

After the table was cleared and the leftovers wrapped up and put in the refrigerator, they all headed to the den. Fluffy followed with a tray of cookies.

"Thank you for the cookies, Madge," Max said as she selected one. "Though it's not like I need one more thing to eat after your wonderful meal."

"There's always room for cookies. Especially Sis's," Ida said.

"Remember when Scarlet and I were little and we'd tell you we were full and then asked for dessert, and you'd say, 'I thought you were full' and we'd answer, 'the dinner side is full, but the dessert side is empty.'"

They all laughed. "My dessert side is always empty," Amber declared, helping herself to a chocolate chip and an oatmeal cookie. "By the way, I'm going to Facetime Scarlet so she can hear how the launch went. I'm supposed to text her so she can be sure to be in a place where she can listen."

"Text her now. Tell her to call us as soon as she can."

Ten minutes later, the phone rang. When Amber tapped the screen, Scarlet's face appeared.

"Hi there. Oh, I see you're all eating cookies." She pretended to be miffed. "I need to come home for a visit. I need a cookie."

"Is your dessert side empty?" Amber asked.

"Always." Scarlet grinned.

"Okay, we're all here. Let's get the news," Fluffy said eagerly.

Max pulled out her phone and searched for something. "Ah, here it is." She stared at the phone for a moment. Amber was getting antsy. It must be really bad.

"We did pretty well for a new podcast. Appears about fifty people listened during the day, and we got several comments on our email. They seemed to enjoy it. Hopefully, they weren't just saying that so they could get free merchandise." Max looked up and grinned.

"I picked one person to send a t-shirt to. That person was the first person to comment and like us. And I picked twelve people to send stickers and magnets to with a note that said if they listened next week and liked us on Facebook, they could win a t-shirt or a mug."

"Fifty? Is that good?" Ida asked.

"It's hard to tell. As I said, we're brand new and we're bumping up against a lot of established true crime podcasts. I believe those listeners will come back and the numbers will grow," Max said. "And don't forget, a lot of people will listen later. On the weekend. These will stay up forever and if people listen next week for the first time, they can always go to the first episode to catch up."

Amber wasn't sure if she was happy or disappointed. Even though she told Scarlet she'd be happy if only one person listened, she'd really hoped for hundreds.

Max was still talking. "I'll continue putting ads on social media, which should help."

"Sounds great," Scarlet said. "Thanks, Max, for everything. We wouldn't have any listeners without your help."

Amber forced herself to smile. "Yes. Thank you, Max. You have been instrumental in getting us out there, and I'm sure this is the beginning of great things."

Scarlet said she needed to return to the library. "I'll see you this weekend when we record the *Romeo and Juliet Murders*."

Before Scarlet disconnected, Fluffy piped up. "I thought we were renaming the podcast. You know I don't like comparing these people to two star-crossed lovers."

"Oh right, Mom. Almost forgot." Scarlet said. "Any ideas, everyone?"

Ida said, "How about *Bonnie and Clyde*? They were rather despicable and seemed to be cold-blooded murderers."

"That's perfect," Amber replied. "What do you think, Mom?"

"I like it. Let's use that title. I'm so excited," Fluffy said. "My podcasting debut."

CHAPTER THIRTY-SEVEN

*F*luffy *stared intently at the* computer screen. She and Amber sat side by side, sharing the microphone. Amber glanced over to check on her mom. She knew they were about to talk about a painful memory from her mother's past, and it could be difficult to dredge those things up. It appeared her mother had taken particular care with her hair and make-up.

"You know this is an audio recording. There is no video. No one can see us," Amber said.

Her mother patted her hair. "I know, but I feel more professional when I'm fixed up."

It looked like her mother had also purchased a new blouse. Amber stifled a laugh.

"I understand, and Scarlet will see us and I'm sure she'll appreciate the extra effort you took."

Amber could tell her mother was nervous. She fidgeted, moving notes around and sipping water from a glass perched on the side of the desk. "I'm glad we came up with a new title."

"Yes. It was a good suggestion from Ida. I agree that these two were more like Bonnie and Clyde than Romeo and Juliet. Only caring about themselves. Killing people in cold blood for money."

Fluffy nodded and continued to pat her hair and smooth her blouse.

Amber needed to get her mom focused. "Remember when we record, you have to be as quiet as possible when you're not speaking, because the recording will pick up everything, including gulping water." Her mom set the water glass down firmly. "Also, remember this is not live. If you mess up, I'll take care of it when I do the edits." Amber gave her mom's hand an encouraging squeeze. "Now time to put on your headphones." Amber hoped it wouldn't mess up her mother's hairdo.

Scarlet's name popped up on the screen, and Amber let her in.

"Hi," Scarlet said. "How are you, Mom? Ready for your true crime debut?"

"Yes. Hopefully. This happened a long time ago, right after I graduated from high school. It was traumatizing and shocking at the time. Hard to believe my best friend was murdered. And by her own sister."

"I can't even imagine." Scarlet said. "By the way, before we start, I want to mention we might not be able to do the part two next week."

Amber stared at her sister. Was she bailing out of the podcast? "Why not, may I ask?"

"Sorry, I do have other things going on. This is finals week and after tonight I will be doing nothing but studying and taking one test after another. The end of my second year of law school is looming."

"Oh dear. How exciting," Fluffy said. "Only one more year and you'll be a lawyer."

"Not exactly Mom. I have to take the Bar first, which is like the hardest test ever in the world. Let's not think about it now."

"I agree," Amber said. "One thing at a time."

"Will you be coming home for the summer?" Fluffy asked.

"It depends. I'm applying for some internships. I'll let you know. Meanwhile, I won't be FaceTiming in for the next Murder crew dinner, and we'll have to push the podcast recording back a week. But we're good.

We have four episodes ready."

"Okay everyone," Amber said. "I'm about to push the record button. I'll do a brief intro and then I'll ask you questions, and Scarlet will pop in to clarify any legal matters we encounter."

"Is that all I'm here for?" Scarlet laughed. "Free legal advice?"

"Pretty much." Amber pushed the button, and the computer voice said, "Recording in progress."

The Podcast

Episode 6: Bonnie and Clyde

Amber: There was some debate over the title of today's episode. Originally, we were going to call it *The Romeo and Juliet Murders* but… this might not really be a tale of star-crossed lovers. More a tale of cold calculated murder with the goal of robbery in mind.

Scarlet: Welcome to Episode Six of *The Murderer You Know*. This week's episode is called *The Bonnie and Clyde Murders*. And in addition to my co-host, we have a very special guest this week. Someone who knew these kids and has first-hand knowledge of this crime.

Amber: Let me introduce this week's special guest, The Mom. And you may wonder why she's called The Mom. Well, it's because she is my mom. And she is the reason I am a true crime junkie.

Fluffy: Really?

Amber: Yes. Remember all those episodes of *Law & Order* and *Dateline*? I spent my childhood in great fear for my life.

Fluffy: Oh no. I did that? Does that make me a terrible mother?

Amber: No, but it explains why I do a true crime podcast: to face my demons. Let us now begin our tale. This story happened over thirty years ago. It was a simpler time. No cellphones, social media, or twenty-four-hour news. And also, a time when murder was not so commonplace. Let's start with a bit about the family.

Fluffy: They were an ordinary family. The dad was a retired army sergeant. The mom worked at the local grocery store, the only one in town. There were two daughters. The older daughter was my friend. We'd just graduated from high school, and she planned to go to nursing school. The younger daughter was wild. Always hanging out with the wrong crowd. My friend told me her parents tried everything and were at their wits' end on how to control her.

The younger girl, our Bonnie, was only sixteen. Her boyfriend, Clyde, was a seventeen-year-old high school dropout. Not the kind of boy parents want their daughter dating.

Amber: Parents have such high standards.

Scarlet: They always want the best for their kids and this guy doesn't seem like the best.

Fluffy: Exactly. I remember her sister telling me she tried to talk to Bonnie, but she was "in love" and didn't want to hear anything bad about Clyde.

Amber: Ahhh… young love.

Scarlet: Teenagers in love can't think straight. It's all emotion and hormones. Remember, the brain doesn't fully develop until the age of twenty-five.

Fluffy: The father was really strict. There were rules for everything, and everyone had to toe the line. Which wasn't hard for my friend, who I'll call Lovely because she was a sweet, kind girl. Unlike Bonnie, who constantly complained about her father, saying their dad ran the house like an army camp. According to her, the father mentally and physically abused her.

Amber: What did Lovely say about her sister's accusations?

Fluffy: She defended her father, saying though he was strict, he wasn't abusive. She said he only grounded Bonnie because Clyde was a loser, and he worried that he would lead her astray. Which seems to be exactly what happened. Bonnie also told people at school she planned to kill her father.

Amber: Wow. If someone had reported those threats, it might have been a game changer.

Scarlet: There's a moment in every crime where if someone said or did something, it could have changed the rest of the story, but that's what we call hindsight bias. The police and the prosecutors are looking at this information after the fact.

Amber: Maybe the dad shouldn't have been adamant about Bonnie not seeing Clyde. Sometimes, if you tell a kid not to do something, it makes them more determined. Bonnie sounds like a kid who wanted to rebel. Attracted to the dark side.

Fluffy: If memory serves, once Bonnie started dating Clyde, she began running away from home. There were several incidents, including one where they took off and made it as far as New Mexico before they were caught. The dad flew out there to get her. They couldn't ignore this relationship.

These two kept running off and behaving badly. The parents finally threw her out and told her she couldn't come home until she followed the rules. I guess they were trying tough love.

Amber: An odd punishment. You keep running away from home, so we're throwing you out.

Fluffy: This devastated Lovely. She came over to my house in tears to tell me her dad had packed up her sister's room. She loved her little sister and worried about her. But she respected her parents and their rules.

Amber: Now we have arrived at the night of the crime. These two came up with a plan to rob the parents and head off to California. They recruited a friend, who we'll call Little Buddy, to help them. Apparently, they involved him because he had a gun, which sounds ominous.

Scarlet: Have you ever seen the movie Bonnie and Clyde? They had a little buddy too. Maybe criminals need friends.

Amber: I'll have to check it out.

Fluffy: Back to that night, Lovely and her boyfriend stopped by my house. He'd just proposed. I was thrilled for them. They left to share the news with her parents.

Amber: When they got to the house, they found her dad outside in the front yard. He appeared angry and agitated, screaming at them to leave.

Fluffy: Lovely couldn't figure out what caused him to behave that way. He liked her fiancé. Still, they left and went to Lovely's fiancé's house. Lovely insisted on checking on her dad. Even though her fiancé objected, she left, promising she'd return shortly. I'll never understand why she went back. Why she didn't wait.

Amber: At some point, Bonnie and Clyde and their little Buddy with his gun arrived. The fiancé said later he thought they were already there, which explained why the father tried to get them to leave.

Scarlet: The events of the night are rather unclear, since it was pieced together from various confessions and surviving eyewitnesses. Each one told a slightly different story. Probably to put themselves in a better light and blame others. The murderers' story agreed that when they arrived at the house, they found the dad drunk and angry. He refused to come outside or let them in.

Amber: They went around back, and Bonnie pounded on the door, screaming she needed to talk to her dad, apologizing and saying she loved him. Dad opened the door, pulled Bonnie into the kitchen and hugged her. Suddenly Clyde ran in and stabbed the dad, not once, not twice but over and over again.

Scarlet: I wonder what was going through Little Buddy's head at this point?

Amber: I'd imagine he'd be wondering what the hell he got involved in. Maybe it was all too surreal, and he couldn't even fathom he'd just witnessed someone being murdered. They wrapped the dad's body in a blanket and dragged it out to the garage. They tried cleaning up but also began frantically ransacking the house, looking for money. Then they saw headlights coming up the drive. Lovely had returned to check on her dad.

Fluffy: The stories the kids told later didn't really match up, but they seemed to agree that when Lovely walked in, she was surprised to see Bonnie. She must have felt something was off and ran into the kitchen looking for her dad and saw a blood bath. She locked herself in the bathroom. Bonnie coaxed her out. Who knows what she said to the sister who loved her to get her to come out? Lovely made a fatal error. She unlocked the bathroom door. In one telling Bonnie attacked her, in another, it was Clyde, but one or both stabbed her to death.

Amber: You said Lovely loved her sister. Protected her. Was distraught when the dad kicked her out.

Fluffy: True. They didn't have to kill her. They could have tied Lovely up. They could have tied the dad up. Stolen what they wanted and left. After they killed her, they wrapped the body and took her out to the garage and laid her by her dad.

The craziest thing is they were searching for money. These people had no money. Her father didn't have gold bars under the bed, or a wall safe with thousands of dollars. What gave Bonnie the idea that there was something of value in the house which would fund their California adventure?

Scarlet: I'm still curious why they invited Little Buddy and his gun along, since both victims were stabbed. It's a bad idea to involve a third person.

Amber: I'm worried Little Buddy might not be long for this world. Why keep him around? He's a witness. He hasn't done anything yet but watch these two kill. If they are caught, he could turn against them.

Scarlet: This crime was so poorly planned. As we've said, criminals often do really dumb things, which is why they're caught.

Amber: We're only doing podcasts on the dumb ones who got caught, not the ones who got away.

Scarlet: True.

Amber: So, here we are. In the middle of the night. There are two dead bodies in the garage, blood all over the kitchen, and the secret stash of gold has yet to be found. And then another set of headlights came up the driveway.

Scarlet: Oh no. I hope not Lovely's fiancé coming to check on her?

Amber: You'll have to find out next week. We are *The Murderer You Know*. Catch us on...

Amber finished the ending and turned off the record button.

CHAPTER THIRTY-EIGHT

During the podcast, Amber's mom became more and more emotional while recounting the events of long ago. Her voice quavered and even broke a few times. Amber jumped in when she thought her mom appeared too upset to continue.

"You okay, Mom?" she asked, handing her some tissues.

"Yes." Fluffy rubbed her eyes and blew her nose. "I'm surprised how it all came back to me. The shock. The horror. The loss." She paused. "When you're young, you never imagine someone you know will die, let alone be brutally murdered."

"I know what you mean." Amber reached out and squeezed her mom's hand. "I felt the same way doing the podcast about my BFF Heather. If someone asked in first grade, 'which one of your friends will grow up to be a murderer?' she'd have been the last one I'd have picked."

"I remember at the time that I simply could not understand Bonnie killing her sister. Her sister who loved her." Fluffy paused and looked at Amber. "Can you imagine doing that to your sister?"

"Mom! No. Never. But you're right, it just doesn't make sense. I can see the dad because Bonnie obviously hated him, but her sister? Makes you wonder if there was something twisted going on in that family."

"Sadly, there must have been." Fluffy looked off, as if staring into the past trying to discover the truth of what happened.

"I began feeling guilty about thinking Mrs. Laurelwood seemed way too upset at the memorial, since her daughter had died a year ago. Now I'm getting all emotional thirty years later, and it was my friend who died, not my daughter." Fluffy reached out and pulled Amber into a tight embrace. "I can't even imagine losing you or Scarlet. I couldn't go on."

Amber hugged her mom back and whispered in her ear. "Don't worry Mom. Nothing is going to happen to us."

"Oh really?" Her mom pulled back and stared straight into Amber's eyes. "You don't think doing a podcast about murder might be a little dangerous?"

"No. No one knows who we are. Remember, we don't use our real names."

"Not for the podcast but at the memorial you were walking all over handing out cards and saying you were interested in the River Road murders. You do realize the murderer was probably there? As I've learned on *Law & Order*, the killer always returns to the scene of the crime."

Amber smiled. Her mom was literally the best mom on earth. "Yeah. I did that, but it isn't as if I said I had information or suspicions about who the murderer was. I simply said I wanted to talk to the people involved."

"You need to be very careful, Amber. That's advice from your mother."

"Okay, Mom. I will."

"If you meet with any of those people from the memorial who have any connection whatsoever with the family, the victims, the investigation, do not meet them in a secluded spot. Only meet them in a public place in the bright light of day. You hear me?"

"Yes, Mom. I hear you. Didn't I meet Ranger Renn in a public place?"

"Yes, you did. But you're way too trusting. In some ways you remind me of my friend Lovely. Why didn't she think logically instead of with her heart? Why did she go back to the house? You're like that. Look at Bruce and your involvement with him."

Wincing, Amber wondered if her mother knew the extent of her misguided trust in Bruce, which basically resulted in the loss of her inheritance. "I'm older and wiser now. Knowing Bruce taught me some good life lessons."

Fluffy stared at her long and hard. "I hope so. I'm begging you not to be impulsive. Think before you leap."

"I got it Mom."

"What is your next step in the River Road murders? I'm assuming you're still planning on talking to other people?"

"Yes," Amber replied. "However, at this point, I don't know if I should keep waiting for people to call me, show up out of the blue like Renn did, or start calling people myself."

"Are you going to talk to Becky's sister, Suzanne? Or Mrs. Laurelwood?"

"Not Mrs. Laurelwood," Amber declared. "Way too awkward. Plus, I'm not sure she'd have any insights into Becky. The secret life of Becky, if there is one. I still hope to talk to Suzanne. Being Becky's big sister, I feel like they must have talked. Shared confidences. She probably knows more about Becky and possibly Annie than anyone else."

"Do you think she'll get in touch?"

Amber sighed. "That's the million-dollar question. She didn't say no or spit in my face when I handed her my card. If she doesn't call, I'll call her. Though if she doesn't get in touch, she obviously doesn't want to talk."

"Very true. It might be too painful for her. She might feel guilty."

"Guilty? Why would she feel guilty?"

Fluffy sighed, shrugging. "Her little sister has been killed. She probably feels like she should have taken better care of her. Kept her out of harm's way."

"Maybe…" Amber replied.

Fluffy continued. "Suzanne appears to be a caring person. You noticed how she tried to help her mother at the memorial."

"What I noticed more is how her mother tried to brush her off. Like she didn't even want Suzanne to touch her. It really bothered me. And I got this weird vibe when I talked to Suzanne. Something is going on with her."

"One never knows the secrets families have. Or their inner workings. We certainly learned that in tonight's podcast." Fluffy paused. "Maybe Lovely was too sweet. She obviously did not realize what a monster her sister was."

"You're right. We just don't know the whole truth."

"I'm sure it was overwhelming for Mrs. Laurelwood to be at the scene of her daughter's murder. She probably didn't even notice how she treated Suzanne."

Amber nodded. "True. Maybe. What about Mr. Laurelwood? He's a cold fish."

Fluffy looked disapprovingly at Amber. "He's a doctor. No doubt he has to keep a poker face on when talking to patients. Can't be too emotional."

"Okay. I concede. Lovely and loving family," Amber said. "I wouldn't want him to be my doctor. Prefer someone who might hold my hand when he gives me the bad news."

"Your imagination has run away with you. Stop reading more into it than there is. We saw these people all of thirty minutes. Spoke to them for less than five."

Amber laughed. "Mom, you have shamed me. You are quite right. I know nothing about these people, but I am looking for a murderer, so my suspicion radar is on high alert."

$\mathcal{M}$onday *was the start of* a new work week at the library, and Amber was looking forward to a little normalcy. Talking about books with patrons and having fun with the children. The thought of going back to school to become a librarian began to play in the back of her mind. That was of course if the podcast didn't make her an overnight star.

Max was in the staff breakroom making coffee when Amber walked in to put her lunch in the fridge. Looking up, Max's face fell when she saw Amber was empty-handed.

"No pastries from The Nook this morning?"

"Sorry. You'll just have to wait until the next potential murderer takes me there for coffee and breakfast. Though if they all stick me with the tab, I'll be broke soon. Remember I'm trying to save up to buy a car, not cake."

Max laughed. "It's not like you really need a car. You could borrow your mom's in a pinch."

"Yes, but I'm beginning to feel like a bit of a leech. I live rent free. I eat fabulous meals for free, including an endless supply of fresh-baked cookies, and I can borrow my mom's car if I need to go someplace."

"Fluffy loves having you home. She would probably be happy if you and Scarlet moved back in and stayed there forever, with your future husbands and your dozens of future children."

Amber smiled. "You're right, and I am so lucky to have literally the best mom on earth." Amber glanced at Max. "Not to forget the best aunt and the best boss."

"Glad you remembered to throw that in." Max grinned. "By the way, how did your mom do on the podcast this weekend?"

"Great. We went over the story ahead of time and she had a script—not to read word for word, but with notes of things to elaborate on."

"I'm not surprised. She has all that crime experience from watching *Law & Order.*"

"Indeed, she does." Amber laughed. "Speaking of the podcast, any change in our viewer numbers?"

"Yeah, we added a few people over the weekend. I'm thinking things will really go up after the official first episode this Thursday. Once again, I've done lots of ads and teasers on Facebook and our website."

"Remind me again how I am going to make money on this?"

Max's mouth crinkled up as she tried to suppress a smile. "Sorry honey. But there ain't no money in this until you go viral and famous people are talking about you. If that happens, maybe I could even book you a gig on the Today Show. Of course, you'd have to wear a mask or a bag over your head to maintain your anonymity." Max snorted. "And then we could get sponsors. That's where the money is. Sponsors."

Amber slumped in her chair, deflated. She wasn't sure what she had been expecting but it seemed like it was going to take a very long time before she could count herself among the rich and famous.

"Don't stress about it. Even if we don't make it into the big time, we're having fun. Aren't we?"

Amber sucked in a deep breath and straightened. Max had done so much for the podcast. Amber needed to stay positive, so Max didn't think she was criticizing her.

"Yes. I'm actually having a lot of fun. It's nice hanging out with the Murder Crew and recording with Scarlet."

"The best part is dinner at your mom's house once a week." Max grinned. "Are we getting together this week after the podcast airs?"

"Sounds good to me. I'll check with my mom. Should we aim for Thursday or Friday night?"

"Friday would be better." Max said. "Now I need to pay attention to my real job. Let's open this library."

Mondays were often busy at the library. People returned books and checked new ones out. The summer reading program for the kids had been posted and people wanted to be sure to register their children.

The day passed quickly, and Amber was reshelving a cart of books when she heard her name called. Turning, she saw one of the clerks waving at her. There was a man standing in front of the desk. It was John Talley, the police deputy from the memorial.

He smiled and started walking toward her. "Hi there. Good to see you again. I knew you wanted to chat, so I thought I'd track you down."

It was interesting that Amber got none of the funny vibes from John Talley that she got from Joshua Renn. "Aren't you out of your jurisdiction?" she teased. "How did you find me? I didn't list the library on my business card."

"True, but I am a policeman, so I have my sources."

"That sounds a bit scary."

He laughed. "Actually, my car is serviced by your Aunt Ida. I figured there couldn't be that many Steens in Easton, so I called and talked to her, and she said you worked here."

"Nice. My own aunt sold me out. I'm glad to know you were not abusing your position of authority and checking me out on the police computers."

He blushed. He probably had done that but since she didn't even have so much as a traffic ticket, he no doubt hit a dead end.

"Of course not," he stammered. "I wouldn't do that."

"Yeah, I bet you wouldn't." Amber smiled. "Anyway, I'm glad you showed up. I was thinking I needed to start calling people and you were at the top of my list. But give me a few minutes, I have to finish up here. Can you wait out front? I should be done quickly."

"No problem."

Amber noticed Max watching him as he left. As soon as the front door shut, Max hurried over. "Who's that? A person of interest?"

"Yes. He's a Westburg police deputy. I met him at the memorial. He wants to talk."

"Oh, how exciting. The second possible murderer in a week."

Amber shook her head and smiled. "True. Wonder what he will have to say and if it will jive with Renn's stories."

"Well, don't keep him waiting. These books can be shelved tomorrow morning. Get out there." Max made shooing motions with her arms. Amber grabbed her bag from the breakroom and headed outside.

CHAPTER FORTY

The deputy was sitting on the bench by the front door, looking out into the parking lot. When he heard the door open, he turned and smiled at Amber, sliding over so she could sit down next to him.

"I'm really glad you came by," Amber said as she sat down. "I was beginning to think no one was actually going to call me. I mean, I know I'm a nobody, but I was hoping to hear from a couple of people."

John laughed. "You're not a nobody. You're a very nice, concerned citizen, and the police should always respond to the public."

Amber looked into his sincere blue eyes. Goodness, but he had beautiful eyes. Why did men always get the best colors and longest lashes? She shook her head to break the spell. "That's nice of you to say."

"At the memorial you said you wanted to talk to people who were there. At the murder scenes. And I was. At all three, not that I was the first to arrive. That would be Ranger Renn and his cohorts." Amber heard the sneer in his voice.

"Actually, I've already spoken with Ranger Renn. He came to Easton last week and we had a long talk."

"Really?" John looked at her with some concern. "I hope you stayed in a public place and didn't go off with him, maybe for a drive on River Road."

Amber laughed. "You sound like my mother."

The deputy blushed a deep scarlet and looked down at the ground.

Amber put a hand on his arm, and he looked up at her. "I'm sorry. I didn't mean to insult you. My mother was equally horrified that I was hanging out with Ranger Renn. But I had to talk to him. He was there."

Nodding, John said, "That's true. First at all three murders." He spoke with a mixture of disgust and mistrust. "There's something about that guy. Honestly, I wouldn't be surprised if he turned out to be the murderer. I'm sure the FBI is giving him a long look." He paused. "They're probably giving everyone a long, hard look."

"There's a rumor that the murderer is a law enforcement officer. Who better to get people to do what they want than someone in authority? Or maybe a person who looks like a cop. Acts like a cop. Has one of those fake flashing lights and a badge they bought off the internet."

"I've certainly heard those rumors as well," John said.

At that moment the library door opened, and Max stepped out. Holding her keys, she locked the door. Turning, she acted surprised to see Amber and John sitting on the bench.

"Oh Amber, you're still here? I thought you'd gone home. Well, goodnight. See you tomorrow." Max walked across the parking lot, got in her car, and waved as she drove past.

Amber almost rolled her eyes at Max's duplicity. She never left through the front door of the library. She was just checking things out.

John stood up. Amber was afraid he was going to leave. Maybe he realized Max was checking him out. "It's kind of late. Do you want to go grab a bite to eat? I don't spend much time in Easton but there must be something better than a McDonald's around. I'd suggest driving to Westburg, but you probably don't want to be in a car with me on River Road after dark."

Amber felt no trepidation about driving with Deputy Talley. Not like she had with Renn. She chuckled to herself. That probably indicated he was the murderer and Renn was an innocent man. Weren't criminals good at acting innocent?

"That sounds great. I am definitely hungry, and we can talk while we eat. There's the Easton Bar and Grill, which is not fancy, but they make a great hamburger."

"Sounds perfect. You want to drive over and meet me there?"

Now it was time for Amber to blush. "Can you give me a ride? I don't have a car currently. That way I can show you where it is."

He agreed. Amber said she had to call her mom first and tell her she wouldn't be home for dinner. He nodded his approval.

Amber followed John out to the parking lot and climbed into his Jeep. This was the perfect car for him. Not flashy like that noisy machine of Renn's. Her mother would not approve of her getting in the car with a possible murderer, but Max knew that she was with John. Surely, he wouldn't murder her since there was a witness? She hadn't told her mother she was with one of the possible suspects. She'd just said she was going out with a friend. No need to get Fluffy all worked up.

Conversation in the car was limited to Amber saying turn right, go straight, and turn left. They parked a block away. John looked around at Main Street when they got out, then at her. "Cute little town. I should visit more often."

Walking into the restaurant, the aroma of sizzling burgers, onions, and spices engulfed them. "Smells good," John said as they were directed to a booth in the back.

Amber thought about what Renn had said about that déjà vu shit all over again. For the second time in a week, she was in a restaurant with a potential murderer.

"What's good here?" John asked.

"Pretty much everything and anything. They make the best burgers and their onion rings are incredible."

"Onion rings?" John looked up at her with those deep blue eyes. "Haven't had those in a long time. They were my dad's favorite. I thought they were something exotic, like caviar or snails, because the only time he ordered them was when we went to a super fancy steak restaurant."

"He'd like the ones here." Amber suddenly realized he'd said, "were" his dad's favorites, not "are". She felt awkward and decided not to pursue the subject. "My dad prefers to eat at home." She smiled. "I guess he thinks nothing is better than my mom's cooking, so why go out. My mom is a fabulous cook, but I wonder if she'd want a night off, to have someone else cook and serve her."

"You're lucky. Your parents are still together?"

Amber nodded.

"Mine divorced when I was young. My dad moved away, and Mom and I stayed in Westburg."

"So, you're a native Westburgian?"

He laughed. "Yes, I am. And you?"

"Easton born and raised. Only time I lived anywhere else was when I went to college for two years up in the mountains." Amber winced inwardly, thinking she was stretching the truth a bit. She'd only been at college for a year before the whole Bruce-farm fiasco.

"I love the mountains," John said. "It's pretty up there. So different from our neck of the woods."

"Yes. I enjoyed it but I'm happy to be home. No place like home."

"True, if you don't count the recent murder spree here."

Before Amber could respond, the waitress came and took their order. They both ordered burgers and decided to split the large stack of onion rings.

As soon as the waitress walked away, John smiled at her. "I guess that's your stock in trade. Murder? True Crime podcaster?"

Amber blushed. "Yes. My sister and I are doing a podcast on people we know who have been victims of crime."

"Did you know any of the River Road victims? Is that your interest?"

"No. I'm just interested because it's just so out of the ordinary. Happening in our little town. Towns. What about you? Three of the victims were from Westburg. Four if you count Annie Forst. I mean, she wasn't a native, but she was living there. And the college girl, Jenna, was going to school there. The only one from Easton is Kyle Phillips, the latest victim."

The waitress brought John a beer and refilled Amber's iced tea. John changed the subject.

"I know you were handing out cards all over the memorial. Have you heard from anyone else yet?"

"I had breakfast last week with Joshua Renn, the ranger."

Talley's lips curled in disgust. "That dude is creepy as shit. I mean, what are the chances that one guy is the first to arrive at three different murders?"

Amber didn't want to throw Renn under the bus. He'd given her a lot of good information, but she couldn't help but agree with John's assessment of him. "It is a bit of a coincidence, I agree, but I actually got a lot of information from him."

"If you can believe anything he says."

"You said you were you there?" Amber tried to steer the conversation away from Renn.

"Yes. But obviously not first like Renn. In fact, the rangers didn't even call us about the first murder, which they thought was some kind of weird accident or a murder-suicide. They'd already towed the car away. Don't ask me why. But then they contacted Becky's…" He paused, and Amber saw something flit across his face. "…parents, and they totally freaked out and called Chief Wallace and the… shit hit the fan. Pardon my French."

"Then the police showed up?"

"Yes, we went to the scene. Walked around. There wasn't much to see. Just the scorch marks on the grass from the burning car. Other than that, there were tire tracks from all the park vehicles obliterating any other evidence. We talked to that weasel Renn when he was identified as the first person on the scene. He was only interested in showing off. Getting recognized."

The waitress returned with their burgers and the mountain of onion rings. Talley picked one off the stack and waved it around, blowing on it before biting into it. "Oh my. These are amazing." He closed his eyes.

"Try the dipping sauce. It's amazing too."

John poured some of the sauce on his plate and then put a few onions rings next to it. He dipped one and sighed. "You are so right. Sauce is fabulous."

For the next fifteen minutes they concentrated on their food. "That was sooo good," John finally said when he'd cleaned his plate. "You should bring your mom here. She deserves a treat."

Amber laughed. Somehow, she couldn't picture Fluffy eating here. But maybe she'd suggest the murder crew come here to celebrate one night. If there was ever anything to celebrate.

"So, you interviewed Renn? What about the car?"

"Once we took over the investigation, we had the car taken to the state forensic crime lab. They couldn't tell us much. Twigs and leaves had been shoved in the car gas tank and set on fire. Eventually it exploded."

"No one heard anything?"

"Not like there are any houses close by or lots of people driving by."

"Very true."

"When the bodies were taken to the medical examiner, he found evidence it wasn't a bizarre accident or a murder-suicide. The older woman, Annie Forst, appeared to have been strangled. Her hyoid bone had been cracked. And they were both hit with a heavy object. The examiner thought it might be a hammer based on the pattern. Since there was no smoke in their lungs. it meant they were both dead before the fire started."

"What did the Westburg police conclude?" Amber leaned closer.

"Murder by person or persons unknown. What else could we conclude?"

Amber nodded solemnly in agreement. She still knew nothing. "Were you involved in the next two crimes?"

"Yes, though once again not first on the scene. When the second car was found abandoned on River Road, everyone's mind went to a tragic accident. Not murder. We were notified when the state police were called in with their tracker dogs. I got there in time to see them working. I thought it was odd the dogs only walked around the car and the parking lot. Never went close to the riverbank. At the time, I thought, how could those kids have gotten down to the river and drowned if the dogs couldn't find their scent leading there?"

"Did you share your idea with anyone?"

John laughed. "I'm a lowly deputy. The bigwigs already came up with a scenario they all agreed on. Young couple. Drunk. Decide to take a midnight swim and drowned."

Amber shook her head.

"The last one was the strangest. We got there pretty quickly. The jogger who saw the car called 911. They alerted the park rangers and us. Once again, I get there to find Ranger Renn at the center of things." John rolled his eyes and grimaced. "It was odd. He was all jumped up. Nervous. Jittery. All over the place. And this time it was obvious something bad had happened. There were signs of a struggle. Blood."

"So, no thinking it was another tragic swimming accident?"

"No." John stared off into space for a long while before looking at Amber. "You know, I wouldn't be surprised if Ranger Renn was somehow involved in all this."

Amber didn't say anything, but she agreed. It was all too coincidental.

John insisted on paying for her dinner. Such a contrast to Renn, who stuck her with the whole tab for breakfast. When he drove her home, he offered to walk her to the front door to make sure she arrived safely. What a gentleman. Amber assured him she'd be fine. Still, he stayed in the driveway until she opened the door, waved, and stepped inside.

CHAPTER FORTY-ONE

"*Amber, is that you?*"

"Yes, Mom. Who else would it be?"

Walking into the kitchen, Amber saw her mom finishing the dishes.

"You never know. There are murderers about." Her mom smiled, drying her hands on a dish towel. "Who were you out to dinner with? An old high school friend?" Her mother looked at her quizzically.

Amber could not lie to her mother. She could try, but she knew she'd turn red, stumble over her words, and look guilty. "John Talley." Before her mom could even ask, she added, "The Westburg Police deputy I met at the memorial. He came by the library, and we went to the Bar and Grill to talk."

Her mother shook her head, looking sternly at Amber. "Really Amber. You know all these people are potential murderers."

"We were in a public place with lots of other people. He's a nice guy. Not like ranger guy."

"It's still not a good idea to get in a car with a stranger. Especially one tied to murder."

"I know. I'll be careful." Amber pecked her mom on the cheek and headed upstairs to her room. She needed to talk to Scarlet.

Scarlet answered on the first ring.

"Were you expecting me to call?" Amber asked.

"Hoping you might. And if you didn't, I was going to call you. I have some big news."

Amber paused. "I have some big news too, but I want to hear yours first."

"As you might remember, this is finals week up at law school, so I will spend most of the week buried in books, stressing out, and generally being a miserable, angry human being."

"Sounds fun. I'm sorry I dropped out of college." Amber rolled her eyes. Scarlet could be such a drama queen.

"You made a wise choice. That's not my news. I've applied for an internship with the Commonwealth Attorney's office to see if I might like a career as a prosecutor."

"I do vaguely remember you mentioning that. When does it start?"

"After finals are over, the candidates who are chosen will be notified. That takes about three weeks since they need to check grades. They're pretty selective. If I get in, I'll start a week after notification. So... I'm going to have the next month off! I'll be coming home this weekend."

Amber squealed. "Yay! Such wonderful news. I can't wait to tell Mom. No, wait, you tell Mom, then I'll tell Max and Mom or Max can tell Ida, or you could call Ida and fill her in..."

"Amber!" Scarlet almost shouted into the phone. "Chill. I got this. I'll call Mom and Dad and Ida. You can tell Max. I wanted to let you know the reason I won't be at the Thursday night Murder Crew dinner for an update on the podcast. Also, we'll have to wait to tape part two of *Bonnie and Clyde* until I get home. I'm going to be way too busy this next week."

"I understand. I can't wait to have you home. I miss you so much and things are heating up with the River Road murders and I want you here to bounce things off of."

"I just can't wait to have an endless supply of Mom's cookies," Scarlet said with a laugh. "What's your big news?"

"I've met with a second person of interest. Another one from the memorial."

"Ahh. Which one this time?"

"John Talley, the Westburg Deputy who saved me from being crushed by Chief Wallace, showed up at the library today."

"How did he know you worked there?"

"Apparently, Ida is his mechanic. That's the problem of living in a small town. People always know someone, who knows someone, who knows you."

Scarlet snorted with laughter. "Truth. Did he give you any brilliant insights into the murders? Did he know who the murderer is?"

"No, but I enjoyed talking to him. When he found out I'd met and talked with Ranger Renn, he was horrified. He's convinced Renn is the murderer. I'm not sure I disagree."

"If I remember correctly, you described this guy as having blonde hair and beautiful blue eyes. Do you have a new law enforcement crush?" Scarlet teased.

"No. Why do you all always think I'm crushing on guys? I am totally focused on murder," Amber said, miffed at her sister's suggestion.

"Sorry. I know you are. So, you've had two people get in touch already in a week. What's the next step?"

"I'm going to call Duncan Abbott, the reporter. I believe he has information he isn't sharing. He recently wrote an article about what aren't the police and the FBI telling us? It's a good question. It's been a couple of weeks since the FBI took over, and we've heard zilch from them."

"Let me know if you talk to him. Sounds like he could be a gold mine of information, and it would probably be quite different from the law enforcement guys you've talked to," Scarlet said. "Gotta go. I will be incommunicado from now until I see you in a week."

"Don't stress. You got this. You're the smartest person I know."

"Your circle of acquaintances must be pretty small." Scarlet laughed.

CHAPTER FORTY-TWO

S*carlet called and told everyone* the podcast recordings would be taking a week off. The rest of the crew decided to still meet on Friday night to discuss the podcast, check the numbers, and catch up on the River Road murders.

At work Tuesday, Max told Amber, "Hey, I'm not missing a chance to have dinner at your mom's. We don't need Scarlet here for that!"

Amber laughed. "True enough."

"By the way, how was your dinner with the cute deputy? Learn anything new?"

"You'll have to wait until Friday to find out. Not telling my story twice." Amber smiled.

Later that day, Amber called Duncan Abbott. She couldn't wait any longer to talk to him. She had the perspective of law enforcement. She needed another viewpoint. She got his voicemail.

"Hi, this is Amber Steen, true crime podcaster. We met at the memorial for Becky Laurelwood. I'd really love to meet up and talk." She left her number in case he'd lost her card.

A few hours later, he called. "This is Duncan Abbott. Am I speaking to the infamous Amber Steen? True crime podcaster and possible murderer?"

"Yes. That's me. But I believe you are the possible murderer."

He laughed. "That remains to be seen which of us is the most likely candidate. What can I do for you?"

"I'd like to meet with you and talk. Get some of the behind-the-scenes stuff you seem to be so good at."

"Oh. You know I can't reveal my sources."

"I don't care where you get your information from. I want to hear it all. To know what you know. Or what you suspect. I've already spoken to one of the park rangers and a deputy in the Westburg police department. Now I want to hear another angle."

"I cringe imagining who you might have talked to."

"I will tell all, but it has to be at a face-to-face meeting," Amber teased.

"I doubt you know anything I don't already know, but I wouldn't mind getting out of the office. Where and when?" Duncan asked.

"I'm off work on Thursday. We could meet for lunch here in Easton. I'm a bit restricted geographically because I don't have a car."

"What are you, Amish?" He laughed. "What young person in these parts doesn't have a car? You've dropped way low on my list of suspects now. The murderer has to have a vehicle."

"Saved by the lack of a car." Amber smiled even though he couldn't see her face.

"I could pick you up and drive you to Westburg, but you'd have to be on River Road with me. Alone. In a car."

"You don't scare me."

His voice suddenly turned serious. "You should be afraid, and you should be careful about who you talk to and what you say. There is a murderer out there. Possibly two or three. They obviously have no qualms about killing."

Amber's heart began to pound. Her mother had said the same thing. This wasn't a game. "How about we meet at the Carving Board on Lancaster Avenue here in Easton at noon. They have great soups and sandwiches."

"I am familiar. I will see you there."

He hung up, and Amber pulled out her notebook to make notes. She needed to be prepared before Friday. Max walked by and gave her a quizzical look.

"I just talked with Duncan Abbott. We have a date—no, not a date, we have a meeting this Thursday. I should have two updates for the Murder Crew Friday night."

Max sat down. "Great news. He seems to be frustrated with the investigation and is about to unleash an angry editorial, or maybe he found out something he's willing to share. You might be the first to know."

Amber laughed. "I hardly think he is going to give me a scoop."

"True," Max nodded. "Still… you never know what he might say."

"I feel like we are getting somewhere in our investigation. I've already spoken to two people, and Duncan will be the third."

"Other than Suzanne, are you planning on talking to anyone else?"

Amber considered it. "No. I'm running out of ideas about what happened and who the murderer is. It could be you for all I know." Amber laughed.

"It could be." Max gave her a sinister look, arching and wiggling her eyebrows. "As you said, no one is above suspicion. Except for Fluffy. Fluffy has no time for killing except in the kitchen."

Max and Amber burst out laughing.

Wednesday, on her way home from the library, Amber heard the low rumble of a car pulling up alongside her. She closed her eyes and prayed it wasn't who she dreaded it might be.

"Hey babe," a familiar voice rang out.

She stopped and turned. Joshua Renn. Why was he following her again? She'd told him when she was ready to record the River Road podcast, she'd be in touch. She bent down, looking in the window. "Hi Josh. What brings you to Easton?"

Renn put the car in park and stepped out, walking up to Amber on the sidewalk. "I wanted to see you. I drove to your house and knocked on your door. Some old dude answered the door. Your dad? Damn, he's some kind of psycho. I asked for you and he went off in some incoherent rant and shoved me off the porch and slammed the door."

"Yes. That would be my father. He's very protective. Overly protective. You should never come by the house again."

"Don't worry. I won't. He scared the shit out of me. I couldn't understand a word he said but I got his meaning clear as a bell."

"That doesn't answer my question. Why are you here? I told you I'd be in touch."

"Babe." Amber grimaced at the word. "I like you. I want to go out with you. Go on a drive. Have dinner. Catch a movie. You know. A date."

Amber froze. How on earth could she get rid of this guy? Maybe she could lie and say she had a boyfriend? Or that she had taken a vow of chastity until the murders were solved? The gears in her brain locked and her mouth fell open. No words came out.

A car approached from the opposite direction, and she thought maybe she could flag them down and escape. The car screeched to a halt and Amber heard a familiar voice. "Amber. Is this guy bothering you?"

John Talley stepped out of his Jeep.

"Hi John," she managed to squeak out.

"What are you doing here, Talley?" Renn said, angrily turning to face the other man.

"I could ask the same. What the hell are you doing here, Renn?"

"I'm asking Amber out. It's a free world, dude. I can talk to her. I don't need your permission."

If this was a western of old, they'd be facing each other, their pistol holsters slung low around their hips, preparing for the inevitable gun fight. She hoped the two men were not going to fight over her. Were they?

Amber shot John a quick smile. "I'm sorry, Josh. I have a date with John tonight. We're going to talk about the murders. You know. Get the police perspective?"

Josh curled his lip in disdain. "You're talking to him? He wasn't even there. He's a Johnny-come-lately. I was there. I was first. I found the bodies." Renn became more incensed. He took a step toward Amber with his fists bunched.

John appeared at her side. "Time to back off, Renn. She talked to you and now she's talking to me."

Josh's face twisted in anger. Finally, he managed to regain control of himself. "Whatever dude. Just don't go to her house. Her dad will take you out." He stormed around to the driver's side of the car, revved the engine, and roared off.

Amber was shaking badly. John put out a hand to steady her. "This is the second time you've saved me from a rude person. Thank you," Amber said.

"So glad to be your knight in shining armor." He bowed, pretending to sweep a hat down to his feet. "At your service, my lady."

Amber smiled and curtsied.

"Come and sit in my car. You're white as a sheet."

"He's a scary guy," Amber said. She climbed in the jeep.

"I told you. There is definitely something off with that guy."

"I'm glad you showed up in the nick of time. Who knows what might have happened?" Amber shook her head over her narrow escape. "But what are you doing here?"

He looked embarrassed. "I guess same as Renn. I wanted to see you again."

"That's not a bad thing but you're lucky you didn't go to my house looking for me. Apparently, my dad threw Renn off the porch."

John laughed. "Sounds like a good dad and a smart man."

"Drive me home and you can meet him. I'll make sure he behaves."

John parked in the driveway again and Amber took him in and introduced him to her mother and father. Her dad looked highly suspicious. Her mom invited the deputy to dinner. Amazingly, John was able to hold a conversation with her father. She'd never seen anything like it. John talked about some sports team or event and her dad smiled, nodded, and muttered something indecipherable, and John laughed. After dinner, John and her dad ended up watching something sports related on TV.

After the game, Amber walked him out to his jeep. "Probably not the date you had in mind."

"This may sound corny, but I loved it. Your family is obviously close and loving. I really enjoyed meeting your father and talking to him."

Amber chuckled. "You were amazing. I have never seen my father so interactive. He's not the greatest communicator or the most outgoing personality. My friends in high school nick-named him *the Great Silence*."

"Obviously most people don't know how to connect with him. You need to find common interests to bond over."

Amber arched an eyebrow. "What are our common interests? Murder?"

He gave her a lopsided smile. "Yes, for now. In time, maybe we'll discover something else?"

"Maybe…"

"I really enjoyed your mother too. She is an amazing cook. I don't get too many home-cooked meals these days." He held up a bag. "And she sent me home with cookies."

"She's a great one with the cookies," Amber said.

John put the bag in the car and turned to Amber. "I'd like to see you again. Maybe go on a real date?"

He was such a nice guy, but Amber reminded herself looks can be deceiving. "I enjoy hanging out with you and I'd be happy to see you again. However, I need to let you know I'm not ready for any kind of relationship. I've kind of messed up my life and am trying to get it back on track."

"I understand completely." He put out his hand. "Friends."

"Friends," Amber said, shaking his hand. She waved as he backed out of the drive and headed to Westburg. Along River Road.

"He seems like such a nice young man," her mother said when she walked in.

"He does." Amber agreed. "But didn't you say we had to treat everyone as a suspect?"

Her mother stared at Amber. "You're right. He's just as likely as anyone."

CHAPTER FORTY-THREE

*A*mber had spent a considerable* amount of time that morning deciding
what to wear for her meeting with Duncan Abbott. She wanted to look
mature and serious and professional, but she wasn't quite sure what the
proper attire for a true crime podcaster was.

Where was Scarlet when she needed her? Sadly, still in the throes of
hell week, taking her finals. Amber had been sending her encouraging
emojis throughout the week and Scarlet responded with weeping tears and
faces screaming in agony. Amber knew Scarlet was being dramatic. Scarlet
never failed a test in her life.

Soon it would be over, and Scarlet would be home for an entire month
before heading off into Law-Law Land for an internship. That would give
them the incentive to solve the River Road Murders in those four weeks.

Amber chose a nice pair of pants, a patterned blouse, and a solid-colored
sweater. Boring, but hopefully it would make her appear older. She knew
her looks were part of the problem. Everyone who looked at her saw a
young girl. After brushing her teeth vigorously, she looked critically at her
hair. Too youthful. She pulled it back and wrapped it in a bun. Better. Just

a hint of lip gloss, blush, and mascara, and she was ready to go. Too bad she didn't have a fake pair of glasses. Glasses always made a person look more mature and intelligent.

Bouncing down the stairs, she found her mother in the kitchen. "Bye, Mom. I'm off to meet yet another man and possible murderer." She grinned.

"You shouldn't laugh, Amber. This is getting serious."

Amber hugged her mom. "I know. I don't want you to worry about me. Once again, I'll be in a public place in the middle of the day. No midnight assignations to meet unsavory characters."

"All right dear. Don't forget Ida and Max are coming over tomorrow night. Hopefully, you'll learn something of interest today."

Amber stopped by the library for a couple of hours of work before her lunch with Duncan.

Max asked if she'd listened to the podcast yet. "It's really our first episode since last week was just the intro. This is the first murder we've covered."

"I didn't have time. I overslept. I've been thinking about my meeting today with Duncan Abbott. Can't decide if I should have questions ready to pepper him with or lull him into a false sense of security so he'll spill the beans."

Max laughed. "What did Scarlet suggest? Use your feminine wiles on him. It worked with the ranger and the deputy. Loved your description of them facing off like the gunfight at the O.K. Corral."

Amber winced. "That's all I need, another guy fighting for my attention. Duncan is much more mature and professional than those two."

"Aren't you kinda sweet on Deputy Talley?" Max gave Amber a wicked grin.

"He's cute, and he's certainly far more pleasant than Ranger Renn, who is creepy. And Mom and Dad like him. Which makes me worry he's the murderer and good at pretending to be a nice guy. Plus, I've decided I need to focus on my career for now. Men are just a distraction."

"Truth." Max nodded in agreement.

"So, did you listen to the podcast?"

"Yes, I did, while eating breakfast. I set it to drop at six this morning, so people can listen on their way to work," Max said.

"And…? Was it good?"

"I thought so. You told the story very well. You left the listeners hanging, wanting to learn the outcome for your BFF. If they listen today, they're definitely coming back next week."

"I'll listen when I get home. Hope Mom and Ida listen before tomorrow night. We're all obsessed with the River Road murders, but the podcast should be our priority," Amber remarked.

"Of course it is. By the way, I have a special surprise for tomorrow night. Looking forward to dinner at your house."

The library door opened, and the first patron of the day walked in. Amber and Max got to work.

Amber left at noon for her lunch with Duncan. She had to walk to the restaurant. She could have asked Duncan to pick her up, though she wasn't sure if she wanted to be in a car with him. Later, she'd check her bank account again, to see if she was getting closer to being able to get a car.

Duncan Abbott was sitting outside on the bench by the front door. He looked up when he heard her approach. Standing, he put out his hand. "Ms. Steen, I presume?"

She blushed and took his hand. "Mr. Abbott, I presume."

He smiled, opened the door for her, and waved her inside. "Let's sit in the back corner so no one will overhear us talk about murder."

The waitress led them to a booth in the back and handed them menus and a piece of paper. "The Daily Specials," she announced.

Duncan and Amber stared at the menu as if the identity of the murderer could be found on its pages. Amber glanced at the specials. The combo plate with soup and salad or a sandwich looked good. Should she eat light? She should have asked her mother what she was making for dinner.

"What are you thinking of?" Duncan asked.

"Maybe the beet salad and…" Amber paused. What kind of soup went with beets? "Or the tomato soup and the sunflower salad." Amber stared at the sheet. "It all sounds good." She looked at Duncan. "What about you?"

"I'm going with the carved turkey on sourdough with homemade chips."

Her resolve crumbled. "Ummm… I'll do the half sandwich with tomato soup. And the chips."

The waitress returned with their waters and took their orders. Duncan pulled out his notepad. Amber responded by pulling out her notepad. Duncan laughed. "Dueling notepads at ten paces."

"I'm not the seasoned ace reporter you are, but I like to make notes if I hear something I want to follow up on."

Duncan smiled. "Good idea. Have you heard anything of interest? Or spoken to anyone? Any suspects? Other than me, of course."

"I've had quite a productive two weeks. Last week I talked to Ranger Renn. He was full of information."

"More likely full of himself." Duncan rolled his eyes. Amber noticed again what nice eyes he had behind his glasses. Were his glasses real, or did he wear fakes to look more serious?

"Everyone seems to dislike Renn so much, but…"

"You like him?" Duncan asked, curiously.

"No, I mean, I don't like him, but I don't dislike him…" She was blathering. "He was first on the scene at all the murders and I wanted to hear his impressions of what he saw."

"Okay. Fair enough."

"And this week I spoke with Deputy John Talley of the Westburg police."

Duncan raised an eyebrow. "What did he say?"

"He also can't stand Renn and said the Park Service destroyed the crime scene at the first murder. And I guess at the second one too, since they thought it was a drowning accident."

"Yes. As the FBI said, everything was handled badly from the get-go. Good luck trying to find out anything now."

"You think the murders won't ever be solved?" Amber asked in shock.

"Not all murders are," Duncan replied. "But I do believe one or all three of these will be." He gave her a conspiratorial look, but she couldn't ask him why he thought that because the waitress returned with their sandwiches. After asking if they needed anything else, she left.

"Have you heard something? From your secret source?"

Duncan laughed. "Is that the rumor? That I have a secret source?"

"It's what Max and my mother think."

"Who's Max?" Duncan asked.

"My boss. The librarian of Easton. She's a big fan of yours. My mother is too."

"I'm feeling quite full of myself. I have fans." He smiled. "I don't have a source. Sometimes people in law enforcement who are disgusted with the way things are being handled reach out to me. And I've heard a few things from various people this week."

"Such as?" Amber could hardly contain her excitement.

"Poison pen letters have been flooding the FBI office this week, accusing all kinds of people of the murders."

"What? Do you know who has been named?"

"I've heard some of the names. You're one of those who's been accused."

"Me?" Amber's voice squeaked in outrage and shock. "Me? I wasn't even living here when the first murder took place."

"That doesn't mean you didn't start killing at some point. Maybe the third murder is your handiwork? I think the letter said you were obsessed with crime and wanted to make a big splash with your true crime podcast."

"I… umm… I don't… why would…"

"You should see your face," Duncan said, trying to suppress a grin.

Amber got angry. "I'm upset. And outraged and horrified to hear someone thinks I'm a murderer."

"Don't feel so special. I was accused too. It was something about me trying to pump up my ratings by littering River Road with bodies." He smirked. "I suppose I'm trying to win a Pulitzer by killing people and writing about it. Not sure what the upside is, since I'll be in jail. But I'll be famous, so maybe it's a win for me."

"Who else has been accused?" Amber asked.

"Might be easier to say who hasn't. Basically, everyone in law enforcement, from Renn to Chief Wallace. I'd like it to be one of them. Or even both of them. Don't like either one. Renn is high on my list, though he's not very bright. Wallace is smarter, but I can't really figure out his motive. Not solving the murders and having the investigation taken over by the FBI didn't make him look good. For Wallace, it's all about being re-elected and being large and in charge. This could hurt his chances."

"Anyone else?"

"All of Becky Laurelwood's family—mother, father, and sister. Some random former army pals of Annie Forst. Various roommates and frat brothers of the college boy have been accused. A prank gone wrong or something. The mafia or some kind of drug related nonsense for the third murder. Some of the letters seemed reasonable and believable. Others were absurd."

"You said I was accused too?"

"You and your family. Actually, just your mom and aunt. Probably because they were with you at the memorial. You must have rattled the murderer's cage to get your whole clan on the shit list, including your boss at the library, Max Bolger."

"What? That's ridiculous. Why on earth would my mother or my aunt… or Max be out on River Road killing people?"

"Good question, but on the other hand, have you found any logical reason for any of the murders yet? Or any logical suspects? Maybe logic has nothing to do with this. Crazed serial killer?"

Amber chewed thoughtfully on her sandwich. "My mom has a theory. You ever hear about the Tylenol murders?"

"Of course. It's one of the most famous unsolved murders ever."

"My mom said the police suspected only one of the victims was the intended target and the murderer cold-bloodedly killed the others to muddy the waters and cover up the crime."

"Yeah. In fact, the police pretty much figured out who did it but didn't have the evidence to convict them."

"You think that's what will happen with the River Road murders?"

"Maybe. I hope not. I hope the FBI is figuring something out. In fact, be sure to watch the news tomorrow night. Agent Devereaux will be giving an update on the investigation. No doubt he's heard the citizens are getting restless and want some answers."

"How do you know this? I haven't heard anything about an update." Amber asked in exasperation.

"The press does have to be notified so we're there to be sure to cover the story."

"I have one more question for you, since you are so knowledgeable." Amber smiled at Duncan. "Do you think the murders are related? That one person committed them all?"

Duncan swallowed. "No. I don't. I think the third murder is an outlier. There are no similarities between the third and the first two. Different weapon. Messy scene. Maybe the murderer decided to take advantage of the fear of a serial killer loose on River Road, hoping the police would lump it in with the first two."

"I agree. It doesn't quite fit in." Amber nodded.

Duncan smiled. "Great minds think alike."

They finished lunch and made plans to meet the following week. As they left the restaurant, Duncan took Amber's hand and held it.

"I know we've been joking around about one or possibly both of us being the murderer. I'm not and I don't believe you are either. Be very careful. You have attracted the attention of the wrong person. We are dealing with a psychopath who has no qualms about killing. Practice extreme caution. Do not get in a car or meet anyone remotely associated with these crimes. No matter what they say. Even if they say they absolutely know who the murderer is and will only tell you, but you have to meet them alone at night."

When Duncan dropped her hand and walked away, a chill shot through her. So many people were warning her to be careful.

CHAPTER FORTY-FOUR

*A**mber ran into the house*, slamming the door behind her. "Sorry!" she yelled out to anyone who might be listening. In her room, she hurriedly pulled off the clothes she was wearing. She needed to get comfortable. To surround herself with familiar things. Duncan had scared her, and she wanted to crawl into her bed and pull the covers over her head and stay there forever.

"Amber? Are you home?" Fluffy called.

"Yes. Mom. Getting changed. Be down in a minute."

Amber crawled out of bed. She pulled on her sweatpants and a t-shirt and headed down the stairs. Not surprisingly, she found her mom in the kitchen preparing dinner. Even though she wasn't hungry, Amber pulled a cookie from the cookie jar and sat at the kitchen table. Comfort food.

Fluffy glanced at Amber. "Don't spoil your appetite with cookies."

"I just need one cookie."

"How was lunch with Duncan Abbott? Did he share all his secrets?"

"No. Not all." Amber forced a smile. "We had quite an interesting talk, but I don't want to repeat myself, so I'm going to save it for our murder crew dinner tomorrow. Apparently Agent Devereaux is giving an update tomorrow on the evening news."

"It's about time," Fluffy replied, vigorously mixing something in a bowl. "Can't wait to hear what you learned and what the FBI has to say."

"I'm heading back upstairs. Need to write down my notes from today."

"Okay, dear," Fluffy said.

"Also, I'm going to listen to the podcast before dinner. Max said it's really good and our numbers will probably go up again. Have you listened yet?"

"Yes. I listened between breakfast and lunch. It was quite good."

"Wish I could check with Scarlet to see what she thinks but I doubt she even listened," Amber said.

"Don't be impatient. She'll be home in two days," Fluffy said, putting a pan on the stove.

After listening, Amber agreed that the podcast was quite good. She then got busy with her notes. Wasn't sure if she'd drop the bomb about the poison pen letters or wait to see what Agent Devereaux said during the news tomorrow night.

riday night, Max and Ida arrived around five p.m., eager for another update or maybe eager for Fluffy's cooking.

They gathered in the den. Max and Ida carried in three metal easels on which Max unfolded a large, tri-fold cardboard display. The cardboard was covered with a map of River Road. The dates and locations of the three murders were marked on the map. "This will help us get the crimes organized. Like the police do, sticking up photos and stuff."

"Oh, I love it. So, *Law & Order*," Fluffy said. "Do you have photos?"

Ida handed Max a folder from which she extracted photographs of each victim and pinned them to the specific location of their murders. "Yes. As you can see, we have the timeline, the location, and the victims on the map. We can add things as we go along."

Stepping back, she pointed both hands at the board. "Ta-dah! How does it look?"

"Wow. What a great visual. I never realized exactly where each crime took place," Ida said.

"Agreed. You've done an amazing job, Max," Amber commented, quite impressed with Max's handiwork.

"I accept all your praise." Max bowed. "We have photos of the victims. None of the suspects. Do we have any suspects yet? When can we start adding those photos?"

"We might have some information along those lines," Fluffy said. "Amber met with Duncan Abbott yesterday, and I've been waiting to hear what he said."

All eyes turned to Amber and she felt like a bug under a microscope. She considered how best to tell them they were all suspects. "It was an interesting meeting. Two things came out. Duncan doesn't think the same person committed all three murders. He feels sure the third murder wasn't committed by the same person as the first two. I told him I felt the same way."

"You two might be on to something. Unless the murderer is trying to confuse us," Max said.

"Are there any similarities between the first and second?" Ida asked. "Other than there were two people, and they were bludgeoned with a blunt instrument, but in one, they were burned in their car. In the second, the bodies were taken to a remote site and buried. In one, the murderer is almost bragging and showing off, and in the second, the murderer tried to hide the bodies."

"In my gut, I feel the first two are connected," Amber said. "If only because the victims didn't appear to have any enemies."

"Did the third murder victims have known enemies?" Ida asked.

"No, but the kid was a drug dealer, a dangerous profession which attracts other bad people," Amber replied.

"True," Fluffy said. "We should definitely separate the crimes. In *Law & Order*, they always caution against making assumptions."

"Was that everything you learned?" Max asked, arching her eyebrows.

"No." Amber paused again, knowing she had to tell them they'd all been accused of murder. "The FBI and police have been receiving dozens of poison pen letters, basically accusing a whole host of people of the crimes."

"Like who, specifically? Did he tell you?" Max asked.

"Yes. He did. All of us have been accused of one or more of the murders."

There was a collective gasp. "What? Us?" Ida said.

"Duncan said the murderer or murderers were probably at the memorial and basically accused everyone there. Law enforcement. Becky's family members. And then threw in random people, including Duncan and Sandy Foss."

"Sandy?" Fluffy gulped in horror at her hero being called a murderer.

"Why us?" Ida asked. "I know we were at the memorial, but what possible motive could any of us have?"

Amber looked down at her hands. "Duncan thinks I shook the murderer up by handing out cards and saying I was looking into the murders. He warned me to be extremely careful. He said we are dealing with a cold-blooded killer or possible two killers."

"I told you the same thing, Amber. I don't know why you felt the need to involve yourself publicly in these crimes," Fluffy said, shaking her head.

"Maybe I was trying to shake things up," Amber confessed. "Apparently, I shook the murderer more than I wanted. And don't worry, Mom. I'm taking Duncan's advice."

"Have you taken Duncan off the suspect list?" Max asked.

"Good question. I'll think about it. He also told me that Agent D will be making a statement on the news tonight. Maybe to talk about the letters?" Amber said.

"We better get done with dinner so we can watch," Max said.

"First," Amber jumped in, "I'd like to talk about our podcast. Has everyone listened to this week's episode? Our first full episode." Amber looked at Ida.

"Yes, I listened yesterday. I listen on headphones while I'm working," Ida replied.

"Thoughts, comments, concerns?"

Everyone said it was really good.

"I wish we could have heard from Scarlet, though I doubt she's had a chance to listen. Hopefully, she can catch up next week." Amber looked at Max. "What about our numbers?"

"We have a little more than seventy followers now. Even got some likes and thumbs-ups on our Facebook page," Max said.

"I guess the momentum is building," Amber replied. She tried to sound enthusiastic instead of disappointed. It was unrealistic to expect they'd shoot to the top after two episodes.

Fluffy stood up and announced they should eat, since they didn't want to miss the press conference. When they entered the dining room, Amber's dad was already seated at the head of the table, apparently impatient for the evening meal. Another Fluffy-fabulous feast was served, and everyone groaned happily afterwards.

CHAPTER FORTY-SIX

Amber helped her mother take dessert and coffee out to the family room. Tonight's treat was strawberry shortcake with real whipped cream, which was right up there with lemon bars in Amber's mind. Her dad turned up the volume on the TV. A few moments later, a voice announced the regularly scheduled program was being interrupted by a special news report.

On the screen, Agent Devereaux stood at the podium. Local law enforcement fanned out behind him on either side. Everyone looked properly serious.

Agent Devereaux tapped the microphone in front of him and cleared his throat. "Good evening. I know many of you have been concerned about the progress of the investigation into the River Road murders. Trust me, my agents and your local law enforcement have been working diligently, and we may soon have a break in the case."

Amber, Max, Ida, and Fluffy looked at each other in surprise.

"However, tonight I want to discuss an issue we have encountered on the way to solving these crimes. It appears someone, or possibly several someones, has been sending letters to the FBI address we gave out, accusing dozens of people of committing these crimes.

"This is not helpful, and I am concerned it is not meant to be helpful. Some of the accusations are completely absurd. I'm surprised I haven't been named as a person of interest in these letters." Agent Devereaux looked down at his notes then back into the camera. "Unfortunately, we have to investigate every one of these letters because it is hard to know which ones are meant to deliberately mislead us and which ones might have a grain of truth.

"Starting on Monday, police officers from Westburg and Easton will be contacting and interviewing people who have been named. If a police officer shows up at your door, please cooperate. We are not accusing you. We simply must treat everyone the same and speak to everyone who has been named. We intend to make short work of that so we can move on.

"If someone is doing this as a joke, please stop. This is not a joking matter. Six young people have died. Families are grieving. We shouldn't have to waste our valuable time and resources investigating false leads.

"Thank you for your attention. I will not be taking questions at this time. There will be another press conference next week with major news." Agent Devereaux picked up his papers, tapped them together on the podium, and exited. The police followed him off the stage.

The camera angle switched and Sandy Foss, ace reporter, came into focus. He stood facing the audience with his microphone in hand. "This is certainly an interesting development. Maybe these letters are the work of the murderer trying to create chaos and confusion. I have it on good authority my name has appeared in one of those letters. As I am sure you all know, this is a smear on my reputation as a crime fighting reporter. However, if the police come to my door, I will most certainly cooperate with them, as Agent Devereaux has requested. I hope all of you will do the same." Sandy brushed his hand over his mane of hair. "Thank you. This is Sandy Foss, Channel 9 News, reporting." Sandy gave his signature sign-off salute and the screen went black.

"You heard it first, Amber. I guess we'll all be getting visits from the police next week, since Duncan said our names have appeared in the letters," Max said.

"Surely, they won't waste their time on us," Fluffy responded. "The very idea of any of us committing murder is absurd."

"They have to, Mom. It's like Agent D. said. They have to follow every lead, no matter how unlikely."

"I don't care about talking to the police," Ida said. "I've nothing to hide. I'm more curious about a possible break in the case."

"Right. He kinda snuck that in before getting to the poison pen letters. You think he's telling the truth or throwing out a hope they've cracked the case? Or one of the cases," Amber said.

"All I can say is he better have something to say soon, or people are going to get angry," Max stated.

Well, wasn't that enlightening. I was beginning to worry the FBI would completely ignore my letter-writing campaign. But as our dear Agent D. said, they couldn't do that. And now they have to follow up with every single person I accused.

How should I act when they come to my door? Shocked? Outraged? Horrified? Angry? I'll have to practice facial expressions in the mirror to see which one is more convincing. I think a bit of outrage would not be unexpected. So, I'll start with that and then switch to resignation and play the good citizen willing to help catch the killer.

Though I'm more curious about that little gem Agent Devereaux dropped about a break in the case. Is he trying to frighten the murderer into doing something foolish? Perhaps they solved the copycat murder. I can't decide if that's a good thing. Chasing after the other murderer takes the heat off me. Another murderer muddles things even more and confuses the already confused police.

Either way, I hope I can soon go back to committing more murders. Maybe I should expand my territory. Do a couple up in the mountains on one of the scenic hiking trails. Or the beach. So many places. So many victims waiting for me. They will never ever catch me.

CHAPTER FORTY-SEVEN

Her cell phone vibrated, waking Amber out of a deep sleep. She searched under the covers to find it, to turn it off. Who would be calling this early on a Saturday morning?

Scarlet's name and photo appeared on the screen. Amber hadn't spoken to her in almost a week.

"Scarlet!" Amber shouted into the phone.

"Don't blow my head off," Scarlet responded.

"I'm just thrilled to hear from you. It's been too long."

"It's only been a week," Scarlet said.

"I know, but it's been quite a week. I have tons of stuff to tell you. I've been meeting people and talking to them, and Max made a murder board…"

"Stop. Please stop." Scarlet laughed. "I'm done with exams. Packing up clothes, my computer, and heading home. Now I wait until I hear back from the Commonwealth's Attorney on the internship. For the next three weeks, I want to chill out and eat lots of mom's cookies. And while I am munching, you can fill me in."

"When will you be here?" Amber asked eagerly.

"Hopefully by dinner or maybe sooner. I'm not going to rush. I'm worn out and taking my time packing. I'll see you soon. Tell Mom I'm on the way and I expect a dinner fit for the return of the prodigal daughter."

"I will." Amber jumped out of bed and headed downstairs.

She found her parents in the kitchen. Fluffy was putting the finishing touches on breakfast and her dad sat waiting at the kitchen table, reading the paper. Amber kissed him on the top of his head and sat down.

"Good morning sleepy head," her mom smiled. "Nice of you to join us."

"I come bringing great news," Amber said. "Scarlet is on the way, and she'll be here by dinner if not sooner. She requests a banquet to be prepared in her honor and the cookie jar to remain full while she is home."

Amber's dad looked up and smiled before returning to his paper.

"That's wonderful news," her mom squealed. "I can certainly fulfill those requests."

Amber poured a cup of coffee. She couldn't imagine how she'd fill the next hours until Scarlet arrived.

"Should we invite Max and Ida over for dinner?" Her mom's question broke into her thoughts. Her dad glanced up and snorted. "No. I guess not," her mom said, putting plates of scrambled eggs in front of Amber and her dad. "We'll keep her all to ourselves tonight before we share her."

After breakfast, Amber went upstairs to organize her notes. She had to tell Scarlet about the Renn-Talley face off and John Talley coming over for dinner. And there was the conversation with Duncan Abbott. Oh, and she'd have to check to see if Scarlet had listened to the first full episode of their podcast. Then there was the update from the FBI, the poison pen letters, and that Mom, Ida and Max, along with herself, would probably be interviewed by the police. Scarlet was lucky not to be included in the list of suspects since she'd been up at law school the whole time and hadn't attended the memorial. At least Duncan hadn't mentioned Scarlet's name. Or her father's.

Amber's mind raced. So much had happened, and yet she still was no closer to solving the River Road murders. And neither were the police, though there was the tantalizing hint dropped by Agent Devereaux about more news to come. Was that real or something to pacify the public?

Amber dressed quickly and headed downstairs. "I'm going for a walk," she called out as she went out the front door. She walked along her neighborhood sidewalks, mind spinning. In addition to everything else, she, Fluffy, and Scarlet still had to record the second part of the *Bonnie and Clyde* podcast. No rush, but they couldn't wait too long.

She looked up and realized she was at her Aunt Ida's front door. Did her subconscious bring her here? She walked up to the door and knocked. A moment later, Ida answered.

"Why, Amber. This is a nice surprise," Ida said, opening the door wide and beckoning her in. "To what do I owe the honor of a visit?"

"I don't know. Scarlet called to say she's on the way home. I'm excited to have her back, but I began thinking about all the things I need to catch her up on… including recording the second part of Mom's podcast. At the same time, I'm wondering and worrying when the police are going to show up and talk to all of us. I still can't believe we've been named as suspects… and it's all my fault."

"Whoa. You need to take a deep breath. Come in. Sit down. Let me get you some water."

Amber sat on the couch and waited for Ida to return. Her mind was a whirling dervish. Ida came back and handed her a glass of water. "Drink slowly. Calm yourself."

Amber took long, deep sips, swallowing each one after a pause. She handed the glass back to Ida.

"Better?" Ida asked.

"Maybe."

"I thought you'd be thrilled with Scarlet coming home; instead, you appear to be on the verge of tears."

"I am thrilled. I'm just overwhelmed by my insignificance." Amber frowned. "Scarlet has a month off before she starts an internship. After another year of law school, she'll be a kick-ass lawyer. And what will I be in a year? A third-rate podcaster with 70 followers." Her eyes welled up with tears. "And the River Road murders will remain unsolved, and bodies will continue to stack up."

Ida sat on the couch and hugged Amber tightly. "There, there," she said as she squeezed Amber until she squeaked. "What on earth brought this on? You might never be a rich and famous podcaster, but aren't we having fun? We're the Murder Crew and your mom is keeping us going with her kick-ass dinners. And guess what? You don't need to solve the River Road murders. That's up to the police and the FBI."

"I know," Amber sniffed. "I can't stop feeling guilty, like I threw all of you under the bus and now the murderer knows your names and might be coming after you."

"The murderer isn't coming after us. They're trying to create turmoil and have the police chasing their tails. Which probably means they're scared. Don't worry. No one is coming after the Murder Crew. They'd be fools to tangle with us. We'll take down that psychopath." Ida laughed and gave Amber another hug.

"Thanks, Aunt Ida. You're the best. I'm lucky to have you." Amber paused. "And my mom, and dad, and Scarlet, and Max too.

"I'm glad you included Max. She is my oldest friend, almost like a sister. We probably have more in common than your mother and I do." Ida smiled. "We are polar opposites, Fluffy and I. No one would ever nickname me Fluffy."

"But you and Max are kinda opposite, too. I mean, she's all business suits and you're all work boots," Amber said.

"That's on the surface, kiddo. Underneath we're really a lot alike."

Amber decided to ask the question that had been nagging her for months. "I've been kinda wondering about your relationship because you seem so close and all and I know neither one of you ever married…" Amber ran out of words to say.

Ida threw her head back and laughed. "Oh, my goodness, Amber. Are you trying to ask if Max and I are a couple? That question has dogged us our whole lives, practically since elementary school. It's a sad comment on the world we live in that if you're an unmarried woman with short hair and have a close woman friend, you must be a lesbian. There could be no other explanation as to why you wouldn't want to be in a relationship with a man. In the past, it was worse. If you were old, unmarried, lived alone, and had a cat, you might even be accused of being a witch."

Looking at Amber, Ida smiled. "No. If Max and I were gay, I'd happily declare our relationship to the world. I don't think your mom or dad would care, either. Truth is, we're both independent women who decided long ago we were happier living on our own and making our own decisions.

"Your mom is perfectly happy being married and having kids, and it works for her. I sometimes wish I'd had a kid. They seem like a lot of fun." She looked at Amber. "Though often they're a pain in the butt."

Amber wrapped her arms around her aunt and hugged her as hard as she could. "I'm sorry I asked. It's none of my business. Something Mom said made me wonder if you two might be more than friends. And I'm sorry I'm a pain in the butt sometimes."

"You know I love you. And Scarlet. Your mom did a great job with you two. Now stop thinking you're a failure and go home. Scarlet will be here soon. Don't overwhelm her tonight. You got all of tomorrow to fill her in."

CHAPTER FORTY-EIGHT

*A*t dinner, Scarlet talked about her final exams and her hopes for getting the internship. "While most of my classmates want to go into criminal defense work when they graduate, my experience with the podcast and the current murders in our town have convinced me there is a need for first-rate lawyers to work on the side of justice to convict evil doers."

Their father grunted in approval, and Fluffy patted Scarlet's hand and smiled at her.

After dinner, Scarlet asked Amber to fill her in on the River Road murders. "Let's both take a break tonight," Amber replied. "How about we do our nails and watch one of our favorite Disney movies or, even better, a Hallmark romance? Total mind mush."

The next morning, Fluffy cooked one of her world-famous breakfasts, and after consuming way too much, Amber and Scarlet escaped to the den. Of course, Scarlet immediately spotted the murder board in the corner.

"What's this?" she asked, looking closely at the map and photographs.

"That's Max's murder board. It lines everything out by date and location, murder weapons, etc. We have the victims' photographs, now all we need is to put up some suspects' photos. We have a few people we're looking at."

"Like who?"

"Apparently someone has been sending poison pen letters to the FBI, accusing dozens of people of the murders. Even suggesting motives. The suspects include yours truly." Amber pointed at herself and smiled. "Our mother, Aunt Ida, and Max. You and Dad didn't make the cut."

"What the hell?" Scarlet said.

"Exactly. What the hell. Can you imagine Fluffy, in her shirtwaist dress, sensible shoes, and apron, out on River Road, bludgeoning people to death?"

Scarlet burst out laughing. "No. I can imagine her causing a massive heart attack in someone by overfeeding them but not murdering them. I wonder how you came to the attention of the murderer. Why did they accuse you?"

"The theory is, I rattled the murderer's cage when I was at the memorial, handing out my cards, telling everyone I was a true crime podcaster and wanted to talk to people about the River Road murders," Amber said. "I'm waiting for the police to come pounding on the door to drag us all away for interrogation."

"Stop being a drama queen. It's not going to happen," Scarlet said.

"Agent Devereaux said everyone named in the letters would be questioned."

"Yes. Questioned. Not water boarded. Get a grip." Scarlet walked over and picked up a stack of photos. She leafed through them and looked up at Amber.

"Are these some of your suspects?" She held up one of the photos.

"Yes. We each have our favorites. That's Ranger Joshua Renn. He's the dude who found all the bodies. First on the scene, as he likes to say. He's pretty high on everyone's list because he's so unlikable. He puts off this totally icky vibe. I keep having to remind myself just because he's a creep doesn't mean he's guilty."

"So true. Actually, makes it more likely he's innocent," Scarlet said. "I mean, wouldn't you try to convince people you're a decent guy?"

"Also, he doesn't appear to be very bright, and I think the murderer definitely is," Amber added.

Scarlet stared at another photo. "Is this the deputy, John Talley? He's cute."

"Yes. He's one of the stories I have to catch you up on." Amber told Scarlet how John showed up at the library, went to dinner with her, and later in the week, saved her from Renn. "And Mom invited him for dinner."

"Wow. He got along with Dad? Will wonders never cease?" Scarlet said.

"Exactly. Which is what makes me suspect even more he's the murderer because he's so… nice?"

Scarlet laughed. "Hiding his murderous persona behind those beautiful blue eyes."

"Exactly. And yesterday, I met with the reporter, Duncan Abbott."

"You have been busy. You've dined with three suspects already."

Amber filled her in on Duncan. "He was the one who first told me about the letters. And he also told me we'd all been accused."

"One time you thought he might be involved. Do you still suspect him?"

Amber considered the question. "He seems normal. Not creepy or murderous. And he warned me to be careful because I apparently upset the murderer."

"Wouldn't it be clever of him? To warn you and convince you he has your best interests at heart while planning to do you in?"

"Arrrgh. It's so maddening," Amber groaned.

Scarlet held up a picture of Chief Wallace. "The Westburg police chief?"

"He's Max's pick. She really doesn't like him." They laughed.

Amber told Scarlet about the latest press conference by Agent Devereaux. "He claimed a big announcement, a break in the case, would be announced soon, though I'm wondering if he's trying to scare the murderer into making a mistake."

"Sounds like you had quite the week while my head was buried in books."

"How about we pack a picnic lunch and go on a bike ride like when we were kids and put all of this—law school and murder—out of our minds for the day."

"PB&J and mom's cookies?" Scarlet grinned. "I'm in."

CHAPTER FORTY-NINE

he next morning, Amber and Scarlet told their mother they wanted cereal for breakfast. "I'm not used to these morning feasts," Scarlet said. "It's going to put me in a food coma, and we have things to do, including recording part two of *Bonnie and Clyde*."

"Luckily, I'm off work for a few days," Amber said. "Max knew I'd want to have time to hang out with you. And I agree with Scarlet. If you're up to it Mom, we should probably record tonight."

"Okay. Cereal it is, but at least drink some orange juice," Fluffy said.

There was a knock at the door, and Amber jumped up to answer it. "Wonder who it is this early in the morning."

"It's not early, Amber. It's almost ten. The working world has been at it for hours," Scarlet shouted as Amber walked down the hall.

Amber opened the door and was surprised to see Ida, Sheriff Fenster, and a young deputy standing outside.

"Ummm… good morning. Come in. Coffee's on." Amber led them to the kitchen.

Sheriff Fenster removed his hat and followed Ida down the hall with the deputy trailing behind.

"Good morning Mrs. Steen," he said to Fluffy.

"Buster, don't be so formal. We've known each other since we were kids."

The sheriff blushed deeply and looked down at his hat in his hands. "I'm afraid I'm here on official business, which requires me to be formal."

They all stared at Sheriff Fenster and back at Ida, who held up her hands. "Don't look at me. I just found him on the doorstep when I arrived."

Still staring at his hands, the sheriff nervously rocked back and forth on his feet. "Ummm… I'm sure you all watched the press conference Friday night. About the letters the FBI received. We've been instructed to interview everyone mentioned in a letter."

He finally looked up. "Madge, you and your daughter Amber and your sister Ida have all been accused. I have a list of questions I need to ask each of you. Separately. Is there a place where I can conduct the interviews?"

They all looked at each other. What room should he use? They couldn't use the den since the murder board was in there. If Sheriff Fenster saw that, there was no telling what he might think.

"How about right here in the kitchen?" Fluffy asked. "You can help yourself to coffee and perhaps a little cake while we're talking." She opened a container and cut several slices of pound cake, put them on a plate, and set it on the table. "How do you like your coffee, Buster—oh excuse me, Sheriff Fenster?"

"I really shouldn't," he said, as he reached for a slice of cake. The deputy sat in the corner and Fluffy handed him a plate with a piece of cake on it.

Their mother volunteered to go first. And the other three took refuge in the den. "Fold up the murder board," Ida hissed. "In case he wanders in here."

"Should we call Max and warn her? She was accused too," Amber asked.

"No. We shouldn't," Scarlet said. "If we're all innocent, why would we warn her? Better to let her be surprised when he shows up."

"You're right." Amber said. They sat and stared at the floor.

"So… how was exam week?" Ida asked. "Think you did well?"

"Seriously Ida. Scarlet always does well," Amber snapped.

"Calm down Amber. Don't let it get to you." Ida reached over and patted Amber on the hand. "Just be grateful you're being interviewed by Busted Window and not that over-bearing ass from Westburg, Chief Wallace. I'm sure the FBI considers us pretty low on the list of suspects, which is why they let Sheriff Fenster handle it."

"True," Amber said.

Ida turned to Scarlet. "So, what are your plans for the summer?"

Scarlet chatted about her exams and the potential internship. After a half hour, there was a knock on the door and Fluffy stepped in. She glanced at the Murder Board, clearly relieved to see it tucked away. "Ida, you're next. I can't come in here because I might fill you all in on the questions. I'll be in the living room."

Ida walked out and Fluffy shut the door. Scarlet and Amber stared at each other. They both picked up books and tried to read while they waited. The clock on the desk ominously ticked the seconds away.

Finally, the door opened, and Ida stepped inside. "Your turn Amber. Your mom and I can now sit with Scarlet."

Amber walked into the kitchen and Sheriff Fenster smiled and waved her to a chair. A full cup of coffee and crumbs from the pound cake littered the table in front of him.

He brushed his face with the back of his hand and turned the page on his notebook. The deputy sat with his head down, staring at his notebook.

"We'll start with the easy questions. Where were you living when the first murder took place?"

Amber answered numerous questions, some of which seemed to be repetitive, possibly with the aim of tripping her up. She thought she was doing well by placing herself far from the murder scenes when Sheriff Fenster turned a page of his notebook.

"Why did you go to the memorial for Becky Laurelwood? You didn't know her, did you?"

Amber's stomach lurched. "No. I didn't, but my boss at the library, Max Bolger, knows the family and she suggested we go to show our support. My mom decided she wanted to go too, and Ida joined us."

Sheriff Fenster scribbled in his notebook.

"And why did you walk around the memorial handing out cards saying you were a true crime podcaster and wanted to talk to anyone connected with the crimes on River Road?"

She should have been prepared for this question. But she wasn't. This was Sheriff Buster Fenster. An old friend of her parents. He wouldn't ask hard questions. He wouldn't suspect any of them. It suddenly occurred to her that he hadn't written the questions. They were probably questions designed by the FBI and personalized for individuals. How was she going to explain her behavior, which now seemed quite ghoulish?

"I apologize. In hindsight, I realize it was insensitive on my part. When I returned home from college… ummm… well, not exactly college… I was starting an organic farm with a friend…"

Sheriff Fenster looked at her. "Yes, you already covered that earlier when I asked where you were during the crimes," he said.

Amber blanched. She was babbling, and she recognized Sheriff Fenster was sharper than she'd given him credit for. She glanced over at the deputy, hoping for some sympathy, but he was studiously staring at his notepad and didn't make eye contact.

"Truth is, I'm trying to straighten out my life. I got a job at the library and decided to start a true crime podcast about local murder. I became a bit obsessed with the River Road murders. They're local and obviously attracted a lot of attention. The FBI is here investigating. Foolishly, I believed if I could talk to some of the people involved, maybe I'd crack the case." Amber realized how stupid she sounded. What the hell was she doing?

"Foolish describes it perfectly. You probably talked to the murderer or talked to someone who talked to the murderer and now you're in their sights. So, they're trying to deflect scrutiny by accusing everyone remotely connected with the crime. There was even a poison pen letter sent accusing me."

Amber was shocked. What possible motive could Sheriff Fenster have for randomly murdering people? She'd love to read that letter.

"You need to be careful, Amber Steen. Stop poking the bear. There is at least one and possibly two cold-blooded killers stalking River Road. Don't end up as their next victim."

Sheriff Fenster gathered everyone back in the kitchen and thanked them. "I don't think you need to worry about any follow-up from the FBI, but they might want to interview you again if they see anything that piques their interest. That interview would be at the FBI office in Westburg and would be much more official than our chats here. Thank you for the coffee and cake, Madge. Say hi to Bob for me." He walked out to his police car with his deputy tagging along. Both were carrying bags of cookies.

After waving goodbye, they returned to the den and collapsed into their chairs. "Wow," was all Amber could say.

"That was intense," Ida added.

"I'm almost jealous I didn't get interviewed," Scarlet said.

"Don't be," Fluffy said. "I feel quite unclean being talked to by the police like I am a common criminal."

"Still, wasn't it like being in an actual *Law & Order* episode?" Scarlet asked.

Fluffy perked up. "Why yes. Yes, it was."

"I guess he's heading over to talk to Max. I hope she'll call us afterwards and we can all compare notes," Ida said.

Amber knew she wouldn't share what Sheriff Fenster said about poking the bear. If she poked hard enough, the murderer might reveal themselves.

CHAPTER FIFTY

As Fluffy poured everyone coffee and put out more cake and cookies, they all began speaking at once about being accused and the questions Sheriff Fenster asked. They all thought they'd done an excellent job proving their innocence. Amber took a big bite of a cookie. Nothing like a cookie to make a person feel better.

Ida looked over at Scarlet. "Welcome home, honey. Though this was not quite the welcome I planned, bringing the law in with me."

Everyone forced a laugh.

"It wasn't quite the welcome I was expecting," Scarlet said. "I was looking forward to a quiet time, but you guys have apparently ruffled some feathers."

"Has it been only two weeks since the memorial?" Amber asked. So much had happened since then.

Amber's phone rang. She pulled it out of her pocket and looked at the screen. Glancing up, she announced. "It's Max. Should I answer it?"

"Of course you should. Why not?" Ida said.

"She'll be mad we didn't call and tell her Sheriff Fenster was coming to talk to her as a potential murder suspect," Amber explained, before punching the phone button and speaker at the same time.

"What is going on?" Max did indeed sound angry. "Why didn't you warn me Buster Fenster was coming to interview me as a murder suspect?"

Before Amber could answer, Ida spoke up. "We all agreed it would be best if you appear surprised when he arrived. If we called you, you'd have been prepared, which would have made us all look guilty."

There was silence on the other end of the phone. Max finally sighed. "You're right and believe me, I was surprised, and I think he could tell."

"How did the interview go?" Fluffy asked.

"At first, I was completely outraged. I could hardly disguise my anger. Eventually, I was able to calm down and answer all his questions. Apparently, the theory is the murderer was riled up at the memorial and decided to get the police running around in circles chasing after suspects."

"Same thing he told us," Fluffy said.

"Did you tell him at the time of the third murder we were at book club together?" Ida asked.

"I did. And I was at a council meeting the night of the first murder, so I was covered. He said the murders were committed late at night or very early in the morning, so according to Buster, neither of those is a good alibi."

"Yeah. He told me the same," Ida said. "But at least our stories matched."

"That's one of the problems with living alone. You don't have anyone who can confirm you were there and didn't sneak out of the house in the middle of the night," Max said.

"Bob wouldn't know if I slipped out in the middle of the night. He sleeps like a log and snores like a freight train," Fluffy said.

"Don't tell Sheriff Fenster! You need Bob as an alibi," Max said. "Are you going to tell Bob we were interviewed today as potential murderers?"

"Not a good idea," Scarlet said. "Dad would probably punch Sheriff Fenster in the nose before driving to Westburg to give Agent Devereaux a thumping."

"Oh dear. You're probably right. Don't tell your father, girls," Fluffy said.

They all promised not to share the news with their father.

"Max, come for dinner after work. You deserve a treat. We all do," Fluffy said.

CHAPTER FIFTY-ONE

mber woke to the sound of someone rummaging in her closet. Rolling over, she saw her sister's backside as she bent over, looking for something.

"What the hell time is it and what are you doing in my closet?"

"These." Scarlet said, turning around with a pair of sneakers in her hand. "Get these on. We're going for a jog."

"You have to be kidding me? Why would I want to do that?"

"It's good for you, for one thing. Clears the cobwebs out. Healthy body. Healthy mind. How do you think I manage law school?"

"By jogging? Sounds awful." Amber flopped back down on her bed and pulled her pillow over her head.

"Nope. None of that," Scarlet said, yanking the covers off. "You need this. When the killer comes after you, you need to outrun them."

"Not funny." Amber sat up. "You're really going to make me do this?"

"Yep."

A half-hour later, they were at the breakfast table. Fluffy filled their plates with scrambled eggs. "Protein." Scarlet smiled.

Amber grimaced as she took a sip of coffee. "My stomach is too upset to think about eating."

"So, what's the plan for today girls?" Fluffy sat at the table.

"No big plans. John said he'd like to drop over after work today. He wants to meet Scarlet," Amber said.

"I can't wait to meet the cute deputy," Scarlet teased.

Amber rolled her eyes. "As Mom constantly reminds me, he could be a murderer."

"I'm sure he'll want to stay for dinner. Let me figure out what to make," Fluffy said.

"So, my wants and desires as the returning hero are now taking second place to this guy?" Scarlet retorted.

"You two duke it out. I'm going to take a shower. I've never sweated so much in my entire life."

"You quit after ten minutes," Scarlet said.

"Whatever," Amber replied as she climbed the stairs to her room.

She was sitting on the bed toweling off her hair when her cellphone rang. Recognizing the number, she smiled.

"Hello? Is this the infamous true crime podcaster, Ms. Steen?"

"Yes, it is. And is this the infamous reporter, Mr. Abbott?"

"Guilty as charged. But that's my only crime."

"To what do I owe the pleasure of a call from you? Not that I'm not happy to hear from you."

"I was wondering if you've had your police interview yet as the potential River Road serial killer?" Duncan said.

"Yes. Sheriff Fenster came by yesterday and talked to me, my mom, and my aunt Ida. Then he went to the library to talk to Max Bolger. Thank goodness my father had already left for work. He would have gone ballistic."

"I'm guessing none of you confessed?"

"No. Thank goodness I'd already told them about the poison pen letters and we were all potential suspects. If he had shown up out of the blue, it would have been really upsetting. So, thank you for forewarning us."

"My pleasure."

"And you? Have you been interviewed yet?" Amber asked.

"Yes. I have. I guess because I am an important person, I was interviewed by a real-live FBI agent. He let slip that he'd also talked to Sandy Foss. We media types were lumped together. Maybe they think we conspired to commit the murders to increase our ratings. Though newspaper reporters don't actually get ratings."

"Did you talk to Sandy afterwards?" Amber asked.

"No. I don't want to give the FBI any more ammunition. For all I know they're tapping my phone."

"You're talking to me!" Amber squeaked.

"Oh, yeah. I forgot about that. No. In all seriousness, I've known Sandy for years and we respect each other but we're rivals for the big news stories. I'll let him defend himself against the charges."

"Probably a good idea," Amber said.

"I wanted to see if you survived your interrogation. I'm glad Sheriff Fenster talked to you. He's a decent person. Not like Chief Wallace."

"Thanks for checking."

"And to give you a little something to think about, I've been looking into that little sprinkle that Agent Devereaux dropped about more news coming. Seems like there is going to be a major announcement soon. But keep that to yourself. I'll let you know if I hear any more."

"Wow. Thanks. I won't tell a soul." Except maybe Scarlet, she thought.

Duncan hung up and Amber got dressed and went back downstairs.

The rest of the day was spent helping their mother with housework and laundry. The ordinary things of life that had taken a backseat. Amber did not tell Scarlet about Duncan's phone call. She felt bad but she didn't want to betray his confidence. She and Duncan had been accused of being murderers. Scarlet hadn't. They had a bond.

At five o'clock the doorbell rang, and Amber ran to open the door. John Talley stood there with a sheepish grin on his face and a bouquet. "For your mom. She's so sweet to invite me for dinner."

"You're nice to think of her." Amber took the flowers. "I'll get a vase. Just go into the living room. My father and my sister are in there."

"Look what John brought," Amber said as she walked into the kitchen. "For you Mom. He really appreciates your cooking."

"Oh, how lovely. Put them in a vase and place them on the dining room table. I'll meet you all in the living room."

Amber put the flowers on the dining room table and walked into the living room. She was knocked over by the sight she was met with. Scarlet and John were on the couch, staring into each other's eyes. It was perfectly obvious they had been struck by Cupid's arrow.

"I see you've met my sister," Amber said to break the spell. Scarlet and John dragged their eyes away from each other and looked at Amber as if in a fog.

"Ummm… yeah," John mumbled.

Scarlet blushed violently and jumped up. "I'll check to see if Mom needs any help."

It was a good thing that Amber hadn't fallen for John because it was obvious he and Scarlet had been thunderstruck. Amber wasn't sure how she felt about that. She liked John but there was still something a little too perfect about him.

Dinner went well and John did not stay late. Scarlet walked him outside to his car. Amber waited for her up in her bedroom. When Scarlet waltzed in, she had an enormous smile on her face. She flopped down on the bed and grinned up at the ceiling.

"Well, that's an interesting development," Amber said. "A bit taken with our young deputy."

Scarlet bolted up. "I'm sorry. I'm sorry. I know you met him first. I don't mean to get in your way. It's so strange… the moment I saw him, and he saw me… the world melted away and it was just the two of us." She paused. "I've never had that feeling before for anyone."

"Don't worry about me. John is a nice guy, but I am not interested in him. I do want to caution you that we don't know anything about him, so be careful. Be very careful."

CHAPTER FIFTY-TWO

"*I have to go in* to work for a couple of hours today," Amber explained to Scarlet and Fluffy at breakfast. "I'm needed for the children's program." She picked up her coffee go-cup. "I should be back in the early afternoon. You two talk. We need to record the second part of *Bonnie and Clyde*."

"I know dear." Fluffy handed Amber a bag with a sandwich, cookie and apple inside. "For your lunch. Scarlet and I will make a plan. It just seems that everything has been thrown out of whack."

"True," Scarlet agreed. "Hard to talk about thirty-year-old murders when we're being accused of present-day murders."

"I will remind you, dear sister, that you and Dad were the only ones not accused." Amber arched an eyebrow at Scarlet.

"Who knows," Scarlet snapped back. "There might be a second round of letters, and I could be in that group."

"Keep hoping. See you all later."

As she walked to the library, Amber wondered why she was so angry at Scarlet. Was it John? It wasn't like she had a crush on him, but it did kind of wound her vanity that he so quickly threw her over for Scarlet. It didn't matter, she told herself. She had bigger fish to fry and murderers to catch.

The children's program went well. The library was busy, and Amber and Max had no time to chat but there really wasn't anything new to talk about other than John and Scarlet becoming smitten with each other. And that was news Amber wasn't planning on sharing. Not her story. Not her business.

As she got ready to leave, her cell phone rang. The screen said *unknown number*. She almost didn't answer but she had been giving out her card hoping for people to call her.

"Hello, is this Amber Steen?" A woman's voice asked. "True crime podcaster?"

"Yes. That's me. And who is this?"

"We met at the memorial, the one for my sister Becky. My name is Suzanne Laurelwood."

Amber almost screamed, she was so excited. Suzanne had called at last. She took a couple of deep breaths to calm herself. "Suzanne. I'm glad you called. I've been hoping to hear from you."

"I'm sorry. I debated about calling you, but I would like to talk to someone and sometimes it's easier to talk to a stranger. My parents…" Her voice faded away.

"I know what you mean," Amber said. "Would you like to meet and talk? Whenever and wherever is convenient for you."

"That would be great. How about this Friday? Are you familiar with Westburg? There's a nice coffee shop on Main and 11th. The Coffee Connection. Do you know it?"

"Not really but I'm sure I can find it. What time?"

"Would nine be too early for you?" Suzanne asked.

"Perfect. I'll see you then."

Suzanne clicked off and Amber punched her fist into the air. This might be the final piece of the puzzle. She'd always believed Suzanne had answers that no one else could provide. Amber rushed into the library to find Max.

Max was in her office going over budgetary issues. "Max!" Amber almost screamed.

"For goodness' sakes Amber, this is a library. Quiet voices, please."

Amber almost slammed Max's door but she closed it very slowly and then started squealing, jumping up and down.

"What? Do you have something to tell me?" Max asked.

"Yes! Suzanne called. She wants to meet Friday morning. In Westburg, which is a slight problem because I'll need to borrow a car, but I can use Mom's or Scarlet's or…"

"Calm down before you hyperventilate. You're right. The car's not the problem. That is great news. It will be interesting to see if she has anything important to share."

"Yes. It will. I'm going to be on pins and needles until Friday."

"It's only two days away. You'll make it."

Amber practically ran home to share the news with her mom and Scarlet. They were equally excited. "You really created quite a stir at the memorial. So many people have called to talk to you. Maybe Sandy Foss will call," Fluffy said, patting her hair into place in anticipation of meeting her hero.

"Maybe." Though Amber thought that would never happen.

"I'll have to borrow your car, Mom. She wants to meet in Westburg."

"Oh dear. You'll be driving on River Road all alone?" Fluffy said.

"In broad daylight. Nothing's going to happen."

"Actually, I could drive you," Scarlet said. "Maybe John and I could meet for a coffee or lunch."

Amber had to physically control her eye roll. "That sounds like a good idea," she managed to say with a smile.

CHAPTER FIFTY-THREE

*A*t *breakfast the next morning*, Amber, Scarlet and Fluffy talked about when to record the second part of the *Bonnie and Clyde* podcast.

"Maybe Saturday night? That used to be our recording night. It worked fine, I thought," Amber suggested. "We can spend the weekend focused on our podcast and put the River Road Murders on a back burner."

"I'm going to have to relisten to the first part of the episode. Seems like it's been forever since we recorded that," Scarlet said.

"Yes, so much has been happening, it feels like months ago, though I think it was two weeks. We should all give it a listen again," Fluffy added.

"After breakfast, let's all sit down and listen to the second part of *Your Childhood BFF*. Max said she was dropping the recordings by six in the morning so it should be available."

"Good idea," Fluffy said. "Grab a cup of coffee and we'll listen in the den."

At the end of the podcast, Amber said, "I think that was really good. Though it makes me sad again when I listen to it."

"Yes. Like my friend who was killed in our *Bonnie and Clyde* episode," Fluffy said.

"You know," Amber said, "in both our *BFF* episode and the *Bonnie and Clyde* episode, our victims were murdered by people they knew. People they loved and probably trusted."

"True," Scarlet said. "We kind of talked about that in the very beginning. About how people are always worried about the stranger lurking in the shadows but you're much more likely to be killed by someone you know."

"Right. And it makes me think about the River Road murders and the Tylenol murders that you mentioned, Mom. It seems to me that there is a strong probability that at least one of these murders was personal. And the other two just smoke screens to disguise the original intent," Amber said, taking her last sip of coffee.

"So that means we have to figure out which murder seemed the most personal. Right?" Scarlet said.

"The first one," Fluffy jumped in. "It was very personal. The victims were strangled and beaten. That is as personal as you can get since you are in the victim's face. And the burning of the bodies. That shows rage."

"I think you're right," Amber said. "If we can crack the first murder, I think we've solved the case." Amber stood up. "The answer might be found tomorrow when I talk to Suzanne. She might not know it, but she possibly holds the key to the murders. Knows who the murderer is but hasn't connected the dots yet."

"We're switching the Murder Crew dinner to tomorrow night so you can tell us what you've found out and maybe we can start putting some suspect pictures up on the board," Fluffy said.

"That would be nice." Amber laughed. "The board is great, but it lacks that essential ingredient. I have to head over to the library for a couple of hours to help with the children's program."

"It's wonderful how essential you've become. Hopefully, a full-time job might be in the future?" Fluffy asked.

"That would be nice. I like working at the library. I might go back to school part time and get my degree."

"Who would have thought the little girl who ran through the library screaming like Tarzan would turn out to be a librarian?" Scarlet and Fluffy laughed.

I thought I handled the police interview quite well. I started with anger, followed by outrage, that I, of all people, should even be accused, let alone interviewed. I berated the interrogator and said it was absurd anyone would believe the nonsense in those ridiculous letters.

My interrogator quickly became my supplicant, apologizing to me over and over, saying how sorry he was, agreeing it was an outrage. He explained Agent Devereaux had demanded that everyone who they received a note about had to be interviewed. And of course, he knew I was innocent. It was absurd to even think I could be involved.

Finally, I pretended to calm down and said of course I was willing to help, and he became grateful for my assistance.

This is so much fun. I wonder what the next twist will be.

CHAPTER FIFTY-FOUR

Amber and Scarlet woke early on Friday morning. They needed to shower and get dressed to make it to Westburg by nine a.m. Amber was undecided once again on what to wear to meet Suzanne. Nothing bright or flowery. Nothing that appeared frivolous. She didn't want to wear black though. This wasn't a memorial. She finally decided on the same outfit she wore to meet Duncan. It was a serious outfit, and she wanted to appear serious.

As she put her hair back in a bun, she wished once again she had fake glasses. There must be a place where she could get a pair.

Scarlet walked in as she was putting the finishing touches on her make-up. Very subtle of course. "Are you ready?" Scarlet asked.

"I think so." Amber turned. "What do you think? Have I struck the right tone? Serious. Concerned."

Scarlet tilted her head and looked Amber up and down. "You need one more thing to get the right look. I'll be back."

A moment later Scarlet returned and handed Amber a pair of glasses. "I wear these in class, so my professors think I'm studious and smart."

Amber turned to the mirror and slipped the glasses on. "OMG. This is just what I've been wanting. They are a game changer. I look so much more mature," she said. "I never knew you were so devious."

They headed down the stairs and out to Scarlet's car, calling goodbye to their mother as they left.

Driving along River Road toward Westburg, Amber and Scarlet couldn't help but comment as they passed the sites of each of the murders. "Right here. Along this beautiful road. How could something so awful happen?" Scarlet murmured.

When they got to Westburg, Scarlet dropped Amber off at the coffee shop. "I'll be in the park when you're done. Walk over and meet me there."

Amber stood facing the door for a moment and took a deep breath. Would this interview be the crack in the case? What was Suzanne going to tell her about Becky and, more importantly, about Annie?

The bell over the door tinkled as she pushed it open. She looked around the shop and saw Suzanne sitting in a back corner, staring down.

Approaching her, Amber said, "Suzanne? Hi, it's me, Amber Steen. We met at the memorial."

Suzanne's head jerked up and for a moment she looked confused, as if she wasn't expecting Amber. But then she smiled. "Amber. Yes. Nice to see you again." She didn't have anything to eat or drink in front of her. "I'm afraid if you want coffee or anything to eat, you have to order at the counter, pay, and then they bring it to you," Suzanne said as if in explanation

"Okay. I'll order for us both? What would you like?" Amber asked, realizing she was going to be paying again.

Suzanne gave Amber a complicated coffee order that included oat milk and honey and several other random ingredients. "Let me write that down. I'm a straight up coffee girl myself. Just cream and sugar for me," Amber said.

Suzanne laughed. "It's the number seven. I should have said that first."

Amber ordered, adding a slice of banana bread, paid, and returned to the table.

She pulled out her notebook and adjusted her glasses as if she was focusing on the task at hand. "How have you been, Suzanne? At the memorial, was that only three weeks ago? Seems like ages," Amber said. "You seemed upset. Concerned about your mother and father." She didn't think Suzanne had been concerned about her father in the least, but she didn't want to say that.

"Oh. Yes. The memorial. For Becky." Suzanne stopped speaking.

Amber wasn't sure where this was going. She'd assumed Suzanne had called her to talk about her sister and the murder and maybe any suspicions she might have about a possible suspect. Amber scribbled something in her notebook while she considered her next step. At that moment the coffee and banana bread arrived. Amber took a bite of the treat. "Oh, this is really good. My mother makes good banana bread, but this is right up there."

"That would be nice to have a mother who bakes. My mother is not a baker. The only time we ever had cake or sweets in the house was on our birthdays. And it was a store-bought cake." Suzanne stared over Amber's head as if memories of the past were washing over her. "Our mother is very health and fashion conscious, and she tried to raise us to adhere to her standards."

Amber couldn't imagine anything worse. No cookies?

Suzanne looked at Amber. "I'm sorry. I hope it didn't sound like I was criticizing my mother. She is an amazing person. Actually, the person I admire most in all the world." She took a sip of her coffee and smiled. "This is so good. Anyway, I'm sorry. I had all these things I wanted to talk to you about today, but we had a very upsetting incident yesterday and I haven't quite gotten over it."

"I'm sorry to hear that. What happened?" Amber quickly added, "If you don't mind me asking."

"We, my mother, father, and I, had a visit from an FBI agent yesterday morning. Apparently, they have been inundated with letters accusing people of murdering Becky and the three of us were implicated." Suzanne's voice was tight with anger. "Can you imagine how that made my parents feel? It's one more insult. Becky's been murdered. The police are too incompetent to solve the crime, and now we're being investigated."

Amber muttered something that she hoped sounded sympathetic.

"My mother was devastated. She spent the rest of the day in her room. My father was furious and stormed off for work as soon as the agent left. I tried to stay and help my mother, but she wanted to be alone."

"That is awful. I know about these letters because the police also showed up at our house on Monday to talk to me, my mother, and my aunt. We were also accused of the murders."

"No? Seriously?" Suzanne gasped. "This is crazy. They're questioning the wrong people. Why would they accuse us? Becky's family. We loved her. She was my mother's fav… baby," Suzanne said. "Her death has destroyed us." A small sob escaped, and she stopped for a moment to drink her coffee and compose herself. "Why would they accuse you and your family? You don't live in Westburg. You didn't know Becky."

"I think we were accused because we were at the memorial." Amber almost added that she probably had upset the murderer by handing out her true crime podcaster cards but didn't. "My boss at the library, Max Bolger, was also accused. She was there as well. I believe she is a friend of your mother's?"

Suzanne didn't respond.

"I think the theory is that the murderer is trying to get the police chasing their tails. Did you watch the press conference? As Agent Devereaux said, they have to follow up on every letter, no matter how absurd. So, if they're wasting their time interviewing… dozens? hundreds?… they don't have time or resources to find the real killer."

"I guess you're right. We tried to cooperate. It wasn't easy. My parents were horrified. I was also angry but tried to calm down and help, though I had little to contribute."

Amber and Suzanne sat quietly sipping their coffee. Amber tried to eat her banana bread, but it stuck in her throat. She sipped more coffee to wash it down.

"I want to apologize for approaching you at the memorial and asking you to get in touch with me. That was so unfeeling of me. I don't know what I was thinking," Amber finally managed to say. "I wanted to try my hand at solving the murder even though I have no training in police work. I've always been a bit obsessed with true crime, but I'm beginning to realize that these things don't just affect the victim and the murderer. They destroy families and send ripples through the community."

Suzanne reached over and patted Amber's hand. "It's okay. I admit I was very angry at the time when you handed me your card and I wanted to stuff it down your throat." She gave Amber a weak smile. "But I'm glad I didn't. I'm glad to have someone outside the family I can share my feelings with. I feel even more bonded since you have also been unjustly accused and interrogated by the police."

Amber winced for Sheriff Fenster, who had been so kind and careful. Hardly an interrogation but if Suzanne felt closer to Amber because of that experience, it would work out better.

"Did you hear that little bit at the beginning of the press conference when Agent Devereaux kind of implied there was a break in the case?" Amber asked.

"Yes, but I don't know what to think of it. I've pretty much lost all confidence in the investigation," Suzanne replied.

"I can understand why you feel that way, but I think Agent D is not one to say things for effect. He's not a Chief Wallace."

"Oh my God, Wallace." Suzanne rolled her eyes. "What a waste of space. My dad used to be a big supporter but not anymore."

"Yes, I was talking to someone else involved and they said this whole thing has been a disaster for Chief Wallace since he likes to act like he runs a tight ship, and crime has been practically non-existent under his reign."

"I didn't even think about it. Have you been talking to other people? How self-centered of me to think I was the only one you gave a card to."

Amber blushed. "I'm afraid to admit I was handing them to everyone remotely involved and asking them to call me. In fact, I think that's why my family and I were accused in those letters. I think I rattled someone's cage."

"So do tell. Who else have you spoken to?"

Amber suddenly felt awkward. She didn't really want to "out" her sources. Renn, Talley and even Duncan had spoken to her in confidence. She smiled. "Sorry, but if I want to be a bona-fide true crime podcaster, I can't reveal that information. And you can be assured I won't mention your name to others either. Just some people in law enforcement, the press…"

"I understand. And I appreciate that you won't tell anyone about talking to me."

Except to the entire Murder Crew. Amber had the decency to wince.

A beeping sound came from Suzanne's wrist. She looked down and said, "I'm sorry. I have to leave for work. Thank you for meeting and listening to me and making me feel better."

Amber panicked. She hadn't learned anything. "Yes… this was great. I'm glad if I helped. Can we meet again? Next week? I would love to talk to you about Becky and her friend Annie." Amber thought she saw Suzanne's face tighten at the mention of Annie. "Fill in the blanks, so to speak. You're Becky's sister. You knew her better than anyone."

Suzanne smiled. "I'll call and we can set something up."

After Suzanne left, Amber sat staring at the empty seat across from her. This had not gone the way she had hoped.

CHAPTER FIFTY-FIVE

*L*eaving *the cafe, Amber wondered* how she had lost control of the interview. Did Suzanne manipulate her? No. Suzanne had been distressed. Worried about her parents. Naturally, she wanted to talk about that. Next week, Amber could get to the real story.

She headed over to the park and spotted John and Scarlet sitting on a bench, talking and laughing. That little green monster started blossoming in her and she squashed it quickly down. She hadn't been interested in John and Scarlet needed some fun. A chance to unwind after a brutal second year of law school.

"Hi guys."

They both looked up. "Are you done already with Suzanne?" Scarlet asked. She sounded disappointed.

"Yes. Apparently, she had to get to work. Strange she scheduled us to meet on a workday," Amber said.

"I guess we'll head home." Scarlet looked at John.

"I'll escort you to your car." John smiled.

As they walked along the sidewalk, John sucked in his breath and uttered an expletive under his breath. Chief Wallace, with his usual attendant deputies, was heading their way. He was scowling. He walked right up to John and glared. "Deputy Talley. I assume since you're in uniform you're on duty, so why are you hanging out with these young ladies? Are you conducting business with them?"

John's head fell forward, and he stared at his feet. "No sir."

"What did you say? Speak up," Chief Wallace demanded.

John looked up. "No sir. I met them in the park and was walking them to their car."

"Ahh. I see. Performing civic duties, escorting young women to their vehicles." The sarcasm dripped from Chief Wallace's mouth. "How about you run along now and do your real job and the boys and I will make sure these two are safely delivered to their car."

John nodded and headed quickly down the street to the police station. Amber and Scarlet tried to make a quick escape to their car, but Chief Wallace stopped them and stared at Amber. "You're that girl. That girl that approached me at the memorial and stuck your card in my hand? Amber Steen? True crime podcaster, if I recall correctly."

Amber nodded, completely intimidated by this blustering man. He leaned closer and Amber shrank back. "Are you interrogating my staff to find out crap for your podcast? You gonna drag us all through the mud?" Suddenly Scarlet was between Amber and the Chief. She pushed him with her fingertip. "I have all that on video," she said, holding up her phone. "Unless you want to be charged with assault and intimidation, I suggest you back off, way off, and leave my sister alone."

"Your sister?" Chief Wallace stared at them. "I guess you're some damn podcaster too?" He sneered, trying to regain control of the situation.

"No. I am a lawyer," Scarlet said, pointing to her phone again. "The video? You want that sent to the local news? Or possibly to the Commonwealth Attorney's office?"

Chief Wallace's eyes narrowed, and his lips tightened into an angry grimace. "Get the hell out of my town. And don't come back." He stormed past them, once again almost knocking Amber over.

Scarlet helped Amber regain her balance. "I'm guessing that is the pig that you described from the memorial."

Amber ran her hands up and down her arms. "Yes. What a despicable creature."

"Do you think he'll do something to John? Fire him?" Scarlet said as they got in the car.

"With any luck he'll think John ran into us in the park like he said."

"I hope so." Scarlet started the car and pulled into traffic. "Let's get the hell home."

As they cruised along River Road, flashing lights appeared in their rearview mirror. It was a ranger car. Scarlet pulled over and the ranger pulled up behind her.

"Miss, I had you clocked going at least twenty over. License and registration, please." Scarlet handed over the required items, and the ranger went to his vehicle.

"I wasn't speeding," Scarlet said in disgust. "I never speed on River Road."

"See how easy that would be for someone in law enforcement to commit these crimes," Amber whispered to Scarlet. "Everyone stops for the cops. Or the rangers."

"Stop whispering. He can't possibly hear us," Scarlet snapped. "I'm sorry, it's just such BS. I was not speeding."

"I know. I'm sure Chief Wallace called his buddy Chief Ranger Richardson and told him to have a ranger pull us over and harass us."

"We must be getting close to solving the crimes because everyone is pissed at us," Scarlet grimaced.

The ranger returned and handed Scarlet her papers. "I think you've been drinking, Miss. I need you to step out of the vehicle so I can perform a sobriety test."

"At ten-thirty in the morning you think I'm drunk?" Scarlet tried unsuccessfully to rein in her anger. Amber squeezed her hand to calm her down. "Certainly, I will be happy to." Scarlet stepped out of the car.

"You look like you're weaving and slurring your words," the ranger said. "I'm gonna have to take you in. Hands behind your back."

Amber almost leapt from the car to defend her sister when another car pulled up next to them. Sheriff Fenster climbed out of his car and walked up to the ranger. "Problem? Can I be of assistance?"

The Ranger tried to appear cocky. "No… sir…" he added reluctantly. "Just some drunk drivers joy riding. As if we don't have enough to worry about. I'm taking them to Westburg to book 'em."

"Well, young fellow, considering you're a tad closer to Easton right now, and considering I am the Sheriff of Easton, I believe I will escort them to my police headquarters and book them there."

"Ummm… I don't think… I really need to… I was told…" the young ranger struggled and stumbled over his words.

"You've done a fine job keeping the peace. But I'll take it from here." Sheriff Fenster put Scarlet in the back of his police car and told Amber to drive to Easton. He waved to the ranger who stood by his car, slightly shell-shocked, as they drove off.

Instead of driving to the police station, Sheriff Fenster drove to the Steen house. He parked and opened the back door to let Scarlet out.

Amber jumped out of her car. "Sheriff Fenster, you showed up right in the nick of time. Thank you so much. I know it was a set up between Wallace and Richardson and they made it all up…"

"Calm down. I think you've been poking that bear again, Amber, but I wasn't your only guardian angel today. I got a call from a young deputy in Westburg who said he was worried about you two, so I thought I'd take a drive."

Fluffy flew out of the house and came rushing down the steps. "What on earth, Buster? Why did you have Scarlet in your car?"

"Nothing to worry about. Just keeping the peace." Sheriff Fenster doffed his hat, got back in his car, and drove off.

After a soothing dose of cookies and milk, Scarlet filled Fluffy in on what happened. "If I was convicted of drunk driving, I'd be thrown out of law school. So, it was even worse than you can imagine," Scarlet said.

"I've a good mind to go over there and tell that man off. How dare he?" Fluffy's face was bright red with anger.

"Let's not. I think we need to steer clear of Chief Wallace," Amber said. "We got lucky this time."

At the Murder Crew dinner that night, Amber tried to get into the jovial mood of the others. Everyone said the second half of *Your Childhood BFF* was great. "Numbers ticked up again. I think in a couple of weeks I'll try some more Facebook ads," Max said.

Amber had filled them in on her talk with Suzanne, which revealed nothing, and Scarlet told them about being almost arrested and saved by Sheriff Fenster.

"I shall definitely have Buster over for dinner," Fluffy said.

After everyone left, Amber crawled into bed and stared up at the ceiling. She seemed to be upsetting a lot of people but so far, no clues had fallen loose.

He knows you know

CHAPTER FIFTY-SIX

John *had planned to come* over Saturday but texted Scarlet to say he felt like he was being watched and wanted to let things calm down. He confirmed he had called Sheriff Fenster when he overhead Wallace on the phone with Richardson. "I was very afraid of what he was planning," John said.

Amber, Scarlet, and Fluffy decided to record the second half of *Bonnie and Clyde* right after lunch. First, they listened to part one to remind themselves of what had already been discussed and how the episode ended.

"I'll set up in my room," Scarlet said. "You and mom can be in the den together. It's been so long since we last recorded, I hope I remember what we're doing."

"I'm nervous too," Fluffy said.

"As long as I remember to push record, we'll be fine. We can always edit it later." Amber looked over the script one more time and pushed the record button.

Podcast

Episode 7: Bonnie and Clyde

Amber: Welcome back to episode 7 of *The Murderer You Know*. This is a continuation of last week's show called *Bonnie and Clyde*.

Scarlet: Remember our young Bonnie and Clyde and their friend Little Buddy had just killed Bonnie's father and sister and were busy ransacking the house looking for gold to fund their new lives when they saw headlights coming up the driveway.

Amber: Who was it? Who would be the next victim? Was Lovey's fiancé finally coming to check on her?

Fluffy: No. Bonnie's mother came home from her shift at the grocery store.

Amber: Surely Bonnie knew what time her mother worked and when she got home.

Scarlet: Maybe they lost track of the time.

Fluffy: From here the story is told from the mother's testimony at the trial.

Amber: At least she survived.

Fluffy: Just barely. She said she came home, and the house was dark and quiet. She went to the kitchen with groceries and turned on the light and saw blood on the floor. Then something in the hallway caught her eye and she turned to see her youngest daughter with a gun. Pointed at her. When she asked what was going on, Bonnie pulled the trigger, but the gun jammed.

Amber: She certainly had every intention of killing her mother. Odd she finally decided to use the gun.

Fluffy: Yes. Then Bonnie dropped the gun and started screaming for help. Clyde and Little Buddy came out of the garage and headed to the house.

Amber: She must have known something was really wrong at this point.

Fluffy: Yes. She ran into her bedroom and locked the door. She was trying to call the police. Then she heard banging on the door. Clyde was trying to force the door open.

Scarlet: I can't imagine what was going through her head.

Fluffy: She said during the trial it was hard to remember because it was all so traumatic and horrifying. The door crashed open and a teenage boy she didn't know walked in and smashed her on the head with a metal pipe.

Scarlet: During the trial Little Buddy claimed he didn't remember doing this.

Fluffy: Amazingly, the mother didn't collapse but looked him in the face and demanded to talk to her daughter. Bonnie came in and the mother asked again what was going on. Bonnie confessed to killing her dad and sister.

Amber: I can't believe this next part. The mom has had her skull fractured and she calmly talks to her daughter. She must be in total survival mode.

Fluffy: Bonnie started crying and said something about they're all going to jail. The mom hugged her and said, no that's not going to happen. And she came up with a plan. She acted like she was going to help them escape.

Amber: She gave them all the money that was in the house. A measly hundred dollars. They killed two people for a hundred dollars.

Fluffy: After giving Bonnie the money, she helped them pack a cooler with drinks and a bunch of snacks.

Scarlet: And she's doing all this with a fractured skull. Can you imagine?

Fluffy: The mom then gave them the keys to the dad's car and asked them where they're going, and they said California. The mom says, okay, when you get to California, call me and I can send more money. She told the boys to take care of her baby, reminds them not to speed, to drive safely, and they said their goodbyes and the kids drove off.

Amber: Can you imagine the fear. The horror. And all the while she knew her husband and other daughter were dead.

Scarlet: Apparently the 911 call did go through, because the police finally showed up, but it was too late.

Fluffy: My friend's fiancé, after spending the night worrying about his girl, finally found out what happened. Remember they had gotten engaged just that night. At my house. They were so happy.

Amber: Our three murderers are happily driving off to California with a cooler full of drinks and bags of chips and a whole hundred dollars. They must have thought when they crossed the California border, all would be forgiven, and they would be welcomed with open arms.

Scarlet: Five days after the killings, they were stopped in Nevada on Route 50 for speeding.

Amber: You've gone on a murder spree so maybe you wouldn't want to attract the attention of the police.

Scarlet: The policeman who pulled them over radioed in the license plate and driver's license to the dispatcher. The dispatcher told the police officer they were wanted for murder and not to approach, since these kids were armed and dangerous. Back-up arrived and they were arrested. They were so close to the border.

Amber: From what the police in Nevada said, they surrendered meekly. Didn't put up a fight.

Fluffy: A policeman from our town had to fly out to get them for trial. In Nevada, their only crime was speeding. They had to extradite them.

Amber: During the five days after the crime, rumors were flying about what had happened. The mom was in the hospital. Everyone knew that Bonnie and Clyde had killed her dad and sister, but no one really knew who Little Buddy was. Bonnie's mom had never seen him before. When his name was finally released, his mother was hysterical, thinking he must have been kidnapped by the other two. Imagine her shock to find out her son was a willing participant.

Scarlet: When they were brought to Virginia, they were all indicted. Bonnie was charged with one count of felony murder and one for capital murder. Which at the time was punishable by the death penalty. She was also charged with attempted murder and with robbery and vandalism.

Amber: It's crazy how they throw in so many charges.

Scarlet: They want to be sure they get them on something. Clyde was also charged with felony murder and capital murder. And poor little buddy who kind of innocently, in the beginning, went along because he was happy to be included, was charged with two counts of felony murder and robbery. Originally, he was also charged with attempted murder for hitting the mom in the head with a pipe but for some reason that charge was dropped to maiming.

Amber: Did they try them together or separately? Seems like they always hope that one of them will flip on the others.

Scarlet: I'm surprised Little Buddy didn't offer to testify against the other two for a reduction in sentence.

Amber: I wonder if the mom asked for leniency for her daughter.

Scarlet: It doesn't appear so. She was the key witness against all of them, being the only survivor. Although she could have been sending her daughter to the electric chair, she gave very detailed, compelling testimony.

Amber: How did the trials go? I'm sure they were found guilty but were they given the death penalty?

Scarlet: In the middle of his trial, Clyde ended up pleading guilty. Maybe his lawyer saw the jury was probably going to give him the death penalty. Bonnie also pled guilty to avoid the death sentence. They both received life sentences for the capital murder charge, plus fifty for the first-degree murder charge, ten years for attempted murder, and thirty years for robbery. The sentences were to be served consecutively so they basically got life plus ninety years.

Amber: What about Little Buddy? He had only witnessed the murders but then stupidly stepped up and attacked the mom. Maybe originally, he just thought they were going to rob the dad and steal money and head off on a lovely vacation. But as soon as they killed the dad, he should have run screaming into the woods.

Scarlet: He received a hundred years with fifty years suspended for the first-degree murder charges. The attempted murder was downgraded to maiming for which he received twenty years with ten years suspended. Then he got thirty years with twenty suspended for the robbery. Total time was a hundred and ten years plus twenty.

Fluffy: So many lives ruined. And for what? Interestingly, Bonnie wrote Little Buddy a letter basically saying she was sorry for involving him and ruining his life and his family's lives.

Scarlet: Sadly, he didn't seem to learn anything from his mistake. Apparently, he had a very bad attitude in prison and kept getting in trouble. Maybe he was just angry with himself. Eventually he was given parole after serving twenty-four years. He would have been in his forties. The other two have never been granted parole.

Fluffy: The mom moved away and eventually remarried. She never had any contact with Bonnie again. I can't imagine losing your entire family in such a horrific way. Lovely's fiancé also moved away. I'm not sure what ever became of him.

Amber: I often wonder about that five-day car ride. Were they overcome by horror and remorse over what they had done? Did Bonnie wish she'd never walked into the house that night? Did she want to take it all back? They confessed immediately, which makes me think they regretted everything.

Scarlet: You never know what is in people's hearts or what they are capable of.
Amber: Join us again next week for a new episode of *The Murderer You Know*.

Amber pushed the button to stop recording and flopped back in her chair. "That was emotionally exhausting. For me. It must have been worse for you, mom."

Scarlet walked in the room. "Yes. Hard to believe you lived through that. That must have torn up the community."

"Yes," Fluffy said, wiping away a tear. "It was awful. I buried it for a long time."

"I'm still trying to use these crimes we talk about to figure out what is happening in the River Road murders. What is the motive? What was the motive here?" Amber said.

"Anger and jealousy," Fluffy said.

"I understand that Bonnie, as we call her, was angry at her father. He was trying to keep her from her one true love," Amber said. "But killing her sister? I still don't understand that."

"It's a story as old as the Bible. The first murder in human existence was done out of jealousy. Cain is jealous of his younger brother because he is the favorite," Fluffy said.

"So, you're saying that Bonnie was jealous of her older sister, and it spilled out in a murderous rage?" Scarlet asked.

"Yes. I didn't think that at the time. I couldn't wrap my head around it, but thinking back, my friend, Fran, was the favorite. She was the good girl. The parents liked her boyfriend. She had everything her younger sister didn't," Fluffy said. "I think the original plan was just to rob and kill the father but when Fran showed up, I think all that repressed anger and jealous finally spilled out."

"Be careful Scarlet," Amber teased. "I might go psycho on you."

"Don't joke about that," Fluffy admonished Amber. "It's not funny."

"Sorry, Mom, you're right." Amber felt ashamed. "But have we discussed this before? What are the main motives for murder and how do they possibly relate to the River Road murders?"

Scarlet held up her hand and ticked off her fingers one by one. "Jealousy, revenge, fear, anger, hatred, lust, love, and greed."

"I notice you didn't include crazy," Amber said.

"Psycho serial killers, while they receive a lot of press, are not one of the top instigators of murder." Scarlet held up one more finger. "But maybe we need to consider them in these murders?"

"Let's consider the River Road murders. Do any of these motives fit?" Amber looked at the others. "Jealousy? We've considered that. Someone was jealous of Becky's success. Revenge? That seems more of a stretch but was there someone in Annie's past who wanted to get even with her? Fear? I'm throwing that one out. I don't think the murderer feared for their life."

"Maybe not feared for their life but maybe one of the victims knew something about the murderer and they feared their secret would be exposed?" Scarlet said.

"You're right. Putting fear back in there. Anger? People make us angry all the time. What makes it spill into murderous rage? Hatred can be a motivator but what could any of these young people done to make someone hate them?" Amber asked. "Hate them enough to kill them?"

"And we have that double-edged sword of lust and love, which people often confuse," Scarlet said.

"Greed might be one of the main reasons people kill. Did anyone gain financially from these deaths?" Amber asked.

"I keep thinking about that young boy, Little Buddy, who suddenly found himself in the middle of a killing spree and joined in," Fluffy mused. "I'm sure he never thought for a moment that's why they were going to Bonnie's house. Money, yes. Murder, no. Could something like that be a factor in the River Road murders? Something that just went out of control and suddenly people were dead?"

CHAPTER FIFTY-SEVEN

*O*n *Monday morning, Amber received* two calls. The first was Duncan Abbott. "Just a head's up. Agent Devereaux stated there will be an announcement on the evening news tonight about the River Road murders. He made it sound like a major breakthrough in the case."

Amber gasped. Could this be it? "Do you think the murders have been solved?"

"No idea. I'm sure you'll hear about it, but I wanted to give you a call."

"Thanks. I'll be on pins and needles all day. Do you know what he'll say?"

"No. Not even my sources know. They're playing this one close to the vest. Talk to you later."

Amber went to Max immediately with Duncan's news. Max was surprised. "Wouldn't it be great if the FBI had solved the murders? We could all go back to our normal lives," Amber said.

"True." Max nodded solemnly. "We'll have to wait and see."

Later Suzanne called. "I guess you've heard there is going to be a big announcement tonight."

"Yes. Everyone is talking about it. Are you nervous? Do you think they've solved your sister's murder?"

The silence on the other end of the phone dragged on for so long, Amber wondered if they'd been disconnected. "Suzanne? Are you still there?"

"Yes. Sorry. Lost in thought. I hope so. Can we meet for coffee again? I feel like you're the only one who truly understands what I'm going through."

"Sure. But can we meet here in Easton? I ran into Chief Wallace after our last coffee, and he basically told me I'm not welcome in Westburg anymore."

"What? Why?"

Amber sighed. "After our coffee, I ran into one of his deputies and we were chatting. Chief Wallace spotted us, and he recognized me as the girl who gave him the true crime podcaster card at the memorial. He jumped to the conclusion I was pumping his people for information behind his back." Amber had to admit he wasn't wrong about that, but it wasn't illegal for her to talk to people.

"He's an ass. Where can we meet?"

"There's a nice café on Main Street called The Nook. What time is good for you?"

They settled on ten and Amber went to Max's office. "Can I come in a little late tomorrow?"

Max looked up. "Probably. What's up?"

"Suzanne wants to meet me to talk about tonight's announcement. She's concerned about what might be revealed."

"Sounds great. Ida and I are inviting ourselves over tonight to watch with you, Scarlet, and your mom."

"Are you coming over around dinnertime?" Amber grinned.

"If it could be arranged."

"I'll call Mom and give her a head's up."

"Thanks. See you tonight." Max grinned and returned to her work.

Fluffy easily whipped up a dinner for six instead of four. "What's two more?" she said, adding more pasta to the pot. She planned on making her famous ziti and zucchini casserole.

"Don't forget dessert," Amber said.

"Of course not. What's a meal without dessert?" Fluffy sounded outraged.

"The news said the announcement would be at the end of the local news broadcast, which gives us time to eat," Amber said.

"That will make your father happy. You know what a creature of habit he is. Doesn't like to wait for his food."

Max sat back, rubbing her stomach with a look of ecstasy on her face. "Madge, you really need to open a restaurant."

Amber's dad looked up and snorted.

"Oh, no," Fluffy replied, waving off the praise. "It's all I can keep up with feeding my family. A restaurant would be too much work."

"We could all quit our jobs and help out." Ida grinned. "We'd be rich in no time."

"Please, stop your nonsense." Fluffy rose from the table. "Go into the den and turn on the TV. I'll be right out with dessert."

Amber's dad turned to Channel 9. Fluffy brought in slices of tiramisu. "This goes perfectly with the Italian dinner theme," she said as she and Scarlet handed around the plates.

They all settled in. The regular anchor reminded everyone of the special announcement at the end of the news.

The TV switched to the now familiar set-up with Agent Devereaux standing behind the podium and the array of law enforcement behind him.

Agent Devereaux stared into the camera with a grim expression. For a moment, Amber worried that he didn't really have an update.

"Good evening. I know the citizens of this area have been anxiously awaiting any news on possible suspects in the River Road murders. I was specifically sent here to help solve those crimes. And tonight, I can announce we have arrested a suspect for the third murder involving Kyle Phillips and Brittany Brewster." He quickly glanced down at his notes, although Amber assumed it was a ploy to increase the drama. Everyone in the den looked at each other with wide eyes. Max mouthed "Who?"

Agent Devereaux said, "The suspect is one Joshua Renn, a ranger with the park police. We believe we have enough evidence to charge him with this crime." Agent D looked around at the police behind him before turning to the camera. "I want to emphasize this was a joint operation with all the local law enforcement of the towns of Westburg and Easton, as well as the park rangers. At this time, I cannot release any further information.

"I also want to thank all the citizens who were interviewed by the police this week after we received letters accusing numerous people. We have been able to eliminate most of the people named and will continue to do follow-ups.

"I know everyone is wondering if Renn is a suspect in the first two murders. While we do not believe him to be involved, it is early in the investigation, and we aren't ruling anything out.

"As I said, we will be releasing more information in the coming days. That is all we have at this time."

Reporters started jumping up to ask questions. Amber saw the back of Duncan's head as he waved and shouted out a question to the FBI agent.

Agent Devereaux ignored all of them, collected his papers, and left the stage with the police following.

The camera switched to show Sandy Foss standing to the side with his microphone clutched in his hand. "What a surprise announcement. One of the murders on River Road has apparently been solved and perhaps the others will soon follow. Even though the FBI has stated the accused is not yet a suspect in the first murders, they're probably digging deep to find the evidence to implicate him." Sandy brushed back his gleaming mane. "We will have more information on the late news and over the next few days. Trust your investigative reporter, Sandy Foss, to get to the bottom of this." He then gave his signature salute and signed off.

Amber's dad got up to leave as all the others erupted into questions and comments.

"Joshua Renn?" Amber gasped.

"I told you to be careful, Amber," Fluffy almost shouted. "You were dining with a murderer."

"We all told you to be careful," Max added.

"John was convinced it was him or hoped it was him," Scarlet said.

"I wonder if he did them all? But why? What was his motive?" Ida asked.

"Being the center of attention," Amber said sadly. "Poor Josh. He liked having his moments of fame."

They talked for another hour before the gathering broke up.

Later, as she snuggled under her covers, Amber decided to call Duncan first thing in the morning. She briefly wondered how Suzanne would take this announcement before drifting off to sleep.

Well, well, well. That was quite illuminating. Now I know who the copycat is. Ranger Renn. That pathetic creature. I wonder if he finally decided to try his hand at murder after being first on the scene, as he liked to call it. He didn't learn anything from my meticulous planning though, since he must have left evidence all over the place.

Now I have to decide when to commit my next murder. I have my victims picked out. I just have to set the stage. And figure out how to get them all together out on River Road.

CHAPTER FIFTY-EIGHT

The next morning Amber impatiently waited for Duncan to call. She didn't want him to think she needed his insights. But she did. At nine o'clock, she reluctantly dialed his number.

He answered immediately. "Amber, it's you. Good, I wanted to talk to you first thing, but I've got a meeting. Things are completely wild here with speculation and conjecture. I have to research Renn's background and try to figure out why he murdered two teenagers." He stopped to draw a breath.

"I can only imagine. I'm sure the newsroom is a madhouse," Amber said. "I hope we can get together when you have a moment. I know we all considered him a suspect. Now I'm trying to figure out if he did all the murders."

Duncan laughed. "You and everyone else. Tell you what, let's meet for dinner tomorrow night? In Easton of course. I've heard you've been banned from Westburg."

"How do you find those things out?" Amber retorted. She didn't like Duncan knowing everything about her.

"Never you mind. Gotta go."

Before he hung up, Amber mentioned she'd be meeting with Suzanne that morning and hoped to get her reaction.

"Good. You can fill me in tomorrow." The line went dead.

Amber dressed and popped down to the kitchen, where she knew she'd find her mother. "I just talked to Duncan. He said the newspaper is going crazy trying to figure out why Renn killed those kids and if he did the rest of the murders."

"I completely understand," Fluffy said. "It's been the first break in the case."

"I'm meeting with him tomorrow night to compare notes. Since I'm meeting with Suzanne this morning, I might have something to tell him about how her family is reacting to the news. Though of course he can't print third-hand information, it might give him some ideas."

"All right dear. But remember, Renn might not be the only murderer. You need to be wary."

Amber walked down to The Nook. She got there fifteen minutes early because she wanted to be sure to find a table in the back, where it was always quieter. Luckily, it wasn't busy, and she got a secluded booth in the corner. When the waitress came to take her order, she said she was waiting for a friend.

A few minutes after ten, Suzanne came in looking harried. Glancing around, she spotted Amber and waved. "Sorry I'm late," she said as she plopped across from Amber.

"Hardly." Amber smiled. "The waitress is heading this way. Their coffee drinks are amazing and so are their pastries."

Suzanne looked at the menu in front of her. "I don't often eat breakfast," she said.

"Oh, me either," Amber lied. "Usually, I only have coffee."

When the waitress arrived, Suzanne ordered another complicated coffee drink with oat milk and some sort of flavoring. "I guess I'll have a croissant. The almond chocolate one."

Thank goodness. Amber worried she'd faint without breakfast. "I'll have a large regular coffee and a… yogurt parfait." She felt proud of herself for her restraint.

Once the waitress left, Amber looked at Suzanne and asked her how she was doing. "I'm sure the news last night was extremely upsetting for you and your family."

"Yes. We still know nothing. Agent Devereaux seemed convinced Renn only committed the latest murder." Suzanne shook her head, looking at her hands as tears glistened in the corners of her eyes.

"Hopefully, we'll have more details soon," Amber said.

Suzanne abruptly reached across the table, grabbed Amber's hand, and squeezed it. "Having you here to talk to about this… you'll never know what it means to me. Since Becky… I haven't had anyone to talk to."

Amber tried to squeeze Suzanne's hand back. It was awkward. "The last time we met, I wanted to ask you about Becky's friend Annie. Seems like the police were totally focused on Becky and no one even considered the possibility the intended victim might be Annie. That's if the murder was intended, though it did seem rather personal." Amber cringed. Maybe she'd gone too far. "I hope I'm not upsetting you."

"No. Not anymore. I guess I've talked and thought and dreamt about this so much I've developed a numbness. I know what you mean. Everyone is focused on Becky, but maybe it did have something to do with Annie."

Amber didn't want to stop Suzanne speaking, so she continued to squeeze Suzanne's hand and nodded.

"Everyone acts like Annie was this great person. Graduated at the top of her class, joined the army, still no one ever asked why she quit the military."

"Did Becky tell you?"

"No, but I did some digging. Turns out Annie was accused of sexual harassment of a lower-ranking soldier in her unit. She denied the whole thing, though I guess she was encouraged to leave and say it was her decision."

"Some guy accused her of sexual harassment?" Amber asked.

"No. That's the crux of the issue. It wasn't a guy. It was a woman. A young woman in her teens. She reported it to her sergeant, who then reported it up the chain. The story was Annie had been putting moves on her and telling her she'd have her reassigned to some terrible posting if she didn't comply."

"What? Damn, that's a surprise." Amber considered this revelation. "Maybe that's why her family didn't come to the memorial. Were they ashamed?"

"I don't know. My mother reached out to her mother afterwards and got a short note along the lines of 'sorry for your loss' and implying not to get in touch again."

The waitress brought their coffee and food, and for a few minutes, they busied themselves fixing their coffees.

Suzanne began her story again. "I didn't know anything about Annie. I met her once. I saw her and Becky having dinner together at a restaurant in town and walked over to say hi, who's your friend, the usual. I got a very odd vibe from them. They were both awkward about me seeing them together. I also wondered why this grown woman wanted to hang out with a college student. That's when I did my research. Afterwards I told Becky, Annie was a lesbian who'd used her position of power to demand sexual favors from underlings."

Amber took a huge sip from her coffee mug. It was still boiling hot, and she burned her tongue. Grabbing her water, she chugged down the ice-cold liquid. Finally, she managed to say, "How did Becky respond to that news?"

"She was furious and called me names and told me I didn't know anything about Annie or about anything. She called me an old maid homophobe and claimed there was nothing going on between them. They were only friends. She went crazy on me."

"What did you do then?" Amber asked.

"I called Annie and told her I knew all about her and she better stop grooming my sister to be her next lover."

"Wow," was all Amber could say.

"Then they were murdered a couple of days later." Suzanne stared at her croissant, which she'd been pulling into pieces instead of eating.

"You're thinking maybe someone from her past, a former girlfriend or someone like that, killed her and Becky in a jealous rage?" Amber asked. "Did you tell the police about this?"

"The police are useless. Until the FBI showed up, they didn't want to know anything or pursue any leads. They started with the theory it was a bizarre accident or a murder suicide. When the second couple disappeared, they said it was a tragic drowning. When their bones were discovered and it was like, 'oops,' the cops went with the crazed psycho serial killer as their next theory," Suzanne said.

"I can see you are frustrated."

Suzanne laughed bitterly. "To say the least. Who knows? Maybe Renn is a crazed serial killer and I've been thinking about this all wrong. Imagining there was some motive. That my sister's death wasn't just some random horrible accident. Wrong place. Wrong time."

"It's awful," Amber said. She couldn't even imagine what Suzanne had gone through in the last year. If anything ever happened to Scarlet, she couldn't endure it.

Suzanne's voice interrupted her thoughts. "Didn't you say you have a sister? Then you know exactly how I feel."

At dinner, Amber told her mom and Scarlet she'd finally gotten some more information from Suzanne. "It was quite the story. I'll save it until we have our Murder Crew get-together because tomorrow, I'm talking to Duncan, and I hope to find out more about the Renn arrest."

Wednesday, *Amber had to go* to work. It was children's program day at the library and the only thing Max wouldn't let her skip. "I'm not warm and fuzzy," Max told Amber. "The mere idea of dealing with those small creatures with their sticky hands and runny noses is abhorrent to me."

"Don't be silly," Amber said.

"I'm not joking. I am quite serious," Max stated.

Amber asked Scarlet if she would like to come and help with the program. "I'm sure you're bored sitting around the house."

"Not at all. You can't even imagine how wonderful it is to do nothing." Scarlet smiled. "Plus, John is coming over later.

"Sounds fun. Mom, remember I'm going out to dinner with Duncan. I hope he has some more details on Renn's arrest," Amber said.

"Sounds like no one will be here for dinner except your father," Fluffy snorted. "I'll disguise some leftovers as something new. He'll never know the difference."

Amber loved working with the children. She couldn't understand why Max didn't want to surround herself with kids. They were so enthusiastic.

But she was happy to say goodbye to all the little darlings. They could be demanding and exhausting. After she cleaned up, she popped into Max's office.

"Just heading out to meet Duncan for dinner. Early dinner obviously."

"Are we still getting together tomorrow night to talk about the podcast and the arrest and anything you and Scarlet might find out this week?"

"Yes, I think mom is making her famous enchilada pie. Even dad will eat that." Amber grinned.

"Okay. Can't wait."

Amber walked to the Cutting Board and sat outside on a bench. She was early but it was a lovely evening, and it gave her a chance to once again think about everything that Suzanne had said about Annie.

"Hello there Ms. Steen."

Amber looked up to see Duncan Abbott standing in front of her.

"Good evening Mr. Abbott."

They walked inside and once again found a table in a far corner.

"You've been busy?" Amber asked after they ordered.

"Yes. The FBI issued a statement today to the press about what led them to arrest Renn. Of course, my good friend Sandy Foss will be able to blast it all over the airwaves tonight, so he'll get the scoop, but TV news doesn't have a chance to go into great detail. They have to talk about weather and sports and all the other news. I won't be first, I'll be much better."

"Don't hide your light under a bushel," Amber smirked.

Duncan snorted with laughter. "Not my style. So, I'm sure you're dying to know…"

"Of course, I am." Amber leaned closer. "Tell all."

Duncan ran through the list that the FBI had given out to the press detailing their investigation which led to the arrest of Ranger Renn. "Almost from the first moment, they realized this crime hadn't been committed by the same person as the first two murders."

Duncan held up his fingers. "One. The perpetrator used a gun. Two. The scene was messy and disorganized as if the killer had panicked and then tried to cover up the crime." He stopped holding up his fingers and laughed. "Ha. Well, I guess there were just those two things. Not to mention DNA all over the place, despite the killer trying to drag the bodies off into the river. The FBI actually focused in on Renn pretty early, but they didn't want to spook him. They were still trying to see if they could link him to the other crimes but then they finally decided it was time and they arrested him over the weekend."

The waitress brought their food and Amber tried to eat and ask questions at the same time. "Did Renn confess?"

Duncan nodded but finished chewing before answering. "Yes. Apparently, the minute they sat him down he started crying and confessed to everything. To that crime, not the others."

"But why did he kill those kids?"

"One of the oldest motives in the book. Greed. Renn and Kyle Phillips were in business together. Selling drugs. But that night, Renn confronted Kyle and demanded a bigger cut of the pie. They got into a fight, and Renn shot him in a fit of rage. He didn't know the girl was in the car and saw the whole thing, so he had to kill her too."

"How sad," Amber said.

After they'd covered all the facts about the Renn arrest, Amber filled Duncan in on her meeting with Suzanne. "She told me this crazy story that Annie was gay and was 'grooming' Becky to be her girlfriend. She claimed Annie was drummed out of the army because she had sexually harassed another soldier, a female soldier, under her command."

Duncan tilted his head and sat silently for a moment. "How on earth did she find all that out? I don't think the police found out any of that about Annie."

"Suzanne is not a fan of the local police. She said they basically went with the crazed serial killer theory and didn't do any deep digging."

"So, she thinks it was some jealous former or current girlfriend of Annie's?" Duncan's eyebrows twisted into a quizzical look.

Amber shook her head and sighed. "I don't know. I think she's crazy with grief, worried about her mother, and clutching at straws. She also said that maybe Renn will confess to all the murders so she's basically all over the place."

"Sounds like," Duncan said.

"I can understand how upset she is over losing her sister. She really has my sympathy. And she seems to want to be friends. She says she doesn't have anyone else to talk to."

"You realize, Ms. Steen, we are almost out of suspects? Renn is off the table. Who does that leave?"

Amber stared into space. "I'm beginning to go with crazed killer. I can't find any personal reasons for anyone to kill Becky and Annie."

"Unless it is someone from their pasts." Duncan said, then paused. "Or from the present."

"You really narrowed that down." Amber smirked.

When Amber got home, she told her mother and Scarlet that Sandy Foss would have a special report on the arrest of Renn that night. After watching it, Scarlet said to Amber, "Just like our podcast about drugs and greed."

"My thoughts exactly."

CHAPTER SIXTY

*A*mber and Scarlet *got up* early to listen to their podcast, the first episode of *Drugs Kill In More Ways than One*. Actually, Scarlet had gotten up even earlier for her morning run. After a few attempts, Amber gave up jogging with her sister.

"I don't think running is healthy," Amber said after her last outing. "It gives you shin splints, joggles up your insides, and makes your boobs sag prematurely."

Scarlet couldn't stop laughing.

"It's true," Amber huffed indignantly. "You're always hearing about joggers dropping dead from massive heart attacks."

"Whatever," Scarlet replied and left. When she returned, they both went downstairs for breakfast, to listen with their mom.

At the end, Fluffy said, "Another very good episode girls. There are important lessons in your podcasts. It shouldn't just be blood and gore. There must be a message as well."

"I thought it really related to the third murder, which turned out to be basically the same old story, drugs, greed and murder." Amber took a long sip of coffee. "But I have to get to work. Tonight, when the Murder Crew gathers, I can fill them in on my meeting with Suzanne."

The library was busy that day. Everyone had watched Sandy Foss's report the night before and read Duncan's detailed story in the morning paper. Once again, the crowd was divided on whether the ranger had committed all three murders or just one. Amber didn't join in the chats, but she listened to as much of the talk as she could.

That night when everyone gathered, Fluffy announced she had made her world-famous enchilada pie for dinner. They all groaned in anticipation. After dinner, the Great Silence shuffled off to his man cave and the Murder Crew gathered in the den.

"First an update on the podcast. We released our third episode, part one of *Drugs Kill*. Our numbers aren't skyrocketing but they are moving up steadily each week. We've gotten good reviews and a few comments on our Facebook page. Maybe in a week or two I'll take out another ad and offer more giveaways."

Everyone chattered about how exciting it was. Amber smiled along with the others. She remembered Ida's words about having fun and hanging out together. No, she wasn't going to get rich and famous, but it was wonderful to share this experience with these women.

"And now for our next point of business." Max picked up a photo of Renn and pinned it on the murder board with the word *solved* scribbled above it. "One down, two to go." She announced proudly.

She looked around the room. "Any news, updates, anything to report?"

Scarlet piped up. "We were accosted and run out of town by Chief Wallace last Friday. He thought we were pumping John for information. He's an ass. I hope he's the killer." Everyone agreed and laughed.

Amber almost raised her hand to be recognized. Max sometimes had that effect on her. She moved her hand to her lap, hoping no one noticed. "Yes, I met with Suzanne Laurelwood this week. She seems to really like me."

"Did you learn anything?"

Amber filled them in on what Suzanne had told her, and the women digested the news. Finally, Fluffy broke the silence. "Are you saying she thinks this was some kind of romantic murder? Spurned lover? And Annie was homosexual?"

"If that was true, that might be reason enough for someone to kill them. Some homophobe sees them in town, follows them out to River Road, and murders them," Ida suggested.

"True. That gives us one more reason for the murders," Scarlet said.

"But still doesn't fit a pattern, since the second couple weren't gay."

Amber stood and walked over to the board and stared at the picture of Jenna Frankel, the college student. "Look at her hair. She had a short pixie haircut, and I think they said she was wearing jeans and a baggy t-shirt. Could someone have thought she was a boy?"

They discussed that for a while, coming to no consensus other than they all agreed the first murder had been personal.

"Keep up the good work, Amber," Ida and Max said as they left.

Amber and Scarlet helped their mom with the dishes before heading to bed. "At lunch yesterday Duncan said we were running out of suspects, and I'm afraid he's right. Seemed like there were so many possibilities when we started," Amber said, flopping on her bed.

"I'm guessing you've struck Duncan off the list?" Scarlet grinned.

"I suppose so. No one I've talked to seems like a crazed killer, except Renn of course, and turns out he was a killer."

"Just not the right one," Scarlet said, stepping into the hallway. "Don't worry about it. You have other stuff going on in your life."

Amber lay back on her pillow. Scarlet was right. She had so much going on in her life. The podcast and the Murder Crew. Her job and her plans to pursue a degree in library science that fall. And two new friends, Duncan and Suzanne. And John Talley too. But she still wondered if he could be the murderer as she drifted off to sleep.

Chapter Sixty-One

$\mathcal{S}$aturday, *Scarlet had plans to* go kayaking with John. Amber couldn't help but feel annoyed. Scarlet was supposed to be home hanging out with Amber and the family, but she seemed to be devoting a good deal of her time to John. Amber bit her tongue because she knew Scarlet was simply trying to unwind after a stressful year.

When the mail arrived, the letter Scarlet had been waiting for was finally delivered. She ripped the envelope open and screamed. "I got it! I got the internship. I start in two weeks." She danced around the hallway, clutching the letter to her chest.

Amber tried to be happy for her sister. "Wow. You'll be leaving in two weeks. We better get busy solving those murders." Amber forced a smile.

Scarlet danced over and hugged Amber. "We might never solve them. But as a prosecutor, I'll be able to punish the bad guys. After the police arrest them."

"Cool," Amber said and added a belated grin to her face.

Scarlet looked at her phone. "Ooops, John will be here soon. I better get ready."

"Have you told John that you're leaving?" Amber asked.

"I told him I applied for this internship but didn't know what would happen. He wished me luck. I'm sure he'll be sorry I'm leaving so soon but I'll be back and forth on weekends, and he can come see me."

"Sounds serious," Amber said.

"No, silly. We're friends. Having fun. Enjoying time together. I can't be serious about anything until I'm done in law school. It's nice to have a friend, a guy friend, who is supportive and not all whining about themselves and demanding I give up my hopes and dreams for them."

Amber wondered if that was a comment about her track record with guys, particularly Bruce, who she'd pretty much given everything up for.

John showed up a short time later and Amber waved as they left in his jeep. I was the first one who rode in that jeep, Amber thought. Well, I'm too busy for guys. Scarlet isn't the only one who has a life. I have a job and a podcast and…

Amber spent the day helping her mother can tomatoes and freeze batches of beans.

John and Scarlet returned shortly before dinner, sunburned and happy. Of course, Fluffy invited John to dinner. Amber was annoyed since they would only have fourteen more dinners with Scarlet, and she hoped John wouldn't be at all of them.

The dinner conversation centered around Scarlet's upcoming internship. Even their dad seemed thrilled that Scarlet would be working on what he considered the right side of the law, sending criminals to jail. He smiled and nodded and grunted enthusiastically. He and John fist bumped each other. Amber was stunned.

Everyone went into the den to watch a movie. The murder board had been discreetly folded up before John entered. Amber excused herself, claiming she had work to do on the podcast. She really couldn't take any more of the family's apparent joy over another Scarlet success.

They had planned to record the next podcast on Sunday, which was tentatively titled *Love You to Death*, but Scarlet said she had a lot of forms to fill out for the internship.

Amber looked over the script for the podcast. It suddenly occurred to her that there was another reason to kill someone: money. The husband in this story decided to kill his wife for money. Apparently, you could take out a life insurance policy on someone without them knowing it or fake their signature on a policy. The husband, who Ida worked with, took out a policy on his wife, which paid double if she died on a holiday. Amber couldn't imagine why an insurance company would offer such an absurd policy. No doubt they assumed they would never have to pay out, unless, of course, a greedy spouse decided to take advantage of the situation.

Could someone have taken out a policy on Becky or Annie or the college students? And they were sitting back, waiting to collect their big pay-out? It probably wasn't likely. The insurance company might get suspicious and then the police would be informed by the insurance company, who of course wouldn't want to pay. She wondered if Agent Devereaux had checked into that possibility. She had every confidence in Agent D, knowing he would be looking at everything with a fine-tooth comb.

Dinner that night was just the four of them, which should have made Amber happy, but she was beginning to feel a growing resentment toward Scarlet and her wonderful life. She told herself that was absurd, but she couldn't squash all the negative feelings.

CHAPTER SIXTY-TWO

As *Amber left for work* on Monday, she reminded Scarlet that they had to record the next two episodes of the podcast before she left. "The sands of time are running out."

"Don't be such a drama queen," Scarlet scoffed. "We used to record when I was out of town. We can still do that."

"If you're not too busy." Amber rolled her eyes as she walked out the door.

At the library, Max asked her what the problem was. "You've hardly said a word since you got here. And you're shelving books like you're trying to punish them by slamming them around."

Amber let out a big sigh. "Sorry. I'm being petty and jealous."

"Oh?" Max replied. "About?"

"Scarlet." Responding to Max's quizzical look. "Sometimes I get tired of her being the golden girl. She got this internship with the Commonwealth Attorney's office, and you'd think she'd been appointed to the Supreme Court the way my parents are carrying on."

Max laughed. "I know it's hard living under Scarlet's shadow, but your parents are just as proud of you."

"For what? My part-time job? My part-time podcast? The fact that I have no money, no car, and mooch off my parents?"

"Fluffy loves you mooching off of them. She'd be happy to have both of you live with her forever."

Amber snorted. "I know. Plus, even though I met him first, Scarlet and John Talley are totally wrapped around each other. And I haven't quite exonerated him as a possible murder suspect, and he is acting like such a wonderful guy, not even getting upset that Scarlet is leaving. He's being 'supportive.'"

"Oh, I agree, nothing worse than a supportive guy." Max tried to look serious and concerned.

"Stop. I know I'm being ridiculous. Let me wallow for a while."

"Wallow away my dear, just take it easy on the library books." As Max walked away, she turned and said, "I almost forgot. Call your Aunt Ida. She has news."

That piqued Amber's interest. During her lunch break, she called Ida.

"Can you stop by after work?" Ida asked. "I have something I think you might be interested in."

"Are you going to tell me more?" Amber asked.

"Nope. Just come by." And she hung up.

After work, as she walked to Ida's, Amber's phone rang. It was Duncan. "Hello. I've been meaning to call you."

"That's nice. I've been waiting to hear from you to congratulate me on my brilliant article on the capture and confession of Ranger Renn. But nary a word did I hear."

"I'm sorry, Duncan. Too much going on. Family stuff. My sister got her internship and will be leaving in two weeks. Working on…" She almost said podcast but stopped. "…stuff."

"Yeah. I know all about stuff."

"It was a great article. Well written and researched. You answered every question anyone could ask. Much better than the fluff piece Sandy Foss did on the evening news."

"Thank you so much. I'm glad I did a better job than old Sandy. I have nothing else to report. No breaking news from the FBI but wanted to keep in touch."

"Always good to hear from you, Duncan. We should get together at the end of the week. Maybe?"

"Sure. I'll call."

Amber reached Ida's house and knocked on the front door. Her aunt called out to come in. That's how people get murdered, Amber thought, as she pushed the door open. Yelling out to let someone know the door is unlocked even when you don't know who's there.

"Ida?"

"I'm on the porch." Ida replied.

Ida was sitting on the porch with a tall glass of lemonade next to her. "Grab a glass. I made it fresh. I can't cook like Fluffy, but I can make a damn fine lemonade."

Amber poured a glass and sat down. "So, what's the big mystery? What do you have to tell me?"

"Young people," Ida snorted. "Always in a rush. Drink your lemonade. Chill. Enjoy the lovely breeze."

Amber tried to be calm, but she was impatient.

"Max told me you were having a bit of a bad day," Ida said.

Her blood pressure shot up. Did Max send out an all-points bulletin: *warning—Amber is stressed and might snap.* Her circle of people was too small.

"I have just the thing to perk you up. Come out to the side yard with me."

Amber set her glass down and followed her aunt out the back door. They turned right at the end of the house. An old green Honda Civic sat in the driveway. It reminded her of her old car, the Green Flash, and she felt a tear in her eye.

"It's all yours, Sweetie. The second coming of the Green Flash. Slightly newer but not new," Ida said.

"What?" Amber blurted out. She ran to the car and put her hands on the hood. Then she opened the door and plopped in the driver's seat. If she closed her eyes, she could almost believe she was in her old car.

Ida came over and leaned down. "You like it?"

"What's not to like?" Amber grinned up at Ida. But then reality set in. "But, you know, I don't have any money. I can't pay you for this car. I could pay a hundred dollars every couple of weeks but that would take forever." Her voice cracked.

"Honey, I know that jerk Bruce convinced you to sell your car and then he took all your money." Ida held up a hand. "And no, I never told your parents, but I wanted to do something for you because you've been working so hard and pulling your life together. I know how bad you need a car and you've been so good about walking everywhere. I got this from a client. It was a good deal. We'll work out a payment plan. You can take all the time you want. I don't need the money."

Amber jumped out of the car and hugged her aunt. "Thank you."

"Here are the keys. Take it for a test drive. Actually, drive it home. You can tell Scarlet and your parents you bought it from me. They don't need to know any details."

Amber took the keys and climbed into the car. It started immediately. She closed her eyes. She was back in the Green Flash and the entire part of her life with Bruce was erased.

Scarlet and Fluffy were in the front yard when Amber pulled up.

"OMG Amber. Is that the Green Flash? How did you get that?" Scarlet exclaimed.

"Not the Flash but a twin. Ida found it for me." Amber grinned, posing next to her new car. She knew lots of people would sneer at this old green Civic, but it meant more to her than a brand-new fancy car.

That night it was just the family again and Amber was happy.

The next morning Amber drove to the library for work. She didn't need to, but she felt so much more grown-up driving into the employee parking lot. Max got there the same time as Amber did and took a step back when she realized Amber was driving.

"Wow. Is that Amber behind the wheel of a car? I guess I know what Ida wanted to talk to you about. Did she buy that for you?"

"Not exactly. It's not a gift. I have to pay her back, but I get to use it in the meantime."

"That's wonderful. Good to have a family member in the car business."

Amber worked calmly and happily. Her aunt's kindness had colored her entire outlook. She was still sad Scarlet was leaving but happy that Scarlet had this opportunity. The internship would look great on her resume.

At the end of the day, Amber almost started walking home before she remembered she had wheels. As she settled in the driver's seat, she ran her hands over the steering wheel. She still couldn't believe she had a car. She'd have to check her bank account and give Ida a down payment at least.

Before she turned the key, her phone rang. It was Suzanne.

"Hey there. I was hoping we could meet for dinner this week. We could meet over here in Westburg. You don't have to worry about that big jerk, Chief Wallace. He won't dare assault you if you're with me."

"That sounds good," Amber replied. "I actually just got a car so driving over to Westburg isn't an issue for me anymore."

"Nice. It's always good to have your own wheels."

Amber suddenly flashed on images of the cars on the River Road and their murdered occupants. Having a car hadn't worked out well for any of them. Shaking her head to clear the images, she asked Suzanne when and where she'd like to meet.

"How about six tomorrow night at Cavallaro's? They have really good Italian food."

"It's a date," Amber said and hung up. It occurred to her she'd be driving home possibly after dark alone on River Road. The murderer only kills couples, and I'll be by myself. I'll be safe, she thought.

When she got home, Amber told her mom she'd be out for dinner the next night.

"That's fine dear. I think Scarlet and John have a date. Your father and I are going to the movies and out for pizza. I can cook lots of things, but I do like a good pizza."

Amber was completely shocked. This was a first for her. Her parents going to the movies and eating pizza. Life was full of surprises.

Wednesday was children's program day at the library, Amber's favorite day of the week. She loved the little kids' enthusiasm and enjoyed helping them pick out a stack of books.

At the end of the day, she walked outside with Max, grinning when she saw her car in the lot. A car gave a person such freedom. So many possibilities and opportunities.

"I see you're still driving to work," Max said.

"Yes, but only because I'm meeting Suzanne for dinner tonight in

Westburg. I'm going to start walking again. It's good for me and good for the bank account. Gas is not cheap."

"True." Max's face took on a concerned look. "Meeting Suzanne again? This is becoming a weekly event. I doubt she has anything more to share on the murders. That last stuff she told you about Annie Forst seemed a little far-fetched. Gay lovers from her past hunting her down to take revenge?"

"You're making it sound crazier than it was. Kind of made sense the way she told it but sometimes you get a feeling from someone when they're telling a story that you can't explain when you're telling other people what they said."

"Still," Max said. "I'm kind of suspicious of her."

"She's lonely. Her sister is dead. Her father is a cold fish, and her mother has basically retreated into a veil of grief. She has no one to talk to. She finds it easy to talk to me."

"Be careful, okay? As your mother says, you are too trusting."

"I just pretend to be. Under the surface I am a seething mass of suspicion and distrust."

Max snorted. "Yeah. Right. See you tomorrow night. I'm assuming the Murder Crew is gathering as usual."

"Of course." Amber nodded, started the car, and drove toward Westburg on River Road.

CHAPTER SIXTY-FOUR

Amber found the restaurant easily since it was on the main road. After she parked and got out, she looked around warily. Despite Suzanne's assurances that Chief Wallace wouldn't mess with her, Amber didn't want to run into him.

She sprinted to the restaurant, slipping quickly inside. The gracious Italian waiter greeted her and took her to where Suzanne was already seated with a glass of red wine in front of her.

"Amber, how wonderful to see you. Would you like a glass of wine or something to drink?"

"I better not. I have to drive home and I'd rather not be stopped on River Road by a park ranger. Or by anyone else for that matter."

Suzanne laughed. It was a nice sound. She'd changed so much from that repressed woman Amber first met at her sister's memorial.

They perused the menu for a few minutes. Amber never knew what to order in Italian restaurants because her mother always made the same dishes at home so much better. Suzanne recommended something Amber had never heard of, so she said she'd order that.

While waiting for their meals, they munched on bread and chatted. "I'm trying to wrap my head around all the revelations you gave me about Annie Forst. Wondering how her past might have played into what happened."

"I've been thinking about that too. That was my working theory," Suzanne said, "but maybe I should be looking a little closer to home."

Amber couldn't think of anything to say to that. The police certainly hadn't found any suspects locally.

"Do you know Deputy John Talley?"

Amber's stomach clenched. "Yes. I met him at the memorial, and I've interviewed him. What about him?"

"He and Becky dated in middle school, and he was completely besotted with her. When they got to high school, Becky broke up with him. Said she didn't want to be tied down, but they could still be friends."

"The old 'we can still be friends'," Amber nodded.

"He was devastated. Constantly calling, driving by the house, sending gifts. My father finally called his parents and told them to tell John to knock it off. It stopped but Becky said she still felt like he was stalking her. Threatening guys who got too close. Signing up for the same classes."

Amber chewed her bread slowly. "Did you tell the police? Did they know about the relationship?"

"John is the police." Suzanne laughed and then turned serious. "I like John. I like his family. I didn't want to throw them under the bus. But now I wonder if maybe I should have said something."

Amber wondered if she should tell Suzanne that John was dating her sister. This was getting way too convoluted. She thought about her own suspicions about John. That he was just too nice. Was he responsible for Becky's death? Was he a jealous monster? What would happen when Scarlet left to go back to school? Would he snap?

"Earth to Amber."

Amber looked up to see Suzanne staring at her. "Sorry. I was just thinking about all the new possibilities."

"Speaking of possibilities, your boss, Maxine Bolger, is another one you should keep your eye on."

"Max?" Amber was completely confused. "Why would Max kill Becky?"

"I saw her a couple of times with Annie. Having lunch. Hanging out."

Amber's brain was trying to figure out what Suzanne was trying to say. "What are you suggesting?"

"Seriously Amber. You must have noticed that your boss is a little butch. You don't think she couldn't have been attracted to Annie? Young. Attractive. Vivacious."

All Amber could think about was Ida saying that she and Max weren't a couple but that didn't necessarily mean that Max wasn't gay. Did it?

"I thought Max was a friend of your mother's?" Amber said, not knowing why she brought that up.

"Not friends exactly. They served on some committees. Even though Max is from Easton, she's constantly inserting herself in Westburg affairs."

The waiter brought their food, and Amber was momentarily saved from having to say anything else. It was totally absurd to think of Max bludgeoning someone to death on River Road.

After dinner, Suzanne turned the conversation to Amber's family. "You said you have a sister? Was she at the memorial?"

Amber shook her head. "No. She's in law school. Only one year to go."

"Sounds like another Becky. She got the brains. And the looks?"

Amber bristled. She didn't think she was dumb or ugly, which was what Suzanne seemed to be implying. Suzanne must have realized she'd made a mistake. "I'm sorry. I was joking. But that's the way I always felt with Becky."

Amber relented. "Yes. I know what you mean. Scarlet has always been the hero child. Could do no wrong and I'm just trailing in her wake."

"There's one in every family. But you shouldn't feel that way, Amber. You are a wonderful person. Warm and kind. You don't know how much better you made me feel. I almost feel like a have a sister again." She reached across the table and squeezed Amber's hand.

Suzanne walked Amber to her car and gave her a hug. "Drive carefully."

CHAPTER SIXTY-FIVE

Amber had the next day off. When Scarlet got back from her run, they listened to part two of *Drugs Kill* with their mom.

"Your podcasts get better and better," Fluffy said.

"We have two more in the pipeline. Your debut, Mom, the *Bonnie and Clyde* episodes."

"If that's your subtle way of reminding me we have to record the next podcasts, I know that." Scarlet's tone was sharp. "I only have a week left at home and have things I want and need to do. We can record this weekend or when I get to school."

Amber had been trying to remind Scarlet of her responsibilities to the podcast but the information she had learned about John was laying heavy on her heart and she wasn't sure how she would tell Scarlet that John was possibly or even likely the murderer. And then there was the stranger story that Suzanne had told implicating Max. It was easier to wrap her head around John being the murderer than Max. But who could she talk to about any of this?

If she tried to tell Scarlet that her boyfriend hadn't been completely truthful to either of them since he'd never admitted being in a relationship with Becky at all, how would Scarlet take it? On the other hand, did a middle school crush equate to being in a relationship? What explanation would Max have for being seen around town with Annie Forst?

Her head hurt. She felt very alone. Going up to her room, she decided to work on editing the next two podcast episodes. Then she'd go for a long walk. Scarlet popped in and asked if she'd like to get mani-pedis in town at the salon.

"That sounds lovely. I need a treat. Something to take my mind off murder."

Scarlet laughed but Amber was serious.

They asked their mom if she wanted to go. "No dears. That sounds wonderful but I need to find the perfect dish to make tonight for the murder crew. We have five podcasts out in the world. We are going places."

The house smelled wonderful when they returned some hours later. They found Fluffy in the kitchen with pots and pans, mixing bowls, and measuring cups all around.

"Smells great, Mom. What are you planning for us?"

"I am working on Chicken Cordon Bleu with a salad and homemade bread. That's what smells so good. And I'm making profiteroles for dessert. That was a new challenge for me."

"Why are you doing a French meal?" Scarlet asked.

"French food always sounds so elegant and celebratory, don't you think?"

"Let us know what we can do," Amber said.

"For now, get changed and then set the table. I think we'll use grandma's fine China."

Ida and Max showed up at five thirty and dinner was on the table promptly at six. Their father looked suspiciously at the chicken, green beans, and roasted potatoes but after gingerly taking a bite he settled in, eating with gusto. Everyone raved about the meal and as usual Fluffy acted like it was nothing, though Amber knew she was thrilled that everyone enjoyed it.

After dinner they went to the den. "Dessert is on the way," Fluffy announced. Amber and Scarlet helped their mother serve the profiteroles on plates and brought them in along with a coffee pot and cups.

"Did everyone listen to episode four today?" Amber asked as they dug into the delicate French pastries.

Ida's mouth was full, but she nodded. Max swallowed her bite and managed to say yes.

"Once again, I think you hit the right tone. Describing the arrest and the trial and the consequences," Max said. "Our numbers are up again slightly. Hoping to hit 100 listeners in a month or two. I'm going to start doing ads tomorrow and offer more giveaways. I got some old versions of the Bonnie and Clyde movies to offer in a gift pack. I think that will be fun."

Everyone agreed. Max unfolded the Murder board. "Now to our other crime. Any updates on the River Road murders?"

"Didn't you have dinner with Suzanne last night, Amber?" Scarlet asked. "Last time she filled you in on stuff about Annie Forst. Anything new?"

Amber felt like she had a rock stuck down her throat. How could she tell them what Suzanne had said about John or worse, about Max? She swallowed but the rock didn't move. Everyone stared at her. She grabbed a glass of water and gulped the whole thing down.

"This is not going to be easy." They leaned closer. Amber paused again. She couldn't look Scarlet in the face. "Suzanne told me that John Talley was sweet on, or obsessed with, Becky since middle school. She implied he stalked her and made her life miserable until Mr. Laurelwood made him stop." Amber twisted her napkin into knots. "I know that John was on our early list of suspects, and it does concern me he never said anything about this. Didn't mention that he knew Becky."

Amber glanced up and saw that everyone was now staring at Scarlet.

"Goodness Scarlet. That is concerning," Fluffy said.

Scarlet flushed and her mouth was set in a grim line, which Amber knew meant she was angry and trying to control herself before speaking. "Thank you, Amber, for throwing John under the bus. He told me that Suzanne is a bit…

what's the word? Nutty? Controlling? Overly imaginative? Maybe that's harsh but he has told me all about his relationship with Becky. I didn't share it with you all because I don't think a middle school romance had anything to do with a murder ten years later." Scarlet clamped her lips together and looked around the room fiercely, as if challenging anyone to dispute her.

Everyone looked at Amber. She felt they were watching a tennis match with the ball being lobbed between her and Scarlet. "I'm sorry Scarlet. I'm just reporting what Suzanne told me. Since *you* didn't tell us, how did I know this was basically old news to you and that John had unveiled his entire past, including Becky, to you?"

Heads turned back to Scarlet, who took a deep breath before speaking. She seemed calmer. "You're right. I should have mentioned it. It seemed so benign. Little did I know Suzanne would try to imply he was the murderer."

"I think that's a bit strong. She was trying to suggest other people who might have a motive for murder," Amber said.

"She's a bit all over the place," Max said. "First it was people from Annie Forst's past or present—old girlfriends. Jealous lovers. Or random homophobes who committed a hate crime against two lesbians. Now we're on to Becky's old boyfriends?"

"You're right, she is all over the place. This whole thing has made her crazy. She is so worried about her mother, who has been destroyed by this. The not knowing makes it much worse," Amber said.

"Any other theories from Suzanne?" Ida asked.

Amber let out a huge size. "Yes, but you'll like this one even less." She decided to blurt it all out. "She suggested that Max was in a relationship with Annie and was possibly the murderer. Falls in with the jealous girlfriend theory." Amber shut her eyes to the outraged face of Max, who had turned about six shades of purple.

Max started sputtering. "Me? In a relationship? With Annie Forst? I didn't know the woman. I have my taxes done at the office she worked at and met her there. Just a hi are you new here? Not a hey baby, let's get together. We ran into each other once in the Coffee Connection and sat and drank coffee and she talked to me about moving here and how hard it was to meet people. That's it! Not a date. Not a planned meeting. That's the extent of my relationship with Annie."

Everyone turned from Max to Amber, who held up her hands in surrender. "I am only reporting what Suzanne said. I am not saying I believe anything she said. I thought that was what we were doing here. Kicking around ideas."

"You're right, Amber," Fluffy said, trying to calm the waters. "We can't have any secrets from each other, and we have to say what we've heard no matter how ridiculous, even if someone tells you that Ida and I are the killers."

Everyone smiled and helped themselves to a second serving of profiteroles. Amber noticed Scarlet was not smiling with the others.

CHAPTER SIXTY-SIX

*D*uncan *called Amber and asked* if she would like to meet for lunch at The Carvery.

"Okay, I have a late day at the library so that would work. Just have to be done by 2:00," Amber said.

He was waiting on the bench in the front when Amber arrived. He stood and gave her a slight nod. "Ms. Steen. A pleasure as always."

Amber grinned. She liked Duncan. It would suck if he turned out to be the murderer, though she didn't believe he was. They went inside and got a seat in their usual booth. After ordering, Amber asked Duncan if he had heard anything new.

"No, sadly not," he admitted. "I think the FBI is happy to have solved one of the murders. But I believe they may be packing up soon and slinking out of town. There is not one new piece of evidence in the first or second murders other than those random poison pen letters which led nowhere. They interviewed dozens of people. They went over everything, but they can't manufacture something out of thin air. They've probably even interviewed Renn a hundred times hoping he'd crack, but they got nothing."

Amber was shocked. "I thought you said you were sure the murders would be solved."

"I think I said I hoped they would be but not all murders are solved. That's why there are so many cold cases. I guess these will be shelved away and looked at again in ten years. Of course, if the murderer kills again maybe there will be something new to go on. And you? Anything to report?"

Annie updated him on her lunch with Suzanne.

"She seems to be throwing all kinds of people under the bus," Duncan said.

"That was the consensus of everyone at dinner last night. I feel sorry for her. She's so upset by what happened and I can understand it. I'd be crazy if someone killed Scarlet."

"So why have I never been invited to these dinners you mention? I'm hurt." Duncan tried to look sad.

"We don't invite suspects."

Duncan burst out laughing. "Am I still just a suspect to you, Ms. Steen? I was hoping I was more." He leered at her and waggled his eyebrows.

"Yes. You're comic relief." Amber grinned.

They finished their lunch and both headed back to work.

Amber was counting the days down until Scarlet left. Originally, she had high hopes they'd solve the River Road murders in the month Scarlet was home. How absurd. The FBI with all their resources was giving up, according to Duncan. She didn't even have any sources in the police departments like Duncan did, and he'd apparently also given up hope. Nine days. Scarlet would be gone in nine days. They had one weekend, five workdays, one last Saturday, and then Scarlet would pack up and leave on Sunday to be at work on Monday. And she'd be sharing Scarlet with John during those nine days. Amber frowned.

Walking into the library, Amber felt awkward, wondering if Max was still upset with her. She was in the break room putting her purse in a locker when Max walked in. "Max, I'm sorry..." she began.

"Don't be silly Amber. I'm sorry for getting so angry last night." Max sighed. "You were only telling us what Suzanne said."

"I know but I felt like I was accusing you."

"That's the problem with murder. Everyone is under suspicion. People's lives are ruined because the crime is never solved, and distrust remains."

"I hope not," Amber said.

"People will continue to talk about this. They'll whisper and point fingers and make subtle accusations and no one will ever feel safe."

"I saw Duncan today. He seems to think the FBI is giving up and that unless there is another murder, there's not enough evidence to solve these crimes."

"He could be right. On the other hand, maybe the killer got what they wanted. Maybe there were always three killers, and the crimes aren't related. Maybe this will eventually become old news and occasionally the newspaper will write articles about the anniversary of the River Road murders and remember when."

"By the way, I wanted to ask you about something else Suzanne said. I mentioned something about you and her mother being friends and she kind of scoffed at that and made some rude comment about you two had served on some committees together and there wasn't much more to it than that."

Max blushed furiously. "I guess I did exaggerate the friend angle when we were going to the memorial. Though there was a time I thought we were friends. I was thinking of moving to Westburg. Felt I didn't have much of a future here in Easton, so I joined committees and began to mingle with the 'right' people." Max rolled her eyes when she said *right*.

"I had the idea I could become the head librarian in Westburg, which would have been a step up. I met Helene Laurelwood, and we seemed to hit it off quite well. I thought I had the job in the bag when I found out she was on the interview committee." Max paused. "I couldn't have been more wrong. A question came up about book banning, though they didn't quite use that word, in public libraries. I made the mistake of thinking I was among educated worldly people and spoke freely about how I was opposed to censorship. I think some books about gay teenagers were specifically mentioned, and I said that group needed all the support they could get, even if it was only from a book.

"As I spoke, I could see Helene's face change as if she was seeing me, the real me, for the first time." Max looked at Amber. "She called a week later to thank me for applying but wanted to tell me personally someone else had been hired for the job. She said how sorry she was. She didn't sound the least bit sorry.

"It was a wake-up call. Just because people live in nice houses doesn't mean they're nice. Or open minded or kind. I can only imagine how she would have responded if she found out her daughter was friends with a lesbian."

"That's probably what Suzanne was afraid of," Amber said.

"Agree," Max said. "And now, to work. We do get paid to work here."

Ahh. The plot thickens. Well, not really but I think I've decided on my next murder. I've selected my victims, including that little know-it-all Amber Steen. Or maybe I'll set her up as the murderer. This might be my swan song. Leave people wondering about these crimes for years to come.

CHAPTER SIXTY-SEVEN

Scarlet's last weekend at home passed quickly. Once again, they did not record the next podcast, and Amber was getting nervous. They only had the two *Bonnie and Clyde* episodes lined up to air and then nothing for the weeks after. She had dropped numerous hints about recording, but Scarlet continued to blow her off, saying she'd do it when she got back to school. Amber doubted that would happen because knowing Scarlet she would dive deep into her internship and have no time for anything else.

And despite Scarlet claiming she wasn't upset with her over dropping the revelation about John's relationship with Becky in front of the entire murder crew, Amber noticed a chill in the air. Scarlet seemed to be avoiding her. The only time Scarlet sat with her was at dinner, but she was often not there since she and John usually had plans.

Monday morning, Duncan called. "Can you meet at our place at noon?"

"I love that we have a place." Amber laughed. "See you then. I'm hoping you'll give me the news I'm dying to hear."

Amber found Duncan in the back booth and quickly sat down. "So. You got any good news for me?"

Duncan paused when the waitress walked up. They both ordered and after she walked away, Duncan said, "I have news for you but not good, or at least not what you're going to want to hear."

Amber's stomach lurched. "What?"

"As I suspected, the FBI is pulling out. No big press conference this time. No 'Sandy Foss reporting' as he strokes his gorgeous mane of hair." Duncan grinned. "Just a small article in tomorrow's paper that the FBI will keep the office here open and will continue to investigate any leads that come in. But it won't mention Agent Devereaux and most of the agents are leaving. And we know there will be no new leads."

"Unless there's another murder," Amber said.

"Hopeful, are we?" Duncan laughed.

"Frustrated, I guess." Amber's lips twisted in a frown. "I don't know why I thought I was going to be the one to solve these murders. I'm a nobody with absolutely no crime solving experience."

"You're a True Crime Podcaster. That counts for something," Duncan said. "By the way, do you actually have a true crime podcast on the air or were you just working on this one hoping to break the case?"

Amber blushed. "I do have a podcast. It's called *The Murderer You Know*. New episodes drop on Thursday mornings, but you can listen anytime."

"Impressive. I'll have to give it a listen."

"Not very impressive when you realize that was how I hoped to make my fame and fortune." Amber smiled sadly.

"Everyone has to start somewhere."

The waitress brought their sandwiches, and they ate quietly. Leaving the restaurant, Duncan shook Amber's hand. "Ms. Steen, it has been a pleasure knowing you and working on this crime together. I do hope we will see each other again. Take care of yourself." He turned and walked down the sidewalk to his car.

At dinner, Amber told her parents and Scarlet, who was spending a rare evening home, what Duncan had said. "The FBI is slinking quietly out of town. I guess the evidence is too cold. Or maybe they'll try to blame it all on Renn at some point and call it a day."

"So, your crush is taking off." Scarlet sneered. "Whatever are you going to do?"

Amber was shocked at Scarlet's mean and hurtful behavior.

"He is not my crush. I never even spoke to the man." Amber tried to keep the anger out of her voice.

"The FBI didn't seem to do anything but upset everyone all over again," Fluffy snorted. "I think even our local police could have solved the third murder."

"It all seemed so promising when they first arrived," Amber said. "I guess we'll never know."

Her father snorted in agreement. The rest of the meal continued in silence.

CHAPTER SIXTY-EIGHT

Tuesday, she told Max about the FBI leaving. Max nodded. "Yeah, I saw a small article by Duncan on page two of the paper this morning. Basically, says nothing. The usual blah-blah-blah about keeping the cases open. Not giving up."

Amber nodded sadly then brightened. "Maybe they're trying to lure the murderer into a false sense of security. Claiming to be leaving but setting a trap?"

"Anything is possible," Max agreed.

Wednesday, Suzanne called. "OMG, you have to come meet for lunch today."

"What's up?" Amber asked.

"I'll tell you at lunch. Meet me at the Coffee Connection."

Amber drove to Westburg. Having her own car again was wonderful. The wind in her hair. Freedom to come and go as she pleased. It suddenly occurred to her if she got into the library science program at Westburg College, she'd be driving this road a lot. By herself. Sometimes after dark. It would make her feel so much better if the murderer was caught.

Walking into the café, she spotted Suzanne in the back corner and squeezed into the seat across from her.

"I guess you heard the FBI is giving up. Probably gone by now," Suzanne said.

Amber nodded.

"That was just some dog and pony show. I think they knew all along they wouldn't be able to solve the murders but acted like they were coming in with guns blazing. That the murderer would break down in fear and confess when he found out the FBI was on the case."

"I'm beginning to think the murders will never be solved," Amber said. She paused as the waitress came up to take their orders. She ordered a salad and water. Suzanne ordered some overly complicated coffee drink.

"Is that all you're getting? Coffee?" Amber asked.

"Yes. I'm too wrought up to eat. I have more news I can't wait to tell you. John Talley came bursting into my office yesterday and started yelling at me about telling you about him and Becky. I had to drag him into the back room since everyone was staring."

Amber felt like a deer caught in headlights and only nodded.

"I had no idea how he knew I told you since I knew you wouldn't have told him and then he dropped his big bomb shell. Apparently, he's dating your sister? Scarlet?" Suzanne's voice was shrill. "Is that true? Why didn't you tell me?"

Amber's brain went into gridlock. This was getting too complicated. "I didn't think about it. I met him at the memorial, which I told you, and he dropped by one night after Scarlet came home and they really hit it off and started dating. Didn't seem worth mentioning."

"Not worth mentioning?" Suzanne tried to keep her voice down, but it wasn't working. "He is a dangerous man. I'm convinced he killed Becky and you're letting your sister be alone and drive around with him?"

A chill shot through Amber. "My sister is leaving this Sunday. Going up to school for an internship so… I think she'll be safe. That's only four nights away."

"She's leaving Sunday?" Suzanne seemed momentarily confused. "I didn't know it was that soon…" She quickly recovered. "That's good but you need to keep an eye on them until she leaves."

Amber knew that wasn't going to be possible.

"Or at least warn her," Suzanne said.

"To be honest, Suzanne, Scarlet is angry with me for suggesting that John is a murderer. I'm kind of mad at her. I was just reporting his relationship with Becky, and she went ballistic. I think she thinks I'm jealous that John liked her better than me." Amber paused. Was she jealous? She didn't think so. She didn't have time for a relationship. Though neither did Scarlet and she managed to squeeze in time for one. Amber sighed. "Though of course I don't want her to be hurt, so I'll keep an eye on her until she's safely away from here."

"I know how you feel," Suzanne said. "As much as I loved Becky, I don't think she felt the same way about me. And my parents were just gaga over her, and it sometimes got to me. Do your parents treat Scarlet like the hero child and you're nothing?"

Amber thought about it. "No…" She paused. "My parents are good about not treating Scarlet that way. Or treating me like a failure. Which I kind of am… but I'm getting my life together. But it was hard sometimes living under her shadow."

Suzanne reached across the table and took Amber's hand in hers. "Believe me, I understand how you feel. I am so glad to have you as a friend. It fills in some of the emptiness."

"Thanks." Amber smiled and squeezed Suzanne's hand back. "I don't have many friends. Any friends? So, I'm glad too."

Driving home, Amber wondered, could John be the murderer? She had suspected him from the beginning. How could she make sure Scarlet stayed safe until Sunday? There was no point in trying to talk to her, she'd only get mad again.

CHAPTER SIXTY-NINE

Thursday morning Amber, Scarlet, and Fluffy listened to the first episode of *Bonnie and Clyde* together while they ate breakfast and drank coffee.

Both Amber and Scarlet praised their mother and said it was the best episode to date. Fluffy waved off their compliments, blushing deeply, but Amber knew she was secretly thrilled.

At the library, she and Max discussed the latest episode. "Your mom is a natural. I think this will really put our numbers up," Max said.

Once again Amber didn't know whether to be happy or angry. It was her podcast, and her mom was going to get them noticed? Well, she realized, not many murder podcasts had sweet cookie-baking guest hosts.

She told Max what Suzanne had said about John and how worried she seemed about him dating Scarlet. "Should I be worried? Sometimes I think she's borderline hysterical. She does seem to have it in for John."

"Scarlet is leaving on Sunday, right? She has three nights left here. Tonight, we have our Murder Crew gathering, so she's safe there. What's she doing her last two nights?"

Amber grimaced. "Saturday we're having her goodbye dinner with the family, but she is going out with John for their last dinner tomorrow night." She paused. "Should I be worried?"

"Seems unlikely he would kill Scarlet when everyone knows they're out together," Max said, curling her lips. "Maybe we can talk about it tonight."

"Oh no!" Amber exclaimed. "Please don't. She's already mad at me, and I'm hoping we can bury the hatchet before she leaves. Last thing I want to do is say anything about what Suzanne told me or said about John."

"Okay. Mum's the word." Max put her finger to her lips.

The last full cast Murder Crew dinner went off without a cross word. Fluffy made tacos with all the fillings and Spanish rice. For dessert she had baked a tres leches cake. Amber noticed her father grumbled less about these exotic meals since he still got steak and potatoes most evenings.

In the den over dessert, they congratulated each other on another successful episode. "The numbers keep climbing each week," Max announced.

Amber suggested while she was doing her internship, Scarlet could guest host on the second part of the two-part podcasts. That would keep the pressure off her. "The second part is the evidence and the trial, and that's where we need you," Amber said. "Mom, Ida, and even Max can guest on the first part. But only if that works for you, Scarlet. Don't want to add additional stress."

"Yeah. Maybe that will work," Scarlet said.

Amber felt deflated. She had hoped for something more from Scarlet. Some kind of appreciation that Amber was thinking of her and trying to ease the burden. But all she got was a lukewarm response.

Amber tried to focus on the happy conversation, but she couldn't help but feel angry. Two more nights and then Scarlet would be gone.

Friday morning, Amber found her mother in the kitchen with cookbooks spread out all over the kitchen table and countertops. She poured herself a cup of coffee and watched her mom opening and closing cookbooks with resigned sighs.

"What's up, Mom? Planning the next State dinner at the White House?

Or tea with the Queen?"

"No. Scarlet's goodbye dinner tomorrow night. I want to find the perfect recipe."

Amber's anger boiled over. Maybe she had been wrong about how her parents treated her and Scarlet. She didn't remember any elaborate dinners when she went off to school. "Good grief, Mom, she's not leaving to spend a year at the International Space Station. She'll be a couple of hours away at school. She can even visit on the weekend. You can talk on the phone."

Fluffy looked up. "I know, dear. But she is well on her way to becoming a full-fledged adult." A tear briefly glistened in Fluffy's eye. "After this internship and one more year of school, she'll become a lawyer and who knows where she'll go."

"Yeah. She might go as far as working in Westburg." Amber grabbed a banana and marched out of the kitchen. She sat on the front porch with her banana and coffee. As she sat there angrily munching on her banana, John pulled up in front of the house. Amber waved but he seemed to be deliberately ignoring her, acting like he was fiddling with some dial on his dashboard. The door opened and Scarlet came running out. She shouted bye before turning and seeing it was Amber on the porch not their mother.

"Oh… ummm… going out with John. See you later," she said as she ran to John's jeep. They pulled away and disappeared around the corner.

Amber shoved her banana peel into her empty coffee cup and stared off in the direction they had driven. She felt… betrayed… angry… sad, and maybe a little jealous. Not of John. She didn't care about that but of Scarlet in general. She had her life so together. She had been such a good sister to Amber, helping her come up with the podcast idea but she didn't even seem interested in continuing with that. No doubt once she got to school, she wouldn't even record with Amber anymore.

She walked into the kitchen, threw the peel in the trash, and rinsed out her cup and put it in the dishwasher. "I saw Scarlet heading out the door and driving off with John," she said. "I thought they were going out tonight."

Her mother didn't look up from the cookbook. "I think they wanted to spend the whole day together since tomorrow she'll be with us and then she's leaving Sunday."

"Nice," Amber said and hoped she didn't sound too bitchy. "I'm going for a walk." She paused. "Unless you need some help." She didn't really want to help but she didn't want to leave her mom in the lurch.

"No dear. I'm fine. Might need you later. Enjoy your walk."

Amber walked around the downtown area, staring in shop windows but not going in. She didn't need anything. She was trying to distract herself from thinking about Scarlet. She began to think about Suzanne instead. About what she said about being friends. Amber smiled. She needed some friends her own age. Well, closer to her own age. She'd spent the last few months with her mom, Ida, and Max. She loved them all, but they were… old. Maybe Suzanne would like to be on the podcast. Another young voice would be nice since it didn't seem like she'd have Scarlet with her anymore.

When she got to the house, her mom was gone. She found a note on the counter: *gone to the store. Back soon.* Amber slumped down in one of the kitchen chairs and put her head in her hands. She felt totally alone and abandoned. She went up to her room and flopped on her bed. She started thinking about what Suzanne said about John and about keeping an eye on Scarlet. How was she going to do that? She'd let them drive off this morning and had no idea where they were or what their plans were.

Bolting up, she grabbed her phone. In high school, she and Scarlet had put location tracking apps on each other's phones so they could keep an eye on each other. Were they still active? She pushed the button and there was a flashing dot. Scarlet and, she assumed, John were in Westburg at the botanical garden at the college. That seemed innocent enough.

She would check again later. She closed her eyes and fell into a deep sleep. Amber heard her mother's voice calling from a great distance. It was dark and she couldn't find her mother. She realized she was on River Road and was searching desperately. "Mom!" she called, over and over.

"Amber, wake up. I think you're having a nightmare."

Opening her eyes, Amber saw her mother leaning over her. She sat up.

"God. I was having a terrible dream. You were lost on River Road, and I couldn't find you."

Fluffy sat on the edge of the bed and hugged Amber. "That sounds awful. But I'm safe and you're safe. I don't think we need to worry about River Road anymore. A terrible chapter in our lives but I think it's over now. My personal feeling is Renn did them all, but they don't have enough evidence to charge him. He's locked up and that's the end of it."

"You're probably right," Amber said. "I feel awful. I hate napping. It makes me so groggy." Amber stood up and stretched. "What time is it?"

"Almost four."

"I slept that long? Let me grab a shower. That might wake me up." As soon as Fluffy left the room, Amber checked her phone. Scarlet and John now seemed to be at the movie theater. As long as they were moving around, they were safe. But they were in Westburg and had to drive home via River Road.

Amber showered and dressed and headed to the kitchen. The cookbooks were all put away but there were stacks of notes on the table. Amber picked them up and started going through them.

"Oh, no, you don't." Fluffy snatched them away and smiled. "I want you to be surprised as well."

"Okay, Mom. You're in charge. What's for dinner tonight?"

"Actually, you'll have to settle for leftovers. Your dad has some kind of work function, a goodbye party I think, so I didn't make anything."

"I'm always happy with your leftovers. Let me see what we have in the fridge." Amber was starved since she'd only had a banana for breakfast and nothing for lunch.

After she ate, she went up to her room to check her phone with an impending sense of dread. She kept remembering Suzanne saying to keep a watch on Scarlet. She searched for Scarlet's location. Looked like they were at dinner in Westburg. It was past six, and they had to drive back on River Road. Amber paced. She didn't know what she should do.

CHAPTER SEVENTY

mber's phone rang and she was so startled she almost dropped it. "Hello," she almost shouted into the phone. She thought it might be Scarlet calling her for help, but it was Suzanne.

"Do you know where your sister is?" Suzanne asked.

It sounded like a line from a very old, very bad movie. "In Westburg," Amber replied. "Having dinner at the Steak Palace with John."

Suzanne groaned. "What did I tell you? You need to be watching her."

"I am kind of watching her. I have a trace on her phone location."

"Okay. Good, but not great," Suzanne said. "Get in your car and drive to Westburg. Meet me in the town square. At least we can follow them home when they start back to Easton."

Suzanne hung up abruptly and Amber stared at the phone. This seemed so over the top, but Amber couldn't rid the uneasy feeling in her gut. She grabbed her jacket and ran down the steps. "Hey mom, I'm going to Westburg to hang out with Suzanne."

Fluffy started to say, "I don't think you should be out on River Road…" but Amber had shut the door and was in her car before her mom could finish her sentence.

Traffic was unusually heavy on Main Street. Friday night in Easton, Amber rolled her eyes. Seemed like the only thing to do was cruise up and down the street and slow down to wave to people you knew. She got caught by every light. It was dark by the time she entered River Road. She knew she couldn't speed but it was hard not to drive a hundred miles an hour to Westburg.

Her phone rang again. She prayed it was Scarlet, but it was Suzanne again. "They've left the restaurant. Where are you?"

"On River Road," Amber answered.

"Pull over and check Scarlet's location."

Amber did as Suzanne said. She slowed down and pulled into one of the scenic outlooks. She opened her phone and clicked on the app. A chill shot through her. They seemed to be parked on River Road in one of the pull-offs close to Westburg. She stared at the phone, but the dot did not move. She immediately called Suzanne. "Oh no," she said. Her voice trembled. Her hands shook. "They're parked on River Road. Near Westburg."

"Keep driving," Suzanne said. "Meet me at the outlook by milepost five. I think that's where they are. Dim your headlights and pull in. I'll be there. Then we can sneak up to the car."

Amber could barely drive, she was shaking so badly. It was a cloudy night and seemed to have gone dark in seconds. She finally got close to milepost five. She dimmed her headlights, slowed her speed, and coasted into the parking lot.

She didn't see Suzanne or her car. Had she not arrived yet? She quickly looked at her phone. Scarlet had not moved. The dot still blinked in the same spot.

A knock at the window almost made her scream in fear. She turned to see Suzanne looking in with a finger over her mouth to indicate Amber should be quiet. Amber had to take a few deep breaths to calm her pounding heart, then she slowly opened the door and got out.

"Where on earth did you come from?" she whispered fiercely.

"Don't worry about that. I've found John's Jeep. Follow me." Suzanne turned and walked into the woods. Amber realized after a few minutes that Suzanne was following a trail. When they got to the edge of the trees, Suzanne put her hand out to stop Amber from stepping out into the open. She put her finger up to her lips again and whispered, "Hush. Right there."

Amber stared but couldn't see anything. The moon suddenly emerged from the clouds and light bounced off the hood of John's Jeep.

"You see it," Suzanne whispered.

"Yes. But why are they just sitting there?" Amber whispered back. She couldn't imagine that they would pick a lonely spot on River Road to make out.

"Think about it. Young. In love… or maybe they fell asleep?" Suzanne grinned. Her appearance gave Amber an odd feeling. She remembered when she first met Suzanne and couldn't quite put a finger on her expressions. There was something off about the entire scene.

"Let's sneak up and catch them in the act?" Suzanne snickered.

Amber did not want to catch Scarlet in the act. She wanted to call her sister and make sure she was all right and then go home.

"I'll call her. She doesn't need to know we're here. I'll make up some excuse. We can still watch them until they leave. Keep an eye on them."

"Sure. Brilliant idea. Why don't you do that?" Suzanne said.

Something in Suzanne's tone bothered Amber. She ignored the feeling, attributing it to her concern about Scarlet. Upset because Scarlet was leaving. Upset because Scarlet was mad at her. Upset that Scarlet was parked on the murder road with a potential killer.

Amber pulled out her phone and pushed Scarlet's number. Amber could hear the phone ringing inside the car. Scarlet did not answer, and Amber couldn't see any movement in the car.

"Oh my God," Amber almost shrieked. "Are they dead? Have they been killed?" Amber was on the verge of hysteria and tears.

"Oh, no, I hope not," Suzanne said. "How awful. Maybe we should check." Again, her tone was off. There was no genuine concern in her voice.

They walked out of the woods and Amber ran to the car.

"Don't get carried away," Suzanne's voice came from behind her.

Amber rushed up to the side door and grabbed the knob, yanking with all her might, but the door was locked. She stared inside the car and could see Scarlet and John slumped over in their seats. A scream almost erupted from her lips. She was too late. Scarlet was dead. She looked closer and could see Scarlet move a little. John appeared to be breathing, though neither one responded to her pounding on the car window.

"Oh dear. What could the matter be?" Suzanne whispered in her ear. Amber whirled around in fear. Suzanne stood with a hammer in her hand. "I'll take your phone now," she said, snatching it out of Amber's hand.

"What the hell is going on? Scarlet and John are locked in a car, apparently unconscious, and you're not worried?"

"No," Suzanne replied with a bit of a smirk. "I guess not. Since I'm the one who knocked them out. Thanks for the heads-up where they were. I pretended to run into them and apologized for saying stuff about John and Becky. I had a bottle of cider and asked them to drink a toast and forgive me. So absurdly easy. Even though neither one of them likes me and probably had their suspicions about me, they didn't want to be rude." She snorted. "People are such fools. I laced their drinks with tranquilizers that I stole from my mom."

Amber's mind bounced wildly all over the place. What was Suzanne saying? Why had she drugged John and Scarlet? Why had she dragged Amber out to River Road? The full horror of the truth began to slowly dawn on her. "It's you. You're the murderer," she gasped.

"Bingo." Suzanne gave her a triumphant smile. "Aren't you proud of yourself? You solved the murders, just like you hoped to do. Unfortunately, it's kind of all downhill from here. You won't achieve fame and glory. In fact, I'm considering setting you up as the murderer."

Amber went completely ice cold. She should have recognized the insanity from the moment she met Suzanne. At the memorial, she wasn't mourning the death of her little sister, she was trying to cover up her role in her sister's murder.

"You killed Becky?" Amber asked.

"You're getting smarter and smarter. Just a little too late sweetie." Suzanne grinned.

"I understand why you did it. We talked about this. Having sisters who are the hero kids while we get the leftovers." Amber tried to hide her fear. "I don't blame you. I'm all in for doing in John and Scarlet. Maybe you and I can form a team. They'll seriously never catch us."

Suzanne burst out laughing. It took her awhile to control her laughter. "You're seriously so pathetic. Trying to suck up to me and claim you want to become my partner in crime. Guess what? I lied again. I did not kill Becky out of jealousy." Suzanne's face twisted and her voice became mean and bitter. "I killed her because she was a lesbian. I killed her because it would have horrified my mother to have a gay daughter. She'd have been so ashamed. Never again able to hold her head up in Westburg society. But, come to find out, losing Becky was just as devastating. Maybe more so." Suzanne stopped as if overcome by anger. "I did it for her. For my mother, and she barely knows I exist."

Amber was trying to come up with a plan, not only to save herself but to save John and Scarlet.

"So, you killed her out of love?" Amber said, hoping to keep Suzanne talking while she figured out what to do. "What about the college kids?"

Suzanne choked out a bitter laugh. "More pathetic puppies. I stopped and asked them to help me with a flat tire. I discovered after killing Becky and Annie, I kind of liked the thrill of it. I saw some tail lights passing on the road, so I threw them in my trunk. That weekend, I drove up to the woods and tried to bury them. In hindsight, I should have thrown them in the river. Digging two human-sized holes is not easy."

Amber didn't interrupt. Why hadn't she told her mother where she was going? Or Max. Or Ida. She was out here all alone in the woods with a psycho serial killer.

"I was rather upset," Suzanne continued, "when the third murder took place. I'd been planning my next one since it was the six-month anniversary, but then that idiot Renn killed those kids. However, it did confuse the police even more, so in a way it worked out. Now," Suzanne looked at Amber, "it's time for my six-month killing."

Amber's mouth was dry and she couldn't speak.

"Since you are my dearest friend, I'm going to give you some possible scenarios and see which one you prefer.

"In the first, I bludgeon you and Scarlet to death with my favorite little murder weapon, my hammer. Afterwards, I shoot John with his service revolver and make it look like suicide, setting him up as the killer, who after one last murderous rampage, is overcome by remorse and kills himself. That one is pretty good, don't you think?"

Suzanne didn't wait for Amber to answer. "In the second, you go ballistic and kill John and Scarlet. Out of jealousy, psychotic rage, whatever. I'll let your buddy Duncan Abbott figure the motive out when he writes his wrap up of the River Road Murders.

"But if you supposedly kill John and Scarlet with my hammer, and set their car on fire, for old time's sake, what happens with you? How do I dispose of your body? You don't have a gun to kill yourself. I guess you could use John's? Or do I just make you disappear into the sunset? Maybe you could walk into the river to kill yourself?

"I really needed more time to figure things out properly. Unfortunately Scarlet's impending departure moved the timeline up. Couldn't let her get away, could I?" Suzanne laughed. "I even considered inserting myself into the final act. I could say I was driving by and saw the fire and in my fear and confusion I hit you with my car? But what if I don't kill you? I can't drive back and forth over you. Doesn't really look like an accident that way. Plus, I'm not sure I want to draw any attention to myself.

"Any thoughts? Preferences? Would you prefer to be beaten to death, shot, or run over with a car?"

"My mom knows I was driving to Westburg to see you," Amber managed to say.

This seemed to cause Suzanne some momentary concern before she laughed. "No problem. I'll say you never showed up. The hour grows late. Since you are my dear, dear friend, I'll let you choose the manner of your death. However, you must choose fast or I'll make the decision for you." Suzanne tapped the hammer on her palm.

Amber imagined the first whack from the hammer, wondering if it would kill her instantly or at least knock her out so she wouldn't feel the rest of the blows. Never in her wildest dreams had she imagined dying this way. She closed her eyes. She didn't want to see the hammer in motion. Unexpectedly, a loud piercing sound came from John's Jeep. Suzanne jerked her head around and Amber's eyes shot open and she pounced.

She slammed into Suzanne, knocking her backwards. While not a particularly muscular person, the months of walking and moving piles of books had toned Amber. She grabbed at the hammer while forcing Suzanne backwards. They struggled. Suzanne wouldn't let go. Amber was desperate because she was fighting for three lives.

Suzanne suddenly tripped backwards over a tree root and fell with Amber on top of her. Amber got her hands on the hammer. Suzanne scratched, bit, and kicked Amber, who finally wrenched the hammer out of her hands. Amber stumbled to her feet and raised the hammer to strike, but hesitated. Maybe she could convince Suzanne to surrender. Amber didn't want to smash someone's head in, even someone as vile as an apparent serial killer.

"Don't move. If you do, I'll hit you with the hammer," Amber panted. She worried she might faint from the fear and exertion. A jolt of adrenalin kept her up.

"I'm sorry… I'm sorry… don't hurt me," Suzanne cried, covering her head with her hands.

Amber heard a sound behind her and momentarily turned away from Suzanne to see if someone else was sneaking up. Maybe Suzanne had a partner. John stumbled out of the Jeep, falling on his hands and knees. A movement caught her eye, and she turned back to see Suzanne leaping toward her, hands stretched out like talons in front of her. Without hesitation, Amber swung the hammer. She hit Suzanne in the arm which slowed her down for a moment, then she roared and attacked again. Amber hit her in the head, and she went down like a slab of meat.

Staring at Suzanne's crumpled form, Amber wondered if she should hit her again for good measure. She almost felt the same thrill Suzanne must have experienced when she killed her sister and Annie. She raised the hammer but she stopped when she heard John call out, "Don't hit her again. Use my handcuffs. Cuff her and call 911."

John sat on the ground, leaning back on the Jeep. He weakly handed Amber the cuffs. "I feel awful. What happened?"

"Let me take care of Suzanne and I'll tell you the whole story." Amber cuffed Suzanne's wrist to her ankle. No way could she run away now. She was still unconscious. Amber found her phone on the ground and called her mother. When Fluffy answered, Amber explained where they were and told her to call Sheriff Fenster and some ambulances. She asked her not to call the Park rangers or Chief Wallace. Then she ran back to the car to check on Scarlet.

CHAPTER SEVENTY-ONE

*A**mber sat on the back* of an ambulance, her arm around Scarlet. John sat on the other side of Scarlet. They had been checked out by the EMTs, and other than some scratches and bruises on Amber and the after-effects of the drugs on Scarlet and John, the EMTs said they were fine.

A chaotic scene surrounded them. The police cars all had their lights flashing, which added a surreal glow to the scene. Thankfully, Sheriff Fenster arrived first, followed by the ambulances. Police cruisers from Westburg carrying Chief Wallace and park ranger vehicles with Chief Ranger Richardson in tow arrived a few minutes later. Sheriff Fenster probably called them.

Amber saw Suzanne in an ambulance being tended and watched carefully by two deputies. She reportedly had regained consciousness and was ready to be transported to the hospital or jail.

Ida, Fluffy, Max, and even Amber's dad had shown up. The police tried to stop them from parking but luckily Sheriff Fenster stepped forward and escorted them to the ambulance where Amber and Scarlet were sitting. Fluffy fussed over her daughters and their father stood watch as if to warn anyone away from hurting his daughters again.

A black sedan drove up with Agent Devereaux and several other FBI agents. He walked the perimeter of the crime scene, which had been taped off. John's Jeep sat in the dead center. After consulting with various officials, Agent D approached Amber. "So you're the young lady that finally broke the case?" He shook her hand. Amber sensed her father stepping closer.

"I'm not sure if I broke the case or the case almost broke me." Amber's voice cracked. She suddenly felt overcome by the horror of what happened and thought she might faint.

"Thank you. We all thank you."

Amber noticed Chief Wallace and Ranger Richardson standing in the background. They did not look happy or thankful.

Sheriff Fenster stepped up and said to Agent Devereaux. "Amber's an Easton girl, born and raised. Smart and determined."

Fluffy handed out bags of cookies to the EMTs, deputies from Easton, and even Agent Devereaux. "You look like you could use a cookie," she said. Agent Devereaux tried to hide his smile.

A news van pulled up and Sandy Foss and his camera person set up and began a live news report. After he finished, he asked Amber if she might give him an exclusive. He stared at her and said, "Aren't you the True Crime Podcaster from the Memorial? I should have called you." He laughed and brushed his hair back.

Amber smiled. "You should talk to my mom and her assistants, my aunt Ida and my boss, Max. Without them, I could never have solved the crime." Fluffy blushed and handed Sandy a bag of cookies.

Sandy took the cookies and said, "You're my number one fan, as I remember. Let's go over to where it's quieter and we can talk." Fluffy, Max, and Ida walked over to the news van.

Amber squeezed Scarlet, who hugged her back. "Thanks, sis," she whispered. "Thanks for saving all of us and solving the murders. I knew you could do it."

Amber sensed her father moving over and turned to see Duncan Abbott standing next to her. "It's about time you showed up, Ace reporter Abbott." She smiled.

"I've been here. It's been hard to get close to the Golden Girl. I did get a bag of cookies from your mom when I introduced myself. I even got an invite to the next Murder Crew dinner. I can only say, it's about time." Duncan grinned.

"Remember you were a suspect up until a few hours ago. Suspects don't get invites. Now you're in the clear, Mr. Abbott."

"And so are you, Ms. Steen. I hope you'll give me that exclusive interview."

"Only if you promise to guest star on my podcast when we feature the *River Road Murders.*"

"I look forward to it."

Amber smiled at Duncan. He had the warmest brown eyes behind his fringe of hair.

THE END

Acknowledgements

First to my family—my husband Greg and my daughters Allie, Elena and Leah.

They have read my books and encouraged me from the beginning.

And as always, thank you to my wonderful editor/publisher Narielle Living of Blue Fortune Enterprises, LLC. This is our fourth book together and I think we're getting better at this with each one!

Thank you as well to my critique group: Peter Stipe, Dave Pistorese, Mark Greene, Diana Caron, Tish Brown, Sandy Hicks, Jennie Kelly, Jan Marry, Kelly Ronayne, and Dave Wolfe. Some of them have been there from the very beginning helping to make my books better.

And finally to *The Murderer You Know* podcast, who happily agreed to let me use their logo and some of their episodes, though somewhat shortened and altered. If you'd like to check out the original podcasts that appear in this book:

Episode 2: Your Childhood Best Friend

Episodes 5 & 6: Murdered – Your Classmate

Episodes 33 & 34: Bonnie and Clyde

Episodes 27 & 28: The Crime that Made Us Obsessed with True Crime – The Parkway Murders

Episode 77: Update on the Parkway Murders

About the Author

Patti Gaustad Procopi is a former army brat who lived all over the world before settling in the rural community of Gloucester, Virginia. She and her husband, Greg, raised three daughters and numerous cats and dogs in their home on Cedar Bush Creek.

After retiring from two area history museums, Patti finally had the time to do the things she always wanted to do, including writing. Moving constantly made it difficult to make friends and form lasting relationships. Patti's writing is about emotional connections, friendship and family.

In addition to writing, Patti fills her days with gardening and researching her family's genealogy. There are stories there yet to be written. She volunteers with a wildlife rehab facility and enjoys nature photography, especially of her beloved osprey family in their nest on the creek. She and Greg love to travel and have been busy checking off their bucket list.

Patti can be found on Facebook and Instagram. She loves hearing from readers and is available to meet and talk with book clubs and other organizations.

Patti.pro@cox.net
Pattiproauthor.com